D0886792

A Legacy of
Murder

Also available by Connie Berry

A Dream of Death

A Legacy of Murder

Murder

A Kate Hamilton Mystery

CONNIE BERRY

CROOKED
LANE

NEW YORK

Published in the United States by Crooked Lane Books, an imprint of The Quick Brown Fox & Company LLC.

Crooked Lane Books and its logo are trademarks of The Quick Brown Fox & Company LLC.

Library of Congress Catalog-in-Publication data available upon request.

ISBN (hardcover): 978-1-64385-154-9
ISBN (ePub): 978-1-64385-155-6

Cover design by Lori Palmer
Book design by Jennifer Canzone

Printed in the United States.

www.crookedlanebooks.com

Crooked Lane Books
34 West 27th St., 10th Floor
New York, NY 10001

First Edition: October 2019

10 9 8 7 6 5 4 3 2 1

For Bob

I cannot fix on the hour, or the spot, or the look or the words, which laid the foundation. It is too long ago. I was in the middle before I knew that I had begun.

—Jane Austen, *Pride and Prejudice*

Chapter One

～

Saturday, December 5th
Long Barston, Suffolk, England

I woke to the point of a sword in my thigh.

"Ow." I glared at the boy—a child of seven or eight—his face partially obscured by a plastic Saxon helmet. I hadn't actually been sleeping. I'd been standing up, resting my eyes. And it wasn't a real sword, but the plastic tip still hurt.

"Surrender or I'll run you through."

Fortunately, I'd raised two children of my own and knew how to play along. "Please." I raised my hands in the air. "Can't you just take me prisoner?"

"I'm a Viking raider. We don't take prisoners."

"If you're a Viking, why are you wearing a Saxon helmet?"

He grinned with pride. "Stole it."

I might have believed that, except I'd just seen his mother buying the set in the gift shop. Where was she, anyway?

I huddled with the other members of the two-o'clock tour group, ten of us in all, in the shelter of the Dovecote, the gift shop and ticket office where I'd handed over my twelve pounds and received a round red sticker to wear—"clearly visible at all times."

Our tour guide was late.

Another swipe of the boy's sword threatened to sever the arm of an older woman in a beautifully cut woolen coat. She neatly disarmed the young tyrant. "I think ve put away the lovely svard until after the tour." The accent was Scandinavian—possibly Danish, I thought.

"That's mine," the boy howled in protest. "Give it back."

The woman shook her head firmly.

"Cow." He stomped off in his Saxon helmet toward the fountain in the center of the courtyard.

The boy's mother approached us. "Sorry." She reclaimed the sword and tucked it in the belt of her fake-fur-trimmed jacket. "Danny's fascinated with weaponry."

So was Genghis Khan. I rubbed my thigh.

"I hope he didn't hurt you," she said.

"I'm fine." I shivered in my puffy down jacket and imagined what Donald Preston would write in his Sunday column in the *Jackson Falls Gazette*. KATE HAMILTON, LOCAL ANTIQUE DEALER, WAS MAULED BY A PLASTIC SWORD YESTERDAY WHILE WAITING IN LINE FOR A TOUR OF FINCHLEY HALL, A STATELY HOME IN SUFFOLK, ENGLAND. Preston, an acquaintance from my college days and not one of my fans, was now managing editor of the *Jackson Falls Gazette*.

Safe for the moment from little boys with pillaging on their minds, I tucked my freezing fingers in my pockets and surveyed my surroundings. Across the gravel courtyard, Finchley Hall glowed rose-red in the bright December sun. Irregular panes of glass set into tall banks of mullioned windows reflected the light like a patchwork quilt of mirrors. A forest of chimneys pointed toward an ice-blue sky. The house and courtyard were surrounded by brick walls laid in an eye-catching diagonal pattern. The bricks had been recently repointed, I noticed, contemplating the massive piles of cash required to keep a place like Finchley Hall from falling down. No wonder Lady Finchley-fforde opened her estate to paying guests every Saturday afternoon.

Signs of the holidays were everywhere. Strings of fairy lights circled the trunks of the copper beeches lining the long drive. Wreaths of holly and mistletoe adorned every door. I'd always dreamed of spending Christmas in England—snow falling softly outside, the yule log in the hearth, steaming cups of wassail. Is wassail served hot? I didn't actually know. It was an image stuck in my head from an *Ideals* magazine I saw as a child.

This was as close as I was ever likely to get to an English Christmas. Two weeks in December visiting my daughter, Christine, an intern at Finchley Hall; then back to the United States in time for Christmas Eve with my mother. My father was killed in an auto accident on Christmas Eve when I was in high school, and my mother and I mark the date together every year. This year it would be just the two of us. Christine would be staying in England. My son, Eric, was in Italy doing research for his thesis—something to do with spent fuel rods and boreholes.

I pretend to know what that means.

The tour was seventeen minutes late. I was about to inquire in the gift shop if we'd been forgotten when a strikingly beautiful young woman with a sleek black ponytail and skin the color of a caramel macchiato appeared with a purple clipboard in her hand. She wore a name badge on a lanyard and the same green quilted vest I'd seen on the saleswoman at the ticket counter.

"Welcome to Finchley Hall. Sorry for the delay. My name's Alexa Devereux. Call me Alex. I'll be your tour guide today." Her voice and the fluid grace of her movements spoke of palm trees and spice-scented breezes, but the name, Devereux, was solidly Norman and her accent posh boarding school. I pictured a romance between a British aristocrat and an island goddess in the South Pacific.

"Sorry for the late start. Let's get acquainted." Alex consulted her clipboard before turning her unusual green-gold eyes on me. "Kate Hamilton, is it? Where are you from, Kate?"

"Ohio. Near Cleveland." *Exotic.*

The others answered in turn. Besides the older couple, Danish as I'd thought, we had a pair of male university students on a hiking holiday, a trio of middle-aged Englishwomen from Cambridge, and of course Glenda and Danny—the mother and sword-wielding son. They lived in a nearby Suffolk village.

"You've been to Finchley Hall before?" Alex asked the Danish couple.

"I'm afraid not," said the woman.

"Oh, we have—several times," said one of the middle-aged Englishwomen. "Lovely day out."

"You're all very welcome. Follow me, please." Alex's ponytail swished as she turned on her booted heel and strode through the courtyard toward the fountain, where the small Saxon warrior appeared to be calculating the height of the retaining wall. "Our tour will begin at the lake," she said. "Then we'll circle back through the park and finish with the house and what you've all come to see"—she shot us a look over her shoulder—"the Finchley Cross."

The Finchley Cross, I'd learned in the gift shop, was Anglo-Saxon, a stunning gold-and-garnet pectoral brooch, buried the night of the Peasants' Revolt in 1549. The cross, together with some fifteenth-century coins and several objects from the Finchley Hoard, unearthed on the estate in 1818, were kept on permanent display in the Hall library. A much larger exhibit, celebrating the two hundredth anniversary of the discovery of the Hoard, was planned for December nineteenth, the Saturday following the Eve of St. Æthelric, a local saint and patron of the village church. I would be there to see all those amazing objects, one of those strokes of good luck that happen when you're least expecting them. At least I don't expect them.

I stifled a yawn. The airplane from Cleveland to London Heathrow had been jammed. I'd given up my aisle seat to a young woman with an infant—good as gold he was, the whole flight. But the switch

4

had put me between a woman who dealt with her flying phobia by chatting and a man with a tiny bladder (window seat, naturally).

Didn't the guidebooks recommend fresh air and sunshine for jet-lag? I lifted my face to the sky and breathed in the crisp air, infused with the herby scent of boxwood. I had exactly five hours to recover before dinner with Tom Mallory, the Englishman I'd met a month ago in Scotland and fallen in love with.

Or not. It's complicated.

We'd reached the fountain. The lanky chaps in hiking gear had moved to the front of the pack, their interest fueled less, I suspected, by a love of history than by male hormones.

"First a bit of background." Alex turned to face us. "The Finchley estate was originally part of Clare Priory. With the dissolution of the monasteries, the land passed to Sir Oswyn Finchley, who built a timber-frame house here in 1542, burnt to the ground in the Peasants' Revolt of 1549. The much grander house we see today was built in 1588 by his grandson, Sir Giles Finchley. The current resident is Lady Barbara Finchley-fforde, daughter of the Marquess of—"

"Danny, *no.*" Glenda dashed toward the fountain, where her son had hiked one leg over the retaining wall. She dragged him back, her round face pink with embarrassment. "Sorry. He's hyperactive."

"No problem," Alex said, managing to convey with her tone that if Mum didn't get her act together, it might very well be a problem. "Finchley Hall is famous for three things—its fine Tudor brickwork, the magnificent treasure trove discovered here in the early nineteenth century, and"—she paused dramatically—"for murder."

"Ooh, murder." Danny danced in a circle, his wet shoe leaving damp patches on the gravel. "Were the bodies covered in blood and all those creepy-crawlies?"

"Danny never misses an episode of *Silent Witness*," Glenda whispered to me. "We think he's going to be a forensic pathologist."

Or a serial killer.

Alex soldiered on. "Finchley Hall has witnessed four murders, all under unusual circumstances." She flashed us a mysterious smile, a practiced part of the spiel, no doubt. "Follow me as we delve into lost treasure and murder most foul."

We'd started moving again. Danny skipped along the path, kicking up stones.

"You're American," Glenda told me. "Here on holiday?"

"I'm visiting my daughter. She's a student at Oxford, but she has an internship at Finchley Hall between terms." I might have added that I was in England on a buying trip for my antique shop—also the truth—but that would lead to more questions, and I really wanted to hear what the tour guide was saying.

". . . addition of the estate offices in 1830." Alex was describing the other buildings on the estate.

One of them, a stable block, had been converted into housing for the interns. I'd lucked out. An intern had withdrawn at the last minute, and my daughter, Christine, had managed to co-opt the small private room and bath for me. That would save me a bundle—money I could better invest in antiques.

"Your husband isn't keen on old houses?" Glenda asked.

"He was," I said. "I'm a widow." Even after three years the word still jarred, like something referring to little old ladies with tight perms. I braced myself for the usual *you're too young to be a widow*.

Fortunately, Alex interrupted. "Watch your step. The path is uneven."

We'd moved from the courtyard to a narrow flagged path bisecting a wide swath of lawn flanked by perennial borders. Hellebores and intrepid snowdrops pushed through glossy mounds of winterberry. I envied the English their temperate climate. My garden in Jackson Falls was currently hibernating under a blanket of lake-effect snow.

Beyond the lawn, high walls of rose brick enclosed a garden. A maze of neat gravel paths divided islands of soil, laid out in geometric symmetry. Newly planted boxwood hedges defined a circular bed in the center of the garden. An elderly man in a peaked cap leaned on his shovel. Seeing us, he flicked the cigarette he'd been smoking and began to dig. A strong smell of manure wafted on the air.

"*Eww*. That's poo." Danny held his nose and made fake gagging sounds.

"The Elizabethan Garden is being prepared for early spring planting," Alex said. "Restoration began last summer when the original diagrams were discovered in the estate archives. One of our long-term interns is directing the process as part of his doctoral thesis."

Leaving the garden area, we passed through an iron-studded door in the brick wall to a lovely park, acres of woods and shrubs planted over several centuries. We crossed a fishpond with a red wooden bridge built in the Chinese style and passed a miniature Greek temple—the Folly. From there the path sloped sharply downward to a small lake on the edge of a wood.

A black-feathered bird swooped in to perch on the branches of a hawthorn.

"We've arrived at Blackwater Lake." Alex stopped near a large smooth boulder jutting from the soil. "So, who were these unfortunate victims of murder? Number one"—she held up her index finger—"Sir Oswyn Finchley, killed on the Eve of St. Æthelric in 1549. Local peasants protesting an increase in rents swarmed up from the village carrying torches. Realizing the danger, Sir Oswyn gathered his valuables in a large sack, which he entrusted to his servant, Tobias Thurtle, with instructions to bury it until the danger had passed. Unfortunately, one of the torches set the timber-frame structure alight. Badly burned, Sir Oswyn escaped to Blackwater Lake, where he succumbed to his injuries—right about where you're standing, Kate. The Hoard was lost for nearly three hundred years."

"But vhy didn't the servant dig it up?" asked the Danish woman.

My question exactly.

"No one knows." Alex consulted her clipboard. "Perhaps Tobias Thurtle was killed that night as well. What we do know brings us to victim number two—Susannah Finchley, wife of Sir Oswyn's great-great-grandson, the Marquess of Suffolk, murdered on the twelfth of October, 1638, while walking in the park. The perpetrator, a local beggar sometimes fed by the Hall cook, was taken up for the crime but found to be of unsound mind. The authorities assumed he was after the blood-red ruby ring Susannah was known to wear. You'll find a portrait of Lady Susannah in the small parlor, wearing what is thought to be the very ring. Now, victim number three—"

Danny scrambled up the boulder and leapt off with an ear-splitting whoop.

Alex Devereux set her jaw. I couldn't blame her. Danny was getting on everyone's nerves.

"—victim number three, Jim Thurtle, descendant of the servant who buried the Hoard, shot on the fifteenth of December, 1818."

Danny pulled at his mother's arm. "Can I throw stones in the water, Mummy? Can I? Can I? Please, please?"

I could almost hear the silent prayer rising from the group.

Alex lifted one perfect eyebrow. "Okay, Mum?"

"All right," Glenda said uncertainly. "But stay where I can see you. And don't get your shoes wet again."

"I promise." Danny skipped off.

Right. If Danny was anything like my son, he'd be wet to the knees in less than a minute. And in this weather, it wouldn't take long for hypothermia to set in.

Alex cleared her throat. "Back to our story. A Thurtle family legend claimed the location of the buried treasure had been marked by a cross of stone. No such cross was ever found—*until* Jim Thurtle discovered this." She drew our attention to a crude Celtic cross etched into the boulder. "An image of the Finchley Cross? Perhaps. As you can see, the main leg points in a southwesterly direction, toward the lake. Jim Thurtle took this as a clue, and after a night of digging, he located the treasure trove, still wrapped in its moldering sack. Unfortunately, he was spotted by the gamekeeper, who, believing he'd caught a poacher, fired a warning shot. Jim seized as much of the treasure as he could hold and made a dash toward the woods, where he tripped a spring-gun wire concealed in the tall grass. He died five days later, and the Hoard was returned to the Finchley family."

"Not the Crown?" I asked, remembering from my graduate school days that English kings, scorning the ancient Roman law of finders-keepers, claimed buried treasure for themselves.

"Not when the rightful owners can be proved and still own the property. By 1818, the Lost Finchley Hoard was already a local legend." Alex propped one foot against the boulder. "For victim number four we fast-forward to 1996—Catherine Kerr, a curator at the Museum of Suffolk History in Bury St. Edmunds. She'd come to Finchley Hall to arrange a special exhibit of the Hoard. Her body was found in Blackwater Lake by the gardener—the same man, as it happens, we passed earlier. The killer was never—"

A shriek pierced the air.

"Danny." Glenda dashed toward the lake.

Several of us followed.

The little boy stood with a rock in each hand, his shoes submerged in the shallows along the lakeshore. His eyes were open wide. His mouth formed a perfect O. At his feet, wedged against a half-sunken log, was the body of a young woman wearing khaki riding pants and another of the green quilted vests. Long blonde hair fanned out around her head, wreathed with swirls of reddish pink. Sightless eyes stared toward the sky.

Alex's hand flew to her mouth. "It's Tabitha."

A wave of nausea made me light-headed. Then I remembered the boy. "Get Danny away from here—now."

Glenda scooped him up and clambered toward the boulder.

My eyes went to the bank, where a slip of mud and rocks led from the grassy verge, about a foot above the lake, into the water itself. Could Tabitha have slipped and fallen into the lake? I tried to see if she was wearing shoes, but a tangle of twigs and leaves shrouded her feet. What had she been doing so close to the edge?

Something about the scene struck me as wrong, but my thoughts scattered like the leaves on the ground.

"Someone call the police," shouted the Danish woman from the crest of the rise.

The tallest of the three Englishwomen fished through a capacious handbag. "I left my mobile in the car." The other two stood beside her, weeping.

One of the hikers rushed to the edge of the lake and vomited. The other waved his phone in the air. "No signal."

Alex fumbled with some kind of paging device. "The coverage down here is crap."

I raced up the bank. Glenda crouched next to her son, rocking him in her arms. The Danish woman had removed her coat and wrapped it around him.

Scrambling onto the boulder, I tried to balance while fighting off an all-too-familiar sense of vertigo. Wimpy, I know, but I'm acrophobic. I can panic on a stepstool.

"I've got two bars," I shouted.

"Dial 999," Alex shouted back.

I managed to reach an emergency operator, who radioed for an ambulance and the local police. Then I called a number I'd already programmed into my phone.

I knew it by heart anyway.

Detective Inspector Thomas Mallory of the Suffolk Constabulary.

"Tom, it's me. I'm at Finchley Hall. There's a body."

Chapter Two

I stood with the rest of the tour group near the boulder. Impressions of our shoes had been taken for elimination purposes. Two police cordons had been set up, an inner one for the crime scene team and a second, wider cordon for uniformed police and detectives. Wide-angle-lensed cameras strobed the body in the lake. Anonymous figures in white hooded coveralls, shoe covers, and blue latex gloves shuttled between the lake and a white forensics van parked on the grass at the top of the rise.

The boy, Danny, his mother, Glenda, and the tour guide, Alex Devereux, had been whisked away to police headquarters in Bury St. Edmunds. A kindly policewoman had explained that when a witness is a child, the interview is filmed and conducted by someone specially trained to work with children. A good thing. He was clearly in shock.

The temperature had dropped—at least it felt colder. I pulled up my collar and slid my hands into my pockets. A picture of the body I'd discovered a month ago in Scotland flashed in my mind. Finding one body could be considered bad luck. Finding two within the space of thirty days was beginning to look like destiny.

Tom paced back and forth along the taped-off perimeter, a tall, lean figure with dark, silver-flecked hair. His face—long nose, high chiseled cheekbones—burned with an intensity I'd glimpsed but never fully seen until now. He wore the same brown waxed cotton field jacket I remembered from Scotland, but this wasn't *my* Tom—the one with the quick half smile and hazel eyes that crinkled at the corners, the one whose faintly woodsy aftershave made me think of bonfires and starry nights and sent my stomach swooping. This Tom was all business, and his mind wasn't on me but on the pale, very dead young woman in the lake.

Tom walked over and flashed us his badge. "Detective Inspector Mallory, CID. Did any of you touch the body or disturb it in any way?"

We shook our heads.

"It was clearly too late to save her," said the Danish man, speaking for the first time in nearly unaccented English. "I am a pathologist. I recognize death when I see it."

"Did anyone besides the tour guide know this girl? Had you seen her before today?"

We shook our heads again.

A young policeman joined us. He wore the distinctive black helmet of the British police force and a yellow mesh vest over a black uniform.

"I've asked Constable Wheeler to escort you to the house," Tom said. "I'll need to speak to each of you individually. We'll try not to take up too much of your time."

I'd turned to follow the group when Tom stopped me. "Kate, stay for a moment." He squeezed my hand. "Are you all right?"

"I'm fine—or I will be. The dead girl works on the estate, Tom. They all wear those green quilted vests."

"Where's Christine?"

"In an orientation session. I'm supposed to meet her at five thirty at our lodgings. She's going to introduce me to"—my voice caught—"the other interns." I blinked. "Is she in danger?"

"This could be an accident. The coroner will know more once he examines the body." He gave me a quick smile. "There's someone I want you to meet."

He signaled to a youngish man in rumpled khakis and a dark trench coat that had seen better days. In his midthirties, I guessed, with a thatch of brown hair, pink cheeks, and ears that stuck out like saucers.

"Sir." The man climbed the rise, his scuffed shoes coated with mud.

"Kate, this is Detective Sergeant Ryan Cliffe. Cliffe, this is my friend, Kate Hamilton."

"Pleasure, ma'am." Sergeant Cliffe blushed to the tips of his ears. His tie was skewed and the collar of his shirt wrinkled. He reminded me of an unmade bed.

"I'll see you at the house later," Tom told me. "Can you make it there on your own?"

"Of course. Listen, Tom—do you need to cancel tonight? Because of the case, I mean. I'd understand."

"Not on your life. I'll pick you up at seven as planned, but we'd better stick to one of the village pubs in case something comes up." He gave me his half smile, and I felt a flutter of anticipation. Silly, I know. I'm a woman of forty-six with two adult children. But our hearts have seasons, and mine was emerging from a long hibernation that had begun three years ago when my husband died.

Leave it to me to fall for a man who lives thirty-seven hundred miles away.

Or not. It's complicated.

I passed the Folly and crossed the Chinese Bridge. A bank of clouds had moved across the sun, flattening the landscape's winter hues. I shivered, and not just because of the falling temperature.

Inside the high brick walls of the Elizabethan Garden, the air felt warmer. Near a shed at the rear of the garden, the old gardener, the one with the peaked cap, warmed his hands over a fluted brazier. A young man with broad shoulders and short-cropped blond hair joined him. He wore one of the green quilted vests over a faded plaid shirt and a pair of dark-olive cords. He was probably the long-term intern Alex Devereux had mentioned, the one supervising the garden restoration. Even at a distance, I could see his hands were dirty and his cords streaked with mud. The old gardener handed him something—it might have been an envelope or a piece of paper. The young man's reaction was immediate and violent. He ripped it into pieces and threw them on the fire. The old man raised his hands, clearly exasperated, but the young man turned and disappeared into the shed.

What was that about?

Finchley Hall loomed ahead. Strange how bricks that had looked so rosy in the sunlight had taken on the dull, rusty color of—

No, I wouldn't say it, even to myself.

The image of the girl in the lake, her dead eyes staring sightlessly at the sky, made me queasy. It also raised a point of logic. How had she ended up on her back with her feet pointing toward the middle of the lake? If she'd slipped and fallen, had she—in an attempt to right herself—done a sort of flip? And where had the blood come from?

I took a deep breath. A month ago, when Tom and I had met in Scotland, it was a death that had drawn us together. He and I had been outsiders, drawn into the investigation by circumstance. This time, Finchley Hall was on his patch. Were we doomed to spend our time together, once again, caught up in a murder investigation?

Because if the young intern with the long blonde hair wasn't the victim of a tragic accident, she might very well be Finchley Hall's murder victim number five.

* * *

The formal drawing room at Finchley Hall made me feel like a Lilliputian. The space was massive, dominated by an enormous carved marble fireplace, above which the Finchley coat of arms stood out in high-relief, lime-plaster pargeting. A bird perched on the crest—a finch, no doubt—and the shield, quartered in blue and white, pictured a griffin rampant, that mythical beast with the body of a lion and the head and wings of an eagle. He stood on his hind legs, his forepaws in the air, claws extended, wings unfurled. A banner above the shield bore the Latin words FIDELIS, FASTU, FORTITUDO.

Loyalty, pride, courage.

The scent of beeswax polish mingled with the mustiness of old wood, the dust of the ages, and a hint of mildew—an antique dealer's perfume. Two long serpentine-back sofas flanked the hearth, their green velvet upholstery so thin in places you could see the stiff canvas underlayer. Dried thistle heads on the triple cushions advised visitors to sit elsewhere.

The other members of the two-o'clock tour group sat stiffly in chairs scattered around the room. I chose a Chippendale-style armchair, resisting the urge to flip it over and examine the construction.

Someone cleared his throat. I looked up. A man in pin-striped trousers and a black morning coat strode through from the entrance hall. His hair, suspiciously dark for a man of his age, was slicked back over a high forehead. He looked so much like an actor playing the part of an English butler, I almost laughed. Except he wasn't acting. He held a silver tea tray in white-gloved hands and looked down his nose at us, as if serving the hoi polloi was below his dignity. Or his pay grade. He must have dressed in a hurry, though. His black tie was crooked, and one of the buttons on his dove-gray vest was undone. He'd probably been pressed into duty at short notice and was none too happy about it. I couldn't blame him.

"Lady Barbara regrets the shock you have endured," he said, "and wishes to make you as comfortable as possible whilst you wait. Hot water for tea is available, plus a selection of biscuits. If you prefer coffee or a soft drink, pull the bell cord near the fireplace. We shall do our best to accommodate you."

The *we* included a middle-aged blonde in a maid's uniform—black dress, white apron, thick black stockings. She'd followed him into the room, pushing a rolling cart. They set out the refreshments on a long oak table and left us to ourselves.

The male hikers fell immediately on the refreshments. The rest of us followed their lead. In a crisis, there really is nothing like hot, sweet English tea.

Absolute silence reigned, except for an occasional slurp and the snap of playing cards. The Englishwomen had found a deck—or brought their own. They'd pulled their chairs around a coffee table to play a game that seemed to include a lot of discarding and triumphant looks.

I sat back and sipped my tea. I'd have to call my mother in Ohio before she read about the murder in the local newspaper. And she would—no question. Donald Preston, was sure to find out about my involvement (I couldn't imagine how, but he always did), and a snarky article would appear in the *Gazette*. Last October when I had unmasked a killer in the Scottish Hebrides, his headline read JACKSON FALLS' OWN MISS MARPLE. He'd managed to get the details right while making me sound like an interfering busybody who had stumbled into a murder investigation and survived through a combination of naïveté and dumb luck.

No comment.

I'd never figured out what Preston had against me. Unless it was the letter I'd published years ago in the student-run college newspaper, shredding the logic in his op-ed about limiting foreign enrollment. Or the fact that I'd turned down a second date after he tried to maul me at a fraternity hayride. He should have been grateful I hadn't reported him to the campus police.

Today I would.

An hour passed. One by one, beginning with the hikers, the other witnesses gave their statements and left. At last, with the afternoon sun casting bright rectangles on the worn Oriental carpet, I sat alone, nursing my third cup of tea and wondering what I'd do if I needed the powder room.

Tom and Sergeant Cliffe entered the drawing room.

"Water still hot?" Cliffe eyed the urn.

"It was fifteen minutes ago."

He plopped a tea bag in a dainty porcelain cup and reached inside his jacket for a notebook.

Tom pulled up a chair. "We saved you for last, Kate. Now, tell me what you saw. Every detail."

I began with Danny and the swordplay and ended with the body and the slip of rocks and mud. "I assumed she'd fallen and hit her head. But now that I've had time to go back over it in my mind, I think—from the position of the body—she must have gone in backwards and feetfirst. That seems odd."

He raised an eyebrow. "You noticed that, did you?"

"Something else struck me as not quite right, but I can't think what it was."

"Not surprising. You were in shock." He took my hand in his, and the warmth of his touch brought tears.

I swiped at my eyes. "The whole thing was so bizarre, Tom. The tour guide had just been telling us about Finchley Hall being famous for murder, and then Danny screamed and—" I stopped and took a breath. "In 1996 another girl, a young museum curator, was found dead in that lake. And the gardener who found the body is still working here."

"We'll take formal statements from the staff in the morning." Tom rubbed his chin with his thumb and looked up at me. "The young woman's name was Tabitha King, one of the long-term interns. She was a student at the University of East Anglia, working toward a graduate degree in museum studies. She came to Finchley Hall in September, specifically to design and prepare an exhibit to open later this month."

"The Finchley Hoard exhibit. I read about it in the gift shop."

"The tour guide, Alex, told us Tabitha hadn't seemed herself lately. In fact, she was scheduled to lead your tour group today but never showed up. Alex had to step in at the last minute."

"So that's why the tour was late."

"We've contacted Tabitha's parents. They told us she'd been taking antidepressants for almost a year. It's possible her death was planned."

"Suicide?" My hand flew to my heart, imagining what a verdict of suicide would do to those parents. "What a tragedy—if it's true. Whatever had gone wrong in her life would have mended. She had every reason to look forward."

I wasn't exactly the poster child for that statement, but Tom didn't say so. He gave me a one-armed hug. "Where shall I pick you up? I'm looking forward to meeting your daughter."

"Follow signs for the Stables. There's a small parking area across from the entrance."

Sergeant Cliffe shoved his notebook in his jacket and threw down the last of his tea.

Tom gave me that charming half smile. "See you tonight."

I stood at the windows and watched them drive off in a white Ford Focus with the distinctive blue-and-yellow Battenburg markings of the British police.

At nearly four o'clock, the light was fading fast. Christine would be back from her orientation session in an hour or so. I'd have time to shower and change. Maybe even catch a power nap. I set my teacup on the oak table and took a last glance at the drawing room. Portraits of long-dead Finchleys gazed at me with smug equanimity. Had they really been that pleased with life? Grief must have invaded this house many times in the four-hundred-plus years of its existence. Now there was a new tragedy to add to the weight of sorrow.

My heart ached for Tabitha's parents. Burying a child is a parent's worst nightmare. I thought of my own children. Losing my husband, Bill, had left me stunned and profoundly grieving, but I still had Eric and Christine.

Gratitude washed over me. Soon I'd hold my daughter in my arms, look in her eyes, hear her voice. That thought led to another. Christine had been at Finchley Hall only a week, but she would have met Tabitha, spoken with her. Had she noticed anything that would explain the girl's death?

My daughter may not be the best judge of men—let's be honest—but her perceptions of women are usually spot on.

Chapter Three

The Stables, which—glad as I was to have a free place to live—had sounded rather primitive, turned out to be a comfortable and surprisingly attractive living space for the interns. Along with the original stone floors and thick, plastered-brick walls, the builder had incorporated the original ironwork and stable doors into the design. I found the combination of clean lines, pale colors, and historic details attractive and soothing.

The Commons, a gathering place for the interns, occupied the center of the U-shaped building. Two long hallways set at right angles to the central block contained the living quarters. Some of the interns—Christine, for example—had a roommate. My suite was a single. Besides a platform bed covered in a crisp white duvet, I had a built-in desk, a small dresser, a metal swing-arm lamp, and a love seat slipcovered in off-white denim. Next to a tiny kitchenette, a freestanding closet divided the bedroom from a tiled bathroom and shower. A deep-set window looked out on a brick terrace. Two large skylights in the slanted ceiling let in the sun and the stars.

After showering and changing clothes, I decided I was too restless to sleep and caught up on my emails. At six twenty, with no sign of Christine, I wandered into the Commons. A young man sprawled on a gray IKEA-style sofa. He was watching something sporty on TV. His stocking-clad feet rested on a tack box repurposed as a coffee table.

"Hi," I said, expecting no more than a wave of acknowledgment.

He clicked off the TV and sat up. "Oh, hullo. You must be Christine's mum. I'm Michael Nash, one of the new interns." Shaggy red hair, an upturned nose, and slightly pointed ears gave him a puckish look.

"Glad to meet you, Michael."

"I suppose you heard about the . . . death." He grimaced. "Tabitha, one of the interns."

"Did you know her well?"

"Not really. I mean, I'd met her, but I only arrived last week."

"Have you seen Christine? She was supposed to be here forty-five minutes ago."

"She and Tristan stayed after the meeting to chat to the man in charge of the guildhall project."

He meant Tristan Sorel, Christine's latest boyfriend. Tristan, an architecture student, had come to Suffolk to study the preservation of timber-framed buildings. He'd be working, Christine had told me, at a medieval guildhall in Long Barston. To say I was looking forward to meeting him would be an exaggeration. Christine has a habit of falling for guys she thinks are too good to be true, and they usually prove her right.

"Where will you be working?" I asked Michael.

"The Rare Breeds Farm. I'm studying to be a veterinary surgeon." He grinned. "Real farm animals, not lapdogs and budgies."

"You've come to the right place then." I'd noticed the Rare Breeds Farm on the Finchley Hall guide map. "Who runs the farm?"

"A couple of local farmers, in exchange for grazing land for their own herds. We don't have many animals at present. Just a few sheep and chickens, several pigs, a donkey, two Dexter bullocks." He swung his legs off the wooden tack box. His eyes shone with excitement. "Finchley Hall received a grant last year from the Rare Breeds

Survival Trust. I'll be identifying and sourcing some of the early breeds—those at risk and those closest, genetically, to the animals one might have seen centuries ago on a Suffolk farm."

"I'll stop over someday. I'd love to see the animals."

Our conversation was interrupted when Christine burst in, followed by a young man I recognized from his photos as Tristan Sorel.

"Mom." Christine threw herself into my arms. "Sorry I'm late." She pulled back to look at me. "Did you hear about Tabitha? Everyone says it was suicide." She shivered, and not only because the T-shirt she wore under her jacket revealed several inches of bare belly.

"Unfortunately, I was there when her body was found." I brushed back Christine's thick, dark hair to look at her face, seeing distress but not anguish. I'd wait to ask about her impressions of Tabitha until we were alone.

Christine reached for her companion. "Mom, this is Tristan Sorel." She took a quick breath. She was afraid I wouldn't like him.

I was afraid of the same thing.

Tristan was taller than he'd looked in his photos, six feet, maybe. He wore a close-fitting tweed jacket over a buttoned sweater. The striped scarf I remembered from the first photo Christine had sent was tucked under both jacket and sweater, leaving the ends to trail out the bottom. His hair, shaved at the sides, fell in a mop over his eyes. He looked like someone who might bring a manual typewriter to a coffee shop for the effect.

"Mrs. Hamilton." Tristan made a formal bow and took my hand. I was afraid for a moment he was going to kiss it, but he let it drop. "I am happy to meet you at last, *Maman*. I can see the resemblance—those so charming blue eyes, that chestnut hair—*une belle femme*, as we say in France." His accent wasn't quite French, and I must have looked confused, because he added, "My family is from Strasbourg. We speak French, of course, but German is our native tongue."

Oh, I could see the attraction, all right. Tristan had the kind of looks Christine always falls for—dark and mysterious with a hint of the misunderstood bad boy.

"Hiya, Tristan." Michael Nash reached out, and they exchanged some kind of double fist bump.

"Will you join us at the Arms tonight?" Tristan asked him.

"Brilliant." Michael's face clouded. "That is, if everyone's going. I thought . . . under the circumstances . . . well . . ." He trailed off.

"Tonight we shall toast Tabitha's memory. All we can do, no?"

"You, too, Mom." Christine said. "Come to the pub with us. Around eight."

"I'm sorry. I'm having dinner with Tom. Another night?"

"Sure. Fine."

I can read my daughter's face as easily as the marks on old silver. She'd loved her father very much, and the thought of another man in my life wasn't something she was prepared to accept. Yet.

A young woman slammed through the door, threw off a striped wool poncho, and burst into tears. "Sorry, sorry." She waved one hand as she wiped her eyes on the sleeve of a long, loosely woven dress.

"My roommate," Christine whispered before introducing us.

Prue Goody was the stocky young woman who'd sold me the tour ticket. She had a round pink face and curly brown hair that she appeared to be coaxing into dreadlocks.

"I can't believe it." Prue dropped onto the sofa beside Michael Nash. "Poor Tabitha."

"Were you close?" I asked gently.

"Not really." Prue looked at Christine. "I don't think she even liked me."

"Alex says she was depressed," Christine said. "She was taking pills for it."

Prue wrinkled her forehead. "That can't be right. I offered her a paracetamol the other day—she had a headache—and she said she didn't take drugs."

Strange. Why would the girl's parents say she was taking an anti-depressant if she wasn't? Or was Tabitha one of those patients who pretend to take her medicine and then bury the pills in a potted plant? "What was Tabitha like?"

"I would have said reserved." Prue's eyes fell to her lap. "Of course, Alex knew her best. They were roommates for a while, although I don't think they got along. Tabitha moved in with me for a week or so before she got her own room."

"What if it wasn't . . . well, suicide?" Michael's forehead creased with concern. "Tabitha mentioned seeing a strange man near the Folly a few days ago—remember?"

"A strange man?" I didn't like the sound of that.

"Just someone she didn't know." Christine dismissed the thought with a flap of her hand.

"She told the butler at the Hall," Michael said. "He blew her off."

"Of course he did," Christine said. "Lots of people walk in the park. It's open to the public. There's a footpath from the village."

"I saw Tabitha this morning." Prue snuffled and wiped her eyes. "I'd come out to get coffee. She said she was on her way to the archives. Same as always."

The estate archives building, I'd seen on my map of the grounds, was set off by itself, east of the main house and skirting the northern perimeter of Finchley Park.

"Were you and Tabitha going to work together, Christine?"

"Same building, that's all. Tabitha worked downstairs with the Hoard artifacts. My office will be upstairs in the family archives."

Without any of us noticing, Michael Nash had made Prue a mug of tea. He handed her the mug and mumbled, "Thought you might . . . well."

Prue smiled gratefully.

Christine looked at Michael with a kind of puzzled admiration. Tristan saw the look and laid a proprietary arm around her shoulders. Did he see Michael as a threat?

Headlights swung an arc across the bank of windows.

"My ride's here." I grabbed my coat and handbag and gave Christine a quick hug.

Christine could meet Tom later. I'd had just about enough drama for one day.

Tonight I'd keep him for myself.

Chapter Four

~

I watched Tom juggle a pint of beer, a pitcher of water, and a glass of white wine to our table in the Finchley Arms. "Just so you know, I did ask for Chardonnay." He set our drinks on a couple of stained beer coasters. "The barman said wine comes red or white."

"No problem." I scooted my chair farther into the corner to make room at the tiny table. The pub was jam-packed, and the low-beamed ceiling, rather than lending an old-world ambience, made me feel slightly claustrophobic. The only signs of Christmas were a string of colored lights drooping over the bar and a sparse tree decorated with tinsel and beer coasters. We'd chosen a spot in a narrow side room, away from the dartboard and the patrons standing two deep at the bar. Among them, seated at the end of the counter and staring into his pint, was the old gardener from Finchley Hall. He'd removed his peaked cap, revealing a sparse comb-over.

"I thought I was going to meet Christine tonight," Tom said.

"She had plans." My conscience made a sly reference to lies and half-truths. "That is, she did, but the truth is, I didn't feel like sharing you just yet."

A slow smile spread across his face. "In that case, I can wait." He kissed my hair. "Oh, I've missed you, Kate—more than you can imagine."

I smiled, afraid my voice wouldn't work. In the month we'd been apart, there'd hardly been an hour when I hadn't thought of him. If one of us fell short in the imagination department, I was pretty sure it would be him.

"How are things on Glenroth?" he asked. "Have you spoken with Nancy Holden?"

Nancy Holden and her husband were the cook and groundskeeper at Glenroth House, the country house hotel in the Scottish Hebrides previously owned by my husband's sister. I'd gone to the island to patch up my relationship with my sister-in-law. Tom had gone there for a break after a homeland security conference in Glasgow. We'd run into each other in the middle of a snowstorm. Literally.

"Everyone's fine, she says. The new owners are surprisingly easy to work with."

"Glad to hear it." He lifted his pint. "How's the wine?"

I took my first sip. "Fingernail polish remover."

"I was afraid of that. Something tells me this pub isn't known for its cuisine."

Something was telling me the same thing. A sign behind the bar said HOT WOMEN SERVED FIRST. GET USED TO IT. A fire burned in the stone hearth, but the effect was spoiled by a line of gaming machines. Our table felt sticky.

"How did you choose the Finchley Arms? Didn't we pass another pub on the way?"

"Yes—the Three Magpies. Sergeant Cliffe's grandmother lives in Long Barston. She warned us off that one. I believe her exact words were, 'Opened three year ago. We don't take to newcomers round here.'" Tom's imitation of a Suffolk accent made me laugh.

"How long has the Finchley Arms been around, then?"

"Since the Norman invasion, apparently." He grinned. "They say the proprietor has spies, taking down the names of locals disloyal enough to try the competition."

"Well, we wouldn't want that. Let's see what this place has on the menu." I craned my neck to view the chalkboard behind the bar. "Fish and chips, chicken tenders and chips, and pizza."

Tom groaned. "I'd planned to take you to a special place, Kate—the Trout, near my village—but I'm waiting to hear from the coroner. If he calls, I may have to leave."

"Never mind," I said, putting on my optimistic face. "I'll try the chicken tenders." Tom got up to place our orders, and I imagined the wonders of the Trout. Since the term *gastropub* entered the British lexicon in the nineties, fine cooking has made its way into almost every village in England. Almost.

Tom lived in Saxby St. Clare, a village fifteen miles north of Long Barston and thirty miles south of Bury St. Edmunds, where he worked. His household included his daughter, Olivia, currently taking her gap year in East Africa, and his mother, Liz, who'd moved in four years ago when his wife died of cancer.

"My mother's not keen on Americans," Tom had confessed during one of our transatlantic phone calls. "You'll win her over."

"*Win her over?*" I'd said. "Remind me again why I have to meet her?"

"Because I love you. Because I want her to love you. Because you'll win her over." His confidence in me was touchingly naïve.

Tom returned. "One chicken tenders and one fish and chips, coming up."

"We can try the Trout another night. Come sit. Any news about Tabitha?" I wondered how much Tom would tell me about the investigation.

"We had a preliminary chat with the butler and the cook. We'll take their formal statements tomorrow, along with Lady Finchley-fforde and anyone else present on the estate that day. The butler, Mr. Mugg, is making a list."

"*Mugg*. Sounds like a character in an Agatha Christie novel."

"He wasn't best pleased we'd be speaking with his lady, I can tell you. He fancies himself as her gatekeeper. Only too happy for us to question the interns, though. He managed to imply we'd find the answer among them."

"They did know Tabitha best." I told Tom what Prue Goody had said about Tabitha not taking medication. Then I pointed out the old man at the bar. "There's the gardener I told you about, the one who found the body of the young museum curator years ago."

"On our list."

"Tom," I said, picking up my wine glass and considering a second sip, "do you think it's significant that both murders—Tabitha and the one twenty-three years ago—involved young women working on an exhibit of the Hoard? It's almost as if someone didn't want the exhibit to happen."

"Certainly a line of enquiry."

"And then there's the old gardener. I saw him yesterday with a young man—another one of the interns, I think. They seemed to be arguing."

Tom took a swallow of beer and wiped his mouth. "It's odd."

"That they were arguing?"

"No." He laughed. "I was thinking about us. In Scotland we were outsiders, able to see things others couldn't because they were too close. Now I'm on my own turf. Your insight could be helpful."

"I'm not a trained observer."

"You've already seen what others haven't—the position of the body, for example. In Scotland it was your ability to notice details and patterns that led to the killer. If you see patterns now—like the museum thing—I want you to tell me. Don't get me wrong. I'm not suggesting you involve yourself in the investigation. No offense, Kate, but I don't want you in harm's way again."

"Believe me." I took his arm. "That's the last place I want to be."

A frowsy woman in patterned tights and a less-than-pristine apron appeared with two plates of food. She plunked them down and snagged a bottle of vinegar from the next table.

"That was quick," Tom said.

Too quick. I pictured pans of premade chicken and fish drying out under heat lamps.

"You're police." The waitress eyed Tom with a knowing look. "'Ere about that girl what's been found in Blackwater Lake." She'd rimmed her small, round eyes with thick black liner, making them look even smaller.

"That's right," Tom said.

"You 'eard about the stranger, then—one's been 'angin' round the village."

"I haven't heard," Tom said. "What about him?"

"Just that 'e's not English, is 'e? Foreigner—sort of Mediterranean, if you know what I mean."

"Has he done anything to cause concern?"

"No," she said in a voice that meant *yes*. "Only what's 'e doin' 'ere? That's what we want to know. 'E shows up, and a young woman is found dead." She raised her chin as if scoring a point.

"What does he look like?"

"Fifties, maybe. Rough. Funny cap, pulled low over 'is face. Come in 'ere night b'fore last." She gave Tom that knowing look again. "Drank a few pints, slapped down 'is coins, an' left without so much as a by-your-leave."

A criminal, obviously—or worse yet, a newcomer.

"Do you know where he's staying?"

"'As to be the Three Magpies, doesn't it? Only place with rooms—'cept that new place on the A road toward Sudbury."

Tom reached inside his jacket and pulled out a card. "Thank you, Miss"—he glanced at the name badge pinned to her apron —"Briony."

"It's *Mrs.*—Mrs. Briony Peacock." She flicked her head toward the bar, where a tall man with a meager gray ponytail was pulling a pint. "We own the place, me and Stephen."

"Order's ready," Stephen Peacock snarled. "No time fer chattin' up the punters."

Tom handed her his card. "If this stranger breaks any laws, give me a call."

Briony flung herself off with a shrug of her shoulders.

"What do you think?" I asked when she was out of earshot.

"A dark stranger who drinks alone? Very suspicious indeed." He speared a chip with his fork. "That's the trouble with a village, Kate. They don't trust strangers. I will have to look into it, though."

"Michael Nash, one of the interns, mentioned a stranger on the Finchley Hall estate. Actually it was Tabitha who saw him near the Folly. No mention of his looking Mediterranean." Three spears of dry breaded chicken lay on my plate. I cut off a bite and popped it in my mouth. Followed by a swallow of the fingernail polish remover.

Tom had just tasted his fish. "I *am* sorry, Kate. Do you want to leave?"

"And risk getting written up for disloyalty? Let's eat what we can—the chips aren't too bad—and when we get back to the Stables, I'll make you an omelet."

He gave me that half smile, and I went all wobbly inside.

He sprinkled his chips liberally with vinegar.

"How's Olivia?" I asked, remembering the photograph of his daughter he'd shown me in Scotland. She was in East Africa, taking her gap year at an orphanage for AIDS babies.

Tom shrugged. "She was meant to come home in July, only we got an email last week. She says her time at the orphanage has caused her to rethink her decision to study chemistry."

"Caring for orphans is an admirable thing to do."

"I agree," Tom said, "and I want Olivia to do something worthwhile with her life. But she did well enough on her A levels to get a place at King's College, Cambridge. I wouldn't like to see her throw that opportunity away." He speared another chip but seemed to think better of it and put the fork down. "How's Eric?"

"Still in Italy, finishing up his research at the nuclear waste facility. I thought he'd be home for Christmas, but he met a girl, a fellow student. She invited him to join her family at their ski lodge in the Italian Alps. How do I compete with that?"

"It's not easy parenting young adults, is it? Just when we feel most compelled to give advice, they feel least inclined to accept it."

A cold draft blew in as the pub door opened. Michael Nash entered, followed by Prue Goody, Christine and Tristan, and Alex Devereux.

"Mom?" Christine and Tristan threaded their way to our table. "You didn't tell me you were having dinner at the Finchley Arms."

"I didn't know."

Tom stood, and I introduced them.

"Great to meet you," Tom said. "I understand you're at Magdalen College. I was at Trinity."

"Were you really?" Christine's smile was as sincere as a Chinese Rolex.

Tom didn't notice. Or was too polite to show it. "How about you, Tristan?"

"I'm at Oxford Brookes, studying architecture."

"What's your opinion of that new glass building, the one that looks like . . ." The two men began a conversation.

I hugged my daughter. "When do you begin your work?" Christine's internship, she'd explained in one of her rare emails (I'd thought about printing it out and framing it), involved organizing and cataloging a mass of Finchley family documents spanning nearly three hundred years. Luckily for her, organizational skills hadn't been included in the Finchley DNA.

"Monday, officially, but I'm going to spend some time in the archives tomorrow to get a feel for what I'll be dealing with. Why don't you stop by—or will you be checking out the antique shops? Long Barston has three, by the way. All on the High Street."

"I have no plans tomorrow. I'd love to see what you're doing. How about Tristan? When does he begin at the guildhall?"

"Soon. He'd been helping Tabitha with the Hoard exhibit— carrying heavy items, putting up posters, stuff like that. Wasted effort, I imagine. Without Tabitha, I don't see how Lady Barbara can pull it off."

"I hope she has a backup plan."

Christine and I watched Michael Nash shove two tables together. Prue Goody removed some empty pint glasses and carried them to the bar.

My eyes felt dry. I rubbed them with my knuckles.

"You must be exhausted," Christine said.

"At the moment, I'm wide awake. Finding a dead body has a way of doing that."

The jukebox in the corner roared to life. Alex Devereux pushed some buttons, and music—something fast and funky—ramped up the already deafening noise level.

"Christine," Michael shouted. He made a circular motion with his hand, indicating he was buying a round.

She held up a finger—*just a minute*.

The door opened again, and the well-built young man I'd seen in the garden appeared. He'd swapped his work clothes for jeans and a black zip-up fleece jacket. He hesitated for a moment, as if deciding whether to stay. Now that I saw him close up, I couldn't help staring. He wasn't just good-looking. He was gorgeous.

"That's Peter Ingham, one of the long-termers," Christine said. "He's working on his doctorate—the history of landscape gardening. Prue and I think he should dump the plants and take up male modeling."

"I see what you mean."

Alex Devereux saw him, too. Her face lit up. "Peter," she shouted over the noise. "Come join us."

He shook his head and nudged his way toward the end of the bar, where the old gardener gave him a clout on the back. Either their argument had ended amicably or I'd misunderstood what I'd witnessed earlier. That's the problem with noticing details. You don't always interpret them correctly.

"Is Peter always so unsociable?"

"Pretty much." Christine made a little moue of regret. "He hangs out with the gardener mostly. I think he's avoiding Alex. I heard there's some history between them."

Loads of history here, I thought, *and not all the kind that makes it into books.* "What did you think of Tabitha?"

"Nice girl. Serious. Religious, I think. At least she spent a lot of time at St. Æthelric's. But that might have been because of the dishy vicar."

"Do you really think she killed herself?"

The question brought a frown. "I couldn't say. She was secretive. She had a look that said *I know something you don't.*"

"Come, *chére*," Tristan said. "We're ordering food."

"See you later—when you get back, maybe?" I said.

"Okay—bye, Mom. Nice to meet you, Tom."

"Your daughter is lovely," Tom said as we watched them join the other interns.

"And Tristan?"

"Nice chap. Serious about architecture."

A new song began, one I recognized. Christine had played it endlessly the previous summer. The interns got up to dance, if dancing is what you call it these days. Lots of arm movements, posing. No one had a specific partner.

"Wonderful to be young," I said, feeling every one of my forty-six years.

"Oh, yes. We were much more dignified in our day. Remember mosh pits?"

I winced, picturing my big hair and a boyfriend who had been into grunge.

In the middle of the dancers, Alex Devereux stood still, her eyes fixed on Peter at the end of the bar. Then, as if pulled by a magnet, she made her way toward him.

I watched, fascinated by the physical beauty of the two young people—a matched pair. Peter turned toward Alex on his barstool. She held out both arms, moving to the rhythm of the music. *Dance with me.* Her hair, loose tonight, tossed from side to side in a tangle of dark curls.

He turned his back on her.

For the briefest of moments, pain registered on Alex's lovely face. Then she shrugged. And turned her smile on Tristan Sorel.

Another song began, something slow this time, by Bruno Mars. Alex pulled Tristan onto the dance floor, threaded her arm around his waist, and leaned into him.

I couldn't believe what I was seeing. "She's vamping him, Tom. Right in front of my daughter."

"And he's eating it up."

He was, too—like a moth, fluttering around a pretty flame.

I didn't need to see Christine's face. The stiffness of her back told me everything. She whispered something in Prue's ear, grabbed her jacket from the back of the chair, and ran out of the pub.

I thought of the darkness outside—and the killer. "Should I go after her, Tom?"

He touched my arm. "Wait."

It was good advice, because Tristan had seen Christine leave as well. Disentangling himself from Alex, he took off after her.

The music revved up again.

Tom's phone must have vibrated, because he put it to his ear.

He closed his eyes and pinched the bridge of his nose. "Right. On my way." He slid his phone back into his pocket. "I'm sorry, Kate. I'll have to drop you at the Stables. That was the coroner. Tabitha was murdered. And she was three months pregnant."

* * *

Tom and I stood outside the door to the Stables.

"Not exactly the evening I'd planned." He pulled me into his arms.

I laid my head against his chest. "You have to do your job."

"I wanted this night to be special. Great food. Wonderful atmosphere. Just the two of us."

"I can wait."

"For how long?"

"As long as I have to." I made a face. "Well, two weeks, anyway."

He looked at me with those hazel eyes.

I looked at him and felt a little like a moth myself.

He kissed me. Properly.

Then he was gone.

The Commons was dark and quiet. I'd half expected to find Christine, throwing breakable things at Tristan. They would have arrived well ahead of us. The footpath from the village to Finchley Hall cut diagonally through the park, chopping a good two miles off the circuitous drive along dark, narrow roads banked with hedgerows. At night in the English countryside, the maximum safe driving speed is about twelve.

Peeling off my jacket, I switched on a lamp and made my way to my room. As I passed Christine's room, I knocked.

No one answered, but I heard someone sniff.

"Christine? It's me. Are you okay?"

The door opened a few inches. She'd changed into a pair of flannel pajama bottoms and a T-shirt. Her eyes were red.

"I'm sorry," I said, and stopped before saying something I'd regret. Actually, I already regretted saying *I'm sorry*. When Christine is hurt, the last thing she wants is sympathy.

She shot me a stony look and opened the door just wide enough for me to slip through. The room looked like a hurricane had blown through. The twin beds were a jumble of linens. Clothes lay everywhere, along with a scattering of books and papers. She had been throwing things after all.

Christine had always been a mystery to me, even as a child. Happy, outgoing Eric was like his father—steady, even-tempered. You knew where you stood with him. But Christine was a contradiction. Passionate to a fault, impulsive—even reckless—she approached life with the abandon of a runaway freight train. Then, when the inevitable crash came, she'd withdraw into herself and refuse to be comforted. Even a simple *How are you?* might be taken as criticism.

I didn't know where to start. I didn't have to.

"You saw what he did." Christine threw herself on one of the beds.

I sat on the other bed and waited.

She glared at me. "I'm an idiot, right? I should be ashamed of myself—a bad judge of men. That's what you want to say, isn't it?"

"Of course not. You didn't do anything wrong. Alex Devereux is the one who should be ashamed. And Tristan."

"You don't like him, do you?" Her face turned pink. "Another of poor, clueless Christine's disastrous relationships."

"Look. I don't blame you for being angry. But, to be fair, not many men would be immune to what Alex had on offer."

"Leave me alone." She buried her face in the pillow.

I stood. "I love you, Christine. I'm on your side. Never forget that."

I was closing the door to Christine's room when I saw Tristan skulking in the darkened hallway.

"She okay, *Maman*?"

Did he think calling me *mother* would endear him to me? "She will be," I said coldly.

As I turned toward my room, I heard him knock on Christine's door.

"Ma chère? Ma petite? *Je suis Désolé.*"

Chapter Five

Sunday, December 6th

The bells of St. Æthelric's nudged me out of a deep sleep. I stretched and considered emerging from my warm cocoon to face the day. *Oh, not yet.* Rolling on my back, I pulled the duvet to my chin. Back home in Jackson Falls, the time would be . . . well, the wee hours, anyway.

Beside the point. The hands on my clock pointed accusingly to ten fifteen.

Villagers in sturdy tweeds would be gathering outside St. Æthelric's Church in the village. Too late to catch a glimpse of the dishy vicar. There was always Evensong, but tonight I'd been invited to attend Lady Barbara's official welcome dinner for the new interns—that is, if the dinner was still on. I hadn't heard otherwise.

Tom had said he'd try to phone but couldn't guarantee we'd have time together that day—or even the next. He and Sergeant Cliffe would be busy with interviews. The crime scene manager had called in a dive team and a forensic pathologist. Depending on what they found, Tom anticipated some long days ahead.

I nestled further into my pillow and looked up through the skylights. Yesterday's blue skies were gone, replaced by gray clouds threatening rain. No wonder the English greet the brief appearances of the winter sun with deep suspicion.

Christine would have grabbed a mug of coffee and headed for the archives hours ago. Her mood, changeable as English weather, would depend upon Tristan's powers of persuasion last night. I had no doubt she would eventually forgive him. Her temper might have been volatile, but she'd never been one to hold a grudge. I admired her ability to forgive. That and her sense of loyalty. I pictured the stubborn little chin that went up when she, age seven, had taken the punishment that should have been her brother's for hiding the babysitter's iPod. Eric, tortured by remorse, had finally told us the truth. Christine would have kept his secret until doomsday.

Then I thought of Tristan locked in that clinch with Alex Devereux. If Christine *had* forgiven him, I hoped she hadn't made it easy.

Thinking about last night reminded me of Tom's phone call from the coroner. Tabitha had been pregnant, probably the reason she'd stopped taking her medication. She'd been at Finchley Hall since September. That meant the father of her child could be one of the interns. Not Michael Nash—he'd just arrived. The same went for Tristan. I could see Tabitha falling for the gorgeous Peter Ingham, but no one had mentioned they were a couple. I wondered how many male interns had left Finchley Hall in the last two months. Alex would know, but at the moment I didn't think I could have a polite conversation with the beautiful Miss Devereux.

A door slammed somewhere down the hall.

Throwing back the duvet, I slipped out of bed and found my robe. With the whole day free, I'd stop at the archives building to see if Christine was in the mood to talk. First, though, I wanted to take another look at the place where we'd found Tabitha's body. I wasn't naïve enough to think I'd find additional clues—the police had gone over the area with a fine-tooth comb—but seeing the place again might dispel the uneasy feeling I'd been unable to shake. Something about the crime scene hadn't seemed right, and not just the girl's position in the water.

My stomach growled, reminding me I'd eaten almost nothing at the Finchley Arms the night before. I was famished. Fortunately, Christine had stocked my small refrigerator with a few essentials from the Tesco at the roundabout outside the village. I downed a bowl of granola with nonfat milk and two cups of strong coffee.

An hour later, I bundled into my down jacket and wool scarf and made my way through the Elizabethan Garden toward the park. It had rained overnight. Puddles of water dotted the gravel path. Neither Peter nor the old gardener was in sight. Perhaps the soil was too wet to work.

The cold, damp air smelled pleasantly of boxwood and wet earth. I followed the route taken by our tour group, through the walled garden, across the Chinese Bridge, and past the Folly to Blackwater Lake. A fine mist floated on the water's surface, partially obscuring a line of ducks bobbing near the far shore.

Crime scene tape was still in place. I tried to imagine the scene just before Tabitha went into the water. Had she met the baby's father there to break the news of the pregnancy? Maybe he'd insisted she abort the child, and when she refused, lost his temper and struck her. I closed my eyes. How did the slip of rocks and mud fit in?

I was about to leave when I heard a splash, followed by a scream.

Running toward the sound, I spotted an elderly woman in an olive raincoat and wide-brimmed rain hat. She stood at the water's edge, holding a leash from which an empty collar dangled.

"Help," she cried. "My dog fell in the lake."

A small dog—a pug, I thought—fought to keep his head above water, but he was losing ground. I saw panic in his large bulging eyes as he flapped ineffectively.

"He was chasing ducks," the woman wailed. "But he can't swim."

I looked at the cold water. Then at the dog.

I couldn't just let the poor creature die.

Throwing off my jacket and scarf, I picked my way down to the water and waded in. The good news was the shock instantly turned my feet numb. The bad news? The sky chose that moment to open up.

I waded in further, blinking against the pelting rain. The lake bottom fell away quickly, and within seconds the murky water had reached my knees. I felt for solid footing, fearing a sudden drop-off would plunge me into the depths like the struggling animal. If that happened, I'd be helpless, weighed down by my jeans and heavy sweater.

A moment of panic gripped me, but I pushed my wet hair aside and forced myself to focus on the dog.

The pug was vertical in the water now, his front paws still flapping but more slowly. He was running out of steam. His tongue had a bluish tinge.

He saw me coming.

"Hold on, boy. Good dog. I'm almost there."

I reached for him but fell short. I slogged forward through long green tendrils that swirled around my thighs. Feeling for the bottom was no longer an option. My feet were completely numb. Losing my balance was a distinct possibility.

Keep going. Another foot or so.

I reached for the dog again, realizing only then that, without his collar, there was virtually nothing to grab on to. He was a solid little guy with a short, slick coat. And I'd lost feeling in my fingers.

I tried again, but he slipped away, out of my grasp.

Then he disappeared.

The woman on the shore screamed.

Holding back my dripping hair with one hand, I swept my free hand back and forth under the water. Nothing.

Where is he? Am I too late?

My right hand bumped something solid.

Gritting my teeth, I grabbed whatever I could—the loose skin on the dog's scruff, as it turned out—and held on for dear life as I pulled him toward the surface.

When the dog's head broke the surface, he actually gasped.

I edged backward step by step, not daring to turn my head for fear the dog would slip away again. The receding depth of the water told me I was going in the right direction.

At last I reached the shallows. The dog scrambled onto dry land and gave himself a mighty shake.

"Oh, my dear. You saved him." The woman unwound her wool scarf and wrapped it around the dog. She scooped him up and held the trembling animal to her breast.

I was trembling too.

"How can I ever thank you? If you hadn't come along, I'm certain Fergus would have drowned."

"I'm g-glad I got to him in t-time." My teeth were chattering so violently I could hardly get the words out.

"We must get you into dry clothes immediately."

"I'm staying at the Stables at F-finchley Hall."

"Too far. You'll catch your death. My name is Vivian—Vivian Bunn—and my cottage is just over there." She pointed through the trees to a pale-pink, timber-beamed cottage with a steeply pitched thatched roof. "You're coming with me," she said in a tone that would brook no argument. "We'll get you warm and dry in a jiffy."

I squelched after her.

The rain was pelting down, and I was in no mood to argue.

* * *

Rose Cottage—that's what the nameplate beside the door said—was a small jewel box. I sat in my damp underwear, wrapped in a soft blanket, near a crackling fire. The dog, Fergus, lay nearby in his basket, barely visible beneath a plaid shawl. Every so often his body trembled, but he was warming up and beginning to relax. He licked his nose, and I saw his tongue was pink again.

My boots steamed on the radiator. The rest of my wet clothes were tumbling in Vivian's dryer. She'd made a pot of strong, sweet tea and warm chicken sandwiches with peach chutney on brown bread. I'd never tasted anything so marvelous in my whole life.

Vivian, once she'd removed her rain gear and the heavy woolen coat beneath, wasn't quite as elderly or as round as I'd first thought. I would describe her as a healthy, comfortably upholstered woman on the downslope of her seventies. She wore a tweed skirt and wool twin-set that made me think of Miss Marple, but her hair, the color of old pewter, was cut in a short pixie brush-up. Firm lines around her mouth told me she didn't suffer fools gladly, and her eyes were that shade of gray I associate with lively intelligence.

"It was the ducks." She bent to tuck Fergus's shawl around him. He rewarded her with a low, satisfied snort. "He bolted—slipped right out of his collar. Took me quite by surprise. We walk along the lake twice a day—morning and afternoon. He's never done anything like that before."

"Always at the same times?"

She gave me a sharp look. "You're wondering about that young woman. You want to know if I saw her the day she died."

It wasn't a question, but it demanded a response. "I was in the group that found her. My daughter is one of the new interns."

"Ah." Vivian nodded. She considered me for a moment, as if deciding how much to say. "I did *not* see the poor girl the day she died. I wish I had. The villagers say it was suicide."

Another statement that demanded a response, but Tom had warned me to keep the coroner's verdict to myself.

I answered obliquely. "I hope it wasn't suicide, for her parents' sake."

Fergus, close to the fire and swathed in the woolen shawl, began to pant noisily. His long pink tongue lolled to one side.

Connie Berry

"*Tush*, now," Vivian ordered, and to my surprise, Fergus obeyed. She turned back to me. "You're concerned about your daughter."

"One of the interns said Tabitha saw a strange man near the Folly."

"A random killing?" Vivian stiffened. Maybe I'd frightened her. She lived alone, after all, with only a small, obese dog for protection.

"Whatever the reason for Tabitha's death," I said, shifting away from homicidal maniacs, "it won't comfort her parents."

"No. They're arriving today from somewhere north—toward Norfolk, I believe. Lady Barbara has made one of the estate cottages available to them."

"That's kind of her."

"Lady Barbara is a kind woman, generous to a fault. I was private secretary to her husband, Cedru fforde—two smalls *f*'s. When he died in 1999, I received a pension and life tenancy in Rose Cottage. Her doing, I'm certain. The Finchleys have always been loyal employers. Up until the Second World War, most of the local families worked on the estate in one capacity or another."

"Her husband's name, Cedru fforde, is unusual."

"Old Welsh. His family made a fortune in copper and lead mining. Cedru's marriage to Lady Barbara came at the right moment. With death duties and the cost of maintaining an estate as old as Finchley Hall, her father, the Marquess of Suffolk, was nearly forced to sell up. The infusion of cash saved the day. He insisted his daughter retain the Finchley name, so they were hyphenated."

"How long have you known the family?"

"Practically all my life. I was hired just after the engagement was announced. My first task was managing the wedding arrangements." She smiled at the memory. "The social event of the summer, in spite of the fact that the ffordes weren't quite what Lady Barbara's parents had envisioned for her. In the end the choice was between a poor aristocrat and a wealthy tradesman."

"And they chose the wealthy tradesman."

"Oh, Lady Barbara did the choosing. It was a love match. Quite a stunning couple they were, too. She, fair and slim with pale-blonde hair. He, tall and handsome, with coal-black hair and olive skin. It's the Celtic blood, you know. Some say the dark Welsh are descended from Spanish sailors washed ashore after the sinking of the Armada. Malarkey, if you ask me."

Fergus had escaped the confines of his basket. He shook himself and waddled over to me. "Feeling better, boy?" I rubbed his ears. "Me, too."

He looked up and smiled.

Vivian's eyebrows flew up. "Fergus doesn't usually take to strangers. He's too civilized to bite, of course, but he gets his point across. I do believe he's made an exception in your case, my dear." She gazed at the pudgy animal with the fondness of an indulgent parent. "I spoil him, but then I never had children. We all need someone to love, don't we? Do you have a husband?"

The segue took me by surprise. "I'm a widow."

"You have your daughter."

"And a son. Did Lady Barbara and her husband have children?"

"A stillborn daughter the year after they were married. Six years later, a son, Lucien."

Something in the way she pronounced the name told me there was an unpleasant story there. "You don't approve of the son?"

Vivian set her teacup down with a *thunk*. "I've never been a gossip, and I have no intention of starting now."

I could have kicked myself. I know the British consider personal questions rude. Now if I'd asked her about the weather, she'd have given me a full ten minutes, including the shipping forecast.

"I am sorry," I said, trying to regroup. "I didn't mean to pry. It's just that—" I had no idea where that sentence was going. Fortunately, Fergus chose that moment to stand on his short hind legs and hop, begging me to lift him onto my lap. I did, of course, and he rewarded me with a swipe on the nose with his wet pink tongue.

Vivian eyed us. "If Fergus trusts you, I suppose I can as well."

Bless you, Fergus. I stroked his sleek back. He snorted and half-turned in my lap to expose a round, plump belly.

"Lucien was a bonnie baby." Vivian picked up her cup and took a thoughtful sip. "He inherited his father's looks but unfortunately not his character. Having nearly given up hope of children, Lady Barbara was far too indulgent, and Cedru was already . . . well, already out of the picture, fatherwise."

I wanted to ask why Cedru fforde had been "out of the picture, fatherwise," but Vivian pressed her lips together, and I decided not to pursue the subject. Not yet, anyway.

"From boyhood, Lucien was allowed to run wild. I assure you, he made the most of it. He was sent down from Cambridge for a series of peccadilloes involving young women. Yet Lady Barbara continued to coddle him. Generous allowance. Allowed to come and go as he pleased. Until the tragedy."

"The tragedy?"

A bell chimed. "That will be your clothing." Vivian bustled out of the room, leaving me to wonder. She came back with my clothes, warm and neatly folded. "I'll leave you to change, dear."

Placing Fergus on the rug, I pulled on my warm jeans and sweater.

When Vivian returned, I broached the subject. "You mentioned a tragedy."

"Ah, yes." As I listened, Vivian added tantalizing details to a story I'd first heard on the ill-fated tour.

"In 1996, Lucien was twenty-one, recently come down from Cambridge and swiftly gaining a reputation in the surrounding villages as a drunkard and womanizer. A young museum curator, Catherine Kerr, arrived at Finchley Hall to arrange a special showing of the Hoard. Catherine was smitten by Lucien's looks and—it must be said—the money he threw around like confetti. Lady Barbara wasn't happy about the alliance but did nothing to thwart him—or to protect the young woman."

Fergus eyed my lap. I lifted him again, and he settled in with a satisfied snort.

"When the girl's body was found in Blackwater Lake and the inquest returned a verdict of murder, the police naturally looked first to Lucien. No evidence was found against him, and yet the police remained suspicious. Fearing arrest, Lucien fled to Venezuela, where he remains to this day. His mother never speaks of it, except to say he has a good job in the oil industry there and writes every other week. Even so, she sends him money now and again, but they've never had so much as a phone conversation since he left England."

"Couldn't she phone him?"

"Her letters are sent to a tobacco shop in Caracas. Lucien says it's safer if she doesn't know where he's living."

Safer? "And he's never returned to England?" I thought about the dark stranger drinking alone in the Finchley Arms.

"Not even when his father died." Vivian pursed her lips. "He left his mother to cope with everything on her own. I tried to help, but frankly I don't know what she would have done without Mugg."

"The butler?"

"Albert Mugg. He's served the family since he was a lad. There's nothing he wouldn't do for Lady Barbara. The sun rises and sets with her."

I admired Lady Barbara, too. She'd lost a husband and a child—two children, if you counted her runaway son—yet she'd managed to hold the estate together, using the assets she had to reward those loyal to her family.

"Lady Barbara is the finest woman I know," Vivian said as if reading my thoughts. She gave me a sharp look. "I assume I can rely upon your discretion. Her son can have nothing to do with this latest tragedy."

I agreed. Tom wouldn't need me to tell him about Lucien anyway. There'd be more than one person in Long Barston who remembered the events of 1996 and would, no doubt, be thrilled to share them.

"My immediate concern is for the exhibit." Vivian fingered a fine gold necklace that followed the neckline of her wool sweater. "The young woman who died was in charge. I don't wish to sound uncaring—not at all—but this is the worst thing that could have happened right now."

"Will the exhibit be canceled?"

"That would be difficult. The date has been set for more than a year. People have booked in advance. The exhibit was intended to be the centerpiece of a larger holiday celebration that begins on the Eve of St. Æthelric."

"Couldn't the exhibit be postponed? Surely the villagers wouldn't blame Lady Barbara."

"If it were only the villagers, I'd agree, but the exhibit of the Hoard has been publicized nationally. A television crew from the BBC will be there, along with scholars and collectors from all over Great Britain. This will be the first time the Hoard has ever been displayed in its entirety." She broke off, and I realized she was struggling against tears.

I could think of nothing to say that wouldn't embarrass her.

Vivian smoothed her tweed skirt. "I'm not exaggerating when I say the future of Finchley Hall is at stake. The exhibit will generate income for the estate—ticket sales, catalogs, souvenirs, refreshments. The truth is, Lady Barbara needs the money."

Perhaps the internship program was a moneymaker as well. Christine had paid an administrative fee plus room and board. More than likely, the various organizations that employed the interns—the guildhall, for example—paid for the privilege.

"This is too distressing to think about." Vivian's hand hovered over the teapot. "More tea?" When I declined, she poured herself another cup, adding a splash of milk and two sugars. She sat back and watched Fergus snoring softly in my lap. "Tell us about yourself, Kate. What do you do?"

The *us* included Fergus, apparently. His eyes opened, and his short, curly tail beat against my thigh.

"I'm an antiques dealer and appraiser. I'm here to visit my daughter, but I also hope to do some shopping. English antiques are popular in the States."

"You're an antiques expert?"

"My parents were the experts. They trained me."

"What sort of antiques do you specialize in?"

"Silver, porcelain, art glass, furniture—mostly from the eighteenth and early nineteenth centuries."

"Jewelry?"

"Certainly. Anything of age and beauty."

"Age and beauty." Vivian's eyes had taken on a curious gleam. Even Fergus was staring at me with heightened interest.

Why did I find that disconcerting?

As I thanked her and shrugged into my down jacket, a thought niggled at the back of mind.

Vivian had avoided my question about the stranger on the grounds of Finchley Hall.

Chapter Six

With no time left to stop at the estate archives, I returned to the Stables to shower and change for the welcome dinner. I chose a slim-fitting dress in stone-colored wool and added a flowered wool scarf—an outfit chosen by my best friend, Charlotte, an ex–department store window dresser. Charlotte considered me her own private "what not to wear" project. Tonight, I had to admit, the dress and scarf would be perfect. Like most old English houses, even those refitted with central heating, Finchley Hall would be chilly.

I was greeted at the door by Alex Devereux in a black jersey number that managed to cover her from breastbone to midcalf while leaving little to the imagination. "Good evening, Kate. Lady Barbara is pleased you could join us." Alex took my jacket and laid it across a chair. "Christine is such a sweet girl."

Is it my imagination, or did those words just sprout talons?

The reception hall featured oak linenfold paneling and an early Georgian staircase. The old floorboards creaked as we made our way past the massive formal drawing room on the left, the library on the right, and then down a long gallery to what Alex called the private drawing room.

"How many rooms in total?" I asked.

"No idea," Alex said. "We tell visitors there are fifteen fireplaces and five staircases, including a narrow one connecting the kitchen on the lower level to the roof access."

The private drawing room wasn't small, but in contrast to the formal drawing room, where I and the other members of the tour group had waited to be interviewed by the police, it felt warm and intimate. A fire blazed in the Portland stone fireplace. Beneath a plasterwork frieze badly in need of restoration, coral-pink walls featured portraits—more long-dead Finchleys, I supposed—in a variety of gold-leaf frames. Centered above the fireplace was the portrait Alex Devereux had mentioned. A small brass plate read SUSANNAH FINCHLEY 1608–1638. Dark hair fell in loose curls on either side of a pretty face. She wore a silver satin dress featuring full slashed sleeves and a lace bodice. Her left hand pinched the luminous folds of her skirt. Her right hand rested on a book—evidence of her learning, unusual for the time. On the middle finger of that hand was a gold ring set with an oval red stone encircled by rows of what looked like small pearls.

I leaned forward for a better look.

"Welcome to Finchley Hall." A slim woman of medium height stood to greet me. She was probably ten years younger than Vivian Bunn and still attractive in that English-rose sort of way, but frail. Fine lines etched her pale cheeks. Her shoulder-length hair had turned the warm white color natural blondes tend to go with age. She wore a wool dress of the palest blue—chosen, I imagined, to match her pale-blue eyes. She extended an age-freckled hand. "I'm Barbara Finchley-fforde. You must be Kate Hamilton, the mother of this lovely young woman."

Christine sat next to Tristan on one of two high-backed Knole sofas. "Mom, you look terrific. One of Charlotte's picks, right?" Christine's smile and the tone of her voice told me everything in her world was right again.

Tristan had the grace to look sheepish. "She is right, *Maman*. The color suits you."

That *mother* thing was starting to irritate me.

On the opposite side of the room, in an alcove with a bay window, sat Prue Goody and Michael Nash, chatting with Alex Devereux and Peter Ingham. At least Alex was chatting. Peter's head was angled away from the others, his hands in the pockets of his dark trousers. Three couples? If so, Tabitha King would have upset the balance.

"Thank you for including me tonight," I told Lady Barbara. "Spending an evening at Finchley Hall is a real pleasure. And thank you for allowing me to stay in the Stables while I'm here."

"It's the young man who canceled you should thank," she said. "We won't have more interns now until after Hilary term. Then we'll be full again. My friend Vivian says I should open some of the bedrooms in the Hall for scholars. Assuming they'd want to stay in an old pile like this. Corridors leading to corridors."

"They might get lost."

"You're right." Lady Barbara laughed. "When I was a child, the new maids would lay trails of corn to find their way back to the servants' quarters." She tilted her head. "Christine tells me you're an antiques dealer. I noticed your interest in the portrait. Lady Susannah was my late husband's final acquisition, so of course the portrait means a great deal to me."

"Final acquisition? I assumed the portrait had been in the family forever."

"The painting was sold sometime in the early 1800s—no one knows why. We learned of its existence shortly after our marriage, and my husband contacted the owner in London. She refused to part with it, but my husband instructed his attorney to stay in touch. The lady died six months before my husband's own death in 1999. Her estate agreed to the sale, and Susannah finally came home."

"She certainly adds to the mystique surrounding the Finchley Hoard. I'm looking forward to seeing the Finchley Cross in person."

"But I thought you took the tour." Lady Barbara's confusion turned to dismay. "Oh, of course. The tour was cut short." She lowered her voice. "I understand you were among those who found that poor, dear girl, Tabitha. I only wish I'd known how desperate she was. Young people are so passionate these days—not like those of us who grew up in the years following the war. You're far too young to remember, of course, but we had to be practical, to put our futures ahead of our feelings."

I tried not to stare at her. Had Vivian been right about the love match with Cedru fforde, or had Lady Barbara made the practical choice of marrying money after all?

"What happened to Lady Susannah's ring?"

"Ah, the blood-red ruby. Sometime in the past, the ring disappeared. My father feared it had been sold—perhaps along with the portrait, although the lady in London didn't own it. The Finchleys of that generation were more interested in cash than family heritage. My father made me promise never to sell any of the remaining pieces, and I never shall."

We looked at the portrait of Lady Susannah.

"The mystery of the blood-red ring," I said. "Everyone loves a mystery."

"Tabitha planned to move the portrait to the exhibit hall on the nineteenth, so visitors could enjoy a glimpse of the ring." Lady Barbara's hand went to the double strand of pearls around her neck, and I noticed that the elbow of her pale-blue dress had worn thin. "Now that Tabitha's gone, I'm not certain we can go ahead. Only how can we not, at this late date?"

"How many visitors do you expect?"

"Three or four hundred, I imagine. More than a hundred fifty have already bought timed-entrance tickets." Lady Barbara shook her head as if to clear it. "We may be forced to refund the money."

"That would be unfortunate."

I could see what Vivian had meant about the importance of the exhibit to the future of Finchley Hall. If four hundred visitors paid fifteen or twenty pounds apiece—plus extra for the convenience of not standing in line, and possibly more for the right to take photographs—Lady Barbara could reupholster those green velvet serpentine sofas and restore the plaster frieze. With the BBC filming rights, she could make a dent in some of the estate's more basic problems.

"How will the filming work?" I asked. "Won't the crew get in the way of the visitors?"

"Tabitha worked through all that. She sent the producers some preliminary information about the Hoard to help them develop their script. They asked to interview me—no more than ten minutes, I'm told. Thankfully that will happen at a later date, as will a filming session with some of the more noteworthy artifacts. They'll arrive early on Saturday to get a few background shots of Finchley Hall. Then they'll film the crowds waiting to enter the archives. Everything else will be done later. The half-hour documentary will be narrated by a well-known antiques expert and will air on BBC Four in spring."

"Have you spoken to the police about the exhibit? I mean, all those people tramping around a crime scene."

"That nice detective inspector said we could go ahead. That's not the problem. The problem is the exhibit itself. Tabitha planned it out in advance, but her work was by no means complete." Lady Barbara made a helpless gesture. "Who could possibly step in at this late date?"

"If I can be of help, let me know. My daughter begins work in the archives tomorrow. I'll have time on my hands."

Lady Barbara's pale face turned pink. "My goodness. That's generous. Let me think about it, will you? I'll let you know."

A sphinxlike Mugg entered the parlor with a tray of sherry in tulip-shaped glasses. He served Lady Barbara first, and I noticed him subtly guide her hand toward one of the sherry glasses. Was her vision poor?

I wandered to the fireplace, hoping to get a closer look at Lady Susannah's ring. The resins in the old varnish had darkened the image, but even in its present condition, I could make out a design on the deep-red central stone—a griffin rampant. The ruby must have been an intaglio, incised with the image on the Finchley crest.

Mugg offered the tray to me. Then to Christine and Tristan.

Peter Ingham had joined Lady Barbara on the other Knole sofa. Their conversation, from the snatches I heard, seemed to concern the Elizabethan Garden.

Christine joined me in front of the fireplace. "What do you think of Finchley Hall?"

"The place is a treasure," I said, "but to keep a house like this going, Lady Barbara needs money. Lots of it."

"That's why she sponsors interns. It's no secret. In the case of Peter Ingham, she's paid for housing him and gets her garden restored at the same time."

"And in your case, gets her archives organized. What about Alex?"

"Alex was an intern last year. She got her degree in international hospitality and tourism, and now she's a full-time employee. She runs the internship program, supervises the gift shop and the weekly tour groups, and generally lords it over the rest of us."

"And Prue Goody?"

"Prue's here till spring, working at the Anglo-Saxon Living History Museum near Saxby St. Clare. She's from the University of Leeds."

"What do you know about the intern who backed out—the one who would have had my room?"

"Not much. His name was Adam."

"What was his university?"

"I never heard. Why?"

"Just curious. I'm wondering why he decided not to come." It wasn't the whole truth, but it was as much as I could say.

Christine shot me a suspicious look. "What aren't you telling me?"

I shook my head. "It's just odd that he backed out. You know I don't like mysteries."

"There's nothing mysterious about it. He decided not to come."

"You're right." I gave her what I hoped was a conciliatory smile. "I'm sorry I didn't stop by the archives today. I decided to walk by the lake and—"

As I was telling her about Vivian Bunn and Fergus, I noticed Alex drift behind the Knole sofa. With a glance at Peter, she trailed her hand along Tristan's shoulders. Then she bent her head and whispered something in his ear. His eyes widened.

"What's wrong?" Christine had seen the surprise on my face.

"Tristan needs you."

It was the truth.

Something told me Tristan was one moth about to get his wings singed.

* * *

Like the rest of the house, the dining room at Finchley Hall was an amalgamation of periods and styles. The ceiling beams were Elizabethan, the oak paneling Georgian, but the light parquet floors and muted paintwork belonged to the Edwardian era. Over the wide rectangular table, a gaslight chandelier had been electrified. The frayed cord near the canopy told me repairs were long overdue.

Lady Barbara sat at the head of the table with Peter Ingham at the foot. I sat between Peter and Christine with Tristan on Lady Barbara's right. Across the table sat Alex, Michael Nash, and Prue Goody.

Lady Barbara tapped her fork on her water glass. "I wish to extend a warm welcome to our new interns, Christine, Tristan, and Michael. We are all shocked and saddened by the death of Tabitha King. I feel a certain responsibility toward the interns and want you to know that if you have any concerns or should ever simply need to talk, my door is always open. I am not your parent, but I hope you will consider me a friend, should you ever need one.

"Finchley Hall is a place where past and present meet. Each of you, in your own way, will contribute to the continuing life of the estate. I'm sure we all hope the preparations for the Hoard exhibit can be completed on time. I'd like to thank you for your concern, as well as for your part in the festivities planned for the Eve of St. Æthelric. That certainly will go ahead. If you have questions about your role, ask Ms. Devereux." She looked at me. "I hope you will be my guest that evening, Kate—may I call you Kate? And now"—she raised her water glass—"I trust you will all enjoy tonight's dinner."

The interns clapped appreciatively.

Mugg served the meal with the aid of the blonde maid who'd helped him the day Tabitha King's body was found. I hadn't noticed then, but her black uniform hung on her frame. Maybe she'd lost weight. More likely the uniform had once belonged to someone else. It certainly wasn't new. As she bent to serve Peter, I noticed a neatly repaired tear in the pocket. Once we started eating, she disappeared. Mugg remained, hovering protectively behind Lady Barbara.

The dinner, if not gourmet, was well cooked—roast beef with Yorkshire pudding and all the trimmings. All the interns had seconds, except Peter, who appeared out of sorts. I tried to engage him in conversation. He was polite but made it clear he was in no mood for small talk. Alex, at the other end of the table, frequently glanced his way. Remembering their interaction at the Finchley Arms, I wondered about that history between them.

After dessert and coffee, Lady Barbara folded her napkin. "There's brandy in the drawing room for those who would like it. Please make yourself at home. Mugg, convey my compliments to cook."

"It was a lovely dinner," I said. "You're lucky to have such an excellent cook."

"Mrs. Rumple is a wonder. She came to Finchley Hall soon after Cedru and I were married. What dinner parties we had in those days."

Goodness. How old was that cook?

Lady Barbara bade us good night.

The interns headed for the Finchley Arms. I didn't join them. Jet lag and my unplanned polar-bear plunge in Blackwater Lake had taken a toll. I was looking forward to an early night.

"Kate." I was surprised to see Lady Barbara lurking in the long hall. "You offered to help with the Hoard exhibit. Will you let me show you what's been accomplished so far? It's only fair you see what you're in for. Then you can decide."

The comforts of my cozy duvet vied with my curiosity about the Hoard. The Hoard won. "I'd love to see it."

"Grand. Mugg"—the butler must have been lurking with her— "fetch my coat. Mrs. Hamilton's coat is . . ." She looked at me.

"On the chair in the entrance hall."

"Of course, madam," Mugg said. "But I should accompany you. The way is dark."

"No need. Mrs. Hamilton will lend me her arm, won't you, Kate?"

"Very good, madam." Mugg backed out of the room. None too pleased. He shot me a look that said *bring her back in one piece or you'll answer to me.*

Lady Barbara reached for my arm.

In the light of the mirrored wall sconce, her pale-blue irises looked opaque.

Chapter Seven

﹏

"The loss of vision is progressive." Lady Barbara leaned on my arm as we walked through the ill-lit courtyard toward the estate archives building. I kept my eyes peeled. If she so much as scuffed a shoe, Mugg would never forgive me.

"The diagnosis," she said, "is corneal dystrophy, a genetic condition common in the Finchley family. I'll never go completely blind, thank goodness, but each year means an increased loss of freedom. I'm safe enough in my home, but driving is no longer possible, nor even walking alone in the park. I miss that very much, Kate."

"I'm sure you do. The park is lovely."

She smiled. "My consolation will be the Elizabethan Garden. The young man, Peter Ingham, takes great pains to include me in the decisions. I've taken an interest in the plant selections. Even if I won't be able to fully appreciate the forms and colors, I will enjoy the delicious scents."

We arrived at the archives building, a solid Palladian structure with stone columns and shallow steps. Lady Barbara pulled a set of old-fashioned skeleton keys from the pocket of her coat. "I told Mugg you would get me here safely."

"I'm not sure he believed you."

"He never does." Her laugh was as light and silvery as the sliver of moon above our heads. "Mugg can be overly solicitous, but I don't know what I would do without him."

I held her arm as we ascended three steps to the entrance.

"Mugg has been with you a long time?"

"Donkey's years." She laughed. "He came as a boy of fourteen—straight off the farm, although you'd never know it now. He can be quite a snob. I was only a girl myself then." She inserted one of the keys in a large lock and turned it. The door swung open, and she reached for the lights.

The main floor of the archives building had been converted into an exhibit space.

"We had the old wood floor stripped and the walls painted museum white." Lady Barbara slid out of her coat and draped it over her arm. "The display cases were made for us in a workshop in Essex. The price was surprisingly reasonable. Alex will set up a small gift shop in that corner, offering themed items." She pointed toward an L-shaped area to the immediate right of the door. "Years ago, my husband produced colored postcards of some of the Hoard items, but he never got around to doing anything with them. Alex thought we could sell them now—a brilliant idea, don't you think? My biggest concern is a catalog we've committed to produce. We spent money in advance, expecting a profit. The problem is I don't know if the catalogs will be ready in time or even what printer Tabitha used."

"You could always take orders and mail the catalogs out later." I glanced around the room, finding the majority of the display cases empty. I hoped my offer to help hadn't given Lady Barbara false hope.

"We need the money, you see," she said. "Repairs on a house like Finchley Hall can't be delayed forever. Right now we've got rain coming into the east wing. A number of the bathrooms are unusable, and the electrics need work. The staff is too large—I know that—but I won't dismiss those who've been loyal to this family for years. Not without a pension and a place to live. My father would turn over in his grave."

"It looks like Tabitha made a great start." I was trying to be encouraging, and it was true. The exhibit space was clean, spare, and cleverly arranged. The display cases, while attractive, had been constructed of relatively inexpensive materials—white laminate and clear Plexiglas. Cabinets lined three walls of the room. One wall cabinet appeared complete, the clear shelves displaying early pewter plates and tankards, each with an explanatory card. In the center of the room, a number of freestanding plinths would presumably hold larger, more important items encased in Plexiglas cubes. I was encouraged to see numbered slips of paper in the empty display cases and plinths. Assuming the numbers corresponded with some sort of listing, all I'd have to do was find the listing and follow the plan. Paint-by-numbers.

I hadn't noticed before, but a plinth near the rear wall held a bronze-and-silver chalice with splayed feet. As I moved closer, my appraiser brain kicked in.

Early medieval. Near-perfect condition.

My breath caught. Blood rushed to my cheeks. My fingertips tingled.

I knew the symptoms. I'd had them from childhood in the presence of an object of great age and beauty. My father, who'd taught me about antiques, had called me a *divvy*, an antique whisperer, drawn to the single treasure in a roomful of junk. I'd never told him about the physical manifestations. I'd never told anyone—not my mother, not even Bill. How could I explain it when I didn't understand it myself?

I rolled my shoulders and took a deep breath.

The card read 142. BRONZE AND SILVER ANGLO-SAXON CHALICE, CA. AD 800.

"Where are the rest of the treasures kept?" I asked. "Security must be an issue."

"Of course." Lady Barbara was peering at the chalice, and I wondered how much of the detail she could actually see. "The news of the rediscovery of the Hoard, and the unfortunate death of the man who found it, made the front page of *The Times* in 1818. Even so, other than Lady Susannah, the Finchleys have never been robbed—a miracle, really. But Cedru was no fool. After we married, he installed an alarm and purchased a jeweler's safe. Come. I'll show you."

In the rear corner of the room, a flight of stairs led to a lower level. We descended into a large room—an office, furnished with a desk, several file cabinets, a corkboard covered with notes, and a computer.

"The lower level of the archives building is reserved for the Hoard," she said. "Your daughter, Christine, will be working on the upper floor, where the family papers are kept."

A side room off the office was almost entirely taken up by an enormous cast-iron safe, at least six feet high and nearly as wide. Lady Barbara produced a key. "This is for the overlock," she said, turning the key and returning it to her pocket. "Since my vision is poor, I'll need you to enter a sequence of numbers in the combination lock." She spoke the instructions, which involved a series of five numbers with turns of the dial alternately to the right and left.

When I stopped on the final number, something clicked.

"Now turn the wheel."

The nickel-plated ship's wheel operated a system of steel rods, which retracted to free the heavy door. Inside the vault I saw two banks of drawers over open shelves. My eyes popped. The shelves held a dazzling array of artifacts of silver, gold, and bronze. Some were set with precious or semiprecious stones. Others were beautifully chased or inlaid with various materials.

No wonder scholars were excited about the exhibit. If Lady Barbara was telling the truth, these wonderful things hadn't been seen by more than a handful of people since the sixteenth century.

My physical symptoms simmered and bubbled, producing a sense of exhilaration and what I can only describe as a buzz.

Who needs alcohol when you have antiques?

"The safe is burglar- and fireproof." Lady Barbara opened one of the middle drawers. Felt-lined compartments held small objects, mostly jewelry. "Thieves would need a forklift and a flatbed lorry to shift this. I think we'd notice. In any event, we have a security camera inside, plus CCTV cameras outside. Any untoward activity would be recorded." She cocked her head. "If you take this on, Kate, you'll need the key and the latest combination. We change the code frequently. Mugg insists on it."

"Very wise."

"Mugg isn't in favor of the exhibit, if you haven't guessed. He never has been. He says—and I can hardly blame him—that displaying the treasures will encourage burglars. But I see things differently."

"You aren't concerned about theft?"

"Of course I am, but what good are these beautiful objects if no one sees them? If we can pull it off, scholars will be able to view the Hoard with their own eyes. That's why I agreed to produce the catalog. Not everyone who is interested will be able to attend. The Hoard will be studied and written about for years to come. My father and my husband may not have agreed with me—Mugg certainly doesn't—but the Hoard is my responsibility now." Her brow furrowed. "I pray I'm not the last Finchley to bear that responsibility." Her eyes glistened. She was thinking of her son. As if sensing my sympathy, she straightened her spine and raised her chin.

Fidelis, fastu, fortitudo.

Strength is not always physical, I mused, and courage isn't proven in battle alone.

"When did you make the decision to hold the exhibit?" I asked.

"The thought came first when I learned I was losing my sight. I wanted to see the treasure, all of it at once, and I wanted others to enjoy it as well. A young museum curator, Catherine Kerr, was going to make that happen. Then she was murdered, and I put the idea out of my mind until recently. I knew I needed a curator, but that was impossible without funding. So I contacted the University of East

Anglia. They suggested a qualified intern. I advertised. Tabitha was the most qualified applicant." She sighed deeply.

"Where did Tabitha keep her records?"

A smile lit Lady Barbara's face. "Does this mean you will take on the job?"

I looked at those pale-blue eyes. How could I refuse? "Of course, but I'll need Tabitha's spreadsheets and the drafts of the catalog to identify the objects."

"I believe she kept everything on the computer. If you have trouble locating the records, Alex could probably help."

"Count me in. Having a part in the exhibit will be a pleasure."

"I am pleased." Lady Barbara traced a finger along the corner of Tabitha's desk. "Because there's something else I'd like to ask." She looked up. "First allow me to show you the Finchley Cross. Then, if you can spare another ten minutes, I've asked someone to join us in my sitting room."

I got Lady Barbara back to Finchley Hall without so much as a stubbed toe. Once in the house she'd lived in all her life, she moved with confidence. I followed her down the long gallery.

The decor in the oak library was pure Victoriana. Besides the books, the walls were decorated with trophy heads. Several glass cases held the anthropomorphic displays of taxidermy, hugely popular at the time. Cigar-smoking squirrels playing poker. Bunnies at a tea party. Tabby kittens playing croquet. I shuddered, thinking of the adorable litter Fiona, my Scottish Fold cat, had produced one year.

I wasn't interested in taxidermy. Near the carved wood fireplace, another glass cabinet held the object I'd come to see.

The Finchley Cross.

It was magnificent. The arms of the cross were equal in length and flared. Tiny slices of garnet set in gold-wire frames created an intricate design. My symptoms, slowly ebbing since the archives building, built to an alarming new crescendo. My throat tightened. My heart pounded against my rib cage. Was I having a heart attack?

A thought began to unfold, the pleats and tessellations filling my brain. I reminded myself to breathe as emotions distilled into words.

Anguish, grief, emptiness. *Loss.* Yes—that was it.

A great loss.

* * *

Ten minutes later Lady Barbara ushered me, still reeling, into her private sitting room. Oh, I'd had these experiences before—usually no more than a vague sense of joy or sadness or fear, as if the emotional atmosphere in which an object existed had seeped into the joints and crevices along with the dust and grime. But every once in a while these impressions coalesced into something more specific—and unsettling.

I've always blamed my notoriously overactive imagination. Describe a medical issue, and I'm sure to develop the symptoms. Arrive ten minutes late, and I'm picturing smashed cars and sirens. Even so, I've never been able to explain why my brain does these things. Of course, lots of things in life remain unexplained. Like why you always think of the perfect retort when it's too late. Or why teenagers walk around staring at their phones but never actually answer them.

I put these conundrums out of my mind and focused on my surroundings.

The walls of Lady Barbara's sitting room were papered in a vintage design of urns and flowers. Candles flickered on a white marble mantelpiece around which three armchairs had been arranged.

In one of those chairs sat Vivian Bunn, looking enigmatic. "I told Lady Barbara about Fergus and your daring rescue," she said, as if preparing me for further revelations.

"Above and beyond, I'd say." Lady Barbara took the chair in the middle, indicating I should take the third. "We may have more than one reason to be grateful to you."

The atmosphere in the room felt distinctly odd. Two pairs of elderly eyes observed me with what looked suspiciously like guilt.

"There's something more you want me to do?"

The eyes blinked.

"Perhaps," Vivian said.

"If you agree," Lady Barbara added.

The room fell silent.

Vivian scooted forward in her chair. "You mentioned a stranger on the estate. You said the dead girl, Tabitha King, saw him."

"Yes. One of the interns told me—Michael Nash. He said Tabitha told Mr. Mugg."

"Just *Mugg*, dear," Lady Barbara said. "He didn't mention it, but then he *will* shield me from all things unpleasant. In any case, the park is open to the public. Tabitha hadn't been here long enough to distinguish a stranger from a villager. But that's not the point." She fingered her pearls and looked at Vivian.

"The point is," Vivian said, picking up the thread, "Tabitha isn't the only one who's seen a stranger. I hear things in the village."

"What things?" If Briony Peacock was the source of the gossip, I already knew.

"He's male, obviously," Vivian said. "Fiftyish, olive skin, black hair going gray at the temples, dark eyes, medium height and weight. Apparently he wears a funny kind of cap pulled low over his face, as if to disguise his identity."

"Has he done anything illegal?" I asked, echoing Tom.

Vivian put up her hand. I was getting ahead of the story. "After you left my cottage this afternoon, I walked to the village shop to post a letter. The locals believe the stranger is responsible for Tabitha's death."

"On what evidence?"

"The similarity to another death, twenty-three years ago."

"Catherine Kerr," I said, understanding for the first time. "The young woman from the Museum of Suffolk History."

Vivian and Lady Barbara nodded.

"They think the person who killed Catherine Kerr also killed Tabitha? But why?"

"At the time," Lady Barbara said, "the murderer was thought to be . . . mentally deranged." Her pale-blue eyes welled up.

Vivian reached out a comforting hand. "The villagers want someone to blame."

The lamp on the table near Lady Barbara flickered and went out. "Oh, fudge," she said. "That's been happening a lot lately. I'll have to get Mugg to take a gander at the fuse."

I pictured an ancient fuse box plugged with copper pennies. If Lady Barbara did make a profit on the Hoard exhibit, I hoped she'd solve the electrical issues before the cosmetic ones.

"Sometimes I feel quite hopeless," Lady Barbara continued. "When the parents of the interns hear there's been a murder, they'll take their children home. Not that I blame them, but we depend financially on the internship program."

"What can I do about it?"

"Investigate. Look into the rumors. Sort things out." Lady Barbara pulled her cardigan closer around her thin body. "Perhaps you can locate the stranger, find out why he's come."

"But I'm a stranger, too. Why would this man—or the villagers—talk to me? Besides, what makes you think I'd know where to begin?"

"We Googled you," Vivian said.

This time the two sets of eyes looked triumphant.

"I see." I pictured Vivian and Lady Barbara reading Donald Preston's article with my photograph and that ridiculous headline: JACKSON FALLS' OWN MISS MARPLE.

"We'd do it ourselves," Vivian said, "except people will assume we're biased."

"Why would they assume that?"

"Because"—Lady Barbara's chin trembled—"the villagers believe the dark stranger is my son, Lucien. They say he's returned to England and has killed another young woman."

*   *   *

I heard the yelling before I opened the door of the Stables.

Christine and Alex had squared off near the kitchen island. Prue and Michael looked like spectators at a traffic accident, wanting to help but not sure what to do.

"You're a *horrible* person." Christine's clenched hands shook with rage.

"Grow up, little girl." Alex hiked her small handbag over her shoulder and turned to go.

"Don't tell me what to do."

Alex turned back. "I don't care what you do. I'm going to bed. Oh, look—here's your mummy. She can tuck you in."

"*What?*" Christine picked up a ceramic mug and hurled it. Lucky for Alex, the mug missed her and hit the wall, shattering into a thousand pieces.

Alex spun around. "If you ever do that again, you're gone, little girl." Her eyes were slits, her mouth a tight line.

Prue and Michael stared.

Christine burst into tears.

"What's going on?" I said. "Where's Tristan?"

"Dead, for all I care." Christine swiped at her eyes. "Don't mention his name to me again—ever. Any of you." She turned on her heel and marched out of the room.

My throat closed. Hearing secondhand about Christine's disastrous relationships was one thing; watching the train wreck in real time was another.

Later, I lay in bed and stared into the darkness. Every cell in my body ached for my little girl. I thought of her as a lean, wiry infant. She'd cried at the drop of a hat—when the temperature wasn't precisely to her liking, when something she wanted was denied or delayed. Sometimes she screamed for no apparent reason, and when I'd tried to comfort her, her hot little body would stiffen in rage. Now, as a young woman, Christine was bright, passionate, romantic, impulsive, loyal. She could also be secretive, irrational, and—when she'd been hurt—impossible to console.

Trying to sleep was hopeless. Switching on my bedside lamp, I grabbed my laptop, logged on to the wireless network, and tapped out an email to my mother. I'd phoned her to let her know I'd arrived. Now there was more to tell, but I didn't think I could do it without crying. So I wrote it down.

For the second time in as many months, my mother had driven to Ohio from her retirement community in the Kettle Moraine country of southern Wisconsin to keep my antiques shop open while I gallivanted off to the UK. I couldn't have asked for anyone more qualified. For years she and my father had operated an antiques business, earning a national reputation not only for the quality of their stock but also for my mother's meticulous research.

I'LL CALL SOON. LOVE YOU. I pushed send and closed the laptop.

I pictured my mother's face as she read my email. I'd told her about the death of Tabitha King and the village rumors. The dishy vicar. The Hoard exhibit dilemma. Christine's latest romantic fiasco. I'd mentioned Tom Mallory, of course, but I'd downplayed our . . . our what? Friendship? Relationship? *Hopeless cause?*

My mother knew me too well to be taken in by labels. She was a romantic like her granddaughter. But unlike Christine, Linnea Larsen viewed life with a clear eye. If she preferred the rosy version of things and clung to optimism until all reasonable hope was lost, it was a choice, not an illusion. When events took an unfortunate turn, she wasted no time in regrets. She knew as well as I did that a romance between a widow from Jackson Falls, Ohio, and a detective inspector from Suffolk, England, had little chance of going anywhere.

At least I assumed she knew it.

I switched off the lamp.

What I hadn't downplayed in my email were the tensions among the interns and the pressures Lady Barbara faced. Emotional pressures. Financial pressures.

I pictured Finchley Hall, dressed in all its Christmas finery, teetering on the brink of disaster.

Chapter Eight

Monday, December 7th

I made it to the archives building the next morning by eight thirty. The air was crisp. A light frost blanketed the lawn. I let myself in with the key Lady Barbara had given me. From somewhere above, a chair scraped on wood. Christine was already at work.

Had Tristan returned to the Stables last night filled with remorse? Had he gone down on one knee and vowed he'd never again fall for Alex's undeniable charms? Had Christine bought it? I'd know the minute I saw her. I waffled momentarily, wondering if I should run up to find out or respect her privacy. I decided to respect her privacy. At least that's what I told myself.

I turned on Tabitha's computer and checked the document list for her records. There they were, in a file helpfully called THE FINCHLEY HOARD. I opened a document named INVENTORY OCTOBER 2019 and did a mental high five. The spreadsheet listed individual objects, 189 in all, each given a number and a clear description. A small number of objects, no more than twenty, had already been placed in the exhibit. The rest was up to me, but Tabitha had made things easy. The numbers on the inventory list would correspond to the slips of paper in the exhibit hall. Some items included a link to photographs—probably the ones taken for the catalog.

My heart lifted. I could pull this off for Lady Barbara. I really could.

I opened the massive safe, using the key and the number code I'd committed to memory.

Unlike the treasures of Sutton Hoo, two Anglo-Saxon burial mounds dating from the sixth and early seventh centuries, the Finchley Hoard was a collection of objects—coins, jewelry, religious items, household vessels—spanning the late Anglo-Saxon period to the middle of the sixteenth century, a period of some seven hundred years.

The Finchley treasure, lost in a single night and recovered two hundred fifty years later. The fact that the collection was still intact attested to two things—the original wealth of the Finchley estate, with its vast lands and tenants, and the notorious Finchley pride. With all her financial woes, Lady Barbara had never considered selling a single item.

By eleven thirty I'd familiarized myself with Tabitha's system, making comparisons between the descriptions in the database and the items arranged in the safe. I'd also begun to get a feel for the arrangement of items in the exhibit hall. That had required frequent trips up and down the stairs, comparing the numbered slips of paper with the descriptions on the database on the computer. What I needed was a printout.

I pressed print and heard the machine behind me come to life. Nothing happened. Then a message flashed on the screen: OUT OF PAPER.

Drat. Where would Tabitha keep printer paper?

The counter behind me held the printer and an electric kettle with a carton of Yorkshire Gold tea bags and a bowl of sugar packets. I opened the door of a closet. Inside, a heavy wool cardigan hung over a small portable refrigerator. In the refrigerator I found a carton of low-fat milk and a package of water biscuits. Tabitha had probably been battling morning sickness. I pictured the wan face in the lake and felt sick myself. Why would someone want to hurt Tabitha? Because she was pregnant? Because she knew something? Because she was a threat to someone?

What a wicked, pointless waste of life.

After a few more minutes of searching, I found a packet of computer paper in one of the desk drawers. When I pulled it out, I spotted a sheaf of papers held together with a paper clip. Tabitha had already printed out the inventory, and what's more, she'd made a number of remarks in a tiny, precise hand. Most of her notations involved the exhibit plan, referencing cabinets and plinths. I flipped through the pages, knowing that as I worked through the items myself, I would catch the overall vision—Tabitha's vision. We should honor her in some way, I thought, and felt sure Lady Barbara would agree.

I turned to the final page of Tabitha's inventory. In the half sheet left blank, she'd made a list—eleven items, written by hand in letters so small I practically had to squint to make them out:

Small gold and silver chalice
Cloisonné and garnet arm cuff
Gold collar with roped edging
Carved emerald pendant
Gold wirework pectoral cross set with amethysts
Necklace of amber beads
Silver platter with mythical figures
Necklace of pearl and carnelian
Bronze and silver clasp
Hammered silver and gilt communion vessel
Chased silver and filigree Gospel cover

Were these items that needed to be photographed? Objects in need of restoration? None were numbered like the other Hoard objects, and more to the point, none appeared to be alternate descriptions of items already listed. I made a mental note to ask Lady Barbara about them.

Near the bottom of the page, Tabitha had penciled a note: PHOTO FINISH, 14 SHEEP STREET, SAT. I opened a web browser and typed in the address. Photo Finish was a printing company—that was encouraging. The hours on Monday were ten AM to noon and two PM to four thirty.

I looked at my watch. Twelve fifteen. The shop would reopen at two.

Switching off the computer, I relocked the safe, grabbed my handbag and jacket, and ran up the two flights of stairs. I had to face her sometime. "Christine? Have you had lunch?"

No answer.

The landing led to a hallway with three doors. The first was open. I stuck my head in, finding the office empty. Two tall windows looked out over the park. Cabinets painted the color of old linen lined the room. On the soffit above each cabinet, letters of the alphabet had been stenciled—a Victorian filing system. A large square table in the center of the room held piles of rust-brown file folders and old, black fabric–covered account books. I wandered in. On the desk, a half-full mug of coffee and a pot of Christine's favorite lip gloss told me I'd just missed her.

I tried her cell phone, reaching her on the third ring.

"Yes?" Short. Impatient.

"It's me. I'm in your office. I thought we might walk to the village for lunch."

"No. Sorry."

"Are you—" I was about to say *all right* but caught myself in time. "—free later?"

"Why? So you can sort me out?"

"I thought you might want to talk."

A deep breath. "Look, I appreciate what you're trying to do, Mom. Believe me, I'm fine. Okay? I'll call you later. Maybe we can do something tonight."

"I'm on my way back to the Stables. Are you there?"

"No, I'm not." Another silence. "Promise me you won't talk to Tristan. Or Alex."

"Never occurred to me," I lied. "See you tonight."

I stood in Christine's office, watching dust motes float on the air. I imagined leaving her one of the encouraging notes I used to stick in her lunchbox when she was in elementary school.

DON'T WORRY ABOUT THE MATH TEST. YOU KNOW THE MATERIAL. I LOVE YOU.

SEE YOU AFTER SCHOOL. I'VE GOT A SURPRISE! I LOVE YOU.

The surprise that time was the tiny marmalade Scottish Fold kitten I'd rescued from a farm near our house in Jackson Falls. We named her Fiona, and she was currently living the life of Riley with my mother, who insisted on taking her to the antiques shop every day.

What would I write to Christine now? DON'T WORRY ABOUT TRISTAN. HE'S NOT WORTH IT. I LOVE YOU. Or maybe, DON'T GIVE ALEX THE SATISFACTION OF KNOWING YOU'RE HURT. I LOVE YOU.

True but useless.

Light slanting through the window fell on Christine's desk. A fresh December calendar in a green leather frame was blank. Except for the thirteenth, the Eve of St. Æthelric.

REENACTMENT OF PEASANTS' REVOLT, Christine had written. Followed by a heart.

With a dagger through it.

Chapter Nine

With only bagels and granola in my larder, I decided to treat myself to a proper lunch in the village. The walk through Finchley Park into Long Barston was well marked. Passing Blackwater Lake, I waved to Vivian and Fergus. The dog seemed to have recovered from his ordeal, but had he learned his lesson? Ducks honked and took flight, their wings brushing the surface of the water. He strained against his collar.

You're on your own this time, boy.

In Long Barston, the path ended in the churchyard of St. Æthelric's. I headed for the Three Magpies—first to check out their food (it had to be better than the Finchley Arms) but also to ask about the mysterious stranger who might or might not have booked one of their guest rooms. Even Miss Marple had to start somewhere.

The Three Magpies stood on Sheep Street, just around the corner from the Finchley Arms. The exterior was cream-painted brick with white window frames and a dark-blue door. The steep roof, no doubt once thatched, was covered with terra-cotta tiles. Window boxes overflowed with boughs of evergreen, huge pinecones, and sprays of red berries.

A youngish woman, late thirties maybe, crouched on the sidewalk near a freestanding menu board. "Welcome to the Three Magpies," she said, standing. "I'm Jayne Collier." She brushed off her apron and hiked up the sleeves on her heavy wool cardigan. "Lunch for one?"

She was slim and pretty with a long golden-brown braid trailing over one shoulder. She'd been writing on the menu board with a piece of colored chalk. Today's soup was carrot and ginger. The lunch special was herb-roasted pork fillet on a bed of roasted vegetables. *Promising.*

I followed Jayne through the blue door. Inside, under a low-beamed ceiling, a curved bar faced a huge fireplace that hinted at the building's age. Banquettes were tucked under the windows and along the walls. Plain wood tables and chairs. No fake horse brasses. And the best part—no gaming machines.

Beyond the bar, a separate dining room was paneled in sage green, the walls hung with coach lanterns and framed cartoons—from the pages of *Punch*, I guessed, the defunct British magazine famous for political satire.

I was the only patron.

"Where will it be?" Jayne spread her arms. "You have the pick of the tables."

I chose a banquette near the fireplace. Jayne handed me a hand-printed menu card, filled my water glass, and set down a pot of marinated olives before disappearing into the kitchen.

The lunch menu featured the soup of the day, a small selection of inventive-sounding salads and sandwiches, and the pork fillet, served with carrots and courgettes. Along the bottom of the card, I read THE THREE MAGPIES, LONG BARSTON. PROPRIETORS, JAYNE AND GAVIN COLLIER. I pictured the dried-out chicken tenders at the Finchley Arms. Why wasn't the Three Magpies jammed with customers?

Jayne appeared with an order pad. "Any questions, or are you ready to order?"

"It all sounds wonderful. I think I'll try the soup and the green goddess salad."

"Good choice. Something to drink—tea, coffee? Glass of wine, perhaps?"

"Water for now."

After leaving to put in my order, Jayne returned and leaned against the bar. "You're not from around here. Passing through?"

I introduced myself and explained about my daughter and the internship at Finchley Hall.

Her expression darkened. "Where that poor young woman died. It's just awful."

I agreed that it was.

"She was here not long ago—for lunch with the vicar."

"Tabitha was here with the . . . vicar?" I almost said *dishy*. "A date?"

She frowned. "Oh, goodness, I don't think so. I got the impression he was counseling her. She was tearful."

Hmm. I was going to have to meet this vicar. "I'm surprised the village isn't thick with reporters."

"Just wait. They're all in Lowestoft this morning. One of the National Trust properties was burglarized. It was all over the news. The thieves got away with an ivory figurine. Really old, they said. Chinese. Tiny thing—about six inches high."

"A break-in?"

"That's the incredible part. They think the figurine was taken during regular open hours. On one of the tours, apparently."

Outside the window, a Sky News van rolled past.

"You'll have most of the reporters in here for a meal anyway."

"Always a silver lining," Jayne said. "We can't get the locals to give us a try."

"Why is that, if you don't mind me asking?"

"We're new in Long Barston—if you call three years new." She slipped her hands in the pockets of her long cardigan and wrapped it round her slim frame. "In Long Barston there are *locals* and there are *newcomers.* To qualify as a local, you practically have to trace your family roots in Suffolk back to the Domesday Book." She shook her head. "I'm exaggerating, but it's all about loyalty. Gav and I are Londoners. The Peacocks—they own the Finchley Arms—have lived in this village for generations. The cemetery is stuffed with them, no pun intended." She shook her head. "Sorry. I'm boring you with all this."

"Not at all. I'd like to hear more. Do you have time to talk?"

She laughed. "I could say I'm run off my feet, but it isn't true. Not at lunchtime, anyway. We do all right in the evenings. Frankly, that's what keeps us afloat. People come for dinner from as far away as Sudbury. It's the locals who won't warm to us, and it's the local trade we need—regulars, folks who come to see us as a village gathering place. The Arms has the monopoly on that. Always has, always will, I guess."

"How did a couple from London end up owning a pub in Long Barston?"

"Gav and I worked at the Anchor & Hope in Southwark. Gavin was the sous chef. I was assistant manager. The work was exciting, the pay was good, but Gavin has his own ideas about food. So when he inherited money from his grandparents, we looked to buy a place of our own. We found the Three Magpies. The original pub closed after the Second World War, and the building was turned into an electrical repair shop. That closed, too, and the building was up for sale. We bought it, invested money in restoration. Gav designed a simple menu based on locally sourced meat and veg. We thought a real gastropub in the village would be welcome."

"I understand you have rooms as well."

"Four king doubles and two twins. All en suite."

That was my opening. "Do you have anyone staying at the moment?"

"Not at present, no."

"I'm told there's a visitor in town—Spanish, maybe."

Jayne rolled her eyes. "You're talking about the 'mysterious stranger.'" She made air quotes. "It's all over the village. Everyone says he killed that poor girl. And no, he isn't staying with us. Never has, thank goodness. That's all we'd need."

"Have you seen him?"

"Gav did, briefly. Near the Hall."

"Finchley Hall?"

"We sell produce to the cook there when we have more than we need." She turned and called back toward the kitchen, "Gav, can you come out here for a minute. Question for you."

A tall man in a white chef's tunic and toque popped his head through the swinging door near the end of the bar.

"This is Kate Hamilton," Jayne said. "Her daughter's one of the new interns at the Hall. She'd like to know about the man you saw there the other day."

Gavin pulled off his toque. His dark hair reminded me of Tristan's—short on the sides with a brushed-back mop on top. "Caught a glimpse is all." I recognized a London accent.

"Where exactly did you see him?"

"Toward the back of the 'ouse, close to the brick wall. That's where I go—the kitchen. I didn't see him properly, you understand—just a dark shape slipping through the door to the park. Wouldn't've thought more about it, only Mags over t' village shop said everyone's gabbing 'bout a mysterious stranger."

"Would you recognize him again?"

"Doubt it." He glanced at his watch. "Gotta stir the sauce."

Jayne stood. "I'll just check on your food."

I stared into the flames. What was the stranger doing near the Finchley Hall kitchen? Trying to find an easy way into the house—or contacting one of the servants?

My cell phone rang. Tom Mallory popped up on the screen.

"Hey, it's me. Are you free for lunch?"

I felt a bubble of pleasure. Tom's voice had the remarkable ability to turn me into a teenager. "I'm at the Three Magpies. Want to join me?"

"On my way."

"How close are you?"

"Ten minutes. Well, fifteen maybe. I've got news."

"So do I."

*　　*　　*

"No problem," Jayne said when I postponed my order.

While I waited for Tom, I ordered a glass of white wine and thought about the questions swirling in my brain. Reaching for the pen and small notebook I keep in my handbag, I flipped past my notes on the Finchley Cross. At the top of a blank sheet, I wrote QUESTIONS.

1. *Who murdered Tabitha King?*
2. *Who was the father of her baby? One of the interns? The dishy vicar?*
3. *Who is the dark stranger? Lucien? Connection to death?*
4. *Why was T lying with her head close to shore? Slip of mud and rocks?*

That was one question I could answer—at least tentatively. Tabitha hadn't slipped and fallen into Blackwater Lake, and she hadn't waded into its chilly depths to end her life. She'd been carried, dead or unconscious, and tossed into the lake. Perhaps, under the weight of her body, her killer had slipped on the mud and rocks.

These were obvious questions. How about the *un*obvious questions?

I stared at the fire, watching the flames lick the logs.

5. *Why were Catherine Kerr and Tabitha King, two women associated with the Hoard, murdered? Connection other than their profession?*

Better but still obvious. I tapped the pencil against my chin.

6. *Who benefits if the exhibit isn't held? If Lady Barbara loses the Hall?*
7. *What is bothering me about the crime scene, and why can't I remember what it is?*
8. *Why did Tabitha make the list at the end of the inventory?*

I sat back and sipped my wine, trying to recall the list. *Chalice, arm cuff, emerald pendant, amber necklace, Gospel cover . . .*

Ten minutes later Tom brushed through the door of the Three Magpies. "Sorry." He peeled off his waxed jacket and dropped a kiss on my head. "Traffic's brutal."

I couldn't help smiling. In the two months I'd known him, we'd spent less than a week's time together, and yet I felt I'd known him all my life. Since the afternoon we'd almost collided on an icy road in the Inner Hebrides, he'd dominated my thoughts and invaded my dreams.

This wasn't like me—or like the me I used to be.

"Have you ordered?" He slid into the banquette beside me.

"Soup and salad." I handed him the menu card.

When Jayne arrived with her order pad, I introduced them. Tom ordered the soup with a warm turkey sandwich and a pot of tea.

"So what's your news?"

He ran a hand through his hair. "Tabitha's parents arrived today."

"How are they?"

"Shattered. In shock. Determined to find out what happened to their daughter."

"What are they like?"

"Late forties, wealthy, socially prominent—what people these days call the Upper Middleton class. They live in a Grade II–listed Georgian house near Hoxne. Mr. King runs an Internet business and takes an interest in local politics. Mrs. King is a fund-raiser and patron for the local cottage hospital in Aldeburgh. Tabitha was their only child."

I closed my eyes, unable to bear thinking about their loss. "Did you learn anything helpful about her? If you're able to tell me, that is."

He speared an olive. "Nothing we've learned so far is confidential. Tabitha was bright, sheltered, and—until recently—compliant. Last spring she became involved in what they termed an unsuitable relationship. A young man from a working-class family, a fellow student at the university. Tabitha's first boyfriend, and her parents, assuming the young man was after her money, forbade her to see him. Which she agreed to, according to them."

"What was his name?"

"She wouldn't tell them."

"That's odd. They weren't interested enough to find out?"

"If they were, they aren't saying. They believed she'd broken things off. Last August the internship at Finchley Hall came up. They jumped at it. Not only was it a tremendous opportunity for Tabitha, something impressive to put on her CV, but it also took her far away from the young man and, in their words, 'out of harm's way.' They thought she'd refuse to go, but Tabitha seemed delighted. More evidence in their minds she'd gotten over him."

"If she had, he wasn't the father of her baby. How did they react to the news of her pregnancy?"

"Refused to believe it. When I handed them a copy of the coroner's report, they were so shocked they couldn't speak."

"Did they say anything more about her depression?"

"Just that it developed after the break-up. Her local GP prescribed a mild antidepressant. She got better, so they assumed the medication was working. When we searched her room, we found the tablets. She hadn't been taking them—probably because of the pregnancy. She was fourteen or fifteen weeks along."

"When did she arrive in Long Barston?"

"Early September."

I did a quick mental computation. "Which means the baby was conceived just before or just after she arrived. Did you find anything to identify the father—letters, notes?"

"I'm sorry, Kate. I can't talk about that. What I can tell you—because her parents have already informed a local reporter—is they're insisting on DNA testing of all the males at Finchley Hall. Perhaps the whole village. Mr. King has friends in high places. Chief Superintendent Rollins made it clear he expects a swift arrest."

"But doesn't it take weeks for DNA results?"

"Under normal circumstances. We're using a private lab. As I said, Mr. King has friends in high places."

"The police assume the killer was the father of her baby?"

"We're not assuming anything. Her parents are."

"When will you begin?"

"Later this week if we can find the resources. The interns will be tested first, including those who've recently left Finchley Hall."

"One of the interns decided not to come. Adam somebody. He might have known Tabitha before."

"He's on our list. So are a couple of other lads—long shots, but we can't afford to assume anything. That means swabbing the male members of the Hall staff as well, and probably the farmers who graze animals on estate land. If there's no match, Lord help us, we'll begin with the villagers."

"Putting pressure on you."

"I want a fast resolution as well. For the young woman's parents. And for *us*." He put his arm around me and pulled me close. "We were supposed to have two whole weeks together with nothing more urgent than a lost cat or a pub brawl."

"Can't be helped." I leaned my head against his shoulder. "The interns say Tabitha spent a lot of time at St. Æthelric's. She may have been getting counseling." I told him what Jayne had said about the tearful lunch.

"Are you implying her relationship with the vicar was more than spiritual?"

"More likely she needed to confide in someone about the pregnancy. You're the one who asked for details, remember?" I changed the subject. "What about the theft near Lowestoft?"

"You heard about that, did you? That's Eastern Division. Not my patch."

"Any news on the mysterious stranger?"

"Not yet, but I'll have to—"

Tom broke off as Jayne pushed open the swinging door from the kitchen, balancing a tray on her shoulder. Our carrot soup, topped with a dollop of cream and a sprig of dill, was served in small porcelain tureens. My salad was crisp, with slices of avocado, snow peas, and plump ruby pomegranate seeds. Tom's sandwich combined generous forkfuls of turkey with cranberry sauce and melted brie on whole-grain bread.

I took a spoonful of soup and almost moaned. Were the locals crazy? For food like this, I wouldn't care if the Colliers were descended from Lizzie Borden and Jack the Ripper.

Jayne brought a teapot to the table and filled Tom's cup. Then she disappeared into the kitchen.

Tom cut off a triangle of his sandwich. "As long as I'm here, I might as well ask the waitress if she knows anything about the stranger."

"Don't bother. He isn't staying here. Never has. Jayne and her husband are the owners, by the way. He caught a glimpse of someone near the Hall but didn't see enough to be helpful."

Tom put down his fork and stared at me. "How do you know all that?"

"I asked—that's where my news comes in." I told him about Lady Barbara and Vivian strong-arming me into helping with the exhibit and stopping the village rumor mill. "Lady Barbara's desperate. The future of Finchley Hall is at stake—and her family's reputation. How could I refuse?"

"You're doing it again—getting mixed up in a murder enquiry." He shook his head. "No, Kate. Not this time. If anything happened to you, I'd never forgive myself."

"Nothing's going to happen to me—not with you in charge of the investigation." I put down the forkful of salad I was about to eat. "In Scotland, my sister-in-law and my husband's best childhood friend were involved. The police were looking in the wrong direction. This is different." He looked skeptical, but I kept going. "This isn't about the murder. That's *your* job. This is about the Hoard exhibit and Lady Barbara's son."

"What does her son have to do with it?" No one had told him yet.

"Lucien Finchley-fforde was a suspect in the death of that museum curator twenty-three years ago—Catherine Kerr. He fled to South America. Village gossip claims he's back—just in time to kill Tabitha King. Lady Barbara insists he's in Venezuela, and she can prove it. All I did was promise to finish the work on the exhibit and ask a few questions about the stranger."

What about those questions you wrote in your notebook? inquired the voice of conscience.

Mere curiosity, I assured myself—quite convincingly, too.

"So you thought you'd ask questions." He cocked an eyebrow.

"She was telling me about their guest rooms. It was natural."

"Hmm."

"Really, Tom. This is about Lady Barbara, not the murder. Tabitha's death has absolutely nothing to do with me."

He pursed his lips. "I'll check with immigration to see if they know anything about Lady Barbara's son. In the meantime, keep me informed. No secrets?"

"No secrets, I promise."

We finished our food. I left a sliver of avocado, just to prove I could.

He paid the check and held the front door open for me. "By the way, my mother wants you to come for dinner on Wednesday."

So soon?

He gathered me in his arms and kissed me until I pulled back to breathe.

I had no clue where this relationship was going. And at the moment, I didn't care.

Chapter Ten

~

Photo Finish occupied the ground floor of a narrow Tudor building on the High Street, Long Barston's main thoroughfare. Potted fir trees hung with red plaid bows stood on either side of a planked oak door with iron hinges. I stopped to read a sign in the small leaded window: QUALITY DESIGN & CUSTOM PRINTING.

A man behind the counter, youngish and on the wrong side of two hundred pounds, was reading *The Magpie Murders* by Anthony Horowitz. Closing the book, he looked up. "May I help you?"

"I'm Kate Hamilton from the Hall. I'm helping Lady Barbara with the Hoard exhibit."

"We wondered who would contact us. My partner and I were devastated when we heard about Miss King's death. She was a charming young lady. Very organized."

"She planned to contact you—about the catalogs, I assume. Are they ready?"

"I'm afraid not. Miss King was going to stop by last Saturday to pick up the final proofs. We never print until the customer signs off on the proofs. Once printed, there's no going back."

I could sympathize. Once the student-run newspaper at Case Western Reserve University ran with the headline CAMPUS FLASHER CAUGHT ON VIDEO, unfortunately positioned over a photo of the football team's new plush-headed character mascot.

"I guess that means me, now," I said. "I'm not sure what's involved."

"No probs." He dashed off and returned with a packet bound in brown paper. "Read through carefully. Mark any necessary changes and drop off the proofs here. Once we have them, printing and assembly can be completed in a matter of days."

"How many days?"

He rubbed a hand over his head. "Week, maybe. Ten days tops."

"We only have ten days until the exhibit."

"Not to worry," he said in a tone that made me think I should be very worried indeed. "We'll do our best."

Tucking the packet under my arm, I stepped into the sunlight. I'd be able to catch obvious typos, misspellings, and grammatical mistakes, but I wasn't at all certain I could catch errors in terminology. I'd have to compare the wording in the proofs with Tabitha's database. That would take time.

I passed a young Sky News reporter in the process of filming. He spoke in hushed tones. "The village of Long Barston in Suffolk was the scene of a vicious murder last Saturday, when a young woman—"

His voice faded as I walked along the row of shops, their windows festooned with evergreens and sprigs of holly. Long Barston was ready for the holidays. A tall fir near the church had been strung with white lights and golden stars. I sighed. Once the press arrived in full force, the village wouldn't feel so festive.

A woman bustled past carrying shopping bags.

"Oh, hullo. Kate, isn't it?" Glenda and her son, Danny, stood in front of a picture window featuring green-felted elves beavering away in Santa's Workshop. A sign over the door said TALBOT'S TOYS & COLLECTIBLES. Danny wore a school uniform, gray trousers with a navy blazer piped in red. He carried a backpack.

"Hi, Danny. School out early today?"

He scuffed the toe of his leather shoe on the pavement. I couldn't help noticing the difference in him. Where was the exuberant little boy I'd met the day of the Finchley Hall tour?

"Danny had a doctor's appointment this afternoon," Glenda said.

"Everything okay?"

"Fine. Or it will be, right, Danny?" She patted his head. "Why don't you go check out the Legos? Mum will be there in a minute."

Danny trudged off and Glenda blew out a breath. "I promised to buy him a new Lego set if he was nice to the doctor."

"Is Danny sick?"

Her chin trembled. "The doctor is a psychologist. Today was our second visit. Danny's been having night terrors."

"Oh, dear. I'm sure that's normal. He had quite a shock—we all did, but he's so young. I hope the doctor was encouraging."

"He was." Glenda's eyes looked puffy. "It's only Danny's not sleeping much, which means I'm not sleeping either. What with his school and my job, we're knackered. The doctor gave us some pills."

"Well, good luck."

"Thanks." Glenda waved and headed inside the store.

On my way to the footpath, I passed the Finchley Arms. They'd put out a signboard, too. No Cuisine. Real Pub Food. Soup of the Day: BEER.

I shook my head. The Peacocks were going to have to come up with something better than frozen pizza and dried-out chicken tenders to compete with the Three Magpies. That is, if the locals plucked up the courage to give it a try.

Then I saw it, a small shop, tucked between Cate's Cattery and Pen to Paper, Stationers . The sign read The Cabinet of Curiosities. A collection of early silver tea caddies filled the narrow front window.

I looked at the package of proofs I was carrying, then at the mullioned window. Did I mention I'm a world-class procrastinator?

A spring-loaded bell jangled as I stepped into a world I knew and loved. *My* world, with the musty smell of old wood and even older dust. *My* world, where the relics of the past, from the humblest hand-made doll's quilt to the finest examples of porcelain and silver, offer the closest thing we have to time travel. At least that's what an antiques shop does for me—that and the tantalizing prospect of a find so incredible it would make episode of the year on *Antiques Roadshow*. Not that I find amazing things on a regular basis. It's the possibility.

"May I help you?" A small man peered at me from behind a counter. He couldn't have been more than five feet tall, with round, pink cheeks and sparse white hair frizzed out like a halo. Straight out of a Dickens novel.

I must have been staring, because he said, "Sorry. Didn't mean to startle." He straightened up and shot me a curious look. His eyes were a bright electric blue. "You're in the trade. I can always tell. Something about the flushed cheeks." He chuckled as if he'd just said something delightfully droll.

"Guilty as charged," I admitted. "Do you mind if I have a look around?"

"Be my guest. Ivor Tweedy here. I was examining a brooch. Norse. What do you think, hmm?"

I leaned over the counter to inspect what looked like a broken circle, bisected by the shaft of a pin. "It's a fibula brooch," I said, "used to fasten clothing. It looks like gold. Where did you find it?"

"Definitely gold. And it found me, so to speak. Brought in by a picker. Unusual fellow . . . hmm, yes. Stops in every few weeks." Ivor Tweedy's head popped up. "What did you say your name was?"

I hadn't, so I told him.

"Kate Hamilton . . . hmm. All right, Kate, what's your professional opinion? Shall I buy this pin or not?" He fixed me with his blue eyes, and I got the impression this was some kind of test.

"That would depend on the price, of course. And whether or not you have a buyer."

"Yes, yes." He nodded encouragingly, as if I'd gotten my multiplication tables right. "And?"

"And"—now I really did feel like a schoolgirl—"whether or not it's genuine."

"And, and—?" He rolled his hand to spur me on.

"Or stolen."

Ivor Tweedy clapped his hands and bounced, bringing a grimace of pain. "Exactly so. Those are the questions I must ask. Now, the picker is a careful lad. Never known him to deal in stolen goods."

I knew about pickers. My parents had one for years. Pickers are a subculture in the antiques trade, combing small sales and auctions for items to buy and sell at a profit. They provide an invaluable service to dealers who constantly need fresh stock but don't have the time or energy to attend every auction and estate sale. Some dealers, like my parents, form long-term relationships with certain pickers and depend on them.

"What questions are *you* asking?" I said, turning the tables on him.

He grinned, revealing a sliver of gold tooth. "Is it the real thing, of course. I have buyers who specialize in this stuff—Anglo-Saxon, Viking, early Norman. If I were to offer a reproduction, my reputation would be ruined." He handed me the brooch, the pin threaded through a square of soft fabric.

"I'm no expert on medieval jewelry," I said, turning the pin in my hand. "But I've seen these before. They're usually bronze or silver." The flattened circle of gold was embellished with a distinctive design of dots and triangles. "If this was found in Britain, it probably dates from the ninth or tenth centuries—before the Norman Invasion, anyway."

He beamed at me. "So the question I ask next concerns *provenance*—the history of the piece, where it was found, the chain of ownership."

"And?"

"Dug up in a garden near Beccles, I'm told. The owners, assuming it was bronze, sold it for two hundred pounds."

"And it's worth, well, close to—"

"Ten times that amount." He chuckled.

I laughed, too, but not at him. I knew what he meant. I would never knowingly cheat a seller, although I could. I know all the tricks. But sometimes things just fall into your lap. "How long have you owned the shop?"

"All my life, you might say. I was born in this house." He nodded toward the upper floors. "Joined the Merchant Navy as a lad. Traveled the globe. Acquired a taste for history, other cultures. I began collecting things—unique things, rare things. I wanted to know who made them and why. I found I had an aptitude for research."

"Research?" He and my mother, whose near-Sherlockian principles of observation and deduction had made her a legend in her day, would get along like a house on fire.

"Objects have a past, a history—like people," Ivor said. "Take this snuffbox, for example." He opened a drawer and lifted out a small tortoiseshell snuffbox, which he held to the light. "Eighteenth century, extraordinary craftsmanship. A jewel in its own right. But proving it belonged to the English poet Alexander Pope—now, that will double or triple the value." He laid his forefinger on the translucent brown-and-amber shell.

"What makes you think the box belonged to Pope?"

He opened the chased gold clasp and removed a scrap of paper, upon which was written in a faded Spencerian script:

Given me on the death of A. Pope.
F. Redfern. 30ᵗʰ May 1744.
Oh Grave! Where is thy victory? Oh Death! Where is thy sting?

"Lines from the New Testament," I said.

"They also happen to be the final lines of Pope's famous poem 'The Dying Christian to His Soul.' The date referenced, May thirtieth, 1744, is the date of the great poet's death. If I can identify F. Redfern, and if he is connected in some way to Alexander Pope, Bob's your uncle."

"Good luck." I had more immediate topics on my mind than Alexander Pope. "You must know the village well, having been born here."

"Not much escapes me." He sucked in his cheeks and thrust out his chest.

"What do you know about Lucien Finchley-fforde?"

"Why do you ask?" He narrowed his eyes.

"My daughter is an intern at Finchley Hall. Lady Barbara asked me to look into rumors about a stranger in the village. Have you seen him?"

"Maybe yes, maybe no. I did see someone, but whether he is *a* stranger or *the* stranger, I couldn't say."

"What did he look like?"

"Didn't get a good look. Dark clothing, some kind of cap. Saw the back of him, not his face. He was in the churchyard of St. Æthelric's, near the entrance to the footpath."

"The villagers say he's Lady Barbara's son, returned from Venezuela."

"To murder another young woman, yes." Ivor Tweedy pursed his lips. "I've heard the rumors. That's all they are."

"How can you be sure?"

Ivor Tweedy replaced the tortoiseshell box in the drawer and closed it.

"Because Lucien Finchley-fforde is dead."

Chapter Eleven

"How does he know Lucien Finchley-fforde is dead?"

I'd phoned Tom on the way back to Finchley Hall. "He doesn't know it. He believes it. Lucien and Ivor Tweedy went to the village school together until Lucien was sent to a public school near Bury St. Edmunds."

"All right, so why does he *believe* Lucien is dead?"

"Because, according to Mr. Tweedy, if Lucien were alive, he'd be bleeding Lady Barbara dry. He never believed the story about Lucien making it big in the oil business in Venezuela. He insists Lucien lacked the ambition and the business sense. I liked Mr. Tweedy, Tom. I really did. I don't think he'd say something without good reason. Ivor believes he's dead because Lucien has made no attempts to *tap the keg*, as he put it."

"Do we know for sure he hasn't tried to tap the keg?"

"Vivian told me Lady Barbara sends her son twenty pounds every once in a while, but that's hardly tapping the keg."

"No, but how does Tweedy explain the fact that Lucien writes his mother every week?"

"You'll have to ask him."

Tom made a noncommittal sound. "We've contacted the police in Venezuela. Things are in chaos there at the moment. Another coup attempt. But they should be able to confirm Lucien's presence in their country. We're waiting to hear. In the meantime, our immigration service has no record of his entering England legally."

"So what's next?"

"We ask around. The stranger's been seen, all right, but he hasn't been back to the pub, and he hasn't rented a room anywhere within thirty miles as far as we can tell. He may be sleeping rough. Not a crime. He's probably some poor sod who happens to be in the wrong place at the wrong time."

"Any more information on Tabitha?"

The line went silent. "This is confidential, Kate. She drowned, but she was probably unconscious when she went into the water. She'd sustained a significant blow to the back of her head. Traces of adhesive were found on her hands and mouth. She'd been restrained."

"Adhesive?" I shuddered. "Was she . . . ?" The phrase that came to mind was *interfered with*, a ridiculous euphemism you read in those classic murder mysteries of the twenties and thirties.

"She wasn't raped. Which underscores my feeling about the stranger. He drifts into a town and murders a girl he doesn't know for no apparent reason? It doesn't make sense."

"Have you asked her parents? Could this be some sort of revenge killing?"

"They're completely in the dark."

"You believe them?"

"I do, Kate. Until there's a reason not to."

"What kind of weapon was used?"

"Some sort of flat, heavy tool. Steel, probably. No traces of rust or wood fibers."

I pictured the old gardener leaning on a spade. "Wouldn't the killer have gotten blood all over his clothing?"

"Destroyed if he had any sense. Probably burned."

I pictured the fluted brazier outside the gardener's shed.

* * *

Back at Finchley Hall, the first thing I did was stop at the archives building to grab the spreadsheet Tabitha had put together. Then I ran up the stairs to Christine's office. She wasn't there, but she had been. The coffee mug was gone. So were the account books. The file folders on the square table were neatly stacked.

I stood for a moment at her window. Dusk was settling on the estate. Who would ever guess this idyllic place had been the scene of several brutal murders? Tall oaks and spreading limes stretched sheltering limbs over blackthorn and shrubby hazel. Stately yews and clumps of pines formed islands of green. Vivian's fairy-tale cottage stood in the shadows. Behind it, in the distance, a long black car moved slowly along the road. I imagined it was Tabitha King's parents, returning from the police station in Long Barston. How long would they have to wait to take their daughter home for burial?

That evening in my room I worked on the proofs of the Hoard catalog, making it through the first few pages. I found a few minor typos, which I corrected, and a misspelling—Tabitha's mistake, not the printer's. The work was necessarily slow and detailed. The catalog would be sold not just to interested amateurs, but to scholars and collectors. Every word, every description, had to be perfect—checked and rechecked, not only against Tabitha's inventories but also, in some cases, online. Fortunately I'd brought my computer.

The technical nature of the listing brought up another question. What sources had Tabitha used? She'd been a museum designer, not an expert in medieval art. If she'd hired an art expert to help, there was no mention of it in the catalog. Had she consulted some earlier inventory? For the first time, it occurred to me that the handwritten list might be a record of discrepancies.

I reminded myself to ask Lady Barbara—after I'd finished going through the proofs. Completing the catalog on time was the most important task. If I could get the corrected proofs to Photo Finish by

Wednesday, there was a good chance the catalog would be ready for the exhibit on the nineteenth.

At eight PM, realizing I was starving, I made myself scrambled eggs and bacon on the half-size Rayburn cooker. I hadn't spoken with my daughter since noon, when she had insisted she was just fine, thank you, and said she'd call me. She hadn't.

I took a bite of toast and flopped on the love seat.

My trip to England, the one I'd dreamed about for more than a month, wasn't turning out as I'd hoped. I'd imagined spending time with Christine, establishing a new relationship—more friend to friend than parent and child. We'd go to pubs together, I'd thought. We'd laugh, take walks, do a little Christmas shopping in the village. I'd visit her at work. She might join me on a few antiquing trips.

I would like Tristan—or try my hardest.

Well, that was a no-go, and perhaps no longer an issue. Unless Christine had forgiven him. Again.

One of Christine's problems with men was admitting she'd made a mistake. She'd hang on to the bitter end, making things worse. I'd always suspected her loyalty had more to do with pride than affection.

I shut down that line of thought. It made me crazy.

And then there was Tom. He'd wanted us to get to know each other better, to see if our relationship had a future. Instead he was knee-deep in a murder investigation, and the best we could do was an occasional phone call or a hurried meal.

Except for Wednesday night. Panic fizzed in my chest. On Wednesday I'd see his house in Saxby St. Clare, the house he'd shared for years with Sarah. On Wednesday I'd meet his mother. The one who didn't like Americans.

I picked up the phone and dialed the number of the antiques shop in Jackson Falls.

"Antiques at the Falls," came the familiar voice. "This is Linnea Larsen."

Oh, I missed her. "Hi, Mom. How's it going?"

"Splendid. Fiona is the hit of the shop. Today she sold that double-chairback settee, the one with the caned back and seat."

I laughed, feeling better already. "Now, how did a cat sell a settee?"

"By curling up in it. A customer saw her dozing in the sunlight and said she could picture her own cat doing the same. Had to have it."

"Well done, Fiona. Could we get her to curl up on that horrible Victorian mirror?"

"Even Fiona might not be able to shift that thing."

The previous autumn I'd purchased a heavy Victorian mirror at auction. The silvered glass was in good shape. The horrible part was the frame—fourteen inches of gilded gesso, encrusted with floral garlands, quivering arrows, and fat little putti with disagreeable faces. My client, a woman with more money than taste, had shown me a mirror she loved in one of those *Victoriana* magazines. I'd found its first cousin at an auction in Cleveland and texted her the photo. She adored it. Had to have it. Price was no object. Then she changed her mind, leaving me with a piece so ugly I refused to display it on the shop floor. I do have my pride.

"How are you, Mom? I hope the shop isn't too much. Why don't you take an afternoon off? Call Charlotte or one of the other part-timers." My mother is a healthy, youthful seventy-something, always ready to drive down from Wisconsin to help me out. But when she arrived this time, two days before my flight to England, I'd thought she looked tired.

"I'm fine. Enjoying myself. Have they found the killer of that young woman?"

She was redirecting the conversation, a tactic I use with Christine. Learn from the best, they say.

"Not yet." I told her the latest, including the medical examiner's verdict of murder, the proposed DNA testing, and the rumors about Lucien Finchley-fforde. "I told Lady Barbara I'd finish setting up the exhibit. It shouldn't be difficult. Tabitha had everything well organized. Lady Barbara is depending on the exhibit to bring in cash. Maintaining a house like Finchley Hall is a monumental task, but she's determined to make it work. And I promised to ask a few discreet questions about the stranger in the village."

"Kate, darling, you won't get mixed up in the murder, will you?"

Had she and Tom been talking? "Absolutely not. I promise. All I'm doing is finding the source of the rumors and putting a stop to them if I can. The stranger can't be Lady Barbara's son. She just got a letter from Venezuela. Besides, why would he return to England and not contact her?"

"Is there a statute of limitations on murder in the UK?"

"Probably not. I'd have to ask Tom. But that's another reason Lucien wouldn't return. According to his mother, he's afraid the police will arrest him."

"What about the Hoard? Didn't you say the treasure trove was connected to all the previous murders?"

"Not all the murders. Not Susannah Finchley. The man who attacked her was after her ruby ring. Susannah spoils the pattern."

"But are you seeing the *whole* pattern, Kate? Sometimes it's the outliers, the anomalies, that bring a picture into focus. Like looking at a photograph of what you assume is a dry, cracked riverbed and then noticing, way up in the corner, the elephant's amber eye. That tiny detail changes everything."

"I'm not investigating the murders, remember? Tom's got that well in hand."

"And I'm very grateful. Just be careful. Love you, darling girl."

"Love you too."

I held the phone to my chest and pondered the question of anomalies and outliers. When Tabitha's body was found, the police had considered the most likely scenarios first. A tragic accident. The suicide of a desperate young woman with a history of depression. An unwanted pregnancy and parents with impossibly high standards.

Now that they knew Tabitha was murdered, the pregnancy had taken on a different significance. Was the father of the baby a violent young man with no room in his future for a wife and child? Was he a married man with too much to lose if their affair went public?

What was the outlier in this case—the detail that seemed not to fit but put the whole picture in perspective? Could it be Tabitha's handwritten list?

None of the items on the inventory matched the handwritten list. So far.

I grabbed the proofs and settled back on the love seat.

Only eighty-nine to go.

Chapter Twelve

Wednesday, December 9th

I stared into my closet. What if Tom's mother wore a long dress and I didn't? What if she didn't and I did?

Be yourself, I heard my mother say. *She'll love you.*

Sometimes my mother can be touchingly naïve.

Like Tom. He was so sure I'd charm Liz Mallory. How was I going to do that? Would she be impressed with my knowledge of antiques or the fact that I owned my own business? Would she sympathize with my status as a widow or warm to me because we'd both raised teenage girls? Maybe if I tried to be less American. I imagined myself slipping into the Scottish brogue I'd perfected in the early years of my marriage to Bill. *Right*—wouldn't that just seal the deal. Liz's unfaithful husband had been Scottish.

I stared at the closet again.

Just don't look like you're trying too hard.

I pulled out my black midi-length tube skirt and the cherry-red cashmere sweater Tom had liked in Scotland. The one Christine had bought for my birthday. With my Visa card.

Thinking about Christine brought a pang of worry. We hadn't had a real conversation since our phone call on Monday. Oh, I'd spoken with her all right, at the Stables and the archives building, and she'd seemed back to her usual self. She was fine. Everything was fine. But I'd seen the gate, the one she puts up when I get too close. *This far and no further.* Whenever I brought up the topic of Tristan, she'd change the subject. My daughter has the ability to project the image she wants to create.

I stepped into the skirt and slithered it up to my waist.

Christine. Maybe this time I was seeing what I feared rather than what was real. She'd stopped in my room the previous night, full of a story about finding some fascinating old family papers in a mismarked folio in the archives. She'd asked about her grandmother, and we'd laughed until our stomachs hurt about the cat selling the settee. Best of all, there'd been no repeat of the blowup with Alex Devereux. And I'd seen Christine and Tristan walking arm in arm toward the Folly.

Was it too much to hope that the rest of my time in Suffolk would include no more drama—and (please) no more bodies?

I buttoned my red sweater and sorted through my makeup kit for the red lipstick I wear on special occasions. Usually I make do with a swipe of mascara and cherry-colored lip gloss. I glanced at my image in the mirror, trying but failing to see myself as Liz Mallory would.

Stop creating your own drama.

I should have been looking forward to the evening. I needed a break from catalog proofs and display plans. Not that I hadn't enjoyed the process. Putting the exhibit together was like solving a jigsaw puzzle. But I still hadn't identified any of the handwritten items on the catalog proofs. That was bothering me, but I'd forced myself to stay on track, conscious of the deadline.

So far, I'd said nothing to Tom about Tabitha's list. He had more important things to think about. But the whereabouts of those eleven objects niggled at the back of my mind. Was that tiny detail the outlier?

What's the most important piece of a jigsaw puzzle? my mother had asked me once. *The corner piece,* I'd answered confidently. She'd raised an eyebrow. *The most important piece, Kate, is the cover of the box. The cover shows you the whole picture.*

I would tell Tom about the list tonight, after dinner. I'd promised to tell him everything.

Earlier in the afternoon I'd dropped off the corrected proofs at Photo Finish. The printer had promised to deliver the catalogs to the archives building by the afternoon of the eighteenth, the day before the exhibit. Too close for comfort, in my opinion, but he'd insisted it was the best he could do.

The afternoon had been clear and mild, and the evening promised to follow suit. I wouldn't need my down jacket—just my flowered wool scarf that doubled as a shawl.

Ignoring the queasy feeling I'd had since lunch, I wrapped the scarf around my shoulders, grabbed my handbag, and walked to the Commons.

Just in time to see Tom's car swing into the parking area.

Showtime.

* * *

"Have another shrimp puff." Tom's mother held out a platter of puff pastry rounds topped with shrimp and goat cheese. Liz Mallory was an attractive woman in her late sixties with an athletic build and a head of thick, shoulder-length hair in that lovely silver color few are blessed with but everyone admires.

I took a shrimp puff. "Absolutely delicious. Did you make them?"

"Of course." She looked at me with surprise, like I'd asked if she brushed her own teeth. She served Tom and set the plate on a side table. "Do you like to cook, Kate?"

"Cooking was never my strong suit. I don't do it much since my husband died." An understatement. My freezer was stocked with Lean Cuisine, and I had a running tab with Dinners2Go, the local restaurant delivery service in Jackson Falls.

"I suppose you don't have time, running your antiques shop," she said. "Working women have other priorities, don't they? Now, I simply love to cook. So did Tom's wife, Sarah. She loved being a homemaker."

"Sarah did work, if you remember," Tom said. "Until her illness."

"Only part-time at the estate agent's," Liz said dismissively. "Her real love was cooking. She was a true gourmet, Kate. Always trying out new recipes." She smiled at her son. "Sarah always made sure there was something delicious when you came home after a long day." She turned her cool gray eyes on me. "I try to live up to her example."

"Not that policemen are home for a family meal all that often." Tom laughed unconvincingly. Was that sweat I saw on his brow? "Policemen live on fast food."

"There's a policeman's life for you." Liz shrugged. "Family takes second place."

"Now, that's not true. I always make time for you and Olivia. Don't tell me you feel neglected."

"Of course I don't." Liz Mallory waved away the suggestion. "I know you do your best."

Battle lines were being drawn, and I was in the middle of the field.

Liz turned to me. "What do you think of our little cottage, Kate? Not what you're used to in the States, I imagine. We always picture Americans living in enormous, multi-story homes on postage-stamp lots."

"We don't all live like that," I said, feeling slightly defensive. And more than a little guilty. I lived in a house exactly like that—a three-story Victorian on a quarter acre in Jackson Falls' historic district. I'd thought about selling it, now that the children were grown, but I'd never taken the step of calling a realtor.

"We live simply here," Liz said, "but this is all we need. Four rooms on the ground level. Three bedrooms and a bath up. A small garden."

"Your home is charming." I said, and meant it. The Grade II–listed farmhouse stood well back from a road on the outskirts of the tiny village of Saxby St. Clare. The exterior, Tom had explained as we drove up the gravel drive, was the typical Suffolk flint and chalk with red-brick quoins and lintels and a pantile roof. When he and Sarah had purchased the property, the house was in need of updating and repairs, something Sarah had poured herself into until her diagnosis of cancer.

I took in the large, beamed room. The woodwork was painted glossy white, the walls a soft butter yellow. A comfortable sofa and upholstered chairs were covered in loose, rose-striped slipcovers and arranged around a brick fireplace. A Christmas tree stood in the corner, trimmed with pinecones and garlands of red berries. The effect was less fussy and feminine than Vivian's little chocolate-box cottage, but I was reminded of the country homes featured in British design magazines.

Not only had Sarah Mallory been a gourmet cook, she'd been a talented decorator as well. Of course she had. She would have played the violin and spoken several languages. And I probably would have loved her.

Liz led the way into a dining room with a polished oak table and sideboard. Through the open door to the kitchen, I caught a glimpse of milk-colored cabinets and a cream Aga cooker.

The meal Liz had prepared—roasted chicken with tiny round potatoes and bright-orange carrots—was so tasty, I almost promised myself to sign up for one of the organic food delivery services when I got back to Ohio. Almost.

"Do you have special holiday traditions, Kate?" Liz Mallory turned her cool gray eyes on me. "I know you don't pull Christmas crackers or celebrate Boxing Day."

Finally something I could talk about. "My happiest memories involve spending Christmas Eve at my grandparents' farm in

Wisconsin. It was wonderful. We usually had snow—lots of it—and we'd build snowmen and snow forts. Grandpa would harness up the horse, Magnus"—I smiled, remembering the huge, gentle giant—"and he'd pull the grandkids around all afternoon in the hay wagon. After dinner we'd sit around the tree and open our presents."

"Presents on Christmas Eve?" She frowned. "What happened to Father Christmas?"

"Santa comes early in Wisconsin—one less thing to do later."

Tom laughed, but my attempt to be funny fell flat.

"Too bad you won't be spending an English Christmas this year. When is it you leave?"

"The twenty-second." Man, this was uncomfortable. Tom looked desperate, and there was something in Liz's eyes that made me uneasy. So much for my charming personality working its magic.

I glanced at my watch. Eight forty. The evening would be over soon. *Please.*

Liz wouldn't let me help clear the dinner plates. She brought in a fancy layered fruit trifle in a footed glass bowl. "Tom tells me you're involved with the Hoard exhibit. I'm sure Lady Barbara is pleased. It must be interesting work for you. I've seen the Hoard, you know."

"Really? I understood this would be the first showing." I took a generous helping of trifle.

"The first showing of the *entire* collection, yes. But every month Lady Barbara chooses several new objects to put on display with the Finchley Cross. People come from all over England to see them."

I thought about the handwritten list. Were these items Lady Barbara had chosen to put on display? I hadn't seen them, but maybe they were stored somewhere in the house rather than the archives. Another question for Lady Barbara.

"Do you know Lady Barbara well?" I asked.

"Not as a friend, no, although we were on a committee together a few years ago. She's a charming woman, living a privileged life."

"She's had her share of trouble."

Tom gave me a pointed look. Which I ignored. This was not about the murder.

"I don't listen to gossip," Liz said, implying that delving into other people's personal affairs must be one of my hobbies. "Besides, all that business with her son happened years before we moved into the area." Liz set down her spoon and gave me her full attention. "Tell me about *your* family." Tiny lines around her eyes and mouth gave away her age, but not those clear gray eyes. I imagined her looking straight into my heart, searching for my insecurities.

Why couldn't I project an unruffled image like Christine?

After explaining about my husband's unexpected death of a massive heart attack three years ago, I told her about Eric's studies in Italy and Christine's internship at Finchley Hall. "This trip is a chance to spend time with her. The mother-daughter thing is never easy, is it?"

"Isn't it?" Liz's eyes opened, and the corners of her mouth turned down. "You don't get along with your mother?"

"Of course I do. We're best friends now, but I wasn't the easiest child to raise." It was true. Even my patient, uncomplicated mother had struggled with parenting a teenager.

"I never had a daughter, as you know. Tom is an only child. But Olivia and I get along very well. And she adored her mother." She turned to Tom. "Sarah and Olivia were inseparable, weren't they?"

"I wouldn't say inseparable." Tom shifted in his chair. He looked miserable.

"Seconds?" Liz passed the glass bowl.

I took another spoonful to please her. *Coward.*

"Who's keeping your shop open while you're in England?"

"My mother. She and my father were antiques dealers. That's how I got my start."

"Your mother lives with you?"

"Oh, no. She lives in a retirement community in Wisconsin."

"I see." Liz gave me a look that hovered between pity and accusation. "I give her credit. I really do. I'm afraid I couldn't live in a home for the aged. No privacy. And that awful antiseptic smell."

"That's not how it is at all." I swallowed a bite of trifle, feeling a lump forming. "Oak Hills is a wonderful place. Mom has a lovely apartment and—" My throat closed. I broke off, afraid I might cry.

Tom grabbed for my hand under the table.

That was all it took.

I stood. "I'm sorry, Mrs. Mallory. Everything was lovely tonight. Simply perfect. But I'm afraid I don't feel very well. Tom, would you mind driving me back to the Stables?"

"Shall I call a doctor?" Liz asked. She looked genuinely concerned.

"Jet lag," I said. "I need sleep."

* * *

"Oh, Kate." Tom reached across the gear shift. "I don't know what got into my mother tonight."

"I do," I said in a small voice. "She's afraid I might whisk you away to the Midwest."

He didn't answer.

The road was dark and narrow with hedgerows that seemed to claw for my side of the car. A pheasant with a death wish flew up in our headlights, missing the windshield by inches.

"It's obvious. Your mother doesn't like me."

"That's not true. She has to get to know you. Give her time."

"We don't have time. I'm flying back to the States on the twenty-second."

"We could try again. Dinner at the Trout. Neutral territory?"

"No." The firmness in my tone surprised me. "I'm not going to spend the time I have left in England defending myself against your mother's hostility."

Tom downshifted as the road took a sharp turn. "That's a bit harsh, isn't it? It takes her a while to warm up to people, to trust them." His face was in deep shadows. "She's been through a lot. My father's affair, raising me by herself, now raising her granddaughter."

"The problem is I can see her point, Tom. You're not going to move to Ohio, and I'm not going to move to England. We have jobs, families, responsibilities." I'd said the same thing in Scotland, but now that I'd met Liz Mallory, I was certain of it. "She doesn't like me. Olivia probably won't like me either. And Christine, in case you hadn't noticed, wasn't that keen on you."

"Really?" He frowned. "I hadn't noticed."

A rush of warmth for this man flooded in. He took people at face value—non-criminals, anyway. If men can be clueless about emotional subtext, they can also be readier than women to forgive and move on. There weren't many ways in which Tom was like Bill, but this was one of them.

"Families are important," I said. "Bill's sister resented me from the first. She blamed me for his move to the States, even though he'd left Scotland years before we met. Maybe she assumed he'd eventually move back, I don't know. Bill never let it affect his love for his sister, but he was hurt by it."

"Parents can't choose who their children fall in love with."

And I can't choose for Christine. "But there are repercussions. Think about Tabitha King. What if she'd lived and married the boy from the working-class family? Would her parents have accepted him?"

"We don't know he was the father."

"That's not the point. The point is, would a decision like that have driven a permanent wedge between Tabitha and her parents?" I shook my head. "Your mother will never accept me. It's hopeless."

"No. It's irrelevant. *I* accept you. That's all that matters." He squeezed my arm. "I love my family. I'm not sure I can live without you."

My heart bounced into my throat. His hand felt warm, familiar. I felt my reservations slipping away. We'd turned onto the A131. I looked at his profile, the way his hair curled slightly around his ears and at the nape of his neck.

I felt a lump in my throat as I faced the consequences of my own words.

If our relationship really was hopeless, we should break it off now, before either of us got hurt. Or had we already passed the point of no return?

I slid as close to him as the gear shift would allow and put my head on his shoulder. "Can we talk about something else?"

"Definitely."

"This may not be relevant, but you said to tell you everything, so here goes." I explained about the handwritten list at the end of the Hoard listing. "Eleven items. None show up in the proofs of the catalog, and none show up on the spreadsheet she produced. I've been trying to figure out why Tabitha wrote them."

"Are you saying they're missing?"

"I'm not saying anything at this point. All I know is Tabitha listed a hundred and eighty-nine objects on her inventory. Then she listed eleven more by hand, and I can't find them anywhere. I'm going to ask Lady Barbara, but if they're missing, how did Tabitha know about them in the first place? She must have consulted some earlier inventory. I haven't found one."

"Would the woman from the Museum of Suffolk History have made a listing?"

"Catherine Kerr? I haven't heard that she did, but tonight your mother said Lady Barbara displays a few of the objects from the Hoard each year along with the Finchley Cross. Never the same ones, so people have a reason to return. I'm wondering if the eleven items are ones Lady Barbara had on display and then never returned to the safe."

"You'll have to ask her."

"I will. But what if they're really missing?"

"And that's why Tabitha King was murdered?"

"Not necessarily, but if Tabitha noticed objects missing, wouldn't she have reported it to the police?"

"She didn't. I would have heard. But I think she'd have mentioned it to Lady Barbara."

"Then why didn't Lady Barbara contact the police? I'm going to have to ask her that, too."

"Planting the fear of burglary in her mind?"

"Mugg's already done that. He's been trying to talk her out of the exhibit on the grounds that it's too much of a risk."

I thought of the ivory figurine taken from the National Trust property near Lowestoft. No break-in. No holdup. Sleight of hand, and no one noticed until it was too late.

"The thing is, Tom. Mugg could be right."

Chapter Thirteen

Thursday, December 10th

The late-afternoon sun pooled on the bare floor of my room at the Stables. I propped a pillow behind me on the love seat and swung my feet up, feeling a pull in my lower back. I'd spent most of the day carrying objects from the safe on the lower level to the display space on the ground floor. Nothing was heavy, but I'd gone up and down those stairs enough times to merit several gold stars at the gym. And a couple of Advil.

Luckily, I'd found the cache of white cotton gloves Tabitha had purchased from a museum supply website. Oils on the human hand will damage metals over time, and these objects had to be protected. She'd also researched and used time-tested and time-consuming methods for cleaning and conserving objects of gold, silver, and bronze, meticulously documenting each step. She'd done all the preparatory work. All I had to do was follow her plan.

Following Tabitha's plan was a joy. During the last few days, I'd marveled over her sense of proportion, color, and form. She'd seemed to know instinctively which objects would appear to best advantage when grouped with others and which would shine best in their own space. I'd felt energized by the buzz I always experience when handling fine antiques. The only spoiler was my concern over the brazen theft at Lowestoft. And my unsettling experience with the Finchley Cross.

A great loss.

What was I supposed to make of that?

I don't like things I can't explain—like my daughter's relationship with the feckless Tristan Sorel. The previous evening Tom and I had been cuddled on the gray sofa in the Commons when Christine and Tristan showed up, happy and in love again after a rollicking Quiz Night at the Finchley Arms.

"Guess what the final question was." Christine, teetering on her impractical high-heeled boots, didn't wait for us to guess. She flung out an arm and adopted a voice that sounded remarkably like Stephen Peacock at the Arms. "Final question: Wot is Johnny Depp afraid of?" Hooting, she grabbed Tristan's shoulder for support.

"Well," I said. "What *is* he afraid of?"

"Clowns," Tristan said, sending Christine into fits of laughter.

She gasped for breath. "After all those scary people he's played in the movies, he's afraid of clowns."

"Aren't we all?" Tom had whispered in my ear, making me laugh, too.

Outside, somewhere on the lawn, a blackbird chattered.

My phone rang. *Tom*—as if my thoughts had conjured him.

"Thought I'd give you a quick call," he said. "Cliffe and I are on our way to police headquarters at Martlesham Heath. The press are camped outside, and Chief Superintendent Rollins is getting twitchy. He's eager to hold a press conference, but we have nothing concrete to tell them. Strategy session in the morning."

"Any progress at all?"

"DNA testing is set for the sixteenth. At the moment we're searching the databases for similar murders in the surrounding counties. No matches so far. How are things in Long Barston?"

"Quiet if you don't count the press. No more reports of strangers, Spanish-looking or otherwise."

"Good. If he's left the area, the rumors will stop. How's the work going?"

"Great. Done for the day. Will I see you tonight?"

"Afraid not—nor the next. We received a tip that the thieves who stole the ivory figurine at the National Trust property are part of an organized gang. I hate to say it, but they may be headed our way. After Martlesham Heath, Cliffe and I will drive over to Lowestoft. I'm sorry, Kate. After that, things should settle down."

"Will you be back for the Peasants' Revolt on Sunday? I'm looking forward to the reenactment."

"Wouldn't miss it. But let's cut out early, all right?"

"Nothing I'd like better."

The warm glow I felt would tide me over until Sunday.

I eased off the love seat, praying my back didn't seize up. I knew how Tom felt, being pressed for information he didn't have. Lady Barbara had invited me for a light supper before the Peasants' Revolt reenactment on Sunday. She and Vivian were sure to ask what I'd learned about the stranger. I had nothing to tell them they didn't already know.

Leave no stone unturned—my mother's mantra when it came to research. Follow every trail, open every door. When you come to a dead end, go over the whole thing again.

I sighed. A walk to the village would do me good.

Most of the press cars had departed in search of the latest headline. The shock of Tabitha's murder was receding. Life in Long Barston was slowly getting back to normal.

I stopped first at the Three Magpies. Neither Jayne nor Gavin had seen the stranger again.

"I must say, we haven't been paying attention." Jayne's bright smile told me business was on the upswing. "Gav's making some wonderful food for the party after the Peasants' Revolt. Sadly, we won't be able to attend. We're full up with overnight guests."

Second stop, the Finchley Arms. The place was already crowded with villagers stopping off for a drink before heading home. I ordered a glass of sparkling water with lime (impossible to ruin) and sipped slowly as I sat at the bar.

Briony Peacock was washing glasses. She eyed me with suspicion. "Wot'cher doin' 'ere then?"

"I wondered if you or your husband had seen the stranger again?"

"Scarpered off, 'asn't 'e?" she said knowingly. "Too 'ot fer 'im with the press and police swarming the village."

She was probably right. Even if the stranger had simply wandered into the wrong place at the wrong time, he would have been spooked by all the activity. Loners don't like attention.

I finished my water. Maybe Ivor Tweedy had heard something new.

Leaving the Finchley Arms, I turned up the collar of my coat. The wind bit my cheeks and turned my fingers to ice. The possibility of snow was forecast.

Ivor Tweedy's shop was closed. A sign on the door said Open by chance or appointment. I stood on the walk, wondering what to do next, when I remembered promising Michael Nash I'd stop by the Rare Breeds Farm. Michael had actually spoken with Tabitha about the stranger. Maybe there was some small detail he'd forgotten to mention.

No stone unturned.

* * *

I found Michael mucking out the pigsty. From an adjoining pen, a huge sow with black spots on rust-colored skin observed this atrocity with ill-concealed outrage. Michael wore high rubber boots, gloves with gauntlets covering his forearms, and a thick woolen sweater under his green quilted vest. The smell was unbelievable, but he didn't seem to notice. His ears and upturned nose were red with the cold and his hair shaggier than ever.

"Hello, Mrs. H," he said, wiping his nose with his upper arm. "Meet Judith, a Sandy and Black. And that distinguished gentleman"—he indicated an incredibly shaggy donkey staring at us over the fence—"is Casper."

"He's got dreadlocks," I said. "And beautiful eyes."

"He's a Poitou, one of the rarest donkey breeds in the world. Scholars believe they came over with the Romans. Only about sixty in the UK."

Michael plunged his fork into a pile of straw and manure and pulled off his gloves. He opened the gate so Judith could reoccupy her pen and then jumped the fence before she could take her revenge. "I wish I had more animals to show you. The sheep and the bullocks are in the pasture right now. I might be able to scare up some chickens."

We walked toward the barnyard, where a handful of chickens happily pecked the ground.

"They're Dorkings," Michael said. "The oldest breed of chicken in England."

The male, a handsome fellow with black-and-white markings and a huge red comb, strutted around the females with their more modest coloring.

"Dorkings have two unusual features." Michael grabbed a handful of pellets from a trough and scattered them on the ground. "Five toes instead of four. And they're the only chicken with red earlobes that lays white eggs instead of brown." He grinned and threw another handful of pellets into the yard.

"Michael, you told me earlier that Tabitha saw a stranger near the Folly. When exactly was that?"

"I don't know when she actually saw him. She told me about it the night before she . . . well, you know."

"Did she say anything else—like what the man looked like or what direction he was headed?"

Michael furrowed his brow. "I don't remember—" He broke off. "Hold on. She did mention seeing someone wearing sunglasses, but she wasn't sure if they were together or just in the same place at the same time."

"That's helpful. Anything else—anything at all?"

"Ask Mugg. Maybe she told him something—that is, if she got the chance before she was . . . well, before she died." His puckish face fell.

"I will. How about Prue? Has she said anything more about Tabitha?"

That brought a grin. "You can ask her yourself."

A small red-and-black Mini honked as it circled into a gravel parking area on the other side of the barn. The door opened and Prue Goody clambered out.

"Hi, Michael. Oh, hello, Mrs. Hamilton." Prue's hair hung in long twisted coils. She wore a full linen blouse under a long reddish dress, trimmed in braid and tied around the waist with a length of rope. The upper part of the dress, two squares of coarse fabric, was held together at the shoulders by fibula brooches—reproductions, of course. Strands of glass beads hung around her neck.

"My costume," she said. "Not very flattering, but we try to be as authentic as possible."

"I think you look great," Michael said. "You'd fit right in with the tenth century. I mean . . . well, I didn't mean . . ." He blushed furiously.

"I know what you mean," Prue said. "And thank you."

"Mrs. H is asking about Tabitha," he said, changing the subject.

"Did Tabitha say anything to you about the stranger near the Folly?" I asked.

"Not a word. Of course, we didn't have much interaction after she moved into her own room."

"How about her work on the Hoard? Did she talk about that?"

"Not much. I was busy studying the Anglo-Saxon period at the time. There's a lot to learn."

"What do you do in the village?"

"I'm a domestic. I hang out in the houses and do stuff like cooking over the fire. We're not expected to be experts, but we're supposed to stay in period as much as we can."

"You and Tabitha never talked about your work?"

"I wouldn't say *never*. She brought a book home one day—about the history of the Hoard. She pored over it for days."

"Did she learn anything interesting?"

"I don't know, but she was puzzled about something. I asked her one time, like 'What's the matter?' or something, and she said, 'There's a discrepancy, and I can't figure it out.' We never talked about it again."

"Come on," Michael said. "I've got to get cleaned up."

"Too right," Prue said, laughing. "You're not riding in my car until you've had a long, hot bath and changed clothes."

"See you tonight?" Michael asked me.

"Of course. See you then."

It wasn't much. Someone wearing sunglasses. A book about the Hoard. And, most intriguing, a *discrepancy*.

Chapter Fourteen

❧

Friday, December 11th

I stood in the middle of the exhibit hall, surveying my handiwork. About half the Hoard items were now in their assigned places. Barring unknown factors, I would complete my part of the exhibit well before the opening. Leaving time for Tom—if he did have a free evening—and for the festivities marking St. Æthelric's Eve. I was looking forward to that.

A communal dinner in the Commons the previous night had turned out to be fun and encouragingly drama-free. We played darts—I discovered a latent talent for eye–hand coordination. Christine and Tristan appeared blissfully happy. Only Peter Ingham seemed out of sorts, and I wondered if he was ever *in* sorts. Even Alex behaved herself, keeping her hands off Tristan and treating Christine and Prue with only mild disdain.

I was positioning a small Elizabethan manicure set made of iron and bone in one of the display cases when my cell phone rang. I raced to pick up, hoping it was Tom, calling to say he'd be free tonight after all.

It was Liz Mallory.

"Hello, Kate. Feeling better?"

"I am, thanks. I'm on the English clock now. I'm sorry I had to leave so abruptly." I winced as my conscience reminded me that I wasn't sorry at all.

"I shouldn't have dragged things out so long."

"Not your fault."

"I know we didn't start on the right footing, dear. I'm afraid I didn't put things very well. So easy to misunderstand, isn't it?"

If this was an apology, I wouldn't want to see a reconciliation. Liz was basically blaming me for taking her the wrong way. I didn't respond.

"Anyway," she went on breezily, "I was wondering if you had time today to get together. Just the two of us. I know Tom is off on some assignment, but perhaps you'd join me for lunch or tea in the village. I'll be in Long Barston anyway to pick up some dry cleaning."

Oh, man. "Today? I'm working on the Hoard exhibit."

"Just a half hour or so? We could meet at the Suffolk Rose—that's the tearoom near the bridge. They do a lovely cream tea."

I thought of Tom and his willingness to overlook Christine's rudeness the night they met.

"That would be lovely."

"How about three o'clock? You'll still have time to get back to your work."

* * *

The Suffolk Rose Tea Room was as pretty as its name. The building, a pale-pink roughcast with a dark scalloped roofline and green shutters, sat on the edge of the River Stour. An outside terrace along the water was closed for the season. Inside, the place looked more like a Suffolk grandmother's parlor than a commercial establishment. Chairs of every description were grouped around low tables covered in snowy-white linen cloths. Landscapes and genre paintings of country life hung on the wall. A cupboard displayed a collection of Depression-era teapots.

I found Liz Mallory waiting for me at a table near the deep-set window. She wore a pair of slim wool slacks and a black jacket that highlighted her thick silver hair.

"Kate." She stood to greet me. "I'm so glad you could make it. My treat today."

"That's not necessary, but thank you."

"You're been working hard on the exhibit."

"I wouldn't say hard—just steadily. I want to be able to enjoy the Eve of St. Æthelric without worrying about getting everything done."

"It's going well?" Liz handed me a folded menu. "I've already ordered the Mini Traditional—a sampling of everything. Hope that's all right. I thought it would save you time."

"Perfect. And yes, things are going well. I'm working through Tabitha King's plan bit by bit and enjoying the process. I've truly never seen objects like these outside a museum."

"Some of us think that's where they should be. If Lady Barbara's son does return to England one day, I can only imagine what will happen to them. Pay for his gambling debts or something equally unsavory."

Hmm. I thought she didn't approve of gossip.

An apron-clad waitress brought a three-tiered glass tray with a selection of dainty sandwiches and miniature scones with clotted cream and raspberry jam. She left and returned with a pot of tea, cream and sugar, and two rose-sprigged cups and saucers.

Liz smiled at me. "I'll pour out, shall I?" She did, using a silver tea strainer. Then she replaced the quilted tea cozy and lifted her cup.

We spent fifteen minutes or so chatting about the weather, the stained-glass windows in the church, the crowds expected for the Hoard exhibit, and the press who'd just about given up on a quick resolution to the murder. I hated to be suspicious, but I couldn't help feeling she was biding her time. Or gathering courage.

Finally, after we'd worked our way through all the sandwiches and most of the scones, she turned her cool gray eyes on me and said, "Have you and Tom talked about the future?"

I almost choked on my tea. "Liz," I said, because we'd agreed to call each other by our first names, "I don't want to be rude, but I don't feel comfortable discussing my relationship with Tom." *Gulp.*

I expected her to flare up. Instead she folded her hands and said in a quiet voice, "I know it's none of my business, but I can't help being concerned."

"About what?"

"Well, about your differences, for one thing. You're American. He's English. You have a business to run and a mother to care for in her old age. Tom has his career." Had she bugged my phone? "Did you know he's been put up for detective chief inspector?" I didn't but wasn't going to give her the satisfaction of saying so. "Tom is a gifted policeman, Kate. He could be chief superintendent one day."

"I'm sure he could."

"Don't you see? When you think about it, you and Tom have no future. I'm sure that meeting as you did, thrown together in the wilds of Scotland, was very romantic. But real life is entirely different. Are you prepared to give up everything and move to England?"

I put down my napkin. "What Tom and I decide about our future, Liz, is for *us* to figure out. And why do you assume I'd be the one to move?" I regretted saying that the moment the words left my mouth. I was handing her bullets.

"Oh, Kate." She shook her head sadly. "If you think that, you're setting yourself up for disappointment. Tom will never leave England. And, I may as well say it, he'll never marry again."

I stared at her, unable to speak.

"The reason I asked to meet you today was to warn you. You're a good person. I can see that. Believe me, I know how attractive Tom is. Single women all over Suffolk have tried their hand with him. Even after I moved in, they would bring over cakes and curries. Suddenly there were so many extra tickets—for the symphony or the art show or the village fête. I'm thinking of you, dear." She reached across the table and placed her hand on mine.

"No, you're not." I stood, knocking against the table and sending tea sloshing onto the white cloth. "You're thinking of yourself. You're afraid you'll lose him. And that, I'm *not* sorry to say, is none of my concern. Thank you for the tea. Don't bother calling me again."

I shook as I slid my arms into my coat.

What had I done?

And how was I ever going to explain it to Tom?

Chapter Fifteen

~

Sunday, December 13th
The Eve of St. Æthelric

How I slept that night, I'll never know. Emotional exhaustion, maybe. Or more likely to shut out the thought that Liz Mallory was right and any future I'd imagined with her son was fantasy.

Now, with the morning sun slanting through my window, I lay in bed and went over our conversation in my mind. I wasn't proud of the way I'd reacted—even though she'd had it coming. The bells of St. Æthelric's pealed, calling parishioners to Sunday service. I closed my eyes and took in the majestic strains of "Come, Thou Almighty King."

I'd have to tell Tom about my disastrous meeting with his mother. I would, as soon as he got back from Lowestoft.

Flinging off the duvet, I sprang to my feet. Time to face the day.

I spent the rest of the morning and most of the afternoon in the archives building. The church bells rang again at four. Tom called just as I was leaving.

"On my way. See you at the Hall around eight if traffic isn't too bad."

Should I tell him? He obviously hadn't spoken with his mother yet.

"Perfect. Drive safely." *Coward.*

Walking back to the Stables, I consoled myself with the thought that confessions are best made in person.

Gravel crunched under my feet. The annual recreation of the Peasants' Revolt of 1549 was, I'd been told, one of Long Barston's most cherished traditions. In a little more than an hour, I'd join Lady Barbara and Vivian for a light supper. Then, at eight o'clock, a hundred or so villagers would gather in St. Æthelric's churchyard, switch on faux-flame torches, and snake their way along the footpath through Finchley Park to the Hall. There they would be greeted, not with screams of terror and pleas for mercy, but with overflowing platters of finger food, kegs of the local Suffolk ale, and a wicked spiked punch. Every year on the anniversary of the revolt, the inhabitants of Long Barston commemorated the burning of the Hall, the burying of the Hoard, and the death of Sir Oswyn with good-natured jibes about bringing real torches next year and overthrowing the ruling class. And every year Lady Barbara, who wasn't ruling anything, would demand an increase in the rents no longer paid.

Highlight of the holiday season, apparently. And here was me, picturing carolers and horse-drawn sleigh rides.

Anyway, that was later. For now, I had a few moments to relax and think about what I'd tell Lady Barbara about the stranger—and about my suspicion that some of the Hoard items were missing. What I'd learned was vague, to say the least. Tabitha had listed eleven objects I couldn't identify. She'd made an offhand comment about a discrepancy. And she'd seen a man in sunglasses who might or might not have been with the stranger near the Folly.

Vaguest of all was my impression that something at the crime scene hadn't been right. I hadn't thought about it in days and decided not to mention it. Nor would I mention the theft at the National Trust property near Lowestoft. I needed solid evidence.

Sometimes, when you wish for something, you get it.

* * *

"You're saying there's no way to find out who this man is?" Lady Barbara took a bite of cold roast beef.

Lady Barbara, Vivian, and I sat in her sitting room around a drop-leaf table in front of the fire. Mugg, as usual, hovered behind Lady Barbara. The same blonde maid wearing the same too-large black dress and white apron bustled in and out.

"I didn't say it's impossible. I said it won't be easy. People in the village have run into him a few times, but no one—as far as I know—has actually spoken to him. Now that he hasn't been seen for a couple of days, there's a good chance he's moved on."

Lady Barbara looked stricken. "So we might never know."

Vivian *tsk*ed and Fergus, who lay under the table, snorted.

"Maybe not knowing isn't a bad thing." I was trying to make sense of an odd atmosphere in the room. "If the stranger has left the area, you'll never know who he was, true. But the villagers will eventually stop talking about him, and the rumors will die of neglect."

Vivian reached down to hook Fergus's lead to his collar. "I need to change into something more suitable before the Revolt." She was wearing the same baggy tweed skirt and sweater-set she'd been wearing the day Fergus had decided to chase ducks. I couldn't imagine her in anything else at this point.

"Thank you anyway, Kate." Lady Barbara folded her napkin in thirds. Her long, slender fingers trembled. "I'm sure you did your best."

"I'd like to ask something," I said quickly, before my opportunity vanished. Or my courage. I'd already been rebuked by Tom's mother for poking my nose into Lady Barbara's business. This was Lady Barbara herself, with her own listing in *Burke's Peerage*. No nation on earth is more reserved than the British. Most people don't wear their hearts on their sleeves in public. The British, as Bill used to say, don't even wear them around the house.

Lady Barbara and Vivian stared at me.

Here goes nothing. "If the stranger in the village is your son—that's what the rumors are about, right?—he would contact you. But he hasn't. That's proof right there that he's not Lucien."

Vivian bit her lip. Lady Barbara studied her lap. Was I going mad, or did both elderly women look guilty—again?

"I'm afraid I wasn't entirely honest with you." Lady Barbara looked up at me through her pale eyelashes. She stood and moved to a pretty satinwood side table. She opened the drawer, removed a piece of folded paper, and handed it to me.

WE MUST TALK. TOMORROW 7 PM THE FOLLY. The handwriting was loopy, almost childlike. I looked at Lady Barbara. "Is this your son's handwriting?"

"I can't be sure. I haven't seen his handwriting for many years."

"But you've been receiving letters from him."

"Typed. Only the signature is handwritten. Mugg reads the letters to me now, anyway." She glanced toward a dark corner of the room where Mugg stood like a statue.

I'd forgotten all about his presence.

I handed the note to Mugg. He squinted at it over his wire-framed glasses. "I would have to check, madam."

"We'll do that later," Lady Barbara said with an air of finality. She took the note and put it back in the drawer. "The torch parade is about to begin."

"But when did you get the note?" Unsolved mysteries make me crazy.

"Last Sunday. Mrs. Rumple, the cook, found an envelope addressed to me on the bench near the kitchen door."

A week ago. The same night Lady Barbara had asked me to look into the identity of the stranger. "Do you still have the envelope?"

"I threw it away."

"What happened? Did you meet him?" This was becoming more and more fantastic. Then I remembered Lady Barbara's eyesight. "Wait a minute. How did you get there on your own?"

"Vivian went with me." She looked at her friend. "It was Mugg's evening off. Just as well. I decided a man might frighten him away. Vivian had a torch. I had a rolling pin. "

The thought of two elderly women creeping around in the dark with a flashlight and a rolling pin might have been funny if it wasn't so frightening. "And?"

"And he never showed up."

Chapter Sixteen

That evening, Finchley Hall's formal drawing room felt very different from the silent, cavernous place where, more than a week ago, I'd waited with the other members of the tour group after Tabitha's death. A Christmas tree stood in front of the tall front windows. The green serpentine sofas were gone, making room for several tables piled high with platters of food covered in aluminum foil and cling film. The adjoining entrance hall, three times larger than any room in my house, had been set up as a bar with several kinds of local ale on tap along with two elaborate punch fountains.

I stood with Vivian, watching the final preparations before the arrival of the torch parade.

"You'll want to watch out for the punch on the left." Vivian indicated a fountain filled with a pink concoction. "Looks innocent. More than two glasses and you'll be dancing on the tables."

Personal experience? "How many people will be here tonight?"

She adjusted the bow on her cream silk blouse. "Most of the village. Not all at the same time, of course. The torch parade arrives first. Others drift in and out. The whole thing's over by nine."

"Quite an expense for Lady Barbara."

"Oh, the villagers do everything these days. Women bake. The village shop donates paper products. Both pubs contribute food, plus the Café Bistro and the Chinese takeaway—you *must* try the spring rolls, by the way. Right over there, next to the chicken tenders." She made a face. "I'd skip those if I were you."

From the Finchley Arms, no doubt.

"The Peasants' Revolt is a community effort," Vivian continued. "Kickoff for the holiday season. And this year, with the Hoard exhibit, people will come from all over East Anglia."

The interns had gathered in the center of the room. Tristan's arm was draped over Christine's shoulder, but I noticed his eyes frequently wandered to Alex Devereux. I couldn't blame him. She looked devastating in black velvet leggings with spiky shoes and a silky top. Even Peter Ingham couldn't keep his eyes off her.

Alex lifted a purple clipboard. "Let's go over the assignments one more time. Christine, you and Prue will lend a hand with the food service. You'll have plenty of help from the Women's Auxiliary." She frowned at Prue Goody, who wore a long, shapeless dress in rough gray, linenlike fabric with Birkenstocks and woolly socks. "Is that really the best you could do, Prue? You look like a walrus."

"Shut up," Christine said tightly. "You look like a tart."

Alex huffed. "The truth hurts."

"It's not the truth. It's rude and unkind." Michael Nash moved next to Prue, whose round cheeks had turned a bright pink.

"We're representing Lady Barbara," Alex said. "You know—elegance, sophistication."

"I think Prue looks fine. Wonderful, in fact."

"How sweet," Alex said, making a face. "In that case, you won't mind staying in the house with her. You can check in the coats. There's a rack in the library with numbers to give out."

Michael flushed. "I was supposed to help with the torch parade."

"Tristan will do that, won't you?" Alex flashed him a brilliant smile. "And Peter, you'll be outdoors as well, directing guests. We want them to take the path around the walled garden rather than through it. You'll both need hand torches. Any problems, call my mobile."

They scattered.

"That girl is trouble." Vivian made a moue of distaste. "A little too popular with the male interns. I warned Lady Barbara."

"Where is Lady Barbara, by the way?"

"That's part of the tradition. She remains upstairs until the peasants arrive. They demand an audience with the Lady of the Manor. She descends the grand staircase and announces an increase in the rents. They call for her to be drawn and quartered. Then everyone makes a mad dash for the drawing room, and the party begins."

"With the interns taking the part of servants, I suppose."

"That was Cedru's idea. He decided the interns could fill in with a few extra duties. Saves hiring temps."

Since Vivian had brought up the subject of Cedru fforde, I decided to run with it. "The day we met, you made a reference to Cedru not being there for his son. Why was that?"

Vivian eyed me. "I suppose you may as well know the whole story."

The whole story involved mental illness.

"In his twenties Cedru fforde developed symptoms of bipolar disorder, undiagnosed until years later." She lifted the foil from a plate of stuffed mushrooms. "Sample?" I declined. She took a bite and chewed thoughtfully. "His depressions never lasted long, and in his manic state, with increased energy and activity, he seemed to function well. After his marriage, Finchley Hall became the focus of his interest. He hired workmen to repair the plumbing, the heating system, the roof. All of it needed to be done, you understand, but he spared no expense. *The best or nothing* was his motto."

She popped the other half of the mushroom in her mouth. "At a time when most privately owned estates were devising schemes to stay afloat—you know the kind of thing: tours, lecture series, safari parks, holiday cottages—Cedru decided on the internship program. He hired a firm of London architects to turn the old stable block into housing and contacted universities all over England, promising to find meaningful work opportunities for bright students who wanted hands-on experience. At the same time, his health was getting worse. During his manic episodes, which sometimes lasted for months then, he hardly slept."

We moved to the windows that looked out toward the park. Tiny winking lights bobbed in the distance. The torch parade was making its way to the house. I pictured Sir Oswyn standing at a similar window, watching the approach of death.

Christine and Prue were busy removing cling film and aluminum foil from the food.

"Eventually," Vivian continued, "Cedru's depressions became longer and his manic episodes more intense. In the end he was suicidal. Dementia took hold, and he died, leaving Lady Barbara with heavy debts and limited resources. That was twenty years ago. If you ask me, it was the death of Catherine Kerr and the loss of his son that precipitated his final decline."

"Vivian." I looked at her, trying to convey the compassion I felt. "Does Lady Barbara believe Lucien has come back?"

Vivian hesitated before speaking. "She's certain he has not but fears he has. There's no evidence, you understand. The note wasn't signed. What's worrying her is the fact that bipolar disorder has a genetic component."

"You mean Lucien could be suffering from mental illness, like his father."

"Perhaps." Vivian set her lips in a straight line. "If Lucien has come home, he may not be mentally stable."

"Oh, look." Christine, Prue, and Michael stood at the window. The bobbing lights in the distance gathered in clusters before stringing out again, growing more distinct as they came nearer.

"They're in the park now," Michael said. "Won't be much longer."

"Come on, Prue," Christine said. "Better put on our frilly aprons."

"Wait, look." Michael said. "Something's happening."

He was right. Instead of a loose column, the torch lights had become a single dancing blob. We watched in silence as the blob winked and glowed. Then a single torch broke away and moved quickly toward the house.

Minutes later, a man dressed in medieval hose, tunic, and cap burst into the entrance hall. "Call the police," he gasped. "There's a body."

Mugg sprinted up the staircase.

Just in time to catch Lady Barbara, who'd fainted.

*   *   *

Within minutes of the phone call, the local constables arrived, followed shortly by Tom, Sergeant Cliffe, and a crime scene team.

I sat in the drawing room with Lady Barbara, Vivian, and the interns. The food had been carted off to the kitchen. The punch fountains had been turned off, leaving pools of tropical-colored liquid warming to room temperature.

Edmund Foxe, the dishy vicar of St. Æthelric's, arrived to see if Lady Barbara needed help. He was good-looking—and fit. They sat on one of the green serpentine sofas. I would have liked to introduce myself, but he and Lady Barbara were deep in conversation. She twisted a white handkerchief in her hands. His hands were folded on one knee, not quite in prayer.

Mugg hovered behind her, gray-faced and solemn.

Christine walked to the windows, then turned and sat back down. Prue crossed and uncrossed her legs. Michael sat beside her, looking lost. Tristan was doing something on his cell phone—either texting or playing a game. Peter stood near the windows. Vivian tutted occasionally in disapproval.

Waiting was brutal.

"This is very bad," Tristan said, stating the obvious. He sat beside Christine on the other green serpentine sofa. "I saw it, you know. The man was lying there. I'm sure he was dead."

"Let's not speculate until we hear from the police," I said.

Lady Barbara put the handkerchief to her mouth.

"Do you need a glass of water, madam?" Mugg said. "Or tea perhaps?"

When she didn't respond, I said, "Tea, I think. We could all use tea."

Mugg left the room—glad, I imagined, to have something useful to do. I would have liked to do something as well. Like join Tom at the crime scene, but we'd been told to stay put.

They finally came—Tom, Sergeant Cliffe, and Constable Wheeler.

I assumed Tom would interview us individually as he had after Tabitha's death. Instead he said, "Constable Wheeler will take your statements. Meanwhile, Lady Barbara, is there somewhere we might speak in private?"

She clutched the arm of her chair. "Viv, Kate—I need you." She looked at Tom, her face pinched. "If it's all right. It's just that I . . . that I . . ." She broke off with a sob.

With Tom following, Vivian and I each took an arm and propelled Lady Barbara gently down the hall and into her sitting room. Mugg brought a tea tray, and Vivian poured out. Lady Barbara gripped her cup as if it were a life preserver, but she didn't drink.

Mugg added logs to the fire, which had burned down to ash and embers.

Tom sat beside Lady Barbara on the sofa. "The man in the Folly is dead." His voice was calm and kind. "We won't know how he died until the coroner runs tests, but we suspect he may have been poisoned. He matches the description of the stranger seen recently in the area."

"Did he have any identification?" Vivian asked.

"No ID, but the labels on his clothing were written in Spanish."

Lady Barbara's teacup slid to the floor and smashed.

Chapter Seventeen

~

Monday, December 14th

Vivian and I accompanied Lady Barbara to the coroner's office in the West Suffolk Hospital, about a mile and a half southwest of police headquarters in Bury St. Edmonds. The day was overcast, a fitting reflection of our moods. Tom ushered us into the lobby. A security guard opened a door leading to a long hallway tiled in gray linoleum.

"He can't be Lucien," Lady Barbara said for the fourth or fifth time that morning. "I received a letter from him two weeks ago. Everything was fine. No mention of a trip to England. He was doing well, working hard. He'd had an opportunity to invest in a local business and wanted my advice. "

And your money. "Maybe the letter was delayed."

"Or lost in the mail and then forwarded," Vivian added. "That happens."

Lady Barbara's eyes filled. "But Kate said it—if the man was Lucien, he would have come to the Hall as soon as he arrived. He knows how terribly I miss him." She glared at Tom. "I blame the police. My son had nothing to do with the death of Catherine Kerr. I told you so at the time, but you wouldn't listen. Not you personally. I mean the detective then—Evans. Lucien had his faults, I accept that. But he wasn't a killer."

"You may be right," Tom said.

"I *am* right," she said fiercely. "The police badgered him so ruthlessly he had to leave England. He was afraid you would take him up for a crime he didn't commit." She covered her face with her gloved hands.

We arrived at a small waiting room with a sofa and chairs upholstered in beige tweed. Framed photos of seascapes hung on the walls. A Bible sat on the table in the corner.

"Make yourself comfortable," Tom said. "The coroner should be ready soon."

He left through a door at the far end of the room. Lady Barbara sat on the sofa with Vivian beside her. She clutched her handbag. Her feet pointed straight ahead.

If the man found dead was Lucien Finchley-fforde, at least Lady Barbara could bury her son in the churchyard. Small comfort.

I took the chair on the other side. "Tell me about the death of Catherine Kerr. Were there other suspects?"

"The police interviewed everyone," Vivian said. "No connection to the murdered woman was found. And no motive."

"Including Lucien," Lady Barbara said with surprising force. "They never found a single piece of evidence against him."

"Why was he the prime suspect?"

"First was the fact that he didn't have an alibi for the time of murder. The girl was killed sometime between eight and ten PM. Lucien told the police he'd walked into the village. He'd planned to stop at the Finchley Arms but decided against it. He didn't see anyone and couldn't remember exactly where he'd walked."

"Well, you don't, do you," Vivian said, "when you've done nothing wrong. That should have counted in his favor. If he'd been guilty, he'd have concocted a clever alibi."

"And the second reason?"

"Like his father, my son was an exceptionally handsome man. It got him into trouble."

True enough. Beauty attracts admiration, desire, jealousy. I'd seen those emotions on Christine's face more than once. I'd seen them on Alex Devereux's face when she looked at Peter Ingham. But not, curiously, when he looked at her.

Lady Barbara rummaged in her handbag and brought out a fresh handkerchief. "Catherine and Lucien had been seeing a lot of each other in the days leading up to her death, so naturally the police questioned him first. I don't blame them for that. I do blame them for the rest—taking him into custody, holding him overnight, the brutal interrogation. They assumed a lovers' quarrel, but it wasn't true. My son had a gentle soul. He would never have harmed her."

For the first time, she'd referred to her son in the past tense. "Did Lucien mention anyone else—a rival, perhaps?"

"There wasn't anyone else. No one at all."

The door at the far end of the room opened.

"We're ready for you now," Tom said.

Lady Barbara reached out for our hands. "Stay with me, please. I can't do this alone."

The viewing room wasn't all clinical tile and stainless steel as I'd imagined. It looked more like a motel room. A sign on the door said CHAPEL OF REST. The colors were soothing, the lights mellow. A body, covered by a sheet, lay on a draped platform.

Lady Barbara clutched my arm.

"Steady on, Barbara," Vivian said.

The coroner's assistant, a small man with dark eyebrows and a speckled goatee, pulled back the sheet.

Lady Barbara made a small strangled sound.

Vivian took a step back and covered her mouth.

Was I staring at the bloated face of Lucien Finchley-fforde? I wouldn't have called him handsome, but then a quarter century had passed, and his death obviously hadn't been easy. Sallow skin lay slack along his jawline. His nose, threaded with broken capillaries, looked too large for his face. Dark, puffy circles under his eyes looked purple in the artificial light.

Lady Barbara leaned over the body. She bent down until her face was only inches from his. Removing the glove from her right hand, she ran her fingertips over the contours of the face, feeling the nose, the mouth, the closed eyes. She did it again. And again.

The antiseptic smell brought a rush of nausea.

However I'd expected her to react, this wasn't it.

How much could she see? What was she feeling? I stood ready to catch her if she went down, but this time she didn't faint.

Instead, she straightened up and looked directly at Tom. "This isn't Lucien, Inspector. This man is not my son."

Chapter Eighteen

The Trout, an ancient pub outside Saxby St. Clare, was everything Tom had said it would be and more. Low ceilinged, cozy, and—best of all—no jukebox. We'd shared a fabulous dinner of crab ravioli and lamb kebabs with pomegranate-seed rice and yogurt dressing. At present we were curled up on an ancient leather sofa near the roaring fire, drinking cognac from small lead-crystal glasses.

"This was *such* a good idea. Thank you." I kissed the side of his neck, breathing in the woodsy scent of his aftershave. They say the sense of smell has a direct link to the brain's pleasure center. I believe it. That scent would be imprinted on my brain forever.

He slid his hand down the back of my hair. "We both needed to get away."

Yes, we did, and the one thing we didn't need was an argument about his mother. Call me a chicken, but the decision to postpone telling him about the Suffolk Rose Tea Room was easy. Besides, Liz obviously hadn't told him either. That gave me hope. "Do you think Lady Barbara can be right about the dead man not being her son?" I asked him.

"She is his mother. But then she hasn't seen Lucien in more than twenty years, and she admits her eyesight is poor. The dead man fits the basic description we've been given of Lucien—age, coloring."

"Have you spoken with Mr. Tweedy? Nothing wrong with his eyesight."

"I'll do that. For now, we've sent photos, fingerprints, and DNA samples through Interpol to the authorities in Caracas."

"Wouldn't it be quicker to take a sample from Lady Barbara?"

"She flatly refused, insisting she has no connection whatsoever with the dead man. A response from Venezuela may take some time. The police are underpaid, poorly trained, and often corrupt. The infrastructure is unstable. Life is dangerous. People are fleeing the country by the thousands. Lucien Finchley-fforde may have decided his safest course was to return home and face an investigation."

"Well, if the dead man is Lucien, the question becomes who killed him—and why?"

"There's always the possibility of suicide." Tom stretched his legs toward the fire. "Maybe he decided he couldn't face an investigation after all."

"Lady Barbara said the police found no evidence against him. Was she right?"

"I spent time yesterday reading through the file. The only evidence was circumstantial. He had been seeing the girl, Catherine Kerr—he admitted it. Witnesses had seen them arguing, and he had a reputation for violence. The previous year a young woman in Cambridge had accused him of assault. Never proven, and she withdrew the complaint, but there was a history—brawls, vandalism, that kind of thing. Unfortunately, Lucien fled, and that added to the perception of guilt."

"Why didn't the police ask the Venezuelan authorities to send him back?"

"They did, but that country has no extradition treaty with the UK—probably why he chose it. He arrived in Caracas and dropped out of sight."

"What about the gardener, Arthur Gedge—the one who found Catherine Kerr's body in Blackwater Lake? Was he ever a suspect?"

Connie Berry

"He had an alibi. Can't remember what it was now. I'll check. I know DI Evans was convinced Lucien was the killer."

"Is Evans still alive? Could you ask him why?"

"He died ten years ago. All that remains is the file. I plan to read it again, but I don't think it will help. If the dead man is Lucien, the biggest question is, why didn't he get in touch with his mother?"

"He might have—that note."

"Strange way to greet your mother after twenty-three years."

"Maybe he was afraid she'd contact the police. Or someone else would," I said.

"Like Mugg?"

"Exactly like Mugg. He'd do anything for Lady Barbara—even grass up her son, if he thought it would save her greater pain."

"The victim had been living rough, dossing in an old shed in the woods. We found blankets, some food, and an empty bottle of rather fine whiskey. We're checking around locally. There may be CCTV footage of him purchasing it somewhere."

"When was he killed?"

"No more than twelve hours before he was found."

"Do you think this death and Tabitha's are connected?"

"If they are, I couldn't say how. We're treating them as separate inquiries for now. The man may have been poisoned. We'll know in a day or so, when the lab results come in."

Pubs are usually the social center of an English village, but tonight we seemed to have this one all to ourselves. Tom stood and laid another log on the fire. He poked it, sending a shower of embers up the chimney.

"Tom." I pulled him down next to me. "You said I have a talent for discerning patterns. Well, here's a pattern. All three deaths—and I'm including Catherine Kerr—were connected with Finchley Hall. The first two—both women—had access to the Hoard. Catherine Kerr had been planning a museum exhibit in Bury. Her death ended that. Now, twenty-three years later, Tabitha King was planning an exhibit of the Hoard at Finchley Hall. She died before it could happen."

"Are you implying someone didn't want the Hoard items on display? That puts you in a precarious position, doesn't it?"

"I don't think it's the exhibit itself the killer fears."

"Why not?"

"Tabitha told Prue Goody she'd found a discrepancy. The eleven items on the list might be the discrepancy—eleven items she expected to find in the safe but didn't."

"Have you mentioned it to Lady Barbara yet?"

"Not yet, and I won't—not while she's reeling from the death of the man in the park."

"It's a point, I admit. But so is Tabitha's pregnancy."

"Which is why you're conducting the DNA tests."

"Exactly. The child's father hasn't come forward, which means one of three things. He hasn't heard of her death, he doesn't know he's the father, or—more likely—he doesn't want to be identified. Why is that? What does he have to hide?"

"Will you do the DNA testing at police headquarters?"

"We'll send a lab tech to the Stables. Less intimidating. If we find a match, we'll take that person in for questioning."

"And if you don't?"

"We'll widen the field. Tabitha's romance may have been with someone in the village."

An image of the dishy young vicar came to mind. I dismissed it as the worst kind of cliché. *If there's sex involved, check out the local clergymen.*

I took a sip of cognac. The sweet burn traveled down my throat and landed somewhere in my left thigh. "Remember that night in Scotland when we decided to put everything else aside and just talk?"

"Mmm. That's when I fell in love with you."

"Not possible."

"Yes, it is." He held up his glass to the firelight, swirling the amber liquid. "I remember the exact moment."

"Oh?"

"I fell in love with you when you told me about your brother, Matt. He was eleven when he died and you were five, right? I saw your face when you were telling me about it, and that was it. I was a goner."

"I'm not buying it, but let's do that again."

"Fall in love?"

"No, silly." I poked him in the ribs. "Talk. And not about the murders."

"All right. Tell me more about Matt. How did you cope with his death?"

I took a breath, reminding myself that I was the one who'd suggested we talk. "One Saturday, it must have been a few weeks after Matt died, my mother cleaned out his room. She said we'd take his clothes and toys to the church—'for children who need them,' she said. 'Matt would have liked that.' I didn't buy it. It seemed like erasing him or something. Now I realize how much it must have cost her to let him go."

Tom was staring into the fire, and I imagined him thinking of Sarah. He took my hand in his. "What did you do?"

"When she went to find another box, I rescued some of Matt's things. One of his crazy red socks, his Captain America secret decoder ring, his Bugifier—that's what he called the magnifying glass he used to spy on bugs. I put them in a shoebox under my bed. I'm sure my mother knew." The fire popped in a shower of sparks. "I still have it. She probably knows that, too."

"She sounds like a wonderful mother." Tom brushed a strand of hair from my face.

"She is—kind, wise, sensible, smart." I steeled myself against a massive wave of guilt. I would have to tell Tom sometime that I'd insulted his mother and ruined any possible future relationship with her. *Oh, man. Could I have a do-over?*

"How's the exhibit going? Will you be ready on time?"

"My part's almost finished," I said, grateful for a topic less emotionally fraught. "Tabitha would have made a brilliant museum curator one day. As long as the catalogs are ready in time, everything will happen as she planned."

"What isn't your part?"

"Security, for one thing. Alex has arranged to have a couple of off-duty policemen there as a precaution."

"I heard. Good idea."

"Staffing isn't my problem either. Volunteers from the Women's Institute will do a host of other tasks—selling tickets, handling the catalogs and souvenirs, serving tea. Lady Barbara has agreed to set up a tearoom in the library. The locals are glad to help. The showing of the Hoard will bring tourists to the village. Everyone benefits."

"Let's get back to the subject at hand," Tom said.

"And that is?"

"You and me. We need to talk about *us*, the future."

The fire guttered as the door opened to admit a blast of cold air. A man swathed in a wool jacket, scarf, and flat cap headed for the bar.

"You said once that we should tell the truth." I took another sip of the cognac for courage. "When Bill died, we had unfinished business between us. In Scotland, all that was finally settled. I stopped looking back—I really did, Tom. You're partly responsible for that. But not looking back isn't the same thing as moving forward." I held his hand to my cheek. "We have real challenges. One day we'll have to talk about them. Right now, I'm not ready to make any big decisions, and I can't tell you when I will be."

I studied his face. For what? Agreement? Understanding?

His hazel eyes fixed me with a look so intense it nearly took my breath away. "No pressure, Kate. You're too important to me. We have now, tonight, the rest of your time in England. I'm grateful for that. Just know that I *am* ready to take the next step. Whenever you are, I'm here."

Chapter Nineteen

Tuesday, December 15th

If all went as planned, this was the final day I would spend preparing the Hoard exhibit. Everything was in place except the cabinets against the south wall. These would hold the smallest items—coins, pieces of jewelry, and miscellaneous decorative objects.

I was dreading a planned meeting at eleven AM with Alex Devereux to go over security and finalize plans for the mini gift shop in the exhibit hall. Spending time with Alex was not on my list of top-ten things I wanted to do at the moment. She'd hurt my daughter. But then, working with her on the exhibit didn't mean I had to like her.

Christine and I had planned to have lunch together in her office. She was excited to show me the progress she was making on the Finchley family archives and had implied, rather mysteriously, that there was something in particular I'd find fascinating.

My first destination was the Finchley Hall kitchen. I'd been curious about Mrs. Rumple, the marvelous old cook who'd been with Lady Barbara for more than forty years, but what I really wanted was to ask her about the note left on the bench. Did she know when it was put there? Had she caught a glimpse of the man who left it? Had she recognized him?

Resolving the question of the dead man's identity was all I could do for Lady Barbara now. Her assurance that her son was alive and well in Venezuela and would return to clear his name and take his rightful place at Finchley Hall was touching. And irresistible. I found myself wanting to protect her.

A motivation I shared with Vivian and Mugg.

As I walked from the Stables to Finchley Hall, my mind returned to the conversation Tom and I had had the night before. How could I resolve the disconnect between the Tom his mother had described, the faithful widower who'd never remarry, and the man who'd just told me he'd wait for me as long as it took? He was right. We did need to talk about us. We needed to take the next step or turn back.

That conversation had to take place, but not today.

The kitchen was on the lower level of the Hall, toward the back of the house and the Elizabethan Garden. Frog-green paint on the old French-style double doors was peeling. The bench Lady Barbara mentioned was a simple slated garden bench with rusting iron arms.

I knocked.

"Come," called a muffled voice.

The Finchley Hall kitchen combined the latest in Victorian plumbing with a scattering of more modern additions, like an enameled Redfyre range. Occupying the center of the large, high-ceiling room was a scrubbed pine table.

The blonde maid I'd seen several times stood at the freestanding range, stirring scrambled eggs. "Just a mo'. Nearly done." She gave the eggs another stir, then carried the iron skillet to the wooden table, where she tipped them onto a platter next to slices of fried bacon and a grilled tomato. "Madam's breakfast," she said, covering the platter with a dome and transferring it to a wooden dumbwaiter on the wall. She closed the door and pushed a button. The contraption groaned in complaint as it rose toward the upper floor.

This morning, in place of the too-large black dress and white apron, the maid wore a fuzzy mauve sweater with jeans and clogs.

"Is the cook here this morning? I'd like to thank her for the lovely dinner the other night."

"You're welcome, I'm sure." She laughed and stuck out her hand. "Francie Jewell. Pleased to meet you."

"You're the cook?"

"And the server. And the housemaid. And the laundress." She placed her hands on her hips and grinned at me. "I do it all."

"But I thought—" That was as far as I could go with that sentence.

"You thought the Hall had a proper staff, like the old days." Francie Jewell nodded toward the ceiling. "So does she upstairs. Mr. Mugg says there's no harm in it if it makes her happy. She can't see proper, so let her think it, poor thing."

"What happened to Mrs. Rumple? Lady Barbara said she'd been the cook here for years."

"Oh, she was, right up till her son moved her into a council flat in Sudbury. Died a year or so back. Well over eighty."

"And you took her place?"

"Someone had to step into the breach. If not me, Mugg would have done the cooking himself—well, he does on my day off. He's that tenderhearted when it comes to Lady Barbara. Irons a right treat 'n all. Now me? I draw the line at ironing." She chuckled. "I say that's why God invented polyester."

"Why not just tell Lady Barbara that Mrs. Rumple had to retire? I'm sure she would have understood."

"Oh, she would've understood all right, and kept paying the woman until she died. Like old Arthur—Arthur Gedge. He potters round the garden when he feels like it and calls it work. Gets paid all the same."

I could see what she meant. As much as Lady Barbara wanted to keep up the old ways, she couldn't afford to pay two cooks at the same time. "Has Mr. Gedge been here a long time?"

"Just *Gedge*, love. All his life—an' his father before him. Lots of Gedges at the Hall over the years. Still here, if you think about it. Taking their retirement in the churchyard."

"Is Mr. Gedge married? Widowed?" *Ever shown an interest in the interns?*

"Never married, bless him. Lives alone in a tied cottage on t'other side of Blackwater Lake. The police asked about him. Came for a chat, didn't they? Right after the police divers searched the lake."

"This may be off the subject, but have you ever had a theft at the Hall?"

Francie sucked in the side of her bottom lip. "Not that I recall. Least not whilst I've been here. Wait"—she stuck her index finger in the air—"I tell a lie. Someone stole a bottle of whiskey from the pantry last week." She gestured toward a door near a long porcelain sink. "And an extra meat pie I was savin' for my Harry. Must've been one o' the young lads. They're always hungry, aren't they—and don't mind a drop or two now and again."

A missing bottle of whiskey. The dog that didn't bark in the night. Outliers.

"Is there something you require, Mrs. Hamilton?" A dark shape filled the open doorway.

How did Mugg move around so quietly? His face was inscrutable, but I got the message—belowstairs wasn't a place for the likes of me.

"I stopped by to thank Francie for the wonderful dinner the other night."

He arched an eyebrow.

"And thank you, too. I know how hard you work." With a friendly wave, I left.

Poor Francie. As soon as I was out of earshot, she'd get an earful.

* * *

The final drawer of the huge safe slid open silently, revealing felt-lined compartments filled with small items—rings, ear clips, buttons, shoulder clasps, closures, and toggles. Gold and silver coins—two or three dozen—had been sorted and stored in organza bags tied with ribbons, like the rose-petal bags at weddings.

Pulling on a clean pair of cotton gloves, I began the work of placing each item where Tabitha had planned. She'd been wise to showcase these tiny treasures by themselves. Each was a jewel in its own right—pewter buttons in the shape of lover's knots, acorns, and hearts; chased silver aglets—the tubes of metal clamped to the ends of laces to help thread them through an eyelet; beads of glass, amber, and garnet.

I thought about Francie Jewell and the deception perpetrated on Lady Barbara. Perhaps Mugg's intentions were good—protecting Lady Barbara from hard financial decisions regarding her staff—but deceiving her didn't feel right. In spite of her poor vision and general air of fragility, she was a sensible person, able to withstand the hard things in life as well as anyone else. She'd proven that when she faced the likelihood that her son was dead. Now I was in the position of having to choose: should I keep Mugg's secret or tell Lady Barbara?

I wondered if Vivian Bunn knew that Finchley Hall's so-called *staff* boiled down to two people—Mugg and Francie Jewell. Was Vivian in on the deception? Maybe that's why Mugg disliked me. He was afraid I'd spoil the fiction he had going that Finchley Hall was humming along like clockwork. From what I could see, Finchley Hall was hanging by a thread. But it wasn't my job to set Lady Barbara straight. Was it?

On my fourth or fifth trip back to the safe, I picked up a ring and stopped dead in my tracks. The rolled gold band was slightly dented. On the crown, a double frame of small natural pearls surrounded a bezel-set red gemstone, about a half inch by three quarters, incised with a crude griffin.

Was this Lady Susannah's ring, the legendary blood-red ring in the portrait?

I turned it in my hand. The center stone appeared smaller than the one in the portrait, and the shape wasn't exactly right—rounder, less oval. Maybe the portrait artist had exaggerated the size of the stone to emphasize the Finchley wealth. Or perhaps the portrait had been painted after Lady Susannah's death and after the disappearance of the ring.

On the spreadsheet, Tabitha had listed it as GOLD RING WITH RED GEMSTONE. She could hardly have failed to notice the similarity to the ring in the portrait, nor the small differences. Was this the discrepancy she'd mentioned to Prue?

I held the ring toward the light, waiting for the tingling fingertips, the rush of warmth in my cheeks, the pounding of my heart, the dryness in my mouth.

Nothing happened.

Nothing at all.

Chapter Twenty

I placed the red gemstone ring in its allotted place in the cabinet and followed the curve of the pearls with my gloved finger. The central stone was a deep, clear red with a slightly earthy cast. A gem-quality garnet was my guess. Definitely *not* a pigeon's blood ruby, the designation reserved for the finest of the fine. Or at least it used to be. Today everyone uses the term—even Walmart.

Was this Tabitha's discrepancy—finding a garnet instead of a fine ruby?

At least I had something to tell Lady Barbara. I'd learned nothing about the dead man in the park, but I might have found Lady Susannah's ring hiding in plain sight. *Yay!* Displaying the ring and the portrait together would add to the excitement surrounding the exhibit. But I'd have to be honest about my reservations.

What if this ring wasn't Lady Susannah's ring—just similar? Did it even matter?

Truth always matters pronounced the righteous voice of my conscience.

"I know that," I snapped aloud. "But what if the truth can no longer be determined?"

Perhaps the legend was all that mattered—like the search for the Loch Ness monster. How do you prove something doesn't exist? Finding no evidence leaves the legend intact, and everyone is happy.

Not my call. All I could do was tell Lady Barbara everything, including my reservations, and let her decide what to do with the information. The ring, the portrait, and the legend belonged to her.

At eleven on the dot, Alex came through the door, hefting a large box. She dumped it on the sales counter. "Be right back."

I stood at the window and watched her wrestle another box from the boot of an ancient Land Rover. She wore skintight jodhpurs with an oatmeal-colored sweater under her green quilted vest.

Seeing more boxes in the back of the Rover, I went out to help her.

Once we'd carried everything inside, we unpacked the boxes and spread the contents on the long counter. In addition to the stash of vintage postcards of Hoard objects, Alex had purchased a variety of gifts for those who wished to commemorate their visit to Finchley Hall. The items included T-shirts and tote bags digitally printed with an image of the Finchley Cross, sets of medieval action figures, children's Anglo-Saxon coloring books, adult coloring books featuring Celtic designs, some lovely jewelry, and even food—chamomile tea, oat biscuits, jars of local honey, and lovely, long-necked bottles of golden mead. No plastic weaponry, thankfully.

"I'm impressed," I said, fingering a silver necklace with a Celtic trefoil knot. "You've chosen lovely things."

"I wanted to add silk scarves and some reproduction Anglo-Saxon jewelry, too, but Lady Barbara drew the line. Too bad, because we'll triple her investment on this lot."

We got busy sorting the gifts and adding easy-to-peel price stickers. Tabitha had designed the gift shop so people could enter at will, but to exit, they had to pass a watchful salesclerk. A wise precaution.

I glanced at the exhibit hall. Preventing shoplifting was one thing. Preventing the theft of real treasures was another.

"Alex," I said, putting a sticker on the last of the honey jars, "I'm concerned about security. If a National Trust property can be burglarized, we could be next."

"Have you been talking to Mugg? He's still trying to talk Lady Barbara out of the exhibit. Bit late for that now."

"Why is he so protective?"

"He sees himself as Lady Barbara's defender. His one goal in life is to make *her* life as perfect as possible. He thinks putting the Hoard on public display is too dangerous."

"Aren't you worried?"

"We've taken every precaution. The thieves would have to be thick as two planks to try something here. They've got to know security will be tight."

"This may be a professional gang. Tom believes the thieves send someone in advance to scout the place out. The docents at the National Trust property mentioned a woman, respectable looking, who asked a lot of questions."

Alex frowned, her smooth brow creasing. "An advance person?"

"What are you thinking?"

"Nothing, really." She shook her head. "Just that it's a good thing we've assigned extra people to observe. Forewarned and all that."

"How many people will we have inside the exhibit space?"

"You, obviously. Mostly to answer questions. And Mr. Tweedy if we can get him. Otherwise, several observers will be stationed around the room—three, if you think that's enough—plus a uniformed constable. We're paying him. One or two women from the Auxiliary in the shop. More villagers outside, plus one or two constables and a few community support officers who've volunteered their time."

"Sounds like enough." I said. But were we being naïve? If a valuable figurine could be lifted from a National Trust property, why not Finchley Hall?

"I should go," Alex said. "Lady Barbara wants to chat about the tearoom."

"Do you have five minutes? I'd like to show you something and get your thoughts. Over here, in the small cabinet." I pointed out the garnet ring.

Alex's lips parted. She turned her green-gold eyes on me. "Wherever did you find it?"

I told her.

Alex was already taking photos of the ring on her mobile. "If there's the slightest possibility this *is* Lady Susannah's ring, we should issue a press release right away."

"We need Lady Barbara's permission."

She put the back of her hand to her forehead. "This is huge. Think of it—the ring was in the safe all the time, and no one knew."

"We don't know for sure it's Lady Susannah's ring."

Had she heard me? She pulled up one of the photos she'd taken and turned the screen toward me. "What do you think—good enough for the newspaper?" Her face glowed. "How exciting. Well done, you."

"Just get Lady Barbara's permission before you say anything to the press."

"Of course. But it's so thrilling. This will be the focus of the BBC documentary."

If it wasn't for Alex's shameless flirting with Tristan, I might have liked her. She was intelligent, competent, exuberant. Was I being disloyal to Christine? *The friend of my enemy* . . . Or is it the other way around?

Suddenly Alex's face changed. "Do you think Tabs knew about the ring? She never said."

"Did she ever talk about her work?"

"General stuff. She was excited about the exhibit." Alex tipped her head. "Although now you mention it, she did say something about things not working out."

"What do you mean?"

"Not sure. She said something like, 'It's frustrating. I can't make it work out.'"

"Make what work out?"

"I don't know. I wasn't really paying attention."

"Do you remember if she had a book about the Hoard?"

"I never saw one." Alex zipped up her green quilted vest. "We've got to tell Lady Barbara and get started on the promo."

"Let me do a little research first. I'd like to see if any similar rings have been sold through the major auction houses. Why don't you check the portrait? Take a photograph so we can compare. When we've got all the facts, I'll tell Lady Barbara. If she's agreeable, you can go ahead."

"Just don't wait too long."

"One more day won't matter. I'm seeing her tomorrow."

Alex began stacking the empty boxes. "I'll have Tristan take these to storage until after the exhibit."

"Are you serious about Tristan?" *Did I just say that?*

"Hardly." She made a face. "It's just a bit of fun, isn't it?"

I bit my tongue. Going further with this conversation would be disloyal to my daughter. Christine was going to have to figure this one out on her own.

She glanced at her mobile. "Gotta run. Let me know about the ring."

* * *

Christine and I slid the remains of our turkey sandwiches into the Tesco bag and sat back with two mugs of tea and a bag of crisps between us. We'd pulled chairs in front of the tall windows that looked out on the park. What we could see of Blackwater Lake sparkled in the winter sun.

"The challenging part," Christine said, polishing off a crisp and reaching for another, "is the complete lack of organization. Records had been stuffed in files for years without any attempt to sort them into categories. Birth certificates are stored alongside school records and grocery bills. The first thing I have to do is establish some kind of order, and that means looking at every individual scrap of paper. Some records have been misfiled, put in the wrong year. That's what happened to the ledger from 1892. I found it in a folio at the bottom of the 1937 drawer."

Christine had shown me the organizational system used for centuries at Finchley Hall. Inside the painted archive cabinets, deep drawers were stenciled with successive years. The last year stored in this building seemed to be 1999, the year Cedru Finchley-fforde died. Where the current records were kept, Christine didn't know, but if they were in the same condition as these, Lady Barbara would need a team of chartered accountants to sort things out.

"Who keeps the accounts now?"

"Mugg, I think." Christine rocked back in her chair to grab a thick folio from the square table behind us. She pulled out a black, leather-bound ledger, about eight inches by sixteen. Printed in gold on the cover were the words HOUSEHOLD LEDGER and the dates JAN 1892 TO JUNE 1892.

"These people were paid next to nothing," Christine said, "and they worked from sunrise to the wee hours." She opened the book and spread it on her lap where we both could see.

The ledger was organized by month. Names of individuals, mostly males, were written in rough alphabetical order along with their titles or jobs and their wages.

"Take this guy, for example," Christine said.

The name was George Cuthbert. He was listed as head butler with a bimonthly wage of two pounds, ten shillings, and fifty pence. "Do you know how much that is in today's money?" she asked. "I looked it up. Five thousand three hundred and fifty American dollars a year. Of course, he didn't have to pay for a place to live and food to eat. Once in service, he'd never have been thrown out—at least at Finchley Hall. But he had no hope of betterment—saving enough to learn a trade and leave service. These people were stuck, completely dependent on their employers. And he was one of the higher-paid employees. Look at this one, 'Alice Thurtle, Maid of All Work.'"

"Thurtle? Wasn't that the name of the man who buried the Hoard in 1549? And the name of the man who dug it up in 1818 and was killed by a spring-gun?"

"There were a lot of Thurtles at the Hall. She earned fifteen shillings every two weeks. *Fifteen shillings*, Mom. Think about it. That's only eighteen pounds a year, and she would have done everything from scrubbing floors to peeling potatoes to starching collars. Alice would have been expected to get up before the rest of the household, light the fires, and start the breakfast. If she was caught keeping company with a young man, she was thrown out. And with all this, she was expected to be quiet, good-tempered, and content with her lot in life." She handed me the ledger. "Look at all these names. No wonder the great houses kept going for so long. Practically forced labor."

I thumbed through, stuck on the name Thurtle. "I wonder what happened to Alice."

"If I have time, I'll check."

I'd turned a page when a name jumped out and grabbed me. "Look at this, Christine. 'Arthur Gedge, Head Gardener.'"

Christine leaned over my shoulder to read the entry. "Well, they do call him Old Arthur, but he can't be a hundred and forty-six or whatever that works out to be."

I laughed. "The current Arthur Gedge must be this man's great-grandson. Miss Bunn said many of the local families have worked at the Hall for generations."

"Vivian Bunn? She's a hoot. She was telling me all about the portrait of Lady Susannah with that famous ring."

"*The ring*—I almost forgot. Come downstairs. There's something I want you to see."

I flipped on the lights in the exhibition hall, reminding myself not to mention my conversation with Alex. Why skate on thin ice with hot blades?

We stood in front of the display case. "Remind you of anything?"

Christine stared at the ring, then at me. "It's the ring in the portrait. You found it."

"Maybe. It's close but not a perfect match."

She leaned forward to peer more closely. "It's a ruby, right?"

"More likely a garnet."

"Everyone says it was a ruby. Does that mean it's not valuable?"

"It's valuable, for the history if nothing else. But a ruby would be worth a lot more. Not that Lady Barbara would ever sell it. The house would have to be collapsing around her head before she'd sell off any of the family treasures."

"It practically is collapsing," Christine huffed. "She doesn't seem to notice."

"That's not true. She knows she needs income. That's one of the reasons she agreed to the exhibit of the Hoard."

"She should be worried about all the thefts."

"What do you mean 'all the thefts'? Has something else happened?"

"You didn't hear? Glepping Park south of Mildenhall was burgled last night. It made the front page of the newspaper this morning."

"What did they take?"

"Oddly enough, only one thing. A silver snuffbox. Early seventeenth century."

"Easy to snatch and conceal. Like the Chinese figurine taken near Lowestoft."

"Like that lot downstairs."

I felt a chill.

A great loss?

Chapter
Twenty-One

Wednesday, December 16th

Overnight a line of storms swept across the rolling hills of Suffolk on their way to the North Sea and Scandinavia, leaving behind a damp, bone-numbing chill.

Quintessential English weather.

I pulled on my heaviest sweater and scrunched into the warm turtleneck as I zipped my down jacket and headed for the Hall.

The path was soggy. Low, flat clouds hid the sun.

Today was the DNA testing. Tom had asked the female interns—and me—to stay out of the Stables from ten AM until noon. Privacy concerns.

Lady Barbara was my concern at the moment. Finchley Hall was facing more than financial woes. The murders threatened everything she'd worked for since her husband's death. The ring could make a real difference. If it really was Lady Susannah's.

A robin with a coral breast and white underbelly perched on a bush, gorging on the fat, violet-colored berries. All manner of creatures took shelter and nourishment from the Finchley estate. Generations of local families had depended upon the Hall for survival as well. Some still did. The success of the Hoard exhibit was more than a matter of local pride.

Late the previous evening, Alex had texted me the photo she'd taken of the ring alongside a photo of the ring in the portrait. If not the same ring, they were near-identical twins. One of my unbreakable rules in the antiques trade is to tell the truth, the whole truth. If something has been damaged or repaired, I point it out. When there is a question about provenance, I make it known. Lady Barbara needed the facts. All of them.

I stifled a yawn. Three or four hours of fitful sleep are not enough. I'd fallen asleep quickly, only to wake at three AM—the hour of the wolf, some call it, when worries and fears magnify. Were my misgivings about the ring overblown? Was Christine about to get her heart broken again? Was Finchley Hall next on the thieves' agenda?

Loss was becoming a theme at Finchley Hall. The loss of the Hoard and the rediscovery of it more than two hundred fifty years later. Lady Susannah's portrait, lost and recovered by Lady Barbara's husband. The blood-red ring, lost in plain sight.

Lady Barbara's son, the greatest loss.

In the distance two figures moved in my direction. As they neared, I recognized Albert Mugg and Arthur Gedge. They were probably on their way to the Stables for the DNA testing.

Mugg nodded curtly. "Morning."

"Miss." Old Arthur pulled on his flat cap. He looked almost cheerful, as if the suggestion he'd fathered a child was a fine joke. Or a compliment.

I pushed the doorbell. In minutes the heavy entrance door of Finchley Hall opened.

"Good morning, miss." Francie grinned as she stood back to let me in. This time she wore a gray smock with a white collar and cuffs. Her hair was pulled back into a net-covered bun.

She took my jacket and led me into Lady's Barbara's sitting room. Lady Barbara sat with Vivian. The Bobbsey twins.

"Thank you, Briggs," Lady Barbara said.

Briggs? How many incarnations did that woman have?

"Yes, madam." Francie Jewell shot me a look and scurried out of the room.

Vivian studied her nails.

"Kate, I'm glad you've come," Lady Barbara said. "The police called this morning. Not your Tom. The other one, Constable Wheeler."

"News from Venezuela?"

"Not yet. He called to say if they haven't heard anything by tomorrow, they'll retransmit the request." Her eyes were dull, her cheeks ashen. She'd aged a decade or two since the morning at the morgue in Bury St. Edmunds. "All I can think about is that poor man who died," she said, combing her hair back from her forehead with trembling fingers. "Why had he come? What message did he have for me?"

"*Tush*, now," Vivian said. "You'll get yourself in a twist again."

"I *am* in a twist." Lady Barbara stood and made her way to the window overlooking the gravel courtyard. A fine rain pricked the glass and ran down in rivulets. "This *must* have something to do with Lucien. My son may be in trouble, and now I'll never know or be able to help him."

"Come sit, dear," Vivian said. "Briggs will be here with our tea shortly."

I looked at Vivian and mouthed, *Briggs?*

She gave a little shrug.

Lady Barbara returned and perched on the edge of her chair. "I've written Lucien, of course, but I won't hear anything for days, maybe weeks."

"There's something I need to tell you," I said, changing the subject. "I'm not sure, but I may have found the ring in the portrait of Lady Susannah. The blood-red ring."

Both women stared at me in mute surprise.

"Take a look." I pulled up the photos on my phone. "This is the ring I found. And this is the ring in the portrait."

"I can't make it out." Lady Barbara touched Vivian's arm. "Viv, tell me."

Vivian switched on a lamp. The bulb flickered twice before coming on. "It's the same ring," she said, holding the phone under the light.

"Wherever did you find it?" Lady Barbara asked.

"In the safe. Tabitha's inventory listed it as a gold ring with a red gemstone."

"You're saying she didn't recognize it?"

"It's possible she recognized it but didn't, um, live long enough to tell you."

"Poor child," Vivian said, tutting.

"Kate, you're a marvel," Lady Barbara said. "Lady Susannah's ring was there all the time, and no one knew."

"You also need to know there are subtle differences in size and shape. The resemblance is remarkable but not precise. There's no inscription to identify it as Lady Susannah's."

"Well, I believe it's the same ring." Vivian's chin bounced once. "A fitting time to come home to us as well, with the exhibit a few days away."

"It's like a miracle." Lady Barbara's hands went to her pale cheeks. "What do you suggest we do, Kate?"

"I'd like your permission to issue a press release—and to show-case the portrait and the ring side by side. We'll mention the differences, but the public will love it in any case."

Francie Jewell—*Briggs*—brought the tea tray.

Vivian poured out.

"There's something else." I took a sip of my tea and wiped my fingers on a soft linen napkin. "I think we should honor Tabitha's memory in some way."

"What a wonderful idea." Lady Barbara clapped her hands, nearly flinging the cup of tea Vivian was handing her across the room. "Will you think of the best way to do it, Kate? We'll let her parents know."

"Of course." I eyed a plate of delicately browned scones.

"Apricot and ginger," Vivian said. "One of cook's specialties."

"Briggs, are you still here?" Lady Barbara glanced around the room.

"Yes, madam." Francie had the grace to blush.

"Tell cook she's an absolute treasure, will you?"

"Of course, madam. I'll do that now, shall I, madam?" She winked at me and backed out of the room.

I halved my scone and spread it with a thin layer of butter before biting into the fragrant cakelike texture. I tasted spice with a hint of crunch from a sprinkling of sugar on top. *Cook* was a treasure.

Spots of soft color bloomed on Lady Barbara's cheeks. "I can't help wishing my father had known about the ring. The Hoard was something of an obsession of his. He had the idea we might locate the items that were sold off in the past and buy them back again. Impossible, of course."

Since she'd brought the subject up, I took it a step further. "You said you'd promised to keep the remaining collection intact."

"I would never sell. The Hoard is the Finchley legacy. When I'm gone, my son will become caretaker." Her cup rattled in the saucer.

"How many objects from the Hoard were sold? Do you have a list?"

"There may be something in the archives. I'm not sure. All this happened long ago."

"So nothing has been sold recently, I mean in the past twenty-five years or so."

"Not in my lifetime, nor in my father's, nor my grandfather's. Why are you asking?"

"Tabitha had printed out a copy of the inventory she made. At the end, she'd written a list of eleven items, none of which appear on the inventory or in the catalog. It occurred to me they might be objects she expected to find but didn't."

"Because they'd been sold?" Lady Barbara shook her head. "No, that can't be true."

"Or stolen?" I asked in a small voice.

"Good heavens. The Hoard has been under lock and key for nearly forty years now. If we'd had a theft, Mugg would have told me."

Would he? If Mugg kept the lack of servants from Lady Barbara, what other secrets did he keep? "Do you know of any previous inventories of the Hoard? Did Christine Kerr make one, for example?"

"I wouldn't know. Cedru was alive then. He took care of everything."

"I thought if we could compare the inventory Tabitha made with an earlier one, we'd know if any of the objects are missing."

"I suppose so, but—"

"What about that book?" Vivian said. "You know—the one written by that local chap after the discovery of the Hoard. Didn't he include an inventory?"

Lady Barbara's face lit up. "I'd forgotten about that. We have a copy in the library. I'll ask Mugg to look it out for you, shall I?"

"Something you require, madam?" Mugg had slipped into the room without anyone noticing.

I glanced at his feet, half expecting to see felt slippers. If the ideal maid-of-all-work was unfailingly cheerful in her drudgery, the ideal butler was invisible yet always at hand.

"Yes, thank you, Mugg," Lady Barbara said. "Mrs. Hamilton asked if we'd ever had a theft at the Hall."

"No, madam," Mugg said stiffly. "I would have mentioned it."

"Of course. Well, see if you can locate that book on the Hoard, will you? The one written by . . . who was it, now? Swilling? Shilling?"

"Of course, madam."

He left but returned two minutes later. "Pardon me, madam. Detective Inspector Mallory is here to see you."

Mugg stepped aside, and Tom strode into the room.

He shot me a quick look. "I'm sorry for the intrusion, Lady Barbara, but have you seen Peter Ingham today?"

"Not since the Eve of St. Æthelric. Why?"

"He seems to have gone missing."

"Have you asked Gedge?"

Tom put on his professional face, but the subtle shift in his eyes told me he was glossing over what came next. "Mr. Gedge is on his way to police headquarters. Our divers retrieved a garden spade from Blackwater Lake. We're having it tested for blood."

"Gedge?" Lady Barbara's face crumpled. "You suspect *Gedge*?"

"He may be able to help us with our enquiries."

Lady Barbara put up her hands. "This is all too much. Murder. Theft. Whatever will happen next?"

I was wondering the same thing.

*   *   *

Spits of rain fell from a pewter sky.

"How long has Peter been missing?" I held Tom's arm as we hurried beneath his umbrella toward the Stables.

"No one has seen him since yesterday afternoon."

"And you think Gedge knows where Peter is?"

"He says not. He claims Peter was upset by the DNA test, called it an invasion of privacy."

"That doesn't make Peter guilty."

"That's why we need his sample—to rule him out. If he's not the killer, why isn't he willing to give a DNA sample"

"And Gedge?"

"I think he knows more than he's willing to say. The spade found in the lake matches others in the garden shed."

"What about Adam, the intern who decided not to come?"

"Ruled out. He attends the University of Exeter. Never met Tabitha."

We bobbed along under the umbrella, dodging puddles on the gravel path. Cliché or not, I couldn't help thinking about the handsome young vicar comforting Tabitha at the Three Magpies.

"So if none of the samples match, you'll widen the circle."

I must not have sounded as neutral as I'd meant to because Tom slowed his pace. "Are you thinking of someone in particular?"

"No one in particular." Not the whole truth, but I'd learned in Scotland that casting suspicion on an innocent person can have unintended consequences. Before voicing my concerns to a policeman, I'd find out more about the dishy vicar.

"We got a preliminary autopsy report this morning," Tom said. "The man found near the garden wall was poisoned, as we suspected. The substance matches a powerful herbicide also found in the shed."

"That doesn't mean Peter or Gedge had anything to do with the murder. Anyone might have slipped into the shed. Nothing's locked around here. The grounds are open to the public."

"We're aware of that, Kate, but it's a line of enquiry we have to pursue."

"What questions do you think Gedge can answer?"

"Did he notice the spade was missing? Was he aware of the herbicide? Had the bottle been tampered with? Is he protecting Peter Ingham?"

"You now think the two deaths are related?"

"We're still treating them as separate enquiries. But two murders at Finchley Hall within a week can't be coincidence."

"Yes, and there's the death of the museum curator twenty-three years ago."

"Well, if the same person committed all three murders, Peter's off the hook. He wasn't born yet."

"Arthur Gedge was. He found Catherine Kerr's body."

"What motive? Either the killer is a psychopath with nothing more than the desire to kill, or we haven't yet figured out what the murders have in common."

"Catherine Kerr and Tabitha King were both attacked and their bodies thrown in the lake."

"But the man was poisoned."

"Maybe the killer needed to make sure he couldn't fight back."

"Assuming the three deaths are related, why kill a young woman and then wait twenty-three years to do it again? Serial killers typically have a cooling-off period, but not that long."

"Maybe the killer had no *reason* to kill again until Tabitha. And maybe the stranger was killed because he knew something or saw something."

"Possible. Which brings us back to the unknown motive." Tom must have noticed my puzzled look. "What is it?"

"What did the file on the Catherine Kerr murder say about Gedge's alibi?"

"'Airtight' was the way Inspector Evans put it. The young woman died between eight and ten that evening. Gedge swore he was drinking at the Finchley Arms, and the bartender confirmed it. Except for a few trips to the loo, Gedge was there, on his usual stool, from six thirty until closing time."

We'd arrived at the Stables, where Tom had parked his silver Volvo.

"Take the umbrella."

I held out my hand. "No need. Rain's stopped."

Tom shook out the umbrella and rolled it up. "I should be able to get away tonight." He gave me that slow half smile. "How about dinner in the village? Pick you up at six?"

"On one condition."

"Which is?" He clicked open the car doors and slid into the driver's seat.

"The Three Magpies this time. Please."

I watched him drive away. My mobile pinged. A text from Christine.

Come to my office. You're not going to believe this.

*   *   *

Christine's long, dark hair fell over her shoulders as she bent over several open books. She tucked a strand behind her ear. "Amazing what you can learn from original records. So much could be concealed in the past—names, ages, past crimes. No computer records to contradict you." She looked up. "Then, decades later, secrets are revealed."

Long-hidden secrets. It was true. I'd done some genealogical work on my father's family and found that every time the census takers came through, his grandmother shaved a couple of years off her age.

"What secrets did you uncover?"

"Come see for yourself. No, not that one." Christine pushed a ledger book toward me and pointed to a line on the open page. "Start here."

At the top of each page, someone had written in a formal script, Gifts and Payments 1898 to 1900.

"'Tenth April 1898,'" I read aloud. "'Ten pounds. Wedding gift for Alice Thurtle and Thomas Gedge.'" I looked up. "So the Thurtles were related to the Gedges. Understandable, since they both worked for the Finchleys."

She turned several pages. "Now this one."

"'First November 1898. Five pounds. Burial of infant son of Alice and Thomas Gedge.'"

"Alice was three months pregnant when she married Thomas." Christine opened a second ledger to a place she'd marked. "Now, look at this, four years later—'Fourth April 1902. One pound. Gift for Alice and Thomas Gedge upon the birth of a daughter, Eloise.'"

I was about to remark that the birth of a child to a married couple in 1902 was hardly remarkable when Christine opened a third ledger book with a look of triumph. "Guess what happened to little Eloise Gedge?" She angled the book toward me.

16TH JUNE 1924. £25. WEDDING GIFT FOR ELOISE GEDGE AND GEORGE INGHAM.

"Ingham?" It took me a moment to grasp the significance. "You think Peter Ingham and Arthur Gedge are related?"

"Possible. Likely, even. So why haven't they said?"

"Ingham may be a common name in Suffolk. It could be coincidence," I said, remembering Tom's suggestion that Gedge was covering for Peter. I pictured the argument between them near the garden shed the day Tabitha's body was found in the lake—and their obvious friendship later in the Finchley Arms. Now Arthur Gedge was in police custody and Peter Ingham was missing.

"Is Peter Ingham from this area?"

"He went to the University of East Anglia, but he could have grown up anywhere."

The University of East Anglia. Tabitha's university. "It's worth checking out."

Christine closed the ledger. "I'll do a little more research and see what I come up with. Eloise Gedge Ingham wouldn't be alive today, but her children and grandchildren might be."

"Peter's great-grandparents?" I was having trouble taking it in. "But what would this have to do with the murders?"

"I don't know, but it's interesting."

I had to agree. "I'll mention it to Tom tonight. We're having dinner at the Three Magpies."

"Again? Are you serious about him?" The serrated edge to Christine's voice turned the question into an accusation.

"I haven't known him long enough to be serious." The offhand comment didn't ring true, even to me. I owed her an honest answer. "I do like him, Christine. I like him a lot. If it wasn't for our circumstances, living so far apart, I think I could be serious about him."

"What about Dad?" She folded her arms across her chest. "You just forget him and get on with your life, is that it?"

"I haven't forgotten him. I never will. But what else can I do but get on with my life?'

"It's inappropriate. It's too soon. You're still in mourning."

"What am I supposed to do—wear a black veil?"

"You're supposed to act like a mature woman, not a teenager."

I felt the heat rise in my cheeks. "That's not fair. I've done nothing inappropriate, nothing that would dishonor your father in any way."

"I disagree." She took a sharp breath through her nose.

"That's your right, but you don't have the right to plan my life for me."

"Why not? You're always trying to plan mine."

That hurt. I'd tried so hard *not* to plan her life. I'd stood by and watched her ricochet from one disastrous relationship to another, replaying over and over again in real time what I knew she felt as her father's abandonment. I knew it because I'd experienced it. But where Christine repeated the pattern, expecting a different result, I'd walled myself off from pain. Or tried to.

Christine glared at me. A muscle in her cheek twitched. The portcullis was coming down.

I softened my tone. "I loved your father very much, but he's gone. We can't have him back no matter how much we wish it." I reached for her and felt her stiffen. "I haven't forgotten him, Christine. I never will."

I walked away from the archives building, breathing in lungfuls of cold, damp air.

Could I have handled things differently? Used different words?

No. I was forty-six, not exactly young but far from getting a giant pill organizer and joining the Red Hat Society. There would be another man in my life one day. If not Tom, someone else. Christine would just have to accept the fact that I had a life, as she did, and if there were mistakes to be made, I had to make them.

As she does.

Ouch. I hate it when I'm right.

Think about it later. I punched in the number for Finchley Hall.

Francie Jewell—*Briggs*—answered, and I was put through to Lady Barbara.

"I'm calling about that book on the Hoard. I could stop over now and pick it up."

"I'm glad you called, Kate. It's very strange, but the book has gone missing."

"Could Tabitha have borrowed it?"

"It's possible." Lady Barbara sounded distressed. "I do hope you find it. It was a lovely thing, beautifully printed, bound in soft, pale suede. Not many copies were produced. It would be a shame if—*oh.*" She stopped abruptly. "I just remembered. A man in the village has a copy. Ivor Tweedy. His shop is on the High Street, not far from the church. Do you know it?"

Chapter Twenty-Two

❧

The spring-loaded bell jangled as I stepped through the door of Ivor Tweedy's shop. He stood behind the counter, a small metal can in one hand, a rag in the other.

"Kate, my dear. You've come back so soon." He gestured with the rag. "Come in, come in." He set down the can and wiped his hands. "Such a treat. An unexpected treat."

"How's the hip today?"

"No complaints, no complaints. Cleaning silver." He picked up what looked like a pair of footed scissors with a small box on the blades. "Know what this is, hmm?"

"Candlesnuffer." I was the pupil again.

"And it was used for . . . ?" His blue eyes widened, innocent as a child's.

I didn't fall into the trap. "Not for snuffing candle flames. For trimming wicks before the invention of self-consuming wicks."

"And why were the ends pointed?"

I could tell he was pleased. "To retrieve the wick if it fell into the soft wax. I have two pairs in my shop at the moment. One Georgian, sterling, the other Victorian, close-plated on steel."

"You know your stuff." He screwed the cap on the silver cleaner and folded the rag. "The police stopped in yesterday."

"To ask about Lucien Finchley-fforde, I suppose."

"They wanted to know how I could be so certain he was dead. I told them, if Lucien were alive, he'd have wheedled his mother long ago into giving him his inheritance. Completely self-centered, that man was. And always in need of ready cash. He lost his generous allowance when he left England. He couldn't have survived on his own."

"Lady Barbara insists her son is alive and well in Venezuela."

"Let her think that if it brings her comfort."

I wondered briefly if Ivor Tweedy was part of the conspiracy to shelter Lady Barbara from all things unpleasant.

"What do you know about Edmund Foxe?"

"The vicar? Not a lot. Why do you ask?"

"I'm on my way over there." It wasn't much of an answer, but it seemed to satisfy Ivor.

"Young, enthusiastic—not one of the happy-clappies, but he's done away with the bells and smells."

The Church of England, I knew, is divided between those who hold to the old traditions and elaborate rituals—bells and smells—and the more modern, seeker-friendly services with contemporary music and audience participation—the happy-clappies. Edmund Foxe seemed to be navigating the middle.

"How long as he been in Long Barston?"

"Two years. Maybe longer."

"Do you know where he came from?"

"Essex—Colchester, I believe. Or was it Chelmsford? Hmm." He saw me pick up a carved cinnabar lacquer brush pot, and his eyes lit up. "What brings you to the shop today? On the hunt?"

"I should be. I need stock. But I've come about a book, written by a local man about the finding of the Hoard."

"Ah, you mean Swiggett. Walter Swiggett, a wealthy amateur historian from over Foxearth way. Printed privately in 1822. Only a hundred copies, and"—his eyes glittered—"one of them is mine."

I followed him as he limped through a maze of shelves to a small windowless room in the back of the shop. Books filled the shelves floor to ceiling. More tottered in piles on the floor.

"Now where did I put it?" Ivor Tweedy squinted behind his glasses. "History? Hoard? Something starting with *h*, anyway." He pawed through the books like a squirrel searching for a lost nut. "Ah, yes." He gave a little clap. "Here, I think."

He positioned an iron library ladder against one of the shelves and winced as he climbed.

I moved closer, ready to steady him in case he lost his balance.

"Strange." He ran his fingertips along the volumes from left to right, then from right to left. Frowning, he adjusted his glasses. "It's not here."

"Could you have sold it?"

"I'd never do that. In any case, you're the first to ask about the book in at least ten years."

"Lady Barbara's copy is missing, too."

"Now that *is* odd. Very odd indeed."

"Do you know of other copies?"

"There's one in the Bodleian, but access is restricted to researchers. There's an application process."

I didn't have time to visit the Bodleian, much less go through a lengthy application process. "Are you sure the book wasn't stolen? Maybe there's an obsessed collector out there somewhere."

"If you were talking an early folio of *Hamlet*, maybe. But local history? Can't imagine it."

"Have any strangers come in recently to browse?"

"Just you." He chuckled.

"And yet the book is missing."

"Yes." He stroked his chin thoughtfully.

We walked toward the front of the shop. His limp had become more pronounced.

"You're in pain," I said.

"Old hip joints. Everything wears out in the end."

"Isn't there anything the doctors can do?"

"Replacement. I've been on a waiting list with the National Health for six months."

I pulled my card out of my handbag. "If you find the book, please call me."

"Of course. I'm quite baffled by this."

He was still muttering as I closed the shop door behind me. Ivor Tweedy might have been eccentric—well, let's face it, he was—but he was also a kind and honest man.

A van from BBC News trundled past toward the main road out of town. In a remote Suffolk village, even a second murder had limited national press value.

I turned in the direction of the church. The book that might answer my question about Tabitha's handwritten list had suddenly gone missing. Twice.

Someone, it seemed, was a step ahead of me.

*   *   *

St. Æthelric's was one of the famous "wool churches," built in East Anglia and the Cotswolds with the proceeds of the sheep-farming industry—or, more accurately, the wool cloth–producing industry. I stood, my guidebook in hand, gazing up at the solid stone walls. The classic Norman structure—high square tower, main arch with zigzag moldings—had been built by the wealthy cloth guilds. Among its treasures were the original medieval glass windows, taken down and concealed during the Second World War and brought out with great jubilation on V-E Day.

The graveyard, enclosed behind the red brick wall, spanned centuries. The oldest stones were nearest the church itself, simple tablets inscribed with names and dates. Some leaned at crazy angles, but all were intact, the names legible. As I moved toward the outer walls, the monuments became increasingly elaborate and sentimental, some bearing sculptured designs—willow trees, weeping angels, urns. Some taught a lesson about the brevity of life or the inevitability of death. Some included Bible passages or clever aphorisms. Many were decorated for Christmas with evergreen branches and faux red poinsettias.

I was looking for the names Thurtle, Gedge, and Ingham. And there she was. A stone near the wall marked the resting place of Eloise Ingham née Gedge, age forty-eight: DEAREST WIFE OF GEORGE INGHAM. BORN 4TH APRIL 1902. DIED 4TH FEBRUARY 1951.

Then I read the stone next to hers and did a double-take:

Sacred to the memory of the beloved daughters of Eloise and George Ingham.
Lydia aged 19, Born 29th January 1931. Died 1st February 1951
Margaret, aged 21, Born 11th April 1929. Died 7th February 1951
Thelma, aged 14, Born 19th April 1936. Died 12th February 1951

George Ingham's wife and three daughters had all perished within a two-week period in February 1951.

"Sad, isn't it?" A pleasant-looking woman carrying a small evergreen wreath stood behind me. Her dark hair, just going gray, was tucked behind her ears. She wore corduroy slacks and a pine-green waxed jacket similar to Tom's.

She leaned the wreath against a stone carved with the name NUTHALL and squinted against the light. "I'm Hattie Nuthall, the vicar's housekeeper. Every stone here tells a story. The one you're look-ing at is especially sad. All four taken in the flu epidemic of 1951."

"Were there other children?" If all Eloise's children died in the epidemic, Peter Ingham couldn't be related to her.

"There was a son. Ironic, really, because he'd gone to the Korean War. I'm told his mother lived in terror he'd be killed, but in the end it probably saved him."

"Is his grave here as well?"

"I'd have to check. Are you related to the Inghams?" Her nut-brown eyes registered keen interest.

"Not at all, but I am interested in local history. My daughter is one of the interns at Finchley Hall. She's working in the family archives."

"The Hall—my goodness. More sadness. Shocking for your daughter, I imagine."

"Yes, although she didn't really know Miss King."

"I felt sorry for that girl. Something was obviously playing on her mind."

"You knew her?"

"Not well, but the vicar spent a lot of time with her, especially in the weeks leading up to her death. We were devastated when we heard." Hattie polished the headstone with the cuff of her jacket. "My parents lived in this village their whole lives. I'll be here, too, one day, next to them."

"The history of the village is here, I imagine—if you know where to look."

"The vicar knows a lot about local history. I'm headed there now. Come along. I'll see if he's free."

"Thank you." I checked my watch. Tom wouldn't arrive at the Stables for another two hours. Plenty of time to freshen up and change clothes.

We stepped down to enter the stone-floored church. Hattie bus-tled off to find the vicar.

The nave of St. Æthelric's was lit by a series of tracery windows containing the medieval glass so prized by the villagers. I could see why. The late-afternoon sun slanted through the leaded glass, laying streaks of emerald, ruby, sapphire, and topaz. Four windows depicted the four Gospel writers, each carrying a book and wearing robes in brilliant jewel colors. Lozenges beneath their feet held their identifying symbols—divine man, winged ox, winged lion, rising eagle.

Hattie rejoined me. "Vicar's on his way." She followed my gaze to a window along the east wall. "That one was given to the church in the late fifteenth century by Gilbert Finchley and his wife, Juliana."

A prosperous-looking man with his wife in a high-waisted kirtle and winged headdress knelt with their four children to pray beneath a circlet of the Risen Christ and the Finchley coat of arms.

"Lovely, isn't it?" Today the vicar wore jeans and a clerical collar under a tweed jacket. He stuck out his hand. "Edmund Foxe."

I introduced myself. "I saw you at the Hall the night the body was found, but we weren't introduced. My daughter is one of the new interns at Finchley Hall."

"Ah, yes." He shoved his hands into his jacket pockets.

"I'll leave you to it," Hattie said. "Must finish January's flower rota."

"You may not believe this," the vicar said, "but Long Barston is a quiet community. Crime in the village is usually limited to a bit of shoplifting or joyriding. We've had nothing close to murder in decades." He gazed at the altar screen and inhaled sharply.

I followed him up the main aisle toward the chancel, adorned for Christmas with greenery and a crèche. "Your housekeeper tells me you knew Tabitha King."

"Not well." Emotion crossed his face, gone as soon as it appeared. "Tabitha was searching for something. She thought the church might provide it."

"But it didn't?"

"Let's just say, not in time. On a happier note, Hattie tells me you're interested in local history."

"My daughter is working in the Finchley family archives. We noticed the names Gedge and Ingham."

"Common names in these parts." His smile revealed perfect white teeth. If this young clergyman didn't inhabit the dreams of the village bachelorettes, he most certainly did the prayers of their mothers. "Plenty of Gedges and Inghams in the records—births, marriages, deaths. Someone particular you're interested in?"

"I noticed the memorial to the mother and three daughters who died in the flu epidemic of 1951. Your housekeeper said Eloise Ingham had a son who survived the Korean War. Do you know if he stayed in the area?"

"Married a girl from Norwich, if memory serves. I believe he moved up that way."

We'd reached the altar.

"How old is the church?"

"There was an earlier church here," he said, "mentioned in the Domesday Book of 1086. Construction on the present church began in the middle of the fifteenth century. The oldest part is the tower. Wonderful views of the village and park. That's where I caught a glimpse of the man who was found dead—at least I assume it was him. And the other one."

"The other one?"

"The man he was with."

"The two were together? Where was this?"

"Best if I show you." His eyes sparkled with enthusiasm. "Let's run up there now."

I did *not* want to run up the tower, but he was already halfway toward the door. And I *was* curious. Curious enough to face my fears.

"Seven flights. Eighty-four steps." He threw over his shoulder, "We'll catch our breath at the ringing chamber."

Wooden steps zigzagged upward. I grasped the railing, forcing myself to look straight ahead rather than up or down. That usually helps, but by the time we reached the ringing chamber, I'd started to hyperventilate.

I felt the color drain from my face, but the vicar didn't seem to notice. He flashed me a smile. "The bell chamber is directly above. Then the viewing platform. Come on."

"Are there railings? It's just I'm a bit . . ." I trailed off, feeling sweaty and nauseated.

"Fear of heights?" He grinned. "Not to worry. We'll be inside the tower at all times."

This didn't help. I've been known to get vertigo in platform shoes.

"It's an incredible view. Come on. Trust me, Kate. May I call you Kate?"

I nodded, reminding myself that a clergyman in the Church of England probably didn't harbor fantasies of pushing me off the tower.

Then we were there, and he was right. The view was incredible, even from my vantage point in the exact center of the small room. I looked around for something to hold on to. Finding nothing, I widened my stance. *You're all right. You're safe.* The viewing platform had a sturdy wooden floor and a thick parapet that rose comfortingly to chest level. Even I couldn't throw myself off without a great deal of effort.

"Where's Finchley Hall from here?" I asked, hoping to distract myself with information.

"Just there." He pointed toward a patch of green in the middle distance. "If you come forward a bit—just a step or two, Kate—you can see the roof and the chimneys."

I took a cautious step. Then another. "Is curing phobias part of your job description?"

He laughed. "You don't have a phobia. Most people don't like heights. It's the feeling of vulnerability. The secret is to focus on what you see, not where you are. Here, take my arm. There's the Folly—right there, near that patch of dark green—and beyond it the Chinese Bridge."

The octagonal roof of the Folly was easy to pick out among the treetops. A flash of red identified the Chinese Bridge. He was right. I started to relax and took another step forward. I reached out for the brick parapet but instantly took a step back as a spell of vertigo brought another wave of nausea.

Focus on what you see, not on where you are.

Below me, the long, winding main street of Long Barston curved to the left, crossed the River Stour, and disappeared over a low hill. The buildings, cars, and antlike people looked like the models in my brother Matt's train setup.

"There's the Finchley Arms," Edmund Foxe said. "See it? At the intersection of the High and Sheep Street. Sheep Street marks the route originally taken by drovers, bringing their animals to market. If you lean forward, you can see the tiled roof of the Three Magpies on the next street."

"I'll take your word for it."

He laughed. "The torch parade began in the church parking area." He indicated a small paved area between the churchyard and the edge of the wood leading to Finchley Park. "That's where I saw the stranger. I'd come up here to ring the bells at four. We do that two hours before the torch parade and then again around six—a call to arms, if you will. That's when I saw the man who was killed. Four o'clock"—he stabbed a finger—"right there at the edge of the wood. I couldn't see his face, of course, but I noticed he was wearing some sort of dark head covering. A flat cap, maybe, or something knitted. Someone joined him."

"Who was it?"

"Couldn't say. Couldn't even tell you if it was a man or woman. Just a figure, although I had an idea he—or she—was wearing sunglasses. I remember thinking it was strange because the sun was already low in the sky."

"What happened?"

"One minute they were there, then they were gone."

"Did you tell the police?"

"Should I have? They haven't contacted me."

"I think you should. Every bit of information is important."

"I heard the police found a shack where the stranger was sleeping rough."

As we gazed at the crime scene, a thin plume of smoke rose and hung in the air before dissipating. Then another. "What's that?" I asked.

"I don't know. Burning leaves? Campfire? Do you know the number of rough sleepers in the UK has more than doubled in the past five years? In spite of all the government programs, most refuse to ask for help—fear, mental illness."

The smoke was no longer visible.

"Let's get you to ground level," the vicar said. "I'll go first. Hold on to the railing and put your left hand on my shoulder."

I followed him, step for step.

The vicar looked over his shoulder. "The poor man should have come to us, you know. He would have found a hot meal and a safe place to sleep."

We'd reached ground level. I took a breath and blew it out. One thing was clear. If the figure seen by the vicar the afternoon of the Peasants' Revolt was the murder victim, less than four hours later he was dead.

Was the second person, the man or woman in the sunglasses, his killer?

Chapter
Twenty-Three

❧

The evening menu at the Three Magpies featured three main courses—slow-roasted lamb shoulder with chickpeas and apricots, pan-fried trout with buttered new potatoes, and a wild mushroom–and–mozzarella lasagna with roasted cherry tomato sauce.

This time Tom and I sat in the main dining room.

Jayne Collier brought us glasses of crisp Sancerre. "And to get you started, Gavin's homemade sourdough with lemon and coriander olives." Small purplish-brown olives and larger torpedo-shaped green ones swam in a pond of herbed olive oil.

"You're almost full tonight," I said, noticing that only three of the fifteen or so tables in the dining room were empty.

"Not bad for a Thursday." Jayne smiled. "No locals yet."

"Saxby St. Clare isn't exactly local," Tom said. "But once my mother gets the word out, you'll be turning them away."

The mention of Tom's mother brought another stab of guilt. I really had to tell him about our disastrous tea, but when?

He smiled at me, and his hazel eyes crinkled at the corners. *Oh, not tonight.*

"Have you seen the competition?" Jayne asked. "The Arms has started advertising two-for-one mains with a free bottle of wine."

"We've had the wine," Tom said. "Free is just about right."

She laughed. "Water's free here. Still or sparkling?"

Jayne left and returned with a pair of squat glasses and a cool green bottle of spring water. "Enjoy. Take your time. I'll come back to take your orders."

"Did the vicar of St. Æthelric's call you?" I asked Tom when she'd gone.

"Just as I was leaving. I understand you're responsible. Thank you."

"Does it help?"

"Of course. We suspected the dead man knew someone around here, but this is the first direct confirmation. And, if the vicar was right, it pinpoints the murder to a four-hour window between the first ringing of the bells and the discovery of the body."

I speared an olive. "Any news on Peter?"

"Vanished. If he doesn't show himself by morning, we'll have to call his parents in Norwich."

"Peter Ingham's from Norwich?"

Tom narrowed his eyes. "Why? Do you know something?"

"I might. Christine showed me some old Finchley Hall ledgers. Three families working for the Finchleys—the Thurtles, the Gedges, and the Inghams—intermarried during those years. Not surprising, except that Eloise Gedge and George Ingham had a son who survived the Korean War. The vicar said the son moved to Norwich."

"You're saying Peter Ingham and Arthur Gedge are related? Gedge never mentioned it."

Tom's phone beeped. He excused himself.

By the time he returned, Jayne had arrived to take our orders.

"Sorry about that." Tom slid into his chair and spread his napkin on his lap.

I ordered the trout. He ordered the lamb.

When Jayne left to put in the orders, I asked, "Something important?"

"That was Cliffe. The coroner's report on the male victim came in."

"Are you able to tell me?"

"He was dosed with herbicide all right—paraquat, a highly toxic weed killer banned in the U.K. in 2007. The SOCOs—the scenes-of-crime officers—found an old tin of it in the garden shed. Gedge swears he didn't know it was there. If he had, he would have turned it in for disposal years ago."

"And you believed him?"

"Funny thing, Kate, but I did. There's something he isn't telling us—maybe his connection to Peter—but I don't think he was lying about the spade and the poison." Tom took a taste of the Sancerre. "Someone knew the herbicide was there—and what it would do. If you're going to poison someone, you better make sure they die."

"But how would the killer get the man to take the poison?"

"Laced the whiskey. The bottle found in the shack where he'd been sleeping rough."

"Francie Jewell said a bottle of whiskey went missing from the Finchley Hall kitchen. And someone's been sneaking food."

"The kitchen is rarely locked. Anyone might have gotten in."

"And then put poison in the whiskey."

A well-dressed couple on their way out gave us a shocked look and a wide berth. I might have laughed if the conversation hadn't been so grisly.

I lowered my voice. "Wouldn't the herbicide have changed the taste?"

"Yeah, but that's the thing about paraquat. One small sip will kill you. By the time the man realized the whiskey wasn't right, he'd already have taken a lethal dose. But that's not what killed him. Most cases of paraquat poisoning are accidental—drinking from a soda bottle that once held the herbicide, for example. The victims realize what they've done, check themselves into hospital, and die, painfully, ten to sixteen days later. The killer couldn't risk that, so he waited until the stranger was helpless—probably sweating, having trouble breathing—then smothered him with something. The coroner's report confirmed it."

"Poor man."

Tom took a long drink of water. "Gedge is about to be interviewed again."

"What did he say about the spade found in the lake?"

"Noticed it was missing. Assumed it would turn up again." Tom tore off a chunk of bread and dipped it in the olive oil. "The problem with this case is a lack of cohesion. It's like broken glass. We lay out individual pieces, but we've no clue how they fit together."

"Have you heard from Venezuela?"

"Not a word. We released the results of the pathologist's report on Tabitha to the press today, all but the pregnancy. I'm not sure it was a good idea, but the guv wanted to show we've been doing something. Tabitha's father is a powerful man with powerful friends. He wants results. Can't say I blame him." He eyed me. "Sorry. This isn't exactly dinner conversation. Let's change the subject."

"Good idea."

"Tell me what you did today."

"Climbed the bell tower at St. Æthelric's."

"I thought you were afraid of heights."

"I am. I'm also hopelessly inquisitive. I wanted to see where Vicar Foxe saw the stranger the night of the Peasants' Revolt."

"I climbed that tower once. Couldn't see a thing."

"Why was that?"

"Pitch-black. I raced up and rang the bells a few times. Raced down and shot out of there before anyone saw me."

"Recently, was this?"

He laughed. "I was fifteen. A dare. It was awful. Villagers rushed outside in the middle of the night, assuming there was an emergency."

"What happened when you got caught?"

"Never did. I still feel guilty about it."

"You could confess. I'm sure Vicar Foxe would grant you a pardon."

Our food arrived. The trout was tender and flaky with a sprig of rosemary and wedges of lemon.

Tom cut a slice of his lamb. "Have you figured out the list Tabitha made?"

"Oh, golly—forgot all about that. I may have solved a mystery." I told him about the resemblance between the ring on display and the ring in the portrait of Lady Susannah. "The rings themselves, the settings, are almost identical. The biggest problem is the central stone. Legend says Lady Susannah's ring was a fine Burmese ruby, engraved with the image of a griffin, the legendary guardian of treasure."

"Like the Hoard?"

"Exactly like. But the ring I found is a garnet, a nice one, but it's a far cry from a pigeon's blood ruby."

"What are you saying?"

"I'm not saying anything. I'm wondering if the stones were switched and—" I stopped, unwilling to put my suspicions into words.

"And what? Come on."

"I'm wondering," I said, my thoughts taking shape as I spoke them, "if Tabitha was killed because she figured it out. She must have recognized the resemblance to the ring in the portrait. She was careful, methodical. But she didn't say anything. I can think of two reasons why not. The first is obvious. She was murdered before she had a chance to tell anyone."

"And the second reason?"

"Because she did say something—to the wrong person."

"Does Lady Barbara know?"

"She does now."

I could almost see the gears turning in Tom's brain. "Have you told anyone else?"

"Just the whole world." I moaned. "Lady Barbara authorized a press release to increase interest in the exhibit. Alex put it out. It'll be in all the newspapers tomorrow or the next day."

Tom dipped a bite of his lamb in a pot of green mint jelly. "This may turn to our advantage. Shake things up. Make the killer nervous."

Or desperate. "I told Christine and Alex Devereux. I don't want them to be targets."

"No, that's good. If the killer thinks no one knows his secret, he makes sure it stays that way. If a lot of people know, the danger for each individual lessens."

"That reminds me. Did you find an old book in Tabitha's room? Bound in pale suede, published in 1822 by someone named Swiggett."

"She had quite a few books. None fitting that description as I remember. Why?"

"Only a hundred copies were printed. Two have gone missing— one from the Finchley Hall library and one from Ivor Tweedy's shop. The book may contain the original Hoard inventory. That might tell me if the unnumbered items on Tabitha's list were on the inventory made when the Hoard was found but are now either lost or stolen."

"I'll check in the morning. If we have the book, I'll let you know."

His phone pinged. He frowned at the screen. "Brilliant." He looked up. "I have to go, Kate. You're not going to believe this, but there's been another theft."

I froze. "Where this time?"

"Tettinger Court near Haverhill."

"That's not far from Long Barston. What was taken?"

"A small painting, a court miniature. Sixteenth century."

Old, rare, valuable—and small.

Tom downed the last of his water and stood.

Jayne Collier appeared out of nowhere, holding our coats. "Give me five minutes. I'll pack up your dinners."

"Thanks." Tom pulled on his jacket. "Kate, is it all right if I drop you at the Hall rather than the Stables?"

"No worries."

But I was worried, and it wasn't only the murders and the mystery of Lady Susannah's ring.

Thieves were circling Finchley Hall.

* * *

Tom's car pulled up at the entrance to Finchley Hall. "I'm sorry, Kate. I'm saying that a lot these days."

"Never mind. Just catch the thieves. Finchley Hall could be next." I unhooked my seat belt.

"I wish there was more we could do. With the recent cutbacks, we're reacting to crime, not preventing it. Only the most serious cases can be thoroughly investigated—drugs, organized crime. If a house on one of the estates is burgled, good luck to them. If a car is vandalized or a bicycle nicked, forget it."

"I'll breathe easier when the exhibit is over and the Hoard is back in the safe."

"I'll breathe easier when we catch the killer."

"Of course. That's the priority." I leaned over and gave him a kiss. "Go do what you do best. Well, do some policing, anyway."

He laughed and kissed my hair. "See you soon."

The taillights of his car receded, leaving me alone in the cold night air. Stars pricked the black-velvet sky. Moonlight silvered the fountain in the courtyard. From somewhere in the distance, a dove cooed. Nothing stirred.

I pulled up the collar of my jacket. The path to the Stables skirted the garden wall and headed toward the park before making a sharp right turn toward the estate outbuildings and the Rare Breeds Farm.

The crunch of the gravel under my feet sounded unnaturally loud in the still night air.

I'd been in England almost two weeks, and Tom and I had spent so little time together. No one's fault—certainly not his—but my visit was coming to an end soon. In five days I'd be on an airplane, winging my way back to Cleveland. And then what? I loved him, but could our relationship ever be more than it was now? Did I want it to be?

Liz Mallory was right. The life of a policeman—and a policeman's wife—would always mean the phone call in the middle of the night, the last-minute cancellation of plans, the constant uncertainty, the danger. So different from the calm, predictable life of a university law professor, time measured in syllabi and semesters and scheduled office hours. The closest thing Bill ever got to an emergency was the occasional distraught student turning up at our door to beg for one more chance to take that test or revise that paper. The academic life had suited Bill. It would never suit Tom.

And me?

The question shut down when I noticed the bouncing beam of a flashlight. Someone was walking quickly in my direction from the park. The light stopped bouncing. A snort and a low growl told me I had nothing to fear.

"Fergus, it's me, boy." I met Vivian Bunn and Fergus near the Chinese Bridge. The dog, recognizing me, strained so hard against his collar, he choked.

I bent down to rub his soft button ears.

Vivian patted her ample bosom. "You gave me the willies. What are you doing out here in the dark?"

"On my way to the Stables. Tom was called out on an emergency. What are you and Fergus doing out in the dark?"

"Walkies. The little man hasn't been himself all day, whining and pawing at the door. I thought he might have the collywobbles again. I know I shouldn't give him table food, but when he stares at me with those pathetic eyes . . . Anyway, he still hasn't *done* anything, and now we're almost at the Hall."

The dog winked at me, his pink tongue lolling.

"Going to see Lady Barbara?"

"Oh, dear me, no. After eight she's in bed with her nightly Horlicks and a book on Audible. I just kept walking, and somehow here I was. Isn't that right, boy?"

Fergus averted his eyes.

"Oh, all right," Vivian said. "The truth is I got spooked. I don't take Fergus for a proper walk at night—just around the cottage to do his business. But he kept pulling and pulling, and before I knew it, I was near the Folly. But then I heard something, and—" She broke off.

"And you thought about Tabitha and the dead stranger. I don't blame you."

"Not just that. Fergus was acting strangely, sniffing the air, grousing. I got the feeling someone was out there in the dark. I started to run—well, walk quickly—toward the closest place of safety." She shook her head as if to clear it. "Oh, dear. I'm not usually given to fears and fancies."

"Why don't I walk back with you. You can loan me the torch. I'll return it in the morning."

"Would you? Although I don't like the thought of you walking back alone."

"Got my cell phone." I held it up. "First sign of anyone, I'll dial 999."

We made it to Rose Cottage in ten minutes. Vivian invited me in for a cup of tea, but I declined, saying I wanted to call my mother before she left the shop for the day. It was the truth, although I hadn't planned it earlier. Now, with the discovery of the ring and the thieves inching closer to Finchley Hall, I wanted her perspective.

I said good-bye to Vivian and Fergus and started back.

The wind had picked up. The bare-limbed tree branches above me creaked. The tall grass on the edge of Blackwater Lake sighed in the breeze. Just ahead, the Folly's marble columns gleamed in the pale moonlight. I stopped and squinted as I scanned my surroundings. A three-quarter moon illuminated a swath of mossy grass leading to the trees.

The faint scent of burning wood met my nose. The source of the smoke I'd seen earlier?

Switching off the flashlight, I moved cautiously toward the source.

A pinpoint of light flickered through the trees. I crept forward, trying not to make a sound. Curiously, I felt no fear, although the possibility I'd completely lost my mind did occur to me.

Another fifty yards or so brought me to the edge of a clearing. The moonlight shone on a domed structure built into the side of a raised earthen mound. The old icehouse. Outside, a small fire burned, and near it a man huddled on a log, his short-cropped blond hair gleaming in the soft light.

"Peter."

His head snapped toward me. "Leave me alone."

"The police are looking for you."

"Figured they would." He wiped his eyes on the sleeve of his jacket.

"The DNA testing?"

A quick nod. His face contorted.

"You're the father of Tabitha's baby?"

Another nod.

"Did you kill her?" *Did I just say that?*

"Of course I didn't kill her." I heard the anguish in his voice. His shoulders slumped. "I loved her. We were going to be married."

"Then why are you hiding?"

He hung his head. "Because I'm a coward, that's why. If her father finds out I got his daughter pregnant, he'll come after me. That's why Tabs broke up with me. Her father threatened to find out who I was and make sure I'd never work as an architect anywhere in the UK."

"He told the police he didn't know your name."

"Tabs refused to tell him. She knew what he would do—what he *will* do." He ran a hand through his hair, causing it to stand on end. "Not that I care, now that Tabs is gone, but my parents sacrificed to send me to uni. First one in the family. Dad worked day and night, extra shifts, a second job. Mom cleaned houses, offices, anything she could find. They scrimped, saved, denied themselves everything." He choked on the final word.

"Pregnancy takes two people. The Kings will accept that in time."

He shook his head. "You don't know her father, his expectations. Tabitha had to be perfect in every way."

"All right if I sit?" I took a place near him on a fallen log. We were both shivering, and the fire did little to relieve the cold.

In profile, Peter looked so young. I thought of Eric and wanted to comfort him. The fire flared. He scooped up a handful of dry leaves and threw them on top, smothering the flames and sending a plume of smoke upward.

"How did you and Tabitha end up together at Finchley Hall?"

He stretched his legs, warming his feet near the dying embers. "We met at uni, fell in love. Her parents found out about us—not sure how. They demanded she stop seeing me. She was supposed to finish her degree, get a prestigious job somewhere, meet the right sort of lad." He barked a laugh. "I'm not exactly what they were looking for in a son-in-law."

"And she agreed to break it off?"

"She did it for me. I know that now, but at the time I was gutted. When this internship came up, I jumped at it. It was a chance to get away, to get over her, get on with things."

"But that didn't happen."

"Oh, I tried. I met Alex and . . . well, she can be hard to resist. But I couldn't get Tabs out of my mind, so I broke it off. At the end of August

I went back to Norwich. I had to see her, tell her that I was prepared to wait—as long as it might take. She felt the same. That's when she must have gotten pregnant, although neither of us knew at the time. I told her about the internship program at Finchley Hall. Lady Barbara was looking for someone to design the Hoard exhibit. Tabitha told her parents—not about me, of course—and they agreed. I was over the moon. This was our chance to be together without having to sneak about."

"But you would have had to face them eventually."

"At that point the only thing I cared about was being with Tabs, seeing her every day, spending time with her. We'd sort out her parents later, I thought." He huffed.

"When did she tell you about the baby?"

He swallowed hard. "She didn't. Alex got to her first—told Tabs we'd had a relationship. Alex flaunted it, made it sound like I'd pursued her when it was the opposite. I tried talking to Tabitha, explaining, but she was so hurt." He clenched his fists.

"And when she died . . ." I let the words trail off, wanting him to complete the sentence.

"When she died, I thought—" He choked and tried again. "I assumed she'd killed herself, like everyone else. Do you have any clue how I felt?" Tears trickled down his cheeks. "When I found out about the baby, it was worse. Much worse, because it was my fault."

"Tabitha didn't kill herself, Peter. You know that now. She may have been terribly hurt, but she would have told you about the baby. You would have had a chance to make things right again. You're not the one to blame. Her killer is."

Peter swiped at his eyes. "I can't stop thinking how she must have felt." His eyes filled. "She died believing I'd tossed her aside for someone else. I'm . . . I'm not sure I can live with that." His covered his face with his hands.

That's when I saw the gleam of dark metal in his jacket pocket.

Peter had a gun.

I froze.

Was he planning to kill himself? Or Alex?

What should I do? If I tried to grab the gun, there'd be a struggle. The gun might go off.

I took a steadying breath and held out my hands toward the fire where he could see them. "I thought handguns were illegal in the UK."

His hand flew to his pocket. "The gun's legal. We keep it for foxes, predators."

"What were you planning to do with it out here?"

"Nothing. I—" His voice cracked.

"I'd feel a lot better if you gave me the gun, Peter."

"It's dangerous."

"I know that."

Our eyes met for a long moment. "Peter, I'd like it very much if you gave me the gun."

He seemed to collapse. "What does it matter now?" He handed me the gun, handle first.

I know nothing about guns. This one had a long barrel with a curved, rodlike apparatus protruding from the handle. I laid it on the ground, near me but beyond his reach. "Does Gedge know you took it?"

"Shouldn't think so." His voice was barely audible.

The fire popped. I nearly jumped out of my skin.

We sat for a long time without speaking.

Finally I said, "Right now you feel your life is over. I felt the same way when I lost my husband. You *will* survive, even though you can't imagine it. The important thing to remember is that Tabitha's death wasn't your fault. It wasn't. She loved you. You would have worked things out. Don't let her killer take your life as well as hers. What we need to do is find this person and make sure he—or she—is held accountable."

He nodded.

"Do you know Gedge was taken to the police station for questioning?"

Peter's head jerked up. "Why? He didn't kill Tabs. He tried to convince me to tell the police about the baby."

"Then he needs your help." I was tempted to ask Peter about the spade and the can of paraquat, but even if I'd had the right to ask him—which I didn't—it would be best for Peter if he knew nothing about the murder weapons. "You need to talk with the police. The sooner, the better."

"What a mess."

"Yes, it's a mess. That why you have to go back." I held up my cell phone. "I'm going to call Inspector Mallory right now. Then we'll walk back to the Hall together. Okay?"

He said nothing, which I took as a yes.

"Was there anyone from the village Tabitha spent time with?"

He shook his head. "Just the vicar. I think he was counseling her."

I thought of the vicar's boyish good looks and toned physique. He was probably thirty-five, but he looked younger. "One more thing, Peter. The day of Tabitha's death I saw you and Gedge near the garden shed. He handed you something, a piece of paper. You ripped it up and threw it in the fire."

"Oh, that. It was a note from Alex. She said she was sorry. She wanted us to talk."

"And you wouldn't do that."

"Too right, I wouldn't. Alex might as well have stabbed Tabitha in the back." His fingers clenched and unclenched. "Tabs died believing I'd betrayed her, and that's something I will never forgive. Never. Alex will pay for what she did. I'll make sure of it."

Oh man. This really was a mess, and no soothing words from me were going to solve it.

I pulled out my phone and punched in the numbers.

"Tom, it's me. I'm with Peter Ingham. He has something to tell you."

Chapter
Twenty-Four

⁓

Tom must have flown along the narrow Suffolk roads, because he arrived at Finchley Hall less than a half hour after I called him.

Peter and I watched him, walking alone, toward the Folly, where I'd told him to meet us.

"Hello, Peter. I'm glad you've decided to talk. Much better this way."

Peter hung his head.

"You had us worried," Tom said.

"Sorry."

I gave him Peter's gun, which turned out to be a long-barreled revolver with a wrist brace. Tom gave me a look that said *Did he threaten you?* I shook my head.

"Let's go," Tom said. "My car's in the courtyard."

"Are you arresting me?" Peter asked.

"Not if you haven't committed a crime. As long as you answer our questions, you should be back here later tonight."

DS Cliffe was waiting for us at the car. They drove off and I walked back to the Stables, questions swirling in my brain. Was Peter really the father of Tabitha's baby? She hadn't told him he was. She'd arrived at Finchley Hall around the time she got pregnant. Peter's affair with Alex Devereux might have driven her to the vicar. Getting a vulnerable young woman pregnant would end his career—or should. Did Peter assume he was the father of Tabitha's baby because he couldn't imagine her with anyone else?

The DNA testing would tell.

At just past ten at night, the Stables were quiet and dark. In my room, I undressed and got ready for bed, but I couldn't shut my mind off. I was about to get up and make myself a cup of tea when my phone rang. Pushing up on one elbow, I flipped on the swing-arm lamp.

"It's me. I just wanted to make sure you were okay." Tom's voice.

"I'm fine. Can't sleep."

"Figured that. I knew you'd be wondering."

"What happened?"

"We let them both go—Gedge and Peter. They should be back at Finchley Hall within the hour. No charges."

"Are they related?"

"Distantly. Gedge's grandfather and Peter's great-grandmother were siblings. Something like that, anyway."

"So I was right."

"As always." I could hear the smile in his voice.

"What did they say about the spade and the can of paraquat?"

"They knew the spade was missing; they'd talked about it, assumed one of them had left it in the garden somewhere. We interviewed them separately. Peter was stunned when we told him about the paraquat. Speechless."

"And you believed him."

"No choice. Peter and Gedge say they were together in the garden when Tabitha was killed. Peter was with the rest of the interns when the male stranger was killed. Gedge was in the Finchley Arms. The barkeeper confirmed it. Pays to have a local."

"Did you get a sample of Peter's DNA?"

"No problem."

"When will you get the results?"

"In a few days. Why? Do you doubt he's the father?"

"No, but it will be nice to have one question answered. Have you learned more about the theft at Tettinger Court?"

"Same MO as the others. Guided tour of the house. Lots of questions. The only thing taken was that miniature painting."

"Tom, I think these houses are targeted because they're open to the public and because they can't afford sophisticated antitheft equipment. The objects taken are old, rare, and easy to conceal—not likely to be noticed immediately. The thieves take what they've come for and nothing else."

"You mean a theft-for-hire ring."

"Exactly. Collectors identify objects they want and commit to a purchase price in advance. The odds of the police catching the thieves is low because they never hold on to the stolen goods long enough to be traced. And the collectors are rarely caught because the objects never see the light of day. For an obsessive collector, it's about possession, not publicity. Collecting famous art and antiquities can literally become an addiction."

"Lady Barbara may want to ramp up security."

"If you mean adding electronic surveillance, it's too late, even if Lady Barbara could afford it. The Hoard exhibit is one day away."

"There are measures you can take. Requiring visitors to check their jackets, handbags, backpacks—the obvious places of concealment."

"And we will, but couldn't the police spare a few more constables? Additional pairs of eyes is what we need. The last thing these thieves want is attention. What they do is subtle, sleight of hand. They're good at it, and they rely on the fact that everyone else is looking at the objects. We need more people watching them."

"I'll see what I can do." I heard him yawn. "Try and get some sleep."

We'd hardly said good-bye when the phone lit up again with a number I didn't recognize.

"Hello. Kate Hamilton here."

"Oh, Kate." Ivor Tweedy sounded startled. "I expected to leave a message at this time of night. I should have waited until morning, but I wanted you to know right away, right away."

"Know what?"

"I was searching through my book collection one more time, in case the book on the Hoard had been misshelved."

"You found it?"

"No. Wish I had. But what I did find may be almost as good. A partial manuscript."

"Of the Swiggett book?"

"No, listen. A few years ago I bought several lots of books from an estate sale—the estate of a man who'd been writing a book about the history of Suffolk. He'd planned to include the Peasants' Revolt, the deaths associated with the Hoard, and the rediscovery of it all those years later. He never completed the manuscript, but he used the Swiggett book as a source. I'd forgotten all about it until today."

"Are you saying he made notes about the inventory?" I held my breath.

"No. But the point is, he owned a copy of Swiggett's book. Someone purchased it. Not me. I remember asking at the time. What I'm saying is we might be able to track down the buyer."

"How, if the original owner is dead? He can hardly tell us from the grave who bought it."

"No, but his son might. It was the son selling off the father's things. Nice chap. A barrister, I believe. He might remember the Swiggett book and the person who bought it."

"What's the son's name? Where does he live?"

"That's what I've been trying to recall all evening."

I held my tongue. As much as I appreciated Ivor's kindness, how was a vague memory going to help?

"*Until*," he said, stopping me in my tracks, "I started thumbing through a few of the books." He chuckled. "There it was, big as life on the bookplates. 'The Honorable Ridley Pye, Q.C. The Willows, Lavenham.'"

"Ridley Pye is the son?"

"No, the father. But the son, as it happens, lives in the same house. I spoke with him not twenty minutes ago. Reginald Pye." I pictured Ivor grimacing in pain as he bounced on the balls of his small feet. "I told him what we were after. He promised to dig out the documents from the sale. We could go tomorrow if you have time."

"I'll make time. How far is Lavenham from Long Barston?"

"Forty minutes unless there's traffic. I have an appointment in the shop at nine—a buyer from Edinburgh. How about eleven?"

"As long as we're back by three. I promised to have tea with Lady Barbara at four thirty, and there are a few things I want to do before then."

"I don't see why not. The only thing is . . . ah . . ." He sounded embarrassed. "Well, the thing is, I don't have a car. I don't drive."

"Well, I do. Pick you up at eleven."

I switched off the light, lay back against the soft pillow, and stared up through the rain-dotted skylight. Was the answer to the mystery of Tabitha's handwritten list waiting for me in a banker's box in Lavenham?

Chapter Twenty-Five

Thursday, December 17th

The Willows was a lovely Queen Anne house on the edge of the medieval village of Lavenham. The Honorable Reginald Pye met us at the door, along with four exuberant dogs—two lean springer spaniels, a huge chocolate Lab, and an adorable black-and-white Cavalier King Charles. Dried leaves swirled in, littering the already crowded entrance hall. A mirrored wood–and–cast iron coatrack groaned under the weight of jackets, umbrellas, walking sticks, and leashes.

"Down, girls. That's enough now. Good girlies—*ha-ha*. No, I mean it. No jumping." Reginald Pye was clearly not the leader of the pack. The dogs sniffed and snorted to their hearts' content, bounding and leaping over one another in their delight and ignoring their master's attempts to curb their enthusiasm.

"Sorry," Pye said as one of the springers shoved his nose into my thigh.

"It's all right," I said. "I love dogs."

That's when I noticed Ivor, his face horror-struck as the Lab stood on her hind legs and licked his nose. I grabbed her by her collar and pulled her down, petting her sleek, square head. "Good girl. What's her name?"

"That one's Lucy. The springers are Eve and Betty. And this little girl is Oreo."

Except for his height—he was well over six feet—Reginald Pye bore an uncanny resemblance to Albert Einstein. Or maybe it was just the wild hair, for he had a ruddy face and a wide, gap-toothed smile. His strawberry-colored corduroy pants were covered with dog hair.

"They're friendly," I said, laughing as the King Charles rolled over, exposing a grubby pink belly.

Reginald rubbed the ears of the springers and gave the Lab a playful pat on the rump. "Kitchen. Go." Scooping up the Cavalier King Charles, he strode ahead of us into a room littered with sofas and chairs covered in plush mulberry. And more dog hair.

"My father's library is quite remarkable." He plopped the Cavalier on one of the sofas. Bookshelves lined the walls. Light from three sash windows picked out the gold lettering on the spines. "Long before public libraries existed in Suffolk, libraries like this were open to everyone in the surrounding area—country ministers, doctors, teachers, lawyers, even a schoolchild or two in search of information."

"I believe you sold some of your father's books after his death," I said, attempting to move the conversation forward.

"My father was a brilliant man. Sadly stricken with a form of dementia in his later years. He became disorganized, eccentric, obsessive. That's what prevented him from finishing his book on the Hoard. Books were his particular obsession. He bought them by the yard, without any thought as to where he would shelve them. I sold only the most recent purchases."

"Like the Swiggett book?" I asked hopefully.

"Yes." He tapped the end of his nose. "I do regret selling that one. Quite valuable these days, I understand."

"Have you found the receipts you mentioned?" Ivor chimed in. *Bless him.*

"Ah, the receipts." Reginald Pye raised his right index finger as if dazzled by an epiphany. He dashed out of the room and returned carrying a box, not the banker's box I'd pictured but an ordinary cardboard box, sagging under the weight of its contents. "The receipt, if I have it, will be here somewhere."

"Are the papers in date order?"

"Ha!" He crowed as if I'd meant it as a joke.

I was beginning to wonder if dementia ran in the family.

"Feel free to tiptoe through," he said. "I'll take the lovely girls for a walk while you get stuck in. Tea?"

Two hours later, after drinking three cups of smoky lapsang souchong and consuming several of the fruited cake slices on the tea tray, I stopped and stretched my back. We were nearly through the seemingly endless receipts from the estate sale of the Honorable Ridley Pye, QC. Ivor had previously separated the papers into two great piles on the round table in the center of the room, one for himself and one for me, and we'd begun the tedious process of reviewing each slip of paper, some as small as a Post-it.

"A hopeless cause." I finger-combed my hair off my forehead. "If the current Mr. Pye is a successful barrister, he must have an amazingly organized clerk to keep him on track."

Ivor wiggled his eyebrows. "Let's stick with it. We're nearly at the end."

"As long as we're on the road in a half hour." I flipped over another receipt. FOUR CROQUET SETS, MOSTLY COMPLETE, 10£ EACH TO MRS. CHATHAM, STOKE-BY-NAYLAND.

We worked in silence for another ten minutes. I was about to pack it in when Ivor straightened up.

"Eureka!" He handed me a piece of lined notebook paper.

I read Lost Treasure: The Miracle of The Finchley Hoard, 1822, by Walter A. Swiggett. £20. 07778802451. I flipped the paper over. "Where's the buyer's name? And what's that number?"

"No name. Looks like a mobile number. Mine has the same prefix—077."

"Call it."

Ivor had a flip phone. He punched in the numbers, listened, clicked off. "No answer. No voice mail."

Raucous barking in the entryway alerted us to the return of Reginald Pye. "There you go now, girls. Treats all round, eh?"

A minute later he bounded through the library door. "Success?"

"In a way," I said. "We found a receipt for the book, but there's no name or address." I handed him the paper.

"Ah, yes. Remember the chappie now. Refused to give his name. Said the only way to contact him was by text." He tapped the paper. "Mobile number. Right there."

"Only by text? Do you remember anything else about him?"

Reginald narrowed his eyes. "Very pale, what I could see of him. Wore a scarf over the lower part of his face. A brimmed hat. Tinted glasses. He was interested in another book, now that I think of it. When I told him it wasn't for sale, he said if I changed my mind I should text him."

I copied the mobile number in my notebook. We thanked Reginald Pye for the tea. The dogs chased us all the way to the car and halfway down the drive, barking raucously.

The cell coverage on the way home was spotty to nonexistent.

"I'll text him," Ivor said as we pulled up to his shop. "Ask him to contact me. Then I'll call a few of the pickers I know. See if they can tell us anything about a collector who communicates by text only."

"Thank you for your help, Ivor. I'm grateful."

"No, I should thank you." He leveraged himself out of the car. "The thrill of the hunt. I haven't had this much fun since the monkeys got loose in Ulaanbaatar."

Now that was a story I wanted to hear—but not at the moment. I had barely enough time to freshen up before tea with Lady Barbara.

* * *

I found Lady Barbara in a small sunny room overlooking the Elizabethan Garden. She was alone for once, seated in a chair upholstered in tattered mandarin-yellow silk. In her left hand she held a folded newspaper and in her right a large magnifying glass. A pair of reading glasses sat unused on a side table.

"It's no use," she said as I entered and announced myself. "My vision grows worse every day. Will you read this to me?"

She handed me the newspaper. A headline on the first page announced HISTORIC FIND AT FINCHLEY HALL? I read aloud:

A valuable piece of jewelry known as the Blood-Red Ring, belonging to Lady Susannah Finchley, murdered on the 12th of October, 1638, may have been found hiding in plain sight. The ring, thought to have been lost sometime in the late 19th century, was discovered last Tuesday in a large safe at Finchley Hall by visiting antiques expert Mrs. Kate Hamilton of Jackson Falls, Ohio. "The ring is seventeenth century," said Lady Barbara Finchley-fforde, "and appears to be nearly identical to the ring shown in a portrait of Lady Susannah, wife of the Marquess of Suffolk."
This historic find has increased interest in the 200th Anniversary Exhibit of the Hoard to be held at Finchley Hall on Saturday, December 19, from 10 a.m. until 4 p.m. Mrs. Hamilton, whose daughter is part of an internship program at Finchley Hall, agreed to complete the exhibit after the tragic death of the

Hoard's curator, Miss Tabitha King, of Hoxne. "The exhibit will be dedicated to Tabitha's memory," said Lady Barbara.

The newly found ring will be displayed alongside the portrait of Lady Susannah, painted by an unknown artist in the mid-seventeenth century. A BBC documentary about the Hoard will be aired this spring on BBC Four.

Timed entrance tickets for the Hoard exhibit may be purchased in advance at www.finchleyhoard.co.uk or at the ticket office on the day of the exhibit.

I handed the paper back, wondering how long it would take this newsflash to make it to Donald Preston at the *Jackson Falls Gazette*. I could only imagine the article. The word *snooping* was bound to be in there somewhere.

"Without you, we'd never have pulled it off," Lady Barbara said. "And now this marvelous publicity." She struggled to hold back tears. "There's so much to do here, Kate, not only essential things like plumbing and electrics—those will come first, of course—but updating and modernizing. Grants are available, but funds are limited, and we compete with so many others. In the meantime, Finchley Hall declines."

As if to prove her point, the Louis XVI mantel clock struck a nonsensical thirteen bells.

"England has a rich history and heritage," I said. "I've always been amazed at how much is preserved for future generations—and at such great cost. Please tell me if I'm out of bounds here, but have you ever considered the National Trust or British Heritage?"

"You're not out of bounds, dear, but I was born in this house. I hope to die here one day." Her face softened. "Oh, you should have seen the place in its heyday. Picnics in the park, riding the horses for miles without ever leaving the estate. And the view. Do you know my favorite thing to do as a child, Kate?"

I laughed. "Tell me."

"Climbing up to the roof and just sitting there, listening to the church bells, watching the sheep in the meadow and the wind and sun on the wheat fields. The view is magnificent. You should go up there one day, Kate. There's a staircase leading from the kitchen. Four flights up, round and round, the stairs narrower with each turn. You duck your head, open the hatch, and there you are."

One pleasure I'd gladly forgo. "An idyllic childhood."

"That's why Finchley Hall must be preserved for future generations. When my son returns to England one day, he shall have a home to come to, a home to pass on to his children and grandchildren."

From what I'd heard of Lucien Finchley-fforde, this sounded like fantasy, but it wasn't my place to destroy Lady Barbara's dreams. Nor Mugg's, apparently.

As if on cue, Mugg entered the room with a tea tray, which he placed on a rosewood writing table. "Shall I pour, madam?"

"Lovely. Two sugars, please."

This time, instead of finger sandwiches and petit fours, the tiered glass tray held proper sandwiches, sliced beef on whole-grain bread, and shaved ham on soft egg buns. I was starving. My only lunch had been the fruited cake provided by Reginald Pye.

I bit into a beef sandwich and experienced a nose-clearing explosion of horseradish.

Mugg laid a napkin in Lady Barbara's lap and handed her a plate with half a ham bun.

He cleared his throat. "May I speak my mind, madam?"

"You always do," Lady Barbara answered.

"With this latest theft at Tettinger Court, I must entreat you again to postpone the exhibit. The danger is simply too great."

"That's as may be," Lady Barbara said, "but it's far too late to cancel now. We've taken precautions. I refuse to act out of fear."

"Very good, madam." Mugg retreated into a corner, his sphinxlike imperturbability replaced for once by a palpable anxiety. Everyone,

I've learned, has a redeeming grace. Mugg's seemed to be an unshakable loyalty to Lady Barbara.

"This is the Morning Room," Lady Barbara said, switching gears. "I remember my mother and grandmother retiring here after breakfast to drink tea and write letters. Strange, because I've always liked this room best in the afternoons. Can you see how the sun gilds the brick walls?" We gazed out toward the Elizabethan Garden and the park beyond. "In spring and autumn, sunbeams pick out the ferns on the forest floor." She took a deep, shuddering breath. "It's times like this when I feel my loss of vision most keenly, but then I remind myself that others have suffered more and feel quite ashamed."

"No need." The lump in my throat prevented me from saying more.

"Your friend, Inspector Mallory, phoned this morning to tell me Peter has confessed to being the father of poor Tabitha's child."

I thought of Vicar Foxe and hoped the DNA test would confirm that.

Lady Barbara turned her pale-blue eyes in my direction. "I'm not shocked, you know. I understand Peter and Tabitha were in love. They planned to marry."

"What will happen to Peter now?"

"I hope he will stay. I'm grown quite fond of him. If you see him, Kate, will you ask him to come to me?"

"Of course."

"Inspector Mallory also told me Tabitha's death appears to be unrelated to her pregnancy. Can we be glad about that, do you think?"

"We can be glad she didn't take her own life. Suicide is hardest on the survivors. I don't know about her parents, but as brutal as her loss is for Peter, he won't have to carry the burden of guilt."

"The question now is who killed her and why," Lady Barbara said. "Inspector Mallory didn't mention the poor man in the Folly. Is there news of him?"

"I believe the police are still trying to find out who he was."

"I've never liked the fact that Finchley Hall is famous for murder, you know. It brings the tourists, but that was all so long ago. Now, with two more deaths, people will say the Hall is cursed. And the horrid part is, instead of putting people off the exhibit, I'm afraid it will attract them. I want the exhibit to be a success, of course I do. But the whole thing feels ghoulish."

"Let's hope the police solve the crimes quickly."

"Yes, of course." A slight movement of her eyes told me she was troubled.

"I'd like to talk to you about the exhibit," I said. "And specifically about the publicity surrounding Lady Susannah's ring."

"The one bright spot in all this."

"Not all bright, I'm afraid." Beads of sweat broke out on my forehead. Why was it so hard to tell Lady Barbara the truth? Perhaps it was her aristocratic beauty, still visible in her fine bone structure and erect carriage. Or perhaps it was an air of vulnerability that made others want to protect her. I steeled myself. She had a right to know.

"The publicity surrounding the ring will bring more visitors—that's true—but it might also tempt thieves. Mugg may be right."

A small cough from the corner of the room reminded me that he was still there.

"You mentioned theft the other day." Her brows drew together, creating a deep furrow between her eyes.

"Thieves are operating in Suffolk right now. They're targeting stately homes. The objects taken are valuable and small. The police think it may be a theft-for-hire ring."

Lady Barbara touched her throat.

"I haven't brought this up to frighten you or to persuade you to postpone the exhibit, but to make you aware. We've taken additional measures to protect the exhibit. Tom—Inspector Mallory—has agreed to send two more constables on Saturday. The security camera in the archives building will be positioned to capture every visitor coming through the door. The staff and interns will be on full alert. That's where we have the advantage. We've been forewarned."

"And forewarned, as they say, is forearmed."

I wondered if this was true.

A great loss.

On the way back to the Stables, my cell phone rang.

"Mom, we're meeting at the Finchley Arms. If you and Tom don't have plans, why don't you come along?"

That was a first.

"Tom's on duty tonight, and I just ate. I'll join you for a drink, though. You go ahead. I'll be there soon."

Chapter Twenty-Six

By the time I arrived at the Finchley Arms, it was apparent the interns, my daughter included, had consumed more than their usual share of alcohol. Unfortunate on many levels, not the least of which was the fact that tomorrow was the final day of preparation for the expected crowds that would attend the two-hundredth-anniversary exhibit of the Finchley Hoard. All hands on deck.

I pictured the interns, all five of them—maybe even Alex—showing up for duty with pasty faces and queasy stomachs.

Beer is something I don't normally drink, but a half-pint of Southwold Bitter sounded a lot safer than the wine I remembered from my first visit. I sat back in my chair, took a sip of the deep-amber liquid, and tried to ignore the din of conversation.

The exhibit itself was complete, but now that I'd found Lady Susannah's ring (or its twin), some adjustment was necessary. The portrait of Lady Susannah wearing the ring would be moved to a prime spot at the far end of the room, where an overhead spotlight would focus on the painting and a plinth displaying the ring. Visitors could compare the two and make up their own minds.

Other tasks yet to be completed included setting up ticket booths and establishing roped-off queues in the yard and in the exhibit space for crowd control. Moving visitors along a predetermined path would allow each person a clear view of the objects and, more importantly, give the designated observers a clear view of the visitors.

The catalogs would be delivered in the morning and the gift shop arranged with a sales point and credit card machine. The lighting and outside security cameras still had to be positioned and the interns and volunteer staff trained in their various tasks by Alex Devereux. The tearoom in the library would be furnished with small round tables and chairs borrowed from the Café Bistro in Long Barston. Baked goods were currently browning in ovens all over the village. The exhibit was truly a community effort.

Would Tom be there?

I wished he were with me now. The Finchley Arms was even more packed, if possible, than it had been on my first visit with Tom. Music from the jukebox thumped in my chest. People hoisted drinks over their heads to squeeze through the crowd. I was surprised to see Gedge at his usual place at the end of the bar. Next to Peter Ingham.

The interns had co-opted two tables near the miniscule dance floor.

"Hey, *Maman*." Tristan raised his pint. His face was flushed. "Wanna dance? Bet you were a champion dancer in your day."

In my day? "Sorry. My pacemaker might blow a fuse."

Michael Nash and Prue Goody laughed so hard they spit beer.

"Come on, luv." Tristan grabbed for my arm but missed and staggered backward.

Prue clapped. "Well done." She'd traded her shapeless linen tunic for a pair of jeans and a T-shirt with a map of the London Tube. Her coiled hair was pulled into a topknot. She even wore a flattering coral-red shade of lipstick.

Tristan, looking embarrassed, stumbled off toward the bar.

"Where's Christine?" I asked Prue.

"Loo," she answered. "Oh, there she is."

Christine swayed a bit as she hiked her tiny handbag over her shoulder. "Sorry, Mom. I've had enough. I'm going home."

"I'll drive you."

"No. You just got here. Tris'll walk me home."

You're the only reason I'm here. "Fine. See you in the morning."

I watched as Christine found Tristan at the bar. She whispered something in his ear. He shook his head, holding up the pint of beer he'd just purchased.

That's when I saw Alex. She was talking to one of the local lads, but her eyes, as usual, were on Peter.

"Tomorrow's a big day," Prue said.

"I was beginning to think everyone forgot."

"Just blowing off steam. These past two weeks have been the worst. First Tabitha, then that man. My parents called yesterday. They want me to come home."

"I can understand that."

"Michael says whatever happened won't happen again." She beamed at him, making him flush. "My work at the Living History Museum is important to my future. Why should I give it up?"

"Loo," Michael said, and headed for the toilets.

"Christine feels the same," I said. "And Tristan is here."

Prue scooted her chair closer. "You know about Tristan, right?"

"Know what?"

"He's playing her." She ran her finger around the side of her glass, blurring the rivulets of condensation.

"What do you mean?"

"He's playing both sides. Christine and Alex."

"You mean he and Alex—" I couldn't finish the sentence.

"Obvious. I said we should tell Christine, but Michael said it's not our business. I thought you should know."

No words came. Which was a good thing, because Christine appeared.

"Tristan's staying." Her mouth was tight. "Let's go now."

The ride back to Finchley Hall was painful. Every time I tried to say something, Christine shut me down. "I don't want to talk about it."

"Fine," I finally said, "but the steam coming from your ears is fogging up the windows."

That brought a laugh. Followed by a sob.

As soon as I pulled into a parking spot outside the Stables, she pushed the car door open and ran inside.

* * *

I don't usually go to bed before nine. That night was an exception. After knocking at Christine's door with no response, I felt too drained even to call my mother at the shop, which is what I'd planned to do earlier.

I was settling into the duvet when my cell phone rang.

"Sorry I couldn't phone earlier. How are you?" Tom's voice.

"Knackered, as you English say. Christine just had another blowup with Tristan. I didn't handle it well. She's hurt and embarrassed, and I made it worse."

"How did you do that?"

"By showing concern. She hates that."

"Give her time. She'll come round."

"I'm not so sure. She sees me as her adversary. Or at least her critic."

"You can't help noticing when she's headed for disaster. You can't help caring."

"But do I make it worse? Do I communicate my fears for her, and does she interpret that as not trusting her?" The thought came like a punch in the gut. "She's right, Tom. I don't trust her when it comes to men. Why does she always choose the ones who will let her down?"

"She lost her father, Kate. Like you did—and at almost exactly the same age. You know what it feels like."

"It feels like abandonment. Not logical, I know. When I met Bill, and he was so much older, my mother was afraid I was looking for a father figure."

"Were you?"

"I didn't think so at the time. Now I wonder if Bill felt like the safe harbor I'd lost. Fathers are important to boys, I know, but they're even more important to girls—in a different way. Bill was solid, reliable, predictable, *there*."

"And then he wasn't."

I sighed. "And then he wasn't."

"So Christine is looking for safe harbor, someone who's there for her. Losing someone unexpectedly is like PTSD and can be just as devastating. I wonder about Olivia—if the loss of her mother is what's motivating her to give up her place at King's College and remain at the orphanage in East Africa."

"At least it's a worthy motivation. What Christine is doing is akin to self-harm, replaying the loss of her father over and over again by subconsciously choosing unreliable men."

"But she has you. You're the fixed point in her world."

Was that why Christine had reacted so badly to my relationship with Tom? Did she see it as abandonment? I was too tired to think about that. "Tell me about your day."

"We interviewed witnesses in Mildenhall and Haverhill."

"Anything to go on?"

"Most of them remember a woman—polished, well educated. At Glepping Park she was alone. At Tettinger Court she was with a group of women. In both places, she engaged the docent in conversation, asking questions about certain objects. It might have been completely innocent, or it might have been a tactic used by street thieves all over Europe. One person distracts the target while the other calmly picks his pocket."

"Good to know. Tomorrow I'll alert everyone to be on the look-out for a talker. I feel better knowing that additional uniformed police will be present. Will you come?"

"Can't promise. I'll try." His voice sounded funny.

"What's wrong?"

"You're leaving in a matter of days, Kate. I feel cheated. We've had so little time together."

"Can't be helped."

"No, but we do have a little time left. How about taking a day off? We could drive to the coat or just spend the day roaming around Cambridge."

"That sounds lovely. But how can you do it with all that's going on?"

"I'll fix it. How about Sunday? The exhibit will be over."

"Not Sunday. I may still be moving the Hoard objects back into the safe. What about Monday? Christine will be back at work. I'll be free as a bird."

Would I? Saying it felt like tempting fate.

Chapter
Twenty-Seven

❧

I sat up in bed.

Loud voices and the sound of breaking glass told me there was a fight going on. *Oh, not again.* Throwing a sweatshirt over my Disney flannels, I slipped on a pair of flats and ran toward the commotion.

In the Commons, Michael and Prue stood behind Christine. She had on the leggings and T-shirt she wears to bed. Her eyes were puffy. Her hair was a mess. She'd obviously been crying.

"You steal my boyfriend and then tell me to chill?" Christine screamed.

Alex stood in the doorway, looking thoroughly bored. "I didn't steal him, darling. You lost him."

"Witch." Christine picked up a ceramic mug and threw it at Alex, who ducked. The shattered remains of a glass soup bowl lay scattered on the floor. Alex was lucky. Christine was no athlete, but she used to have a crack pitching arm.

Tristan leaned against the doorjamb, watching the battle for his affections with an amused smile on his face. I felt like throwing something at him. Instead, I said, "Stop this," in my *mother's in charge* voice. "Fighting isn't going to get you anywhere."

"Poor Christine," Alex said, turning the corners of her mouth down in fake sympathy. "She can't face the truth. Tristan fancies me—what of it? They're not engaged or anything."

Christine yanked her arm out of Prue's grasp and lunged toward Alex, who raised the umbrella she was holding and brought it down hard on Christine's shoulder.

Christine grabbed her shoulder and started to cry.

"That's enough, do you hear me?" I snatched the umbrella. "You're acting like children."

"Self-defense," Alex said. "She started it."

Pushing me out of the way, Christine took hold of Alex's ponytail and threw her to the floor. Alex kicked out, landing a blow on Christine's knee.

"Tristan, Michael," I yelled. "Get those two away from each other before someone gets seriously hurt."

Michael grabbed Christine by the arms.

Tristan picked Alex up off the floor.

"Thank you, darling." She threw her arms around him and gave him a long kiss.

"Let's go, Christine," Prue said. "They're not worth it."

Alex took Tristan's hand and led him toward the opposite corridor. "Come on, Tris." She laughed. "Let's have another drink."

Christine spun around. "You'll regret this, Alex. I swear it." She stomped out, trailing a comet's tail of fury.

After cleaning up the broken dishes, I knocked on Christine and Prue's door.

Prue opened it and stood aside. "Be my guest. Maybe she'll listen to you."

I doubted that. Christine lay facedown on her bed, and somehow her silence was more unnerving than her tears.

"Tell me how all this started."

Christine ignored me.

Prue said, "We left the Arms—the four of us. Me and Michael, Tristan and Alex. Alex had been trying to attract Peter's attention all night, but he wasn't having it. So she tried it on with Tristan."

"And he lapped it up." Christine propped her head on one hand. Her face was blotchy.

"Of course he did. We'd all had way too much to drink." Prue moaned and held her head. "Oh, I'm getting the whirly-bats."

"What happened when you got here?"

"Alex was giggling and hanging on to Tristan," Prue said. "Kind of stumbling, you know, and he was holding her up. Then Christine came out and saw them and—"

"And went berserk, right?" Christine's voice was preternaturally calm. "Well, I'm over it now."

I knew this Christine, and it frightened me. Christine in full meltdown mode is alarming. Christine in a cold fury is enough to curdle the blood.

"Let's try to get a good night's rest," I said. Lamely. Sleep rarely solves anything. "We can deal with this in the morning."

"What a good idea." Christine pulled up the duvet and turned over, her face to the wall.

I said good night to Prue and left with a sense of impending doom.

No way I'd get a night's sleep now—good or otherwise.

When Christine promised retribution, she meant it. I thought of the time Eric and Christine argued about who was going to use the family car for the homecoming dance. Eric won the coin toss, and Christine retired meekly to her room. The next morning, I heard Eric pounding on her bedroom door.

"Look what she did, Mom." He held out his favorite jeans. Christine had cut them off at the knees. She was repentant, of course, and used money she'd been saving for months to buy him a new pair.

I checked the clock. A little after midnight. Seven PM in Ohio. The only person I could talk to about this was my mother. As I went to dial my home number, I noticed a text from Ivor: NO RESPONSE YET FROM OUR MYSTERY MAN.

Kind of Ivor to let me know, although Christine's trouble had erased thoughts of the missing Hoard book. Only three days remained until I returned to the States. I might never find out why Tabitha had written out that list of objects. Everywhere I turned was a dead end.

I punched in my home phone number. After five rings the answering machine kicked in.

You've reached the Hamilton residence. Leave your number and—

The message was interrupted by a sleepy voice. "This is Linnea Larson."

"I'm sorry. Were you sleeping?"

"Dozing. It must be late in England. What's happened?"

I gave her the blow-by-blow. And the arctic aftermath.

"Give her time. Her anger will burn itself out. The main thing is to keep Christine and Alex apart until it does."

"That'll be hard. Tomorrow we're all working together on the Hoard exhibit."

"Send them in opposite directions. Give them tasks that don't overlap."

"I'll try."

"Christine will see what she's doing in time and make a change."

"Hope I live to see it."

"You will. Just keep loving and supporting her. Don't let her manipulate you into saying too much. You can't solve this one for her. She's got to figure it out on her own."

"There's something I want to run past you—about the list Tabitha made. The local antiques dealer I told you about has been helping me locate a book on—"

"Kate, darling. Do you mind if we talk in the morning? I've had a headache all day."

"You had a headache the last time we talked."

"Well, it's back. I called Charlotte this afternoon to fill in for me."

"Call my doctor. His number's in the phone book on my desk."

"No need. It's just a headache. I'll be fine."

"We'll talk tomorrow. I love you."

After we disconnected, I reached for my notebook and scanned the list of questions.

1. *Who murdered her?* No answer.
2. *Who was the father of her baby?* Probably Peter. DNA results would tell.
3. *Who was the dark stranger?* No clear answers yet.
4. *Position of Tabitha's body in the water.* Thrown in, but by whom?
5. *Connection between Catherine Kerr and Tabitha King.* Probably the Hoard, but how?
6. *Who'd benefit if the Hoard exhibit was canceled?* Mugg argued against it, but not for his own benefit, and he certainly wouldn't benefit if Lady Barbara lost the Hall.
7. *Why did Tabitha make that list?* Good question—no answer.
8. *What is bothering me about the crime scene?* Good question—no answer.

Good question—no answer. My new motto.

Chapter Twenty-Eight

Friday, December 18th

The day of the setup dawned clear and crisp. Better yet, the weather forecast for the following day was the same. Clear skies, temps around ten degrees Celsius—a nice, crisp fifty degrees Fahrenheit. A perfect English winter's day.

On Saturday, hundreds of visitors would descend on Finchley Hall. No muddy shoes or dripping umbrellas. Nice dry coats, handbags, and backpacks to be checked at a table near the entrance and whisked away to a repository on the upper floor.

I joined a group of villagers waiting near the dovecote for instructions. Miraculously, all the interns had shown up on time. Youth is wasted on the young.

Peter and Arthur Gedge hovered on the edge of the group. The sun glinted off Peter's blond hair. Gedge tossed a cigarette butt into the gravel and ground it in with his boot. The rough old beer-soaked bachelor with permanently dirty fingernails seemed to have a soft spot for his young relative. Good thing. At the moment, Peter needed all the friends he could get.

So did I, come to think of it. Not only was another blow-up between Christine and Alex looming, but I'd felt unsettled since the previous night's phone call with my mother. Linnea Larson was the *fixed point*, as Tom had called it, in my life. I knew she was getting older. I'd watched the lines deepen on her face, the silver take over her hair, but she was healthy and strong, always there for me with common sense and words of wisdom. I checked the time. Nine AM—four AM at home in Jackson Falls. I'd call her later.

Alex came out of the dovecote with her purple clipboard in hand. "Lady Barbara has asked me to express her personal thanks to all who have pulled together to make the two-hundredth-anniversary exhibit of the Hoard a success. Let me begin by giving you an overview of what to expect tomorrow. We've presold more than three hundred tickets now, which means the total number of visitors could be five hundred or more. The parking area in the yard will be reserved for disabled visitors with a Blue Badge permit. Others will park in the churchyard or in the field at the end of the long drive. We open promptly at ten AM. Those with timed tickets will be admitted first in each time slot—others on a first-come, first-served basis, with a maximum number of thirty in each twenty-minute segment."

Alex's beautiful face showed no remnant of the intoxicated shrew of the night before. If I didn't know better, I could almost believe there were two Alex Devereuxs, like Dr. Jekyll and Mr. Hyde.

Christine, standing beside Prue Goody, was avoiding eye contact with me. Tristan slouched near the door to the dovecote, his hoodie pulled up. I hoped he had a doozy of a hangover.

Alex had gotten to the end of her spiel. "Before I divide you into work crews, I've been asked by the local police to say something about security." She flipped a page on her clipboard. "You may have heard about a series of thefts in the area. The criminals will probably not risk another theft so soon, but we can't be too careful. If you see something suspicious, tell the nearest uniformed officer. There will be at least one in every area. We've been told to be on the lookout for a well-dressed woman who may try to distract your attention—asking questions, dropping some personal item, bumping into you or another visitor. Keep your eyes open and say something. You should know your assignments by now, but I'll go over them again just in case."

As Alex began to read names, I experienced a moment of panic. How could I make sure Alex's and Christine's paths never crossed? But I needn't have worried. Christine and Prue were sent to the Hall to help Vivian and the volunteers in the tearoom. Tristan, Peter, and Gedge would set up the ticket booths and the rope barriers between the dovecote and the archives building. Michael and Mugg would help me move the portrait and Lady Susannah's ring into place and make sure the lighting was perfect. After that, Michael would make sure the CCTV camera was focused toward the entrance door. Then he would join the volunteers, marking the footpath from the churchyard.

After my part in the exhibit area, I would join Alex in the gift shop, where I would try very hard to forget she'd attacked my daughter with an umbrella.

That should be fun.

For lunch, the volunteers set up a sandwich buffet and tea urn in the dovecote. The sun was warm enough to eat outside. Groups of volunteers pulled folding chairs into circles and tipped their faces to the sun. The atmosphere was almost festive.

By two o'clock, the exhibit hall was ready. I called my mother at the antiques shop.

"Antiques at the Falls. Linnea Larson speaking."

"Hi, Mom. Can you talk?"

"Of course. No customers at the moment. I'm arranging a display of antique glass Christmas ornaments in the front window."

"Perfect. What's the weather like?"

"Cold. No more snow."

"How are you feeling?"

"Right as rain. Oh—I have to go. Someone's just come through the door."

I felt right as rain, too.

In the gift shop, Alex and Danny's mother, Glenda, were working on the gift displays.

"Hi, Kate." Glenda beamed. "Everything is going so well, isn't it?"

"So far. Can I help with anything?"

Alex was arranging the small round pots of local honey. "Now that you're here, Kate, do you mind if I leave?"

"Not at all." I wouldn't have minded if she hopped a slow boat to the South Pole.

She gathered up her coat. "I should help the volunteers with the timed-ticket schedules. Glenda knows what to do."

Glenda added a tall, slender bottle of mead to the others on the counter and stood back to examine her work.

"Is Danny in school today?" I asked, picturing the little boy knocking over plinths with his sword and claiming their contents as spoils of war.

"Yes, but he's missed a lot lately." She looked worried.

"Still having nightmares?"

"Oh, yes. The therapist has him in art therapy, drawing what he sees in his dreams. They're always the same. He draws the lake and the body—just a blob, really. He draws himself, standing along the shore—another blob. But then there are trees and an enormous dark figure with yellow eyes. A monster." She shuddered.

"That sounds scary. What does Danny say about the monster?"

"He *says* the monster has no face. Just yellow eyes that glow and a voice that sounds like sandpaper. When the therapist asks Danny what the figure represents, he just shrugs."

"What does the therapist think?"

"She says the monster represents Danny's fear, the trauma of finding the dead girl." Glenda hugged herself. "Danny isn't himself. He doesn't want to play with friends. His teacher says he doesn't utter a word at school. That's not like him."

No, it wasn't.

"Would you talk to him, Kate? He's mentioned you. He liked you."

"Of course. Anytime. But do you mind if I tell Inspector Mallory?"

"If you think it's important." She wrote her phone number on one of the sales slips. "But I don't see how it could be. It's not as if monsters are real, is it?"

* * *

Glenda and I spent the next half hour putting the finishing touches on the gift shop displays, getting the receipt book ready, and figuring out the credit card machine. We were finishing up when Tom arrived.

"I've been looking for you." He gave me a hug and kissed my forehead, then my mouth.

"Be still my heart." Glenda patted her chest.

"Good timing," I said. "Tom, this is Glenda . . . um." I realized I'd never known her last name.

"Glenda Croft," she said. "We met briefly the day that young woman was murdered. You probably don't remember."

"I do, as a matter of fact. You're Danny's mother."

"She has something to tell you," I said. "About a monster."

Tom listened intently as Glenda described Danny's nightmares and the art therapy. He wrote a few words in his notebook, thanked her, and gave her his card. "If Danny says something else about the monster or remembers anything about that day, contact me at once."

"Of course." Glenda gathered up her things. "See you tomorrow, Kate."

After Glenda left, I showed Tom the portrait and the ring. "So, is it the same ring?"

"They look the same to me."

"Except for the details. Look at the ring in the painting. If you examine it closely, you can just make out the image carved into the central stone. See?" I pointed out a tiny squiggle of paint. "That's the intaglio. The artist shows us the light hitting the design. I think that bit right there is the wing. And the griffin's raised paw—right there. The design on the ring is similar but not exact."

Tom studied the painting, then the ring. "It might depend on which way the lady wore the ring—with the feet toward her or away from her."

He made a good point. Still, the designs carved into the central stones didn't completely match. I tried again.

"Look at the artist's use of light, shadow, and color," I said. "He communicates both realism and emotion. And that little brush stroke in the intaglio gives the impression of fine detail. Do you see it? Now look at the ring. The image is there but much cruder."

"Maybe the painter took artistic license."

"Maybe."

"You think they're not the same ring?"

"I don't know. The settings are nearly identical. The construction of the band is consistent with the time period. The seed pearls are set in a double row. I counted them. Exactly the number in the painting. But the central stone isn't right. First of all, it's a garnet, not a ruby. Then there's the carving. And then the size and shape."

"Kate Hamilton, solving history's mysteries." He gave me that half smile of his.

I gave him a playful shove. "So why are you here? Not just to tease me, I assume."

"I brought a few of our community support officers to see the place and meet Lady Barbara. They're with Alex now."

He must have read the expression on my face. "What's wrong?"

"Christine and Alex had another fight over Tristan last night. This one got pretty nasty, and it might have gotten even nastier if I hadn't been there." I didn't mention the hurled dishes and the swinging umbrella. Tom was a policeman, after all.

"Fault on both sides?"

"With Tristan in the middle and relishing every minute. I felt like wiping the smirk off his face, but I'm known to the police."

He laughed. "Here's one policeman who'd like to know you better still."

"That sounds like a challenge." I smiled at him. "Are you free tonight?"

"I wish I were." He slipped an arm into his waxed jacket. "Skype conference with the authorities in Venezuela. This is our first opportunity to get information on the murdered man—and Lucien Finchley-fforde, with any luck. But I will be here tomorrow for the exhibit. Let's have dinner afterward."

"Lady Barbara is holding a thank-you reception for the volunteers at seven. I need to be there."

"A late dinner, then."

"It's a date."

Telling myself that things do work out sometimes, I slipped on my jacket and hiked my handbag over my shoulder. As we left, I set the alarm and locked the door.

He wrapped a scarf around his neck. "The best news is we're set for Monday. We'll have the whole day, Kate. Nothing on God's green earth will keep me away. I promise."

Outside in the yard, a team from St. Æthelric's was trimming a fir tree with tinsel and giant red balls. Vicar Foxe stood near the top of a tall ladder, a foot-high angel in his hand.

"Hullo, Kate." He lifted his mirrored sunglasses to grin at me. "Could you climb up here and help me for a minute?"

"What?"

"Sorry—poor joke."

"This is Inspector Tom Mallory," I called back. "Tom, this is Edmund Foxe, the very amusing vicar at St. Æthelric's."

As we walked toward the Hall, I considered telling Tom about the vicar's counseling sessions with Tabitha King but thought better of it. First I'd do a little research—find out what kind of a reputation the vicar had in his previous parish in Essex.

"Almost forgot," Tom said. "We got a little more info on that woman. The people at Glepping Park described her as having a northern accent and wearing an expensive-looking suit. At Tettinger Court her accent sounded more like Devon or Cornwall, and she wore conservative country clothing. Probably two different people."

"What made you think it was the same woman?"

"Same MO. Asked lots of questions. And same basic description—middle-aged, respectable."

"Oh, she'll really stand out in the crowd tomorrow." I rolled my eyes. "Be on the lookout for a curious, respectable, middle-aged woman."

"No, Kate. Be on the lookout for sudden or unnecessary distractions. And keep your eyes on the treasure."

* * *

At five o'clock, Christine, Prue, and Michael took themselves off to the Finchley Arms. Alex and Tristan opted for the Café Bistro—a wise move. With so much riding on the Hoard exhibit, the last thing we needed was another fight. Christine seemed to have cut all ties with Tristan, but knowing her history, I wasn't breaking out the champagne and confetti yet.

All I wanted was a quiet night to myself.

Seeing the vicar on that ladder had given me an idea, a theory that might link the possible thefts from the Hoard with the murders of Tabitha King and the dark stranger. What I liked best was the simplicity.

What if someone—a man, obviously—had taken advantage of Tabitha's vulnerability after Peter's betrayal, and what if that man's ultimate goal was to gain access to the Hoard? It made sense. After winkling the codes for the safe out of Tabitha, he killed her and then killed the dark stranger because he'd witnessed the murder.

The only potential clue to this man's identity was a pair of sunglasses, and the person I'd just seen wearing sunglasses was the vicar. Time to do a little research on Edmund Foxe.

With the remains of an egg-and-cress sandwich on the desk beside me, I sat cross-legged on my bed, my computer open on my lap. The first thing I did was plug Edmund Foxe into a couple of people-finder search engines in the UK. Quite a few Edmund Foxe's lived in Essex. None fit the vicar's age. Then it occurred to me I was looking in the wrong place. It wasn't current information about the vicar I was after, but his history. Pulling up Yahoo UK, I typed VICAR EDMUND FOXE ESSEX into the search bar and waited.

Bingo.

The article had been published three years ago in the *Chelmsford Weekly News.*

Edmund Foxe, vicar of St. Botolph's Church in Chelmsford, was questioned today in connection with an incident alleged to have taken place in July. A woman, age 19, claims the vicar acted inappropriately toward her in his office, where she had gone for counseling. A full investigation is under way.

I followed the link, finding similar articles—then a subsequent article published the following October.

The investigation into alleged improprieties at St. Botolph's Church in Chelmsford was closed today when the woman who brought the charge admitted the incident never took place.

My breath quickened. Had the vicar been falsely charged, or had the young woman, finding the process too stressful and embarrassing, simply given up? In either case, the church higher-ups appeared to have reassigned the vicar to another parish.

To commit murder?

This was going to take some thought.

If Edmund Foxe was innocent, he needed to be protected.

If he was guilty, he needed to be stopped.

Chapter Twenty-Nine

༄

Saturday, December 19th

The day of the Hoard exhibit was more glorious, if possible, than the day before. I stood in the courtyard of Finchley Hall, holding a steaming mug of coffee and watching the sun inch above the horizon. It was eight AM. The sky was a deep purple, shading to crimson and lemon. Blades of grass were silvered with frost. The temperature had settled on a crisp thirty-three degrees.

A film crew from the BBC was setting up a mobile crane shot of the Hall.

I'd managed to sleep in spite of my doubts about the vicar. Instead, Tom's warning about con artists and sudden distractions had played out in a series of bizarre dreams. The jeweler's safe, dangling by a hook from a helicopter. A pack of yellow-eyed monsters smashing and grabbing with huge furry paws. Mazes through which I chased burglars brandishing guns shaped like the Finchley Cross.

Sometimes an overactive imagination bites you back.

Steam from my coffee mingled with the icy vapor of my breath. I wrapped my fingers around the warm mug, feeling oddly comforted. Surely no theft ring worth their salt would risk a heist in the middle of a BBC documentary.

Around eight fifteen, with the sun's rays slanting through the trees, cameramen began to capture what one of the crew members, a friendly young woman in a knitted cap and quilted jacket, called *establishing shots*.

"We're filming the long drive and Finchley Hall now," she said. "Morning light's perfect. Later, when the sun's higher, we'll get the lake and the line of visitors outside the archives building."

I watched her making notes and communicating with the film crew in a language comprised mostly of acronyms.

"This lot does the big, outdoor shots," she told me. "After the holidays, a different crew will come to film an interview with Lady Barbara and take close-ups of the most important Hoard objects."

The whole thing, she said, would then be edited into a thirty-minute documentary with the antiques expert doing voice-overs from a studio somewhere in London.

By nine, the queue waiting for the exhibit to open snaked half-way down the long drive. The air had warmed. The sun caught the neon-yellow vests of the community support officers. From somewhere in the trees, I heard the familiar *chuck, chuck, chuck* of a blackbird.

Still carrying my now-empty mug, I walked toward the archives building. After handing the mug and my jacket to one of the volunteers, I did a final walk-through of the exhibit. Everything was perfect. Tabitha would have been proud.

Ivor Tweedy arrived just before ten. He'd agreed to act as a second docent, answering questions and providing background information as needed. I worried that the hours on his feet would exacerbate his hip pain, but he seemed inordinately cheerful. Even two bad hips couldn't dampen his enthusiasm.

"To think we might catch a gang of thieves," he whispered. "Thrilling, isn't it?"

"I'd be more thrilled if they gave us a miss."

At ten, I peered out the window as the first group, red stickers clearly visible, made their way along the roped lines to the archives building. Was one of these nice, ordinary-looking people a con artist? *Ridiculous*, I told myself. Everyone was on guard. If anything, we suffered from overkill. Besides Ivor and myself, we had three volunteers to keep watch, plus a community support officer and a police constable. The gift shop was staffed by Glenda and another woman from Long Barston.

The doors opened, and suddenly the room was filled with guests. The air took on the smell of wool sweaters, leather shoes, and warm bodies. After checking their belongings, the visitors strolled past the exhibits with their heads bent and hands clasped behind their backs.

An elderly man with Coke-bottle glasses and a goatee approached me. "Pardon me, but does the card say *mammals* or *animals*? I can't quite make it out." He indicated a bronze ornamented disc.

"The printing *is* small," I said, reading the card for him. "Brooch. Anglo-Saxon, early sixth century. Southern Scandinavian influence, decorated with pairs of animal heads and bands of nielloed triangles."

"Nielloed? I'm not familiar with that term."

Was this a distraction? I checked to see if the man had an accomplice. Of course he didn't. He was just a nice older man with poor vision. "Niello is a decorative metal paste used as an inlay. Some of it's been lost, but the rough-textured lines show where it would have been."

He thanked me and walked on.

The stream of visitors was steady. At twelve thirty, Ivor left to grab some lunch. By the time he returned, I'd answered so many questions there'd been no time to stress about misdirection and partners in crime. I needn't have worried. The worst distraction was a lost coat, eventually discovered on the wrong hanger.

At one forty, Alex found me in the process of explaining to two middle-aged sisters the difference between *vermeil*, gilded silver, and *ormolu*, gilded bronze. They were so grateful you'd think I was disclosing the location of the Fountain of Youth. When they finally moved on, Alex said, "Time you took a break. Get something to eat. Relax for an hour or so. I'll stand in for you."

I headed for the library tearoom and found it jam-packed, too. The hall outside was lined with people waiting for a table. Christine spotted me. Like the other servers, she wore black slacks with a white blouse and a crisp apron, borrowed from the Three Magpies. "It'll be at least a half hour before a table opens up," she said. "If you don't mind standing, you can eat at the counter." A portable beverage bar had been set up in front of the windows. She cleared a space for me at one end and brought a bowl of vegetable soup, an individual pot of tea, and a giant wedge of carrot cake with a slice of Cheddar and vanilla ice cream.

Perfect. All the food groups.

I was finishing the last bite when I noticed Vicar Foxe, sharing a table with, of all people, the Danish couple from the ill-fated tour. The fourth chair was empty.

"Hello, Kate." He waved me over. "Come join me." He really was an attractive man.

"I can't," I said. "I need to get back to the exhibit."

"Such an exciting day. Everything is perfect."

So far.

The Danish pathologist stood and made a polite little bow. "We meet again."

"A more pleasant occasion this time," his wife added. She was wearing the same beautifully cut wool coat she'd worn the day of the tour.

"We weren't actually introduced," I said. "I'm Kate Hamilton. This is Edmund Foxe, the vicar of St. Æthelric's Church in the village."

"Dr. Emil Møller," the man said. "And this is my wife, Marta."

"I didn't realize you were staying in the area."

"We spend the holidays with my wife's relatives in Suffolk." Dr. Møller said.

"My *bedstemor*, my grandmother, was English," Marta said. "A nurse who came vith the British troops in May of 1945—*Befrielsesdag*, the day of our liberation."

"And how is the little boy, Danny?" Dr. Møller asked.

"Ve have been vorried for him," Marta said.

"His mother says he's having a hard time."

"Ah, poor child." Marta shook her head. "A terrible shock for one so young."

"Have you seen the exhibit yet?" I asked. "Glenda's working in the gift shop."

"Ve are in the final group—three forty."

"My time slot as well," the vicar told the Møllers. "I was about to take a stroll in the park. Would you care to join me?"

"Thank you, but no," Dr. Møller said. "We are not dressed for walking."

They weren't. His wing tips were polished to a mirror shine. Marta Møller wore a pair of expensive-looking sling-back heels.

She pulled on her coat and a pair of kid-leather gloves. "Ve thought ve might stay here, in the tearoom, until our time, but I fear ve must leave. So many vaiting for tables."

"We shall wait in the warm car." Dr. Møller stood and gave another of his little bows. "We are glad to have met you, sir, and to see you again, Mrs. Hamilton."

"Sure you won't sit?" The vicar smiled up at me.

"Maybe just for a moment." I took a seat, wondering how to turn the conversation to Tabitha King. When nothing came, I dove in headfirst. "I understand you were counseling Tabitha, the girl who was murdered."

The vicar's teacup stopped halfway between the table and his lips. "Who told you that?"

"Is it true?"

"Anglican clergymen respect the seal of the confessional."

"Understood, but if Tabitha confided in you, she may have said something that would lead to her killer."

"Do the police know?"

"I haven't told them. *You* should. In fact, you must."

Something like anger flashed briefly across his face. Then an emotion I couldn't identify, but I got the impression he was struggling with a decision. "I know nothing about her death. Nothing that would identify her killer."

"Will you tell the police, so I don't have to?"

He agreed, reluctantly. I left with the distinct impression he was hiding something, but whether it was an innocent attraction for a parishioner or something more sinister, I couldn't tell.

When I returned to the archives building, Ivor Tweedy was bubbling over. "I got a text from our mystery man," he whispered. "He assumes I have something to sell. I didn't want to respond until I'd spoken to you."

"If he's a recluse, he might not welcome a pair of strangers asking questions."

"You're right. I'll go alone."

"Oh no, you won't," I said. "This may be my one chance to see that book."

He gave me an appraising look. "We could pass you off as an American antiques dealer."

"Ivor, I am an American antiques dealer."

"I mean an American antiques dealer with something to sell him."

"And who will you be? An English antiques dealer?"

"I'll be a picker, helping you find a buyer."

"Do we know what he collects?"

"All sorts, a fellow dealer tells me, but rare and old—mostly before the 1700s."

"Do you have something you want to sell?"

"Let me think on it, dear girl."

Our conversation was interrupted by a woman who wanted my opinion on the red-stone ring. Was it a ruby? How did we know it belonged to Lady Susannah? Good questions, and they were followed by others. Before I knew it, the time was three forty. The final group entered.

"Goodness me," I heard Marta Møller exclaim. "I had no idea there vere so many items."

The Møllers, along with the vicar and twenty or so others, walked from exhibit to exhibit, exclaiming over each precious object, reading the explanatory cards, asking questions.

Suddenly I felt exhausted—probably crashing from the carrot cake sugar high.

Five minutes until four. I breathed a sigh of relief. We'd done it. All that was left now was closing up and moving the objects back into the safe.

Wrong.

The sound of shouting came from outside, followed by a high-pitched scream.

The door flung open. "Someone's hurt," a woman cried, her eyes wild. "I think her leg's broken. Is there a doctor?"

I spun around to find Dr. Møller.

"Take me to her." He rushed toward the door. "Marta, get my bag from the car."

The theft must have happened in that very moment.

* * *

"Are you sure the ring is the only thing missing?" Tom and I stared at the empty Plexiglas cube that had once held Lady Susannah's ring.

"Everything else is still here."

"The ring was mounted on a small acrylic pedestal, right?"

"With a speck of clear museum gel. Just like you saw it yesterday. The thief took the whole thing."

"And got away in the confusion surrounding the accident."

"You mean the pretend accident."

By the time Dr. Møller had arrived at the scene, the so-called *victim* had vanished, as had the woman who'd burst in, asking for help.

"The whole thing was a setup," I said. "Now that I think about it, it doesn't make sense. If there'd been a real accident, why run first to the archives building? Why not find a constable or one of the community support officers?"

"The thieves count on instinct," Tom said. "The natural human desire to help someone in need."

"And the natural human desire not to miss a good crisis. Every single person in that room, me included, turned toward the sound and then rushed to the windows."

"Of course you did."

"But we'd been warned," I wailed. "I'd been vigilant all day, Tom. Then, when my guard was down, when I thought we'd made it through without an incident, someone shouts about an accident, and I forget all about theft and diversions."

"The perfect con. You can't prepare for it. You react as they know you will."

"They must have been shocked when there actually was a doctor on the scene."

"Witnesses said the so-called victim and her helper ran like the devil."

"All planned out in advance."

"Meticulously. We believe each of the recent burglaries involved a team of players with specialized roles—the actual burglar, those in charge of creating the diversion, any number of bit players."

Including a vicar? No, of course not. That was too far-fetched, even for me. The theft couldn't have anything to do with the recent deaths—could it? I felt sick.

One of the SOCOs pulled down his white hood and stripped off his latex gloves. "We're finished here, sir. Several clear prints on the Plexiglas cube."

I had the sinking feeling they'd turn out to be mine.

Outside, Sergeant Cliffe was completing his interviews with the visitors who remained. At the time of the theft—virtually closing time—most had already left the estate.

The members of the final tour group had been searched and questioned. The Møllers had given their statements first and driven off for a family dinner, leaving Dr. Møller's business card in case the police needed to speak with him again. I'd given a description of the woman who'd asked so many questions about the ring. Ivor was sure the thief had been a man with—his words—shifty eyes and a suspicious limp. He'd limped off, promising to spend the evening choosing several items to tempt the elusive collector.

Tom was examining the plinth that had held the ring. I watched him, marveling over the thief's finesse. He or she couldn't have had more than a few seconds to do the deed.

The door flew open.

"Will the tragedies never end?" Lady Barbara, followed by Vivian and Mugg, clutched her rose-wool coat around her thin frame. Her normally pale complexion was tinged with gray. "It's the lives lost that matter, but this latest outrage feels like piling on. How can we ever—"

"Now, Barbara." Vivian cut across her words. "CCTV has shots of everyone present today. The police will find the thieves—I'm sure of it."

Tom rubbed an eyebrow. I didn't think he shared Vivian's optimism. "I have some information, Lady Barbara. Shall we stay here or find somewhere more comfortable?"

"Whatever it is, you may as well say it now."

"We spoke with the authorities in Venezuela. I was on my way here to give you the news when I got the call about the theft."

"About Lucien?" She grasped Vivian's hand.

"Not directly. The Venezuelan police have promised to redouble their efforts to find him—if he's still in the country."

"Of course he's there," she said. "He sends letters."

"What we learned last night, and what we've spent most of today confirming, concerns the murdered stranger. You were right. His name was Carlos Esteva from one of the major crime families in Caracas, well known to the authorities. He dropped off their radar twenty-some years ago. They assumed he'd either fled the country or was dead."

"He'd been in England the whole time?" Vivian asked.

"No. He arrived about a week before he made contact. Paid for the flight with a stolen credit card and was traveling under an assumed name and a fake passport."

"What did he want with me?" Spots of pink appeared on Lady Barbara's pale cheeks. "Have you discovered a connection to Lucien? Did he have a message? Or did Lucien send him to . . . to . . ." She grasped the edge of the counter. "I need to sit down."

Mugg sprang to life, locating a chair in the gift shop.

She slumped into it. "I feel so confused."

"Would you like tea?" I asked. "I have supplies in my office."

"Tea—yes, exactly what I need."

"I'll go," Vivian said. "You stay with her."

"We're still trying to locate your son," Tom said. "We will find him."

The fortitude I'd seen in Lady Barbara seemed to be ebbing away. First the murders, now the theft. How much more could she take?

Vivian returned more quickly than I'd thought possible. "We should cancel the celebration tonight."

"No." Lady Barbara's tone was firm. "The party will go on. Just because an evil person committed a crime is no reason to cancel. This is for the volunteers. Wine and hors d'oeuvres in the Great Hall at seven. Kate, will you make sure the interns know?"

"Of course."

"You, too, Inspector Mallory. If you're free."

Later, Tom and I walked toward the knot of police gathered outside the dovecote gift shop. The crime scene investigators were still processing the courtyard.

The winter sun was dipping below the horizon. Tom tucked my hand into his arm. "How long will it take to put all the items back in the safe?"

"Not long if I have help. Christine will be there—and Alex, I suppose, although asking them to work side by side might not be the cleverest move. I could pull in Mugg, but he's glued to Lady Barbara, and they'll be getting ready for the celebration."

"Do you need me?" His breath hung in the air for a moment.

"Yes, but not for that."

He gave me that slow half smile, and I was aware of eyes watching us. "Will you come tonight? Bring Sergeant Cliffe. I like him."

"We'll try. We're still checking for similar reports of burglary. And we've had a breakthrough in Tabitha's murder. DNA under her fingernails. We've sent samples off to the lab. If the killer has form—if he's known to the judicial system—we'll find a match."

"And if you don't?"

He lowered his voice, and I saw a gleam in his eye. "Every male connected with Finchley Hall submitted a DNA sample, including Gavin Collier from the Three Magpies and Vicar Foxe. This is no longer just about identifying the father of Tabitha's baby. We may already have the DNA of her killer."

Chapter Thirty

⁓

I took a sip of sparkling wine. Bubbles tickled my nose, but the celebration marking the successful completion of the Hoard exhibit felt less than festive.

On the one hand, the exhibit had been an unqualified financial success. The number of visitors had far outstripped estimates, and every catalog had been snapped up. Lady Barbara would have to republish. On the other hand, we'd landed with both feet in the thieves' trap.

I surveyed the crowded drawing room, touched by the villagers' support of Lady Barbara.

Light from the blazing fire reflected off the silver tinsel and shiny ornaments on the Christmas tree. The green velvet serpentine sofas—no thistles this time—were in their normal place. Villagers milled about, holding flutes of sparkling wine or bottles of beer. The hors d'oeuvres provided by Lady Barbara were basic—fruit, crackers, cheese.

Where was Christine? Where were Alex and Tristan? All the interns knew to arrive at seven. It was nearly eight. Only Peter, Michael, and Prue had shown up. My stomach clenched as I pictured Christine and Alex in hand-to-hand combat with Tristan blithely looking on. Or worse.

"Hello, Mrs. Hamilton." Prue Goody brushed crumbs from her mouth. "I'm terribly sorry about the theft."

"We all are. Have you seen Christine?"

"I thought she was with you. She left our room at six thirty. I assumed she was on her way here."

"Did she say anything?"

"Just that she'd see me later."

"Have you seen Alex?"

"No, and Michael's been looking for Tristan as well." Prue gave me a look that reflected my own concern. Then her face brightened. "Oh—there's Tristan now."

Tristan Sorel, wearing a black military-style jacket over jeans, grabbed a bottle of beer from a tub of ice. He popped the cap and downed nearly the whole bottle.

A hand bell rang. Everyone turned toward the hearth, where Lady Barbara stood with Vivian Bunn. Fergus sat at their feet, observing the guests with benign condescension.

Vivian held Lady Barbara's arm.

Mugg, on the opposite side of the hearth, appeared uncharacter-istically agitated. I could understand that. No one had listened to his warnings of theft; now he'd been proven right. He rang the bell again. The room quieted.

The vicar dashed in, a coat over his arm. *Sorry I'm late*, he mouthed to anyone who happened to be looking. Hattie Nuthall, who was already there, took his coat and bustled it out toward the coatracks in the library.

Lady Barbara surveyed the crowd, her eyes shining. "Thank you for coming, and thank you for your loyalty and your generosity." She wore a sapphire silk dress, old but well pressed, with a matching wool cardigan. "We couldn't have pulled this off without your support. Even as we come to terms with the brazen theft of Lady Susannah's ring, the memory of this day will remain a happy one because of you." She held out both thin arms. "The loss of the ring, we can bear. What we cannot bear is the loss of our dear Tabitha King, a gifted young woman who would have made her mark in the world. We shall never forget her or what she did to make this day possible. This exhibit was her doing, and I refuse to allow the tragic way her life ended to tarnish her memory. Please join me in a toast." Lady Barbara raised her wine glass. "To the memory of Tabitha King."

"To Tabitha." Glasses clinked.

Lady Barbara handed her wine glass to Mugg. "I have full confidence in the Suffolk Constabulary," she continued. "They will find and punish the person responsible for Tabitha's death. And I have no doubt they will find the ring and return it to its place in the Hoard." She raised her eyes toward the Finchley crest above the fireplace. "*Fidelis, fastu, fortitudo*. Loyalty, pride, courage."

The audience burst into applause.

Lady Barbara stepped away from the hearth and allowed Mugg to lead her to one of the serpentine sofas.

Briony Peacock sidled up to me. "Too bad all who claim loyalty to the Hall aren't 'ere tonight." Her cheeks blazed with righteous indignation. Or alcohol. "That's newcomers for you. Out for themselves, innit."

"If you're talking about the Colliers, they have a good reason for not being here. Thanks to the Hoard exhibit, they have a full house of restaurant patrons and overnight guests."

Briony sneered. "Long as it benefits them, eh? Now us—we closed the Arms tonight. Locked the doors. There's loyalty for you. We're 'ere."

Along with all your patrons. "I'm sure Lady Barbara appreciates your presence."

I heard Christine's voice across the room. *Thank heaven.*

I found her, laughing with Prue and Michael at the hors d'oeuvres table. I wanted to take it as a sign she was getting over Tristan, but it was always the same with Christine—quick to give her heart, slow to take it back again.

Tristan stood alone, looking smaller, thinner—diminished. Had Alex given him the chop?

Peter had joined Lady Barbara on the sofa. My heart ached for him. If he were my son, I'd insist he come home to grieve. But he wasn't my son, and who was I to say he should give up everything his parents had sacrificed for?

Peter bent his head toward Lady Barbara. She laid her small, wrinkled hand on his. Maybe Lady Barbara was exactly the person Peter needed right now. And vice versa.

Suddenly conversation quieted. Tom and Sergeant Cliffe had arrived.

Cliffe headed for the hors d'oeuvres table, his tie flapping.

I caught Tom's eye. He smiled. *What an attractive man he is.* He wore a pair of beautifully tailored trousers with a checked shirt and warm cocoa V-neck sweater that made his hazel eyes look—

"Sorry we're late."

"No problem." My toes tingled. "Christine just got here, too. Any updates?"

"None I can talk about." He gave me a meaningful look. "We're going through the camera footage inside the archives building. It's a shame the camera was pointed at the entrance, not at the ring and portrait."

"How were we to know which object would be the target? At least the thief will have been photographed."

"Too bad he wasn't wearing a sign identifying himself. The thieves will have to make another move. Contact a buyer honest enough to call the authorities. Attempt another heist." He took a breath. "We did get a good shot of the woman who burst in, saying there'd been an accident. She's our best bet at this point."

"How about the pretend victim?"

"Descriptions are vague. Medium height and weight with non-descript hair and an ordinary face." He looked at me. "You'd never make it as a thief, you know."

"Why not?"

"Too memorable." He put his arm around me and tugged my hair. "Nordic-looking woman with ice-blue eyes and hair the color of mahogany? You'd be caught the same day."

"Are you chatting me up?" I grinned. "Want a glass of sparkling wine?"

"Better not. I have a feeling this night isn't over yet."

Why did that send a chill down my spine?

I handed Tom one of the hors d'oeuvres plates. "I've been thinking about the stolen ring."

"And?" He chose a cluster of purple grapes and a few cubes of Cheddar.

"I'm wondering why the thieves stole the ring rather than one of the more valuable treasures—the Finchley Cross, for example, or that bronze-and-silver chalice I showed you. I could understand if the stone had been a Burmese ruby, but I'm certain it wasn't."

"Maybe they assumed the stone *was* a ruby."

"Maybe. But they planned it out in advance—you said so. They aren't novices. They know what they want. These theft-for-hire rings operate like an Amazon fulfillment center. Someone goes shopping—they see an object they want, either online or in person. They order it. It arrives on their doorstep, metaphorically speaking, in days. A bit of an exaggeration, but I think someone wanted Lady Susannah's ring in particular, even with a garnet rather than a ruby. For some reason it was valuable to them."

Tom rubbed the back of his neck. "Interesting analogy. And if we find the ring, we'll know if you're right. But I don't see how your theory will lead us to the thieves."

"You said you were contacting other police units around the country, asking if they'd had similar burglaries. How about contacting antiques collectors to see if any of them specialize in early Elizabethan jewelry?" I considered telling him about the elusive collector Ivor had contacted, but we knew nothing about him yet. No name. No address. And no grounds to accuse him of anything but eccentricity.

"We might just do that," Tom said.

"Ivor Tweedy's asking around. If he comes up with something, I'll let you know."

"Good, but back to the Amazon thing for a moment. This theft shows all the signs of advance planning. How would a collector even know about the ring? Except for you and possibly Tabitha, no one knew it was in the safe until the newspaper article on Thursday."

"I've been thinking about that. Your mother said Lady Barbara chooses a few new items every month to display in the library along with the Finchley Cross. Maybe the ring had been on display at some point. Someone might have seen it during one of the regular weekly tours."

"And neither Lady Barbara nor anyone else recognized it? Is that possible?"

"Let's ask her."

We caught Lady Barbara just as she and Vivian were leaving.

"I think I've had all I can take tonight." Lady Barbara leaned on Vivian's arm. "Will you join us in the sitting room?"

"We can't—I'm sorry. But Tom has a question about the ring."

She listened. "On display? It's possible. I haven't personally chosen the items for some time—my vision, you know. For the last several months, Tabitha had selected them. I'm afraid I don't remember which ones she chose. Alex might. Is she here tonight?"

"I haven't seen her," Vivian said. "Odd, too, because she promised to help with the party."

"Maybe she's in the kitchen, helping cook with the hors d'oeuvres trays," Lady Barbara said. "Or in the library with one of the guests."

"I'll check." Vivian dashed off, leaving Fergus to mind himself.

Tom and I asked around, but no one had seen Alex since just after the theft.

No one.

I was starting to panic when Vivian burst into the drawing room. Her face was crinkled with concern. "Cook saw her in the kitchen around five."

"Have you tried her mobile?" Tom asked.

"That's just it." Vivian held up a mobile phone. "I found this in the library."

*   *   *

Hand torches bobbing in the dark reminded me sickeningly of St. Æthelric's Eve, the night the Venezuelan stranger had been found dead in the woods near the Folly.

Tom had called in a police search team. Until they arrived, he'd divided the guests into groups, assigning each to cover an area of the grounds or park. The vicar and several others would follow the path between the Hall and the church parking area. Sergeant Cliffe and Mugg would lead a second group toward the abandoned ice house. Peter and Tristan would comb the Hall from top to bottom. The remaining interns—Christine, Michael, and Prue—would search the Stables and parking area. Vivian, Fergus, and Francie Jewell stayed with Lady Barbara.

Tom and I began in the Elizabethan Garden. The sky was clear, but the waning moon gave little light. His torch flicked along the geometric paths and found the contours of the garden shed.

"We'll check here first." He pulled back the bolt and pushed open the wooden door.

My heart thumped. *Please.*

We smelled the composted manure before we saw bags of it, stacked against the rear wall of the shed. Tom directed the torch beam into each corner.

No Alex. I breathed a sigh of relief.

Next we walked the perimeter of the brick wall, finding nothing unusual.

"Let's head into the park," Tom said.

I tripped on the gravel path. "Sorry. I'd have worn boots if I'd known we were going to tramp around in the dark."

"Would you like to go back?"

"No. I'm not good at waiting."

The air smelled of decaying leaves, damp earth, and a hint of pine needles. Voices in the distance sounded concerned but not alarmed.

Tom's pager beeped. "Nothing yet," he said into the transmitter. He slid the pager into an inside jacket pocket. "That was Constable Wheeler. They'll be here in twenty minutes."

At the top of the Chinese Bridge, Tom shone his torch into the pond, revealing a glint of gold among the swordlike grass. The fish formed a clump, their fins flapping dreamily in unison. Confused by the light, they scattered.

No body. No Alex.

"Mallory, over here," shouted a male voice from somewhere in the distance.

My heart lurched.

"Come on," Tom said, taking my hand.

Skirting the Folly, we rushed toward Blackwater Lake, half-sliding down the bank to the place where we'd found Tabitha's body.

Tom directed the beam of his torch along the shore.

My heart nearly stopped when I saw a shape in the water.

"Sorry, false alarm," a man said. "Only twigs and grass."

I thought about Danny and his nightmares. The place was spooky. Bare-limbed tree trunks rose from the lakeshore and disappeared into the black sky. I shivered, imagining a dark shape with glowing yellow eyes.

More lights followed the shore on the other side of the lake—the vicar's team, I supposed, on their way to the church.

"Let's check the Folly," Tom said. "Then we'll go back and wait for the search team."

He pulled me up the slope.

"Maybe we'll find Alex at the Hall, embarrassed by all the fuss," I said.

"Let's hope so." Tom shone the beam of light at the Folly. The octagonal roof, the columns, the steps.

That's when we saw her.

Alex lay curled on her side, her knees bent, her arms drawn into her body. Near her head, a dark pool had formed.

Please, no.

Tom bounded up the steps and knelt at her side.

I held my breath and prayed.

"She's alive," he said. "Get back to the house, quick as you can. I'm calling for help."

Chapter Thirty-One

∼

Flashing blue lights pulsed across the gravel courtyard.

I stood with Lady Barbara and Vivian on the steps of Finchley Hall, watching the EMTs lift Alex into the back of an ambulance. Uniformed police milled about. Several emergency vehicles were stowing equipment.

"Will she be all right?" I asked Tom when he joined us.

"No way to know until the doctors examine her. She sustained a bad blow to the back of her head."

"Did the poor girl say anything?" Lady Barbara clutched her sapphire-blue sweater around her thin body. I was about to ask if I could fetch her coat when Mugg appeared with it.

"She's unconscious," Tom said. "It may be some time before she's able to speak. Even then, she may not remember what happened."

"Thank goodness you found her in time," Vivian said. Fergus snorted in agreement.

"I shall pray for God's mercy." Lady Barbara's hands trembled as she buttoned the top button of her coat.

"I suggest you retire now, madam," Mugg said. "This is too much for you." He wasn't overstating the problem. Lady Barbara looked close to collapse.

"Yes, of course," Tom said. "We'll talk in the morning."

Tom and I followed them inside. Mugg and Vivian helped Lady Barbara up the wide staircase. Fergus followed, grunting with every hop.

Sergeant Cliffe appeared. "We've finished interviewing the guests, sir. I'd like to send them home."

"Of course. What about the interns?"

"In the library, sir. Waiting for you."

Cliffe's expression—and Tom's, for that matter—gave nothing away, but I didn't need facial feedback to know what they were thinking. The interns would be suspects. My daughter in particular.

A felt a knot in my stomach.

"Before you go in, sir, you'll want to take a look at this." Cliffe handed Tom a pair of thin blue gloves, then the mobile phone found in the library.

Cliffe punched something into the phone. "The mobile had been turned off during the Hoard exhibit. Ms. Devereux appears to have turned it back on at four thirty. After that she sent and received a series of texts. No name. Just a number. Take a look at the messages."

Tom and Cliffe exchanged glances.

"What is it?" I asked, not sure I wanted to hear the answer.

"Someone—not one of her regular contacts," Tom said, "made plans to meet Alex in the Folly at six forty-five."

"Won't take us long to find the name, sir," Cliffe said. "Provider records."

"True." Tom punched a series of numbers into the phone. "And sometimes you just call the number and see who answers."

He put the phone to his ear and waited.

From a distance came the familiar strains of "OMG" by Usher.

I froze.

"It's coming from the library, sir," Cliffe said.

We dashed down the hall and rushed through the door.

From somewhere inside Christine's clothing, the sounds of the ringtone gathered to a conclusion.

Followed by silence.

* * *

"Go over it again, please," Tom said. "See if you can remember details, anything at all."

I sat beside Christine on the gray sofa in the Stables. She folded her arms across her chest. Her face was sullen, her mouth a firm line. I knew this expression—all too well. She was shutting down.

"I told you," she said tightly. "After we finished putting away the Hoard, I went to the Stables to change clothes. Alex texted me. She said we had to talk. I didn't agree. That's all."

"Then what's this about the Folly?" Tom leaned forward and turned the phone screen so she could read it. "Alex said she'd meet you in the Folly at six forty-five. You agreed."

"So what? I changed my mind."

"What did she want to talk about?"

"How would I know?"

"Take a guess."

"All right—Tristan. Maybe she wanted to tell me they were engaged. Whatever it was, I didn't want to hear it. I could care less about Tristan."

"If that's true, why were you so angry?"

"Because Alex is a witch—she's evil."

"Christine," I said, appalled. "Alex is badly hurt."

"I'm sorry about that. She's still a witch."

"We know about the fight," Tom said. "You threw things at her."

"And missed," I said pointlessly.

Christine snorted. "I don't feel like that now."

I couldn't just sit there and listen. "Look, she's answered your questions, Tom. She didn't meet Alex in the Folly, and she doesn't know who did."

"Christine is an adult, Kate. I've allowed you to stay out of courtesy." He paused and let that sink in. "If you keep interfering, you'll have to go."

"I'm not going anywhere." I closed my mouth and folded my arms. Christine and I looked like bookends.

"Christine, where were you tonight between six thirty when Prue saw you leave your room and eight fifteen when you showed up at Finchley Hall?"

"Nowhere in particular. I was upset, okay? I thought I'd better chill. So I walked."

"Why were you upset?"

"It's personal."

"Why were you upset, Christine."

"Alex made me mad."

"Where did you walk?"

"I don't remember. On the estate."

"Near the Folly?"

"No. Not there. I just walked."

"You're sure you didn't go near the Folly?"

"Positive."

"Did you see anyone?"

"I don't remember."

"Hear anything?"

"I wasn't paying attention. I had a lot on my mind."

"Like what?"

"Like none of your business," she snapped.

"Christine," I said. "Don't make this worse. Just tell Tom where you were."

They both glared at me.

Sergeant Cliffe arrived. "Sir, may I—?"

"Not now," Tom said. He turned to Christine. "Are you sure you didn't see anyone?"

"Like who?"

"Like anyone at all—one of the interns, someone from the village."

"I told you. I didn't see anyone." Christine set her mouth. "I have nothing more to say."

Sergeant Cliffe cleared his throat. "A *word*, sir?"

"Stay where you are," Tom told us. He and Cliffe went outside.

"Christine," I hissed. "Stop lying and tell them what you were doing."

"I'm not lying."

"Yes, you are. You've never been a good liar."

She shot me a dangerous look.

Tom returned and addressed Christine in that super-calm voice of his. "Were you at the Folly at any time tonight? Think carefully before you respond."

"No." Her eyes flashed with something. Anger? Fear?

I felt a frisson of terror.

"You were seen near the Folly just before seven," Tom said.

Christine's eyes flicked. "They're wrong."

"Someone saw you there."

For the first time, Christine seemed to stumble. "So?"

"You said you didn't go near the Folly."

"Then I was mistaken. I don't remember being there."

"You have no memory of being there?"

"I may have walked past it. I don't remember."

"Why would you walk past the Folly if you had no intention of keeping your appointment with Alex?"

She's hiding something. I felt a twist of panic in my chest.

"Alex made the appointment," Christine said. "I didn't. And I didn't go there."

"But you admit walking past," Tom said. "I think you did meet her, Christine. Tell me what happened."

Christine jumped to her feet. "I didn't meet Alex at the Folly, all right? I didn't see her. I didn't see anyone. You can't make me say something that isn't true. I'm going to bed."

She jumped up and brushed past him.

Tom stopped her. "I'm afraid it's not that easy." He gave me a brief glance. "Alex asked you to meet her in the Folly at six forty-five. You say you didn't keep the appointment, but you were seen there around the time of the attack. You refuse to tell us where you were and what you did."

"I don't remember." Christine set her jaw.

His expression hardened. "This isn't a game, Christine. A young woman has been viciously attacked. She may die."

"I didn't attack her."

"Who did? You have an obligation to help us."

"I have nothing to say."

"I think you do. I've given you a chance to answer questions here. You refuse. I have no alternative but to take you into Bury for further questioning. Is that what you want?"

"*Tom?* You can't do that." I grabbed my daughter's arm. "For pity's sake, Christine. Just tell him what he wants to know."

Cliffe couldn't look at me. He handed Christine her jacket. "You do not have to say anything. But it may harm your defense if you do not mention when questioned something which you later rely on in court. Anything you do say may be given in evidence."

I brushed away tears. "You can't arrest her. Please, Tom."

"She's giving me no choice." His jaw was set.

"Stop. This isn't necessary." I flung myself in front of him. "Christine didn't hurt Alex. You know that."

"Kate, listen to me. I *have no choice*."

"Then I'm going with her."

"No, you're not."

His words sliced through my veneer of self-control. Fear turned to fury.

Who was this man? I didn't even know him.

They headed for the door.

"Mom?" Christine sounded like a little girl.

"As soon as they release you, we're leaving England." I looked Tom straight in the eye. "I swear it."

Chapter Thirty-Two

≈

What do you do when your world explodes into a million tiny pieces?

I stumbled back to my room and slammed the door. For ten minutes I paced the perimeter in a white-hot fury. Something inside me was ripping, cleaving. How could I have trusted him? How could I ever trust him again? At last I flung myself on the bed and sobbed until my body ran out of tears and my heart ran out of anger. Then I lay, paralyzed with fear, as I pictured my daughter, huddled in an interview room with a team of clever investigators hurling questions at her, trying to break her down. I pictured her in a tiny cell, alone and frightened, unable to sleep on a hard slab, thin mattress.

I edged under the duvet.

Something ugly prowled and snarled at the edge of my brain. Where *had* Christine been between six thirty and eight fifteen, and why was she so determined not to tell the police? An innocent person would have been more shocked, would have promised to do anything to help. Christine's insistence that she couldn't remember where she'd been during that time period was ridiculous. My daughter has a near-photographic memory. And an iron will.

I hadn't believed her story. Neither had Tom.

Did he hope the shock of being taken into custody would pull the truth out of her? Or—another thought stopped me in my tracks—did he think she was about to crack?

My teeth started to chatter. I pulled the duvet closer.

I heard my mother's voice, as clear as if she were in the room with me. *Use your brain, darling. Begin with what you know.*

I took several deep breaths and squeezed my eyes shut to better concentrate. The familiar process of applying logic and order brought some comfort. There was an answer. I was going to have to find it.

One. The victims. Three people had been attacked on the grounds of Finchley Hall in two weeks. Two were dead, one was fighting for her life. Carlos Esteva was a mystery that might never be solved.

Two. The theft of the ring. There was no evidence to connect the theft and the attacks, but both young women—Tabitha and Alex—had access to the Hoard.

Three. The killer. The chances of more than one killer roaming the grounds of Finchley Hall were slim to none. Hadn't Tom said once that the simplest explanation was usually the right one? I took another deep breath, forcing myself to consider every possible option. No one had been cleared, not even Peter.

Four. Lady Barbara. She was the one person all the victims had in common—including Catherine Kerr.

Five. Motive. Was the killer trying to frighten her into selling Finchley Hall? To get his hands on the Hoard? Or was there another reason no one had thought of?

Six. Lucien Finchley-fforde. Even if he was in England, why would he kill three people? Ivor had suggested money, but how would killing help? If he asked his mother for money, she'd give it to him. She'd give him everything.

Seven. Money. Lady Barbara needed cash. The house couldn't survive without major repairs. Lucien, according to Ivor Tweedy, always needed cash. I tried and failed to see how this was related to the attacks.

Eight. The Hoard, and the possible discrepancy in the inventory. Had other Hoard objects been stolen in the past?

Nine. The missing books by Walter Swiggett. Two had disappeared under mysterious circumstances. Someone was determined to keep something in that book a secret. The only lead was the reclusive collector who'd purchased a copy of the book from Reginald Pye, and the only way to get to him would be to offer him a treasure. I'd call Ivor first thing in the morning.

Ten. The dishy vicar, Edmund Foxe. I was back to him.

The pieces of the puzzle lay before me, but I had no clue how to assemble them.

I was still thinking about the vicar when my phone rang. *Tom*. My logic dissolved. "What do you want?"

"I wanted you to know Christine's all right. She's still not talking, but she's fine."

"She's not *fine*." I spat the word out. "My daughter is sitting in a jail cell, thanks to you."

"Kate, listen. The custody sergeant on duty, Tamara, is a friend. She's looking after Christine, making sure she's safe and well cared for."

"She wouldn't be there at all if you'd listened to her. She didn't meet Alex in the Folly. She didn't see anyone. She knows nothing about what happened. What about that don't you understand?"

He started to answer, but I cut him off. "Never mind. I don't want to hear it."

"I don't understand you, Kate." His voice was so low I almost couldn't hear. "I'd do anything in my power to protect you, to protect Christine—you know that. But this is beyond my control. If I hadn't taken Christine into custody, someone else would have."

I couldn't speak. I heard myself sob.

Then, before I had time to think about what I was saying, the bitter words that had caught in my throat spilled out. "Scotland was the golden hinge in my life, Tom, the dividing line between past and present. When I met you, all the sadness and loss I'd experienced just melted away. I had a future again." I could hardly speak, but I kept going. "I loved you. I gave you my heart. I trusted you, and *you hurt me*." I sobbed again.

It took him a moment to respond. "I would never hurt you intentionally. You have to know that."

"Why? How can I know that?"

"So what now? Where do we go from here?"

"We don't go anywhere. As soon as Christine is released, we're leaving."

"You can't do that," he said. "You can't just walk away."

But I could. And I would.

I heard him take a breath. "We can hold Christine for twenty-four hours. Assuming there's no additional evidence against her, she'll be released tomorrow evening." He stopped abruptly, then cleared his throat. "I'm not giving up on us, Kate. Not without a fight."

He hung up.

I lay in the dark and let the tears flow. I'd blamed Christine for giving her heart too quickly. Had I done the same, or—a niggling guilt crept in on the heels of my fury—was I being irrational? Did I want a man who would throw integrity to the wind because what he had to do was distasteful to me?

It didn't matter. We'd turned a corner. Now we could never go back.

Suddenly all I wanted to do was talk to my mother.

Eleven thirty in Long Barston would be six thirty PM in Ohio. Mom would be at the house, eating dinner, probably watching something on TV.

Blinking back tears, I punched in my home number.

The phone picked up after two rings, but the voice that answered wasn't my mother's.

"Kate? How did you know?" The voice belonged to Charlotte, my best friend and one of the part-time workers at the antiques shop.

"Know what?"

Silence. Then a tiny sound, like someone swallowing. "I was just about to call you. Your mom's had some kind of attack. She'd phoned me around three to take over at the shop because her headache had gotten worse. I stopped by after work to make sure she was okay. I found her on the floor in your kitchen. The EMTs called it a possible stroke. I'm so sorry, Kate. They've taken her to Jackson Falls Memorial. I'm getting a few things together for her right now. How soon can you fly home?"

How soon? The magnitude of the choice I faced hit me like a sucker punch. Christine was in police custody, a suspect in a vicious attack. My mother was in a hospital in Jackson Falls, paralyzed—or worse.

"When will they know more?"

"Tomorrow. They've scheduled tests. Let me know when your plane arrives. I'll pick you up at the airport. And I'll call you the minute I hear something—I promise. Try not to worry." She broke off. "Except I know you will, only try not to."

I mumbled my thanks, and we hung up.

How could I be in two places at once?

Chapter Thirty-Three

～

Sunday, December 20th

The bells of St. Æthelric's were ringing and ringing. Wouldn't stop.

Panic rose as I tried to descend those zigzaggy wooden stairs, my feet slipping out from under me. Trying again.

My heart pounded. Somehow I had to warn—

The dream evaporated as I realized the ringing was my cell phone. *Christine?* I reached out to answer, but the duvet had twisted itself around my legs.

I turned on the swing-arm lamp and squinted at the call-back number. It was Charlotte. The hairs lifted on the back of my neck.

Fingers trembling, I pushed redial. "Charlotte, what's happened?"

"Nothing yet. I wanted to give you an update."

"It's the middle of the night in Ohio."

"Only one AM. No problem. You know I'm a night owl. Anyway, I just got off the phone with the nurses' station. You can call your mother's doctor Monday after ten in the morning, Ohio time. He'll have the test results by then. Here's the number."

I scrambled out of bed and found the notebook and pen I keep in my handbag. When I'd taken down the doctor's information, I asked, "Any change?"

"The nurses say she's starting to wake up. That's good news. Still too soon to know if she sustained any impairment. She's scheduled for an MRI and Doppler scan in the morning. Maybe an echocardiogram, depending on what they find. When she's fully awake, they'll test her memory and cognition. Doug is making sure she gets the best care."

"Tell him thank you." Charlotte's husband, Doug, a pediatrician, knew every doctor in northern Ohio. I felt relieved to know he was watching over my mother's care.

"Have you gotten your flight yet?"

"It's complicated." I spent the next several minutes explaining everything to Charlotte.

"Oh, Kate. You must be beside yourself with worry."

I started to cry. "I *have* to fly home to be with mom, but how can I leave Christine?"

"Listen, Kate. Your mother is being well looked after. Wait until we get the results of the tests. Talk to the doctor. Then you can make up your mind."

"What about the shop?"

"I'll take care of everything. Don't worry."

We were about to hang up when she added, "This is none of my business, but I'm going to say it anyway. Have you thought about how much Tom must be suffering?"

I hadn't. I couldn't.

All I could think about was the fact that I was far from home with no one to help me. Oh, Lady Barbara and Vivian would sympathize, but what could they actually do to help?

Then I remembered Ivor Tweedy.

* * *

The bells of St. Æthelric's, the real ones this time, announced the end of the Sunday service. Parishioners, bundled in coats and scarves, streamed by as I hurried through the church parking area toward Ivor's antiques shop. If the shop was closed, I'd phone him.

The shop was open. Entering, I heard the bell jangle and smelled the dusty, musty chemical bouquet of the past. This was familiar. This felt like home.

Ivor bounced on the balls of his feet, then pulled a pained expression.

"You've got to stop that bouncing thing. You'll do further damage to your hips."

"Habit of a lifetime. Hips are already shot. If I were an antique, you'd call it patina."

When I didn't laugh, he cocked his head. "Don't tell me there's been another theft."

My eyes filled. "Ivor, I need your help."

We sat in a pair of folding campaign chairs that Ivor claimed had been carried into the Battle of Waterloo. I talked and cried. He listened, made tea, and handed me tissues.

"Your friend is right," he said gravely. "Our first priority is to clear Christine. But how are we going to do that?"

I loved that *we*. It reminded me of my mother. It reminded me I wasn't alone.

"My mother says to knock on the door in front of you. The only door I can see is that eccentric collector who texts. Someone doesn't want me to see the book on the Hoard. That tells me there's something in it we need to know. The collector has a copy—at least we think he has—but how are we going to get him to talk to us?"

"I spent several hours last night thinking about that. We offer him an incentive. Come, take a look. *Ah*." Ivor pulled a face as he pushed himself out of the chair.

He opened the drawer behind the sales counter and removed several objects.

"What do you think?" He handed me a carved lavender jadeite snuff bottle, roughly rectangular in shape, about two and a half inches high. The pink tourmaline stopper fit tightly. Probably original.

My mouth went dry. My fingertips tingled.

"I bought this from an estate sale in Guildford. Chinese, of course. Eighteenth century."

"How much is it worth?" I turned the bottle over in my hand, assessing the value. Jadeite is the most precious form of jade, and lavender is a prized color.

"I paid six thousand for it at auction. I'd say it's worth at least eight."

"I'm impressed, but it may not be old enough for our collector."

"We'll see. How about this?" He handed me a small, carved ivory statuette of the Virgin and Child of a type known in iconology as *Virgo Lactans*. The Virgin sat on a backless throne, offering her left breast to the Child. He rested one hand on her breast while holding an apple in the other.

"The carving is exquisite," I said, feeling my heart thump. "Look how the artist has captured the soft undulations of Mary's mantle and skirt. Tell me about it."

"English. Unknown artist. Last quarter of the thirteenth century. There's one very like it in the Victoria and Albert."

"That may do the trick."

"Just wait." His eyes sparkled as he unfolded a square of snowy-white cloth to reveal a flat turquoise glass profile of a face, made in the distinctive style of the Egyptian Amarna period. My cheeks started to burn. My mouth felt dry. My fingers tingled. I took in the high cheekbones, the almond-shaped eyes, the long neck, the fleshy lips. The forehead was cut at an angle to allow for the now-missing *pschent*, the high double crown symbolizing Upper and Lower Egypt.

"Akhenaten, the heretic king." My voice was barely a whisper.

Ivor handed me the small glass head, resting on a square of black velvet cloth. "Well done, Kate. Eighteenth dynasty, mid fourteenth century BC. The inlay was obviously part of a larger composition, probably set into a piece of jewelry or furniture. Only the head survives—amazing, really, because after Akhenaten's death, the priests did their best to erase all memory of the pharaoh who dared abolish all Egypt's many gods, with a single exception."

"The sun god, Aten. Where did you find it?"

"In Jordan, while I was still traveling. This was one of my first purchases. I gave every penny I had at the time for it."

"And you want to sell?"

"If it means finding a killer and clearing your daughter. Now, don't cry. I've been a selfish person my whole life. Now I have an opportunity to do something really fine. I won't regret it, you know." He winked. "I have a plan."

I wiped my eyes and hugged him. With my fingertips still tingling, I handed him the small glass inlay. "If this doesn't get his attention, nothing will."

"Let's find out. We'll offer him all three objects and see which bait he takes." Ivor spent a minute or so keying a message into his mobile with both thumbs. "There," he said, pushing a final key.

We waited, holding our breath, as if the slightest movement of air might interrupt our tenuous electronic connection with the collector.

"He may not be checking his texts," Ivor said finally. "It took him two days to answer before."

I tried and failed to hide my disappointment.

"If I don't hear back by tonight, I'll text him again."

"That missing book is the only lead I have to the identity of the thief—and maybe the killer. I have to do something to clear my daughter." I pulled on my jacket and slung my handbag over my shoulder. "Call me if you hear from him. And, Ivor, you can't know how much this means to me."

"And to me, dear girl."

Chapter Thirty-Four

~

The walk to the Three Magpies took me past the Finchley Arms. The sidewalk signboard said TODAY'S SPECIAL: NOTHING. YOU'RE NOT SPECIAL.

"Hi, Jayne," I said, sinking into a chair near the fireplace. "Have you seen the sign outside the Arms?"

"Better than the one they put out last week," she said, sliding clean glasses into the slots above the bar. "We're offering family-style dinners on Sundays now. I put that on our signboard. So the Arms put on their sign, 'Leave the kiddies at home. We're a pub, not Disneyland.'"

"At least they have a sense of humor."

"They have that, but what bothers me is the bitterness. No matter what we do, they mock. I know plenty of villages with more than one pub. They do bar food—that's fine. We offer something more. Competition doesn't have to become combat."

"Have you thought about discussing it with them?"

Jayne rolled her eyes. "Briony won't even say hello on the street. If she sees me at Tesco, she turns her cart around and goes in the opposite direction." She handed me the menu card. Her eyebrows drew together. "You look knackered. How is the young woman who was attacked?"

"Alive. That's all we know."

If the village hadn't heard that Christine was helping the police with their inquiries, I wasn't going to tell them. I had to hold myself together, because the only way to prove my daughter innocent was to prove someone else guilty.

I was more convinced than ever that the attacks and the theft were connected. The psychotherapist Carl Jung called it *synchronicity*, the theory that seemingly unrelated but simultaneously occurring events are connected. My mother had a simpler explanation: "When you see things together, things that shouldn't be together, there's always a reason."

That had proven true in Scotland. And now?

Even if the vicar wasn't guilty, only a slight twisting of the theory pointed to a connection between the attacks and the theft. Lady Susannah's ring had been snatched out from under our very noses. And if my theory about Tabitha's list was correct, eleven other precious objects were missing as well. Along with two copies of the Swiggett book. Someone was going to great lengths to make sure the original inventory couldn't be compared to the present one.

The only anomaly in recent events was the murder of Carlos Esteva. Why had he been killed? The only reason I could think of was because he'd witnessed someone attacking Tabitha. Maybe he was the outlier that would put the whole picture in focus.

"Jayne," I said, when she brought the crab salad I'd ordered, "have either you or Gavin thought any more about that man from Venezuela?"

"What do you mean?"

"Have you thought of anything you didn't mention earlier?"

"I never saw him at all, if you remember. Gav just caught a glimpse of him near the garden at the Hall."

I spread my napkin on my lap. "The other day you mentioned seeing Tabitha with the vicar. She was tearful."

"Poor thing. Now that we know she was pregnant, I understand what she must have been going through."

"Did you overhear her conversation with the vicar?"

Jayne's eyes widened. "Kate, I don't listen to the conversations of my patrons."

"Of course not." I shook my head. "But sometimes you hear snatches, right? It could be important."

She tipped her head to one side. "I heard one thing, now you mention it, but it didn't make sense." She bit her lip. "Tabitha was crying. The vicar put his arm around her and said, 'Don't worry. No one will ever know.'"

My cell phone rang. It was Ivor.

He was almost breathless with excitement. "Our collector texted back. He wants to see everything we've got. Tomorrow, eleven AM. His house in Bury. I have the address."

I slid my phone into my handbag.

Knock on the door in front of you.

* * *

"Kate—back for another climb to the top of the tower?" Vicar Foxe's handsome face radiated good humor.

I laughed.

Not sincerely enough, because his face grew serious. "What's wrong?"

"It's my daughter, Christine."

He leaned forward at his desk and listened intently as I told him about her arrest and her refusal to explain where she was when Alex Devereux was attacked.

"And here's me, making stupid jokes. My sense of humor gets me in trouble."

"That's only the first reason I've come. There's more." I glanced at the closed door that led into the office of his administrative assistant, an older woman with a motherly smile. I could hear the *tap, tap, tap* of her keyboard. "I've been doing some research, following leads that might explain why these attacks are happening at Finchley Hall."

"Have you found anything?" He picked up a pen and began clicking it open and shut.

"Maybe." I tried to look at him, but my gaze shifted to the wall behind him with its framed certificates and colored print of Jerusalem's western wall.

I forced myself to look him in the eye. "What I found involves you."

He stared down at the pen, then up at me and exhaled. "Ah, I see. Would you excuse me for a moment?" He picked up the phone receiver and punched in two numbers. After a second or two, he said, "Hattie, would you join me in my office? I'm with Kate Hamilton."

"I'm sorry," I said pointlessly. "I wanted to give you an opportunity to explain before I told anyone else."

"Kind of you." He smiled. "I knew it would come out eventually."

The door opened and Hattie Nuthall appeared, carrying a stack of file folders.

"She found the news articles from Chelmsford," the vicar said. "She wonders if I'm the one attacking young women at Finchley Hall."

Hattie placed the folders on the vicar's desk and took the chair beside me. "We knew it would come out eventually," she said, repeating the vicar's words. They'd braced themselves for this day. "I was there, Kate. The young woman in Chelmsford admitted to her parents and to the police that she'd invented the incident to garner sympathy. She'd made similar accusations before—a teacher, a neighbor driving carpool, a family friend. Her parents have put her under the care of a psychiatrist. If you require confirmation, they've authorized us to give you their name and address."

"I had to know."

"Of course you did."

"I understand."

I watched their faces, seeing concern for me. And yet there was something else, some information they weren't telling me. "You mentioned the seal of the confessional. I respect that, but you were heard telling Tabitha that no one would ever know. You were talking about her pregnancy, weren't you?"

"How do you know what I said?"

I shook my head, declining to answer. "She'd confided in you."

He lay the pen on his desk and flicked it with a finger, causing it to spin. "She told me she was pregnant. She didn't want the father to know. I advised her to tell him but assured her I wouldn't be the one to give away her secret."

"Can you tell me anything that might help the police identify Tabitha's killer?"

Hattie and the vicar exchanged glances.

Hattie pressed her lips together. "Not to identify her killer, no."

"*Hattie*," said the vicar. A warning.

"Well, *I'm* not under the seal of the confessional." She lifted her chin. "I don't wish to speak ill of the dead, but Tabitha misinterpreted the vicar's concern."

"There's no need—"

She cut across him, addressing me. "The vicar is a handsome man."

He shot her an accusing look, then lowered his head. "Tabitha took my concern for her as something more. She'd been terribly hurt. I tried to let her down gently, but when I heard she'd taken her own life . . . well, that turned out not to be true."

Hattie stood and picked up the folders she'd been carrying. "Come Christmas, all that will be over—and not before time, if you ask me."

"Hattie, that's a secret."

She *tsk*ed and patted me on the shoulder. "Kate isn't going to tell anyone, are you, dear? All I'll say is a certain young veterinarian is going to find an engagement ring under her tree this Christmas." She made for the door, stopping to add, "And come January, I'm going to hang a sign outside the church saying, 'Don't bother. He's spoken for.'"

"Is there anything I can do for Christine?" the vicar asked as I slid my arms into my jacket.

"Pray."

Only one door remained now, and I prayed it wouldn't lead to another dead end.

Chapter Thirty-Five

Monday, December 21st

The ancient town of Bury St. Edmunds was laid out according to the old medieval formula of a square for God and a square for man. We found the address Ivor had been given—no name, mind you—on a quiet street outside Bury's medieval grid. I wedged my car into a parking space.

The time was exactly eleven AM. I hadn't told Ivor about my mother's possible stroke. In four hours I'd make the phone call that might change my world forever, but right now I had to put that aside and focus on Christine and the events at Finchley Hall. The man we were about to see might have the answer I'd been seeking—or at least part of the puzzle.

The three-story brick town house blended in with its neighbors—except for the wrought-iron bars. The windows were shuttered from the inside. No name plaque informed visitors of the occupant or occupants inside. A brass letter slot on the front door gleamed in the afternoon sun.

Ivor hobbled up the steps and turned the bell twist. Moments later the door was answered by a middle-aged woman wearing a dark uniform similar to Francie Jewell's in her Briggs incarnation, except this one looked new and crisply pressed.

"Come in," she said without smiling, taking our coats and turning her back. "Follow me."

A narrow entrance hall led to a reception room where a Regency drum table held a spray of white roses. We followed her along a hallway to a staircase descending into darkness.

I glanced at Ivor behind me. *Is this safe?*

He shrugged.

As we descended the stairs, I heard Ivor grunting behind me in pain.

I was contemplating retreat when our guide flipped a switch, revealing a dimly lit corridor. Gilt wall sconces lit the way toward what had to be the rear of the house. The maid opened the door to a room, also dimly lit, with high, barred windows. The room was empty—or rather, almost empty. Two chairs flanked a small wooden desk, behind which sat one of the most unusual-looking people I'd ever seen.

The man's skin, what I could see of it, was nearly translucent, the underlying veins a road map of fine bluish lines. Pure-white hair lay thinly across his skull and gathered in pale clumps at his temples. His head was long and narrow, giving the impression of having been stretched. His lips were thin and colorless. I couldn't see his eyes. He wore a visor and shaded glasses, even in the muted light.

The man was an albino, I realized, probably suffering from the associated photophobia.

He rose, indicating that we should sit. Dark athletic pants and a loose bomber-style jacket hung on his thin frame. He turned his head toward me. "You must be the American collector. Please allow me to see what you've brought." *Curt.*

He opened the middle drawer of the desk and extracted a large magnifier.

"I'm Kate Hamilton," I said. "May I know your name?"

His head snapped up. "Names are irrelevant. If I like what you've brought and we settle on a price, you will each sign a statement promising not to divulge any information you might gather as a result of our interaction, including my address. Theft is a constant concern. Is that agreeable? If not, we have nothing more to talk about."

Ivor smiled beatifically.

"No problem." I watched his face relax.

"Why are you selling?"

Drat. We hadn't planned this part.

I opened my mouth, but Ivor cut in smoothly. "She's a recent widow." He rubbed his thumb and middle finger together and gave the collector a meaningful look. *Needs the cash.*

The collector made a small, satisfied sound. We'd passed the first test.

Reaching into my handbag, I took out three small bundles. I unwrapped the first two and placed the jadeite snuff bottle and the ivory statuette on his desk. Then I unfolded the snowy-white cloth to reveal the turquoise glass head of Akhenaten, resting on the black velvet square.

Ignoring the snuff bottle and figurine, he pulled on a pair of white cotton gloves. "I need light." He reached for a swing-arm lamp on his desk, pulled down the shade, and switched it on. The LED bulb emitted not the sharp white light I'd expected but a warm amber glow. He took a sharp breath. "The heretic king. Eighteenth dynasty. Can you provide provenance?"

"Certainly," I said, handing him the paper Ivor had given me earlier. "The inlay was purchased from a dealer in Jordan in the early 1960s. You can see the name of the shop at the top as well as the attached certificate of authenticity."

He handed the paper back. "Read it, please."

I read. "'This artifact was exported from Egypt prior to the 1970 UNESCO treaty and complies with all international trade laws and restrictions regarding antiquities. Hussaini, Limited, is a member of the Association of Dealers and Collectors of Ancient and Ethnographic Art.'" I pointed to the embossed seal and signature. "It's dated February of 1962."

"I see. And how much are you asking?" He tapped his left index finger lightly on the desk.

I looked at Ivor.

"As Mrs. Hamilton is a collector, not a dealer, she has asked me to represent her in this matter. The asking price is twenty thousand pounds sterling."

I heard a sharp intake of breath. "Outrageous. I could buy any number of objects like this at half the price."

"I doubt that," Ivor said coolly. "And if you could, you would find they were either stolen or reproductions."

"Hmm." The skin around the man's mouth tightened. "Everything I buy is genuine and legal. That's why I insist on provenance, which you have supplied. However, the sum you mention is out of the question." He lifted his long chin in defiance.

"In that case," Ivor said, rising painfully from his chair, "we'll say good day to you."

"Wait," the man said. "I'll make an offer. Sixteen thousand pounds—not a penny more."

I glanced at Ivor, who showed no sign of distress. He made a small moue of satisfaction, and I understood. Our collector would have the head at any price, but negotiations would go more quickly if he thought we were willing to bargain. Ivor had a card up his sleeve. Which one, I couldn't guess.

Ivor allowed the silence to lengthen.

The collector shifted in his chair. "Do we have a deal?"

"Your offer is two thousand less than Mrs. Hamilton is prepared to accept."

"You're not willing to bargain?"

Ivor's blue eyes had that look of childlike innocence again. "We are prepared to bargain—but not for money. I understand you have in your possession a book written in 1822 about the Finchley Hoard. Mrs. Hamilton has an interest in the Hoard and is willing to accept your offer of sixteen thousand pounds and"—he drew out the word—"the book."

The collector frowned. "I own such a book? How do you know that?"

"A barrister in Lavenham sold the book some years ago to a collector who communicates by text only. I believe he meant you."

"Possibly, possibly." He tugged at the collar of his jacket. "I may have purchased such a book, and I'm happy to include it in the sale."

"You're familiar with the book, then?" I asked.

"Vaguely, vaguely." He shook his head dismissively. "Only in the sense that I collect Anglo-Saxon artifacts and thought the book might prove instructive."

"And has it?"

"I lost interest. My vision is poor. In fact, I have no idea where the book is at the present moment." He set his lips in a thin line.

I was about to ask permission to search when Ivor preempted me. "In that case, we shall disturb you no longer. We have another potential buyer. Of course, if you locate—"

"*No.*" Cords in the man's tortoiselike neck stood out like ropes. "You may search for the book yourselves." His nostrils flared. "It's almost certainly among the volumes I keep in my museum."

Ivor shot me a satisfied look, and I understood what had just happened. If I'd asked permission to search, the man, his cloistered existence fueled by anxiety and suspicion, would have denied us. Instead, ratcheting up his fear that the glass head was about to slip from his grasp, Ivor had gotten him to ask us. Ivor was a genius.

He was also slick. In another life and without the tender heart I was learning to appreciate, Ivor Tweedy could sell ice to a Finn in February.

* * *

The museum, accessed through a locked and reinforced metal door, appeared to have been excavated beneath the back garden. We passed rows of showcases in which precious artifacts rested in temperature- and humidity-controlled environments. I've heard of people's eyes popping, but this was the first time I'd experienced it. My *affliction* was in full tilt—fingers and toes tingling, cheeks hot, mouth dry, heart palpitating wildly. Every case held objects so amazing, it was all I could do to keep moving.

Ivor, behind me, gave me a little shove in the back.

Every conceivable type of treasure was represented—porcelain, glass, precious metals, jewelry, ivory, icons and other religious objects, carved stone, weaponry, pottery. I caught Ivor's eye and nodded at a bronze statue of a man holding a silver tray bearing a cluster of natural emeralds. The only comparable statue I'd ever heard of was kept in the fabulous Grünes Gewölbe in Dresden.

Some of the cases were empty, as if waiting to be filled. I wondered where Akhenaten's head would be displayed. I hadn't noticed any Egyptian antiquities. Call me suspicious, but I *had* noticed that most of the artifacts were small, like those taken in the recent thefts.

Unfair. I reprimanded myself. This man insisted on provenance. Just because he didn't collect full suits of armor or life-size marble statuary didn't make him a criminal.

A room behind the museum was dedicated to books, many of them guides to various art forms. I recognized several I had in my own library.

"These books"—he indicated the shelf on our right—"have been organized and documented. The book you seek, if it's here, will be found on the opposite wall or on the table." A long oak table was piled high with books of all sizes.

He watched as Ivor and I got to work. We scanned the spines, looking for a book bound in soft, pale suede. The search didn't take long.

"Success." Ivor held up a slim volume bound in pale suede leather. The leaf edges of the paper had turned a dark butterscotch color.

The collector—it was awkward not knowing his name—exhaled.

Ivor thumbed quickly through the book, closed the cover, and tucked it under his arm. "How do you intend to pay, sir? Check? Money order? Do you need to time to transfer funds?"

"Cash." The collector pulled a cell phone from his jacket pocket, dialed, and spoke two words: "Sixteen thousand."

"Glimpsing your treasures has been a great privilege, sir." Ivor, meek as a lamb, followed the collector out of the room.

"The museum is my life's work, my *raison d'être,* you might say."

He'd turned right instead of left, and we found ourselves in a parallel aisle.

He wants us to see more.

I swallowed hard. Here were the most ancient treasures. Carved figures of wood and stone. Hammered gold and bronze jewelry. Ushabti, the funerary servant figures wrapped in the linen folds of Egyptian mummies. Several *real* mummies—cats, wrapped snugly in crisscross strips of linen with smooth cloth masks painted with whiskers. I pictured the turquoise glass head in that cabinet.

The next case held a collection of black-and-white Etruscan pots from the fifth century before Christ and—I nearly gasped—treasures from ancient Britain. This time it wasn't only my fingers and toes that tingled. My whole brain seemed to vibrate as I took in the objects—a gilded bronze helmet; a glass drinking beaker, amazing if for no other reason than that it had survived roughly ten centuries intact; a finely detailed silver brooch in the shape of a Roman shield. Each object would find space in the British Museum. Could our collector really have purchased them legally?

I leaned in to examine a gold-and-garnet cloisonné cuff. *Wait a minute.* Hadn't Tabitha's list mentioned a cloisonné cuff? Next to it was a silver-and-filigree Gospel cover. And a gold pectoral cross set with amethysts. *Coincidence?*

That's when I saw it—a ruby of the purest red.

My mouth dropped open. The large oval stone, five carats or more, was mounted on a glass plinth. A tiny LED illuminated an intricately carved griffin rampant—an exact replica of the one on the Finchley coat of arms.

"Mrs. Hamilton, are you all right?" The collector sounded suspicious.

I hurried to catch up. "Sorry," I said breathlessly. "I couldn't help myself. Your collection is simply dazzling. What you've achieved is . . . incredible."

Blood rose in his cheeks, shockingly vivid beneath the pale skin. "Perhaps if you were to text in advance, we could arrange—" He broke off. "But of course you'll be leaving England soon. Well." He made a small dismissive movement with his hand.

He's lonely, I thought. *Desperately lonely.* I imagined what life must have been like for him as a child, overly protective parents shielding him from the mockery of his peers. Or, even worse, his parents ashamed of him, hiding him from the public eye. All his life, his unusual physical appearance would have made human contact uncomfortable—children openly staring, adults casting sly glances and whispering behinds their hands.

But I was a fellow collector. We shared a common passion. I was someone who could appreciate his life's work.

As much as I would have liked to take him up on his offer, my most pressing goal at the moment was getting out of there and telling Ivor what I'd seen. The collector showed us to the door. The maid handed us our coats and a rectangular package wrapped in plain brown paper.

"Sixteen thousand English pounds in twenty-pound notes," the collector said. "Would you care to count it?"

"Not necessary." Ivor, trusting soul that he was, handed me the book, took the packet, and tucked it inside his coat.

I was about to ask the collector about the confidentiality agreement we were supposed to sign when it dawned on me that divulging his personal information was exactly what I intended to do. Had the man forgotten or simply decided we weren't a threat? I wasn't going to remind him. Any qualms I might have felt under ordinary circumstances were obliterated by an overwhelming desire to clear my daughter of wrongdoing. And that meant following any lead—however unlikely. If this man possessed items stolen from the Hoard, someone else had done the stealing.

"Before we go," I said. "May I ask where you find these wonderful things?"

Ivor made a small clucking sound. I could tell he was keen to get out of there.

"My condition now prevents me from attending auctions or sales in person. I rely on pickers who know what I want and bring the items to me." Now that we were leaving, the man had become chatty.

"I'm especially interested in the Anglo-Saxon artifacts." Ignoring the pressure of Ivor's arm, I put on what my husband used to call my innocent look.

The collector seemed reluctant to let us go. "There is one picker who specializes in Anglo-Saxon objects. Strange fellow. Always wears a hat. And sunglasses, those reflective amber-tinted kind worn by the military. He comes up with the goods, though—all genuine, all thoroughly documented."

Sunglasses again. "What's his name?"

The collector stiffened. "I told you. Names aren't important."

"Of course not," Ivor said. "Not important at all." He tugged on my arm as he backed out the door. "Thank you again, er . . . sir."

The door shut, and Ivor bustled me down the steps and into the street. "What was all that about?"

"He's got the blood-red ruby," I squeaked.

Ivor's head jerked up. "Are you sure? We have to inform the police. On second thought, let's drive there. The police station is less than ten minutes away."

"Not yet." I started the car and jammed it into reverse. The last thing I wanted to do was accuse someone without evidence. Actually, that was the second-to-last thing. The very last thing I wanted was to run into Tom. "We need proof. He may have purchased the ruby legally. Let's check Swiggett's inventory first."

"Why?" Ivor narrowed his eyes.

"It's not just the ruby. He has several objects that fit descriptions on Tabitha's list."

"*What?*" Ivor threw the packet of notes on the floor and grabbed the book. "You drive. I'll read. But then we really must call the police."

I pulled into traffic. "Not quite yet." The pieces of the puzzle had begun to assemble themselves in my mind's eye. I couldn't see the pattern yet, not the whole thing anyway, but I knew it would come. "I've remembered something, something more important than the blood-red ruby."

"Like what?"

"Like a monster with yellow eyes."

Chapter Thirty-Six

By the time we hit the A134 south, Ivor had confirmed that the origi-nal inventory, made in 1818 and recorded in Swiggett's book in 1822, contained exactly eleven more items than the inventory made by Tabitha King. One of the objects I'd seen in the collector's museum, the ruby intaglio, was a definite match. Three others—the pectoral cross, the silver-and-filigree Gospel cover, and the cloisonné cuff— were definite *maybes*.

"Is that proof enough for you?" Ivor asked.

"All right, we'll notify the police, but there's something I have to check out first."

"The monster with the yellow eyes."

"Glenda Croft's phone number is on a slip of paper in the outer pocket of my handbag. I think Danny's school is on Christmas break this week. Call her and ask if I can speak with him."

As Ivor dialed, I prayed they were home, reminding myself again that things sometimes do turn out well.

Glenda and Danny lived on a housing estate on the outskirts of the tiny village of Little Gosling, ten miles from Long Barston. We arrived at one twenty-five—I admit to a lead foot. Glenda and Danny were finishing their lunch.

"Would you care to join us?" Glenda asked us. "There's tea and biscuits, or I could make more sandwiches."

"Not this time," I answered for both of us. "I'd like to talk to Danny."

The boy sat, sullenly kicking the leg of the table. "Who's that?" He jerked his head toward Ivor.

"A friend. Mr. Tweedy."

"I won't talk to him. Just you."

"Would that be okay, Glenda?" I asked. "I promise I won't take long."

"On second thought," Ivor said. "I wouldn't say no to a cup of tea."

I could have kissed him.

"Wanna see my room?" Danny asked.

I followed him down a short hallway to a room the size of a walk-in closet. A single bed took up most of the space, except for a three-drawer pine dresser, on top of which sat a partially completed Lego project, some kind of spacecraft. Posters of monstrous action figures lined the walls. No wonder the kid had nightmares.

Danny sat on the bed. I pulled up a junior-sized chair.

"Still having bad dreams?" I asked him.

He nodded and hugged his pillow, suddenly shy.

"About the monster?"

He nodded again.

"Can you tell me about him?"

Danny buried his face in his pillow. I was about to conclude this was as much as I was going to get when he raised his head. "I didn't make him up. He's real."

"Okay." I took an even breath, then another. "Tell me about him."

He pointed at a poster of an evil-looking droid, his absurdly muscular arm wielding an enormous sword.

"He's that big?"

Danny shook his head.

"Does he have a big sword?"

"No."

"What does he have?"

"Dunno. He threw it in the lake."

Now we're getting somewhere.

Danny's eyes were on the poster.

Suddenly I knew what had been bothering me since the day we'd found Tabitha's body. My mind went back to the scene—Danny shrieking, a rock in each hand, his shoes submerged in the shallow water along the lakeshore. At his feet, wedged against a half-sunken log, was Tabitha's body. But Danny hadn't been looking at the body.

He'd been looking at something farther along the shore.

"You're saying the monster threw something in Blackwater Lake?"

Danny nodded.

"Like a weapon?"

"Dunno."

"What else?"

"He had yellow eyes."

"Really?" *Yellow. Amber.* My heart rate kicked up. The picker who specialized in Anglo-Saxon artifacts wore amber-tinted sunglasses.

"I'm not lying." Danny's mouth turned down. "Everybody thinks I'm makin' it up, but I'm not." He buried his face in the pillow again.

"I don't think you're making it up, Danny. Tell me about the yellow eyes. Can you describe them?"

Danny sniffled. "They glowed in the sun."

"Think carefully, Danny. Could they have been sunglasses?"

Danny chewed on a fingernail. "Coulda been."

Sunglasses. Mirrored, amber-tinted sunglasses. "Danny, listen. Tell me if I go wrong, okay?" I spoke as calmly as one can while having heart palpitations. "The day we took that tour, the day you found the body of that girl in the lake, you saw a man in the woods wearing yellow sunglasses. He threw something in the lake, right?"

Danny nodded.

"How far away was he?"

Danny's mouth bunched to one side. "Like from here to the kitchen."

About fifteen yards. Pretty close. "What happened to him?"

"He ran away."

"Why didn't you tell your mom?" I put my hand on his arm.

"Scared, wasn't I?"

"I would have been, too. But you should always tell your mom when things scare you."

"He told me not to."

"He spoke to you?"

Danny shook his head.

"So how did you know?"

Danny's normally ruddy face was as pale as his pillowcase. Placing his right forefinger to his lips, he said, "*Shhh.*" Then, with the same hand, he mimed a knife slicing his throat.

"He threatened you."

Danny nodded. Telling me this was costing him something. In his own eight-year-old way, this child was as valiant as the superheroes he admired.

"Well, that's not going to happen," I said confidently. "Your mom won't let anyone hurt you, and neither will the police. I think you're *very brave.*"

One corner of his mouth went up.

* * *

Back in the car, Ivor and I headed for Finchley Hall. I was flying, in spite of the fact that the sun had given way to dark clouds and a spitting rain. Ivor flinched a couple of times as a hedgerow whizzed past him in the passenger's seat.

With Danny's permission, I'd told Glenda and Ivor about the man at Blackwater Lake. When we left, Glenda was on the phone to the police, Danny on her lap.

"Who *is* the man with the amber-tinted sunglasses?" Ivor asked.

"Could be anyone at Finchley Hall—even Gavin Collier or the vicar, I suppose. Until we know for sure, I don't trust any man of any age or description." I put a hand on his arm. "You excepted, of course."

"The one person who *can* identify him is the collector." He pulled out his mobile. "I'm dialing. Pull off the road so you can talk."

I stopped in a lay-by. Ivor handed me his phone.

"This is Kate Hamilton. I'd like to speak with"—I was about to say *Inspector Mallory* but stopped myself in time—"Detective Sergeant Cliffe."

After several minutes, a familiar voice said, "Sergeant Cliffe speaking. Kate, is that you?"

"Did Glenda Croft call?"

"Constable Wheeler is taking her statement right now. We're sending someone to bring them in."

"There's more." I told him about finding the Hoard objects and gave him the collector's address. Then I said, "Where's Christine?"

"At Finchley Hall. Aren't you there? She left with the guv—with Inspector Mallory—forty minutes ago. We've been trying to call you."

I breathed a sigh of relief. "My mobile's turned off. Has Christine been cleared?"

"Not exactly." He lowered his voice to a whisper. "I shouldn't be telling you this."

"Telling me what?" I gulped down a breath.

"The intake sergeant found a scratch on your daughter's arm. We're waiting for the results of the DNA under Ms. King's fingernails. The chief super wanted to keep Christine for another twelve hours."

"And?" This was not good.

"The guv released her anyway. Without permission. Then he took himself off the case."

"Tom took himself *off* the case?" I swallowed hard.

"It'll cost him his promotion. I thought you should know."

* * *

"Christine's been released." I pulled onto the road. "I'll drop you at the shop."

"Marvelous!" Ivor clapped his hands.

My joy was tempered by the knowledge of what this might mean for Tom.

As I drove, Ivor thumbed through Swiggett's book. We were pulling into Long Barston when he said, "My goodness. Listen to this: 'A sad footnote to the tale of the Lost Finchley Hoard involves the family of Tobias Thurtle, the servant entrusted with hiding the Finchley treasure in 1549 and presumed to have perished in the fire that consumed Finchley Hall. His survivors, abandoned by the Finchleys, were left destitute. Still, they never lost hope of finding the Hoard and claiming the reward they believed due them. In 1818, before he died of the injuries inflicted by the spring-gun, Jim Thurtle told police Sir Oswyn had promised Tobias a blood-red ruby set in a gold ring, to be granted upon the return of the Hoard—a promise which, I regret to say, was never kept.'"

An icy hand gripped my heart. "Ivor—the Thurtles, the Gedges, and the Inghams are all one family."

"You suggesting this whole thing—the thefts, the murders—is about Lady Susannah's ring?"

"The beggar who killed Lady Susannah and took the ring—I'm willing to bet he was a Thurtle."

"But why would Peter kill Tabitha? Wasn't he in love with her? Wasn't he the father of her child?"

"We don't have the DNA results yet. Maybe Peter came to Finchley Hall to help his uncle steal what they considered rightfully theirs. And maybe Peter got Tabitha the job as curator of the exhibit for that express purpose."

"If you're right, Gedge and the young man will be long gone."

Five minutes later, I dropped Ivor at his shop. "You call the police again. I'm going to find my daughter." I checked my watch. Still nearly a half hour before I could call the doctor in Jackson Falls.

I turned the car into the long drive toward Finchley Hall. Something wasn't making sense. Why was Christine still refusing to answer questions about Alex? Surely not to protect Peter Ingham. And where had she gotten that scratch on her arm?

I slid the car into a parking spot outside the Stables. Pulling out my cell phone, I switched it on. Four missed calls, all from Tom—and a text.

WHERE ARE YOU? CHRISTINE WILL BE BACK AT FH BY 2:00. DON'T LET HER OUT OF YOUR SIGHT. EXPLAIN LATER.

Don't let her out of my sight? My stomach fell. It was almost three, and I had no idea where she was.

Chapter
Thirty-Seven

❧

Don't let her out of your sight.

Bursting into the Commons, I found Prue, Michael, and Tristan.

"Where's Christine?" I pushed my damp hair off my forehead.

"She changed clothes and left," Prue said.

"Why?"

"Something about a score to settle."

"Tristan, what do you know about this?"

"Why ask me?" He shrunk into the sofa. "Your daughter wants nothing to do with me."

"Prue, Michael—what kind of score? With whom?"

"We asked." Michael shook his shaggy red head. "She wouldn't say."

Tossing my handbag on the counter, I slid my cell phone into my jeans pocket and shot out the door. *Oh man*—what if the score to settle involved Gedge and Peter? All I could think of was finding my daughter.

I raced, splashing through puddles on the gravel path, toward the Elizabethan Garden.

A fire burned in the fluted brazier. I found Peter and Gedge in the shed, sitting on the bags of manure.

"All right, where's Christine?" I barked.

Two faces stared at me in bewilderment.

"She's been released?" Peter said. "We haven't seen her."

"What do you know about the blood-red ruby and Sir Oswyn's reward?"

Peter laughed. "You mean that old family legend?"

"That were a long time ago, missus," Gedge said, chuckling. "I'd rather have a nice tied cottage and a pension than a bloody red stone."

There was more here, but it would have to wait. "Who around the estate wears amber-tinted sunglasses?"

"You mean those wraparound, clear-vision things?" Peter asked.

"*Who?*" I said, more sharply than I'd intended.

Gedge frowned. "Mugg."

* * *

I pushed through the door to Finchley Hall without bothering to ring the bell. No one met me. "Lady Barbara? Vivian? Francie?"

I shrugged off my rain-soaked jacket and tossed it on a chair. The drawing room and the library were deserted. I started to run.

I found Lady Barbara alone in her private sitting room. As I charged in, she sat bolt upright. "Kate, for heaven's sake, you're dripping wet."

"Have you seen Christine?" I gulped air. "She got back here at two o'clock."

"She's been released? I haven't seen her, but—oh, Kate, that's good news, isn't it?"

"I hope so. Look, I'm sorry. I have to go. Where's Mugg?"

"What time is it?" She glanced at her slim gold watch. "I can't see the numbers."

"Three fifteen. Is he here?"

"Cook's day off. He's probably in the kitchen. "

"How do I get there from here?"

"Return to the main hall, turn right, descend the staircase. At the bottom, turn left and continue past the—"

"Never mind. I'll find it." I thought about the new maids with their trails of corn kernels. I sprinted toward the main entrance. Once outside—I'd forgotten my coat—I hung a left and dashed toward the back of the house and the Elizabethan Garden.

There was the bench and the frog-green door to the kitchen. Danger pricked the back of my neck. I opened the door—just a crack. A pot simmered on the old Aga. I smelled chicken and herbs. Christine was there, all right. She huddled between a rack of copper pots and the wide Victorian hearth. My knees went weak.

Her wrists were bound with silver duct tape. A strip of tape covered her mouth.

Mugg stood beside her. With a carving knife.

My legs almost buckled.

I pushed open the door. "What do you think you're doing?" *Stupid question.*

Mugg drew in his breath with a sharp hiss. Moving more swiftly than I'd have thought possible, he rounded the pine table, seized my arm, and yanked me away from the door. Like he practiced this kind of thing every night before bed.

Holding the knife between his teeth, he wrenched my arms behind my back and held my wrists in a viselike grip. Still holding my wrists, he took a set of keys from his belt, locked the door, and shot the bolt.

"You're not getting out of here," he said.

"Neither are you, by the looks of it." Three other doors led from the kitchen. One was for the pantry Francie had shown me. Another, I guessed, led to the hallway and the stairs to the upper floors. That one had been bolted. The third door, on the far side of the hearth, was cracked, about an inch. I felt a surge of hope. Even if it led to another dead end, like the pantry, if Christine could get there, she'd have solid wood between her and that knife, giving me time to—*to what?* I had no idea.

The terror in my daughter's eyes sent a surge of adrenaline pulsing through my veins. My world contracted to a single, all-encompassing ball of rage. I could have gladly ripped his arms off.

Don't be stupid. Use your brain. Was that my mother's voice or mine? Whichever, it was right. I couldn't overpower him. I probably couldn't outmaneuver him. My only chance was to outthink him.

Using his free hand, Mugg snatched a white tea towel lying on the table and began to rip off a strip with his teeth.

Have you ever tried to have a conversation with your eyes alone? Neither had I, but you can do anything when you're left with no alternatives.

Christine's eyes moved from her legs to Mugg. *Should I kick him?*

I gave a tiny headshake and stared meaningfully at the carving knife. *Are you out of your mind? He's got a knife.*

She blinked. *Well, shoot.* Her actual words were probably less polite, but I got the idea.

I looked at her, then shifted my eyes toward the third door. *Way of escape. Not locked.*

She gave me an almost imperceptible nod.

The problem was giving her time to move. My first thought was distraction. Hey, it had worked for the thieves.

"Who's that?" I screamed dramatically and stared at the door behind Mugg.

He couldn't help himself. He spun around, dropping my wrists. Just long enough for me to race to the opposite side of the pine table.

He moved left. I moved left.

He moved right. So did I.

"You can't avoid me forever," he said, stating the obvious. He was the one with the knife, after all. "Now I suppose you're going to tell me the police are on their way and will be here any moment."

"I don't think I will, as a matter of fact. I'll let you guess. What I *am* going to tell you is how utterly despicable you are."

Mugg grabbed the roll of tape. Next he would tie me up, and then—terrifying images flicked through my brain, all involving that huge carving knife.

"What kind of a monster are you?" I threw at him. "After all Lady Barbara has done for you—after the loyalty she's shown you—you *betray* her by stealing her precious inheritance." I shook with rage.

He blanched. I'd gotten to him. "I didn't steal *from* her. I stole *for* her."

"What are you talking about?"

Out of the corner of my eye, I saw Christine take a tiny step sideways toward the third door. *Good girl.*

"Lady Barbara promised never to sell the Hoard. Someone had to." I watched in amazement as his eyes welled. "I didn't take a penny for myself, you stupid woman. All the money went into this house, including some of my own, if you must know. It's never-ending." He ran a ragged hand over his mouth. "Repairs, repointing, new plumbing, new electrics. The roof."

I stared at him, finally comprehending. "You were slowly converting her assets into cash so she could keep living here."

"What else could I do?" He looked at the strip of cloth in his hands with something like horror. "Everything I've done has been for her." His voice caught.

"Killing people isn't love."

"I had no choice." His nostrils flared.

All the puzzle pieces were there now. The thefts, the murders. And the outlier—the tiny detail that put everything else in perspective. The outlier was loyalty—loyalty and love. Twisted and grotesque, certainly, but recognizable. "Catherine Kerr was the first, wasn't she?" My voice sounded preternaturally calm, but my heart thumped against my rib cage so furiously I was sure he could hear it.

Inch by inch, Christine was moving toward the third door.

Keep him talking. Give her time. "Why did you have to get rid of Catherine?"

"She was going to tell Lady Barbara's husband about the missing items from the Hoard."

"So you killed her and let Lucien take the blame. You don't think that hurt Lady Barbara?"

"It was for the best." His lips twisted horribly. "You didn't know Lucien. He would have broken his mother's heart in the end. At least this way she can think of him living happily in Venezuela. A harmless deception." There was more to that story, but I couldn't get off track.

"Like passing off Francie as three different women?"

He *tsk*ed. "Lady Barbara's happiness is all that matters."

"More than the life of a beautiful young woman? Tabitha found out about the missing objects, too, didn't she?"

"That blasted book." He clenched his jaw. "I didn't even know the thing existed until she brought it to me and showed me the discrepancies."

"You took the book from Ivor Tweedy, too?" *How did he not know?*

"Too trusting, that man."

"Why did Tabitha show *you* the book?"

"She realized I was the only other person who knew the codes for the safe. She was giving me a chance to explain. I couldn't, of course." He began to pace in short spans, never moving far from Christine. "That one was the hardest. I had to steel myself."

"So you bludgeoned her with a garden spade and carried her body to the lake."

"She didn't suffer."

I wasn't sure of that. "You met her in the park the day of the tour. Didn't you realize the tour group would arrive soon?"

"She was the tour guide that day. How was I to know Alex would take over?"

Christine moved closer to the door. I tried not to look at her.

"You were still there when the little boy, Danny, went down to the lake. Would you have killed him, too?"

"Of course not. I didn't have to. Even if he told, no one would believe him."

"How did you know about Lady Susannah's ring?"

"Catherine Kerr discovered it. She intended to make the ring the centerpiece of the special exhibit."

"And you switched the ruby for a garnet."

"I took it to a jeweler in Cambridge. He found a garnet of similar size and shape and had it carved with a griffin. He made it fit the setting."

"How did you find the collector in Bury?"

"The jeweler said he knew someone who might buy it, but I'd have to provide a record of ownership. Turned out the jeweler was also an expert in forging documents."

"Weren't you worried the ring would be compared with the portrait?"

"No one knew the ring was there until *you* came along. Not even Lady Barbara." He narrowed his eyes. "That ruby saved Finchley Hall. What good was it doing locked up in a safe?"

He had a point. "So you kept stealing objects and selling them."

"It wasn't stealing," he roared. "I told you—I had no choice. The objects were never missed. No one even knew they were gone until Miss King found that book."

"Now the ring is gone and"—the truth was dawning—"you *knew* it would be. You knew the thieves would be at the exhibit. That's why you were so opposed."

He sighed miserably. "The jeweler in Cambridge had done work for an organized gang from the Continent. Big operation, lots of players. Most of the things I sold went to a collector in Bury, but a few went to the gang, to be sold abroad for a commission. That was my mistake. They got selfish. Decided to cut me out."

"But why would they take the ring? Didn't they know the stone was a garnet?"

His lips curled in a smile. "Never told them. Neither did the jeweler. That was our revenge."

"And Alex? She's still alive, by the way. When she wakes up, she'll tell the police about you."

"*If* she wakes up."

"Did Alex know about the ruby?"

"No, but she'd seen me with the Danish couple—who aren't Danish, by the way. They're part of the gang. I was trying to talk them out of stealing the Finchley Cross."

"But they didn't steal the cross. They stole the ring."

"They changed their minds. Probably the article in the newspaper."

"How did Alex figure it out?"

"She'd seen us together about a month ago. I'd told her they were relatives, come to visit. But when they came back, pretending to be Danish, she recognized them and eventually put two and two together. I had no choice."

"But you didn't finish the job."

"Heard someone coming, didn't I?"

"My daughter?" I stared at Christine. "Have you been protecting *Mugg* all this time?"

"*Mmmf*," she yelped, vigorously shaking her head.

It was time to move things forward.

"What have you got against Christine? She didn't know about the Hoard objects." That wasn't completely true, but why tell him?

Christine shook her head in frustration. "*Umm muumfa umm mumm*."

"She figured it out," Mugg said, translating. "The person who told the police she was at the Folly had to have been there, too."

"Who told her it was you?" I was confused.

Christine's eyes screwed up. *Umm muumf.* Whatever that meant, I'd have to find out later. Assuming we had a later.

Mugg inched toward me, the roll of tape in his hands. If I let him come closer, I might be able to slow him down when Christine bolted. If it didn't work—

"One more thing," I said, holding up a finger. "Tell me about Carlos Esteva."

"I wasn't sorry to kill him," Mugg said flatly. "I did humanity a favor there."

"Why was he in England?"

"Greedy, like the others. Lucien's dead, by the way. Drugs. He was in Venezuela less than a month when he died of an overdose. He and Carlos were friends, if you can call a pusher and his victim *friends.* When Lucien died, Esteva wrote me with a proposition. He'd pretend to be Lucien Finchley-fforde in exchange for the cash Lady Barbara sent from time to time. He was in trouble with his family—he'd been skimming drug money—so he dropped out of sight and took Lucien's identity. He wrote to Lady Barbara, pretending to be Lucien."

"She never suspected?"

"Her vision was bad by that time. She had me read the letters."

"So you let her send this man money? I thought you cared about her."

"Getting the letters made her happy, didn't it? She only sent twenty pounds or so every few weeks. Enough to keep Carlos in whiskey."

"So why did he come to England?"

"Blackmail. He wanted money to keep the secret—thousands. When I refused to pay, he threatened to tell Lady Barbara."

"So you took the whiskey from the pantry and laced it with paraquat."

"I told Esteva the whiskey was a down payment, that I'd have to sell something. I had no choice."

No choice. It was the fourth time he'd said it, and it was making me mad. "You *did* have a choice. You still do. End this now because the police will figure it out, and—

Christine kicked open the third door and vaulted up the steps two at a time.

Oh man. That wasn't a way out—just up. To the roof.

Dropping the knife, Mugg flew after her, pausing long enough to smile.

Crap, crap, crap. The roof had been his plan all along. This was literally my worst nightmare.

I could see the article in the newspaper: SUSPECT IN DEATH OF INTERN THROWS HERSELF OFF FINCHLEY HALL ROOF.

I rushed up the stairs after him. Acrophobia or not, if someone was going to save my daughter, it would have to be me.

Mugg leapt up the stairs like a mountain goat. With Christine's hands bound, she'd either lose her balance or he'd catch her.

Unless I caught him first.

We hit the first landing and rounded the banister. The second flight was narrower and steeper than the first. like climbing a ladder. Or those zigzag steps at the bell tower.

The world tilted. *Focus on Mugg.*

Halfway up the fourth flight, the ceiling was so low we had to stoop.

I grabbed for Mugg's leg and missed. I reached again. This time I caught the hem of his trousers. He kicked back hard, sending me bouncing down on my shins.

That hurt. A lot. But I'd slowed him enough to give Christine a tiny lead.

She opened a wooden hatch to the roof, hiked herself up on one knee, and pushed her upper body through. Landing on her shoulder, she tried to roll away, but Mugg caught her trailing leg and began to pull her back.

I grabbed his belt and yanked with all my strength. It almost sent us both tumbling down the staircase, but it did the trick.

Christine's leg disappeared through the hatch.

Mugg broke free and clambered after her.

I poked my head out. The sky was darkening. Rain drizzled. What I could see of the gray lead roof looked slick. Somehow, Christine had made it to a ladder bolted to one of the roof gables. Mugg wasn't far behind.

I stood rooted to the spot. *Oh man.* I was going to have to go out there. No railing, no parapet. Just a slippery lead surface ending in copper gutters and a sixty-foot drop.

For a moment I thought I might throw up. Then I thought about the courage of an eight-year-old boy. Pushing my dripping hair off my forehead, I forced myself on. Once through the hatch, I crouched close to the structure, my heart beating like a hammer. *Breathe.*

Christine was halfway up the ladder. She moved awkwardly, her hands bound in front of her, leaning her shoulders against the side rails for balance as she climbed. She couldn't have had a clue where she was going.

As Mugg reached for the bottom rung, his leather shoes slipped on the wet lead. *Yay!* Then I thought of my own shoes. They were leather, too.

I shouldn't have looked at the roof's edge. The world began to spin. With a full-blown panic attack threatening, I crawled forward on my stomach.

Something near my hip clunked against the metal roof. *My cell phone.*

I'd forgotten all about it. Should I call Tom? Emergency services?

I was no match for Mugg. Even if rescuers arrived in time—and I had no reason to hope they would—Mugg would carry out his plan. Christine would go over the edge, the distraught attacker. I'd follow, the frantic mother who lost her life attempting to save her child. We were nothing to Mugg.

He was halfway up the ladder now. Christine, at the top, was kicking at him wildly.

There was only one person on earth who could talk him out of this.

Lady Barbara.

Lying flat against the roof, I pulled out my phone, scrolled back through my calls, and pushed redial.

"Kate, is that you?" She sounded so frail. "What's going on?"

"I'm on the roof," I whispered. "Got a bit of a crisis here. Could you come?"

Chapter Thirty-Eight

Lady Barbara's head poked through the hatch. "What's happening?" Without waiting for an answer, she climbed neatly onto the roof. Whatever her health issues, Lady Barbara was agile.

Mugg and Christine had disappeared over the gable. We could hear them struggling.

Someone swore. *Oof.* Something heavy bumped over the ridged lead surface. I prayed it wasn't my daughter.

"Who *is* it? Tell me at once," Lady Barbara demanded.

"Mugg and Christine," I said lamely. "We need to get them down before someone falls." I choked out a hysterical laugh. How else was this going to end with an acrophobic leading a blind woman on a slippery roof?

"Let's go." Lady Barbara started to move.

"Are you sure this is a good idea?" I hissed.

"Don't be silly." She was shivering. "I know this roof like the back of my hand."

"Wait." I reached out for her. Looking back was a mistake. A wave of vertigo sent the world spinning again. In spite of the cold, I broke out in a clammy sweat.

"Use the mop rolls—the ridges—to get purchase," Lady Barbara said. "Lean into the roof or you'll lose your balance. Once we make it over the gable, there's a flat spot."

We inched forward.

My cell phone rang. *Eek!* The phone flew out of my hand, somersaulted in the air, scuttered down the lead roof, and sailed off into the blackness. Still ringing.

We reached the ladder. "You go first," I said, peering at the small figure of Lady Barbara. If she fainted now, I'd try to catch her, and we'd probably both go over the edge.

I needn't have worried.

Hoisting herself up, she shouted in a commanding voice, "Mugg. Whatever are you doing?" This wasn't the frail Lady Barbara I'd heard on the phone a few minutes ago. This Lady Barbara could have led the troops to victory at Waterloo in her ball gown.

She climbed the ladder, hand over hand. I followed, swallowing hard and blinking against the spots swimming in my peripheral vision. Reaching the top, Lady Barbara pivoted, making room for me. We peered over the gable.

Christine had found the level place. She rested on her haunches, sucking oxygen through her nose. Mugg perched on the downside ladder.

No one spoke, so I did. "I'm sorry to tell you this, Lady Barbara, but Mr. Mugg is not the person you think he is. Not only is he responsible for a series of thefts from the Hoard, he's the one who killed Catherine Kerr, Tabitha King, Carlos Esteva. He's the one who attacked Alex Devereux."

Good job breaking it gently.

Mugg's chest heaved. His mouth opened. "I did it for you, madam. Everything for you."

I held my breath.

Then Lady Barbara said the last thing I expected.

"I feel as if I might faint. Mugg, would you help me down from here before I do?"

He swallowed hard. "Of course, madam."

"*Now*, Mugg?"

"Certainly, madam."

I swung my legs over the gable and half-slid down to the flat place where Christine was crouched. I ripped the tape from her mouth.

"Ow," she said, rubbing the skin above her lip.

I held her, but not for long. She pulled away. "Get this tape off my hands."

"I'll need a knife." Not the cleverest statement under the circumstances.

A siren blared in the dusky light. Blue lights raced down the long drive. A small armada of cars and vans skidded to a halt in the gravel courtyard.

Voices called to us from the narrow staircase.

"Albert Mugg," came a welcome voice. "I'm arresting you for the murder of—"

Tom vaulted onto the roof. "Kate, Christine, you're safe."

That's when I lost it.

*   *   *

Lady Barbara, Christine, and I sat, wrapped from head to toe in blankets, on the twin Knole sofas in the private drawing room. I held my mud-streaked phone, which by some miracle had fallen in a planting bed and was still working.

Everyone was there. Peter sat next to Lady Barbara on the sofa. Prue and Michael held hands in the window seat. Tristan slouched in a corner. Francie Jewell was pouring steaming mugs of hot, sweet tea. Even Gedge was there, inside the house for perhaps the first time in his life and refusing to sit on the grounds he might *pong* a bit. Someone had built a fire in the hearth. Probably Vivian.

Tom and Sergeant Cliffe had stopped in before leaving for Bury.

"I never guessed it was Mugg," Lady Barbara said weakly. Now that we were off the roof and Mugg was in custody, she was trembling. People say courage is the ability to do the right thing while you're scared out of your wits. By that definition, Lady Barbara could be counted among England's heroes.

Fidelis, fastu, fortitudo.

Francie handed Lady Barbara a mug of tea.

"Thank you, Francie. Or should I call you Briggs?"

"You knew all along?" I asked.

"I'm not a complete fool." Lady Barbara lifted her cup.

Tom pulled up a chair. "Time for the truth," he told Christine. "We know you saw Mugg near the Folly the night Alex was attacked. What we don't know is why you refused to say so."

Her chin went up.

"Christine, for heaven's sake." I wanted to shake her. "What reason could you possibly have now for not telling?"

"Because she promised." The reedy voice of Tristan Sorel came from the corner of the room. "So I shall."

Everyone stared at him.

"The night before the Hoard exhibit, Alex told me we were finished. Once I was well and truly hooked, she'd lost interest. I was angry and hurt." His mouth twisted. "I assumed she had someone else on the line. I checked her phone messages and found the texts, demanding that Christine meet her in the Folly at six forty-five. I went early, intending to eavesdrop. Instead—" He stopped, stricken. "Instead I found Alex's body."

"That's when I arrived," Christine said. "Seeing him with a bloody garden spade in his hand, his clothes soaked with blood, I assumed he'd murdered Alex. I ran."

"I caught her—told her what happened and pleaded with her not to tell anyone I was there. All the evidence was against me."

"We should have called for help," Christine said miserably. "We thought Alex was dead. We really did."

"Will she be all right?" Tristan asked.

"She has a nasty concussion," Tom said. "With rest and time, she may recover her memory of the attack. We're counting on it." He smiled slightly. "Finish the story, Christine."

"We agreed to arrive at the party separately. We both went to shower and change. I hung out near the Stables until I'd calmed down a bit. The thing is, I'd seen Mugg on the way to the Folly earlier. I didn't think about it until the police told me a witness had seen me. At the police station, I learned it was Mugg."

"So you thought it would be a smart move to accuse him of murder?" I said, flabbergasted.

"It never occurred to me he was the killer." Christine pulled the blanket closer around her neck. "I was going to ream him out for being a snitch."

"Oh, Christine." That's all I had time for, because my cell phone rang.

Memorial Hospital. "Oh, dear Lord—my mother." Dragging the blanket with me, I dashed into the hall.

"Hello, Kate?" came the oh-so-familiar voice.

I couldn't believe what I was hearing. "Mom, is it really you?"

"Of course it's me." Her voice lowered to a whisper. "I'm in the hospital. I'm supposed to be sleeping."

"Why aren't you?"

"I've gotten quite a lot of sleep since yesterday. Seventeen hours, as a matter of fact. One minute I was in the kitchen, deciding if I should take two more Motrin. Next thing I knew I woke up here almost a day later."

"Are you okay?"

"I seem to be. Everything's working. They did some tests this morning. I'm on a blood thinner. They say I had a ministroke, but I don't seem to have any aftereffects."

My mother, the eternal optimist. Look on the bright side. Count your blessings. I was counting them, too, but weren't TIAs sometimes a precursor for another, more devastating stroke?

"Oh, Mom." My voice cracked.

"What is it, Kate?"

My mother's ability to read between the lines is the stuff of legends. And, like my daughter, I'm a terrible liar. So I told her—the expurgated version. Plenty of time later to fill in the blanks.

When I stopped, she said, "Well, that settles it. You must stay in England. Christine needs you, and it sounds like you and Tom have some sorting out to do. You'll have to change your flight."

"But what if you need surgery or something?"

"I'm not having surgery. I'm being released."

"All the more reason why I should be there to take care of you."

"I'm in excellent hands. Charlotte will make sure the shop is covered. She's taken Fiona to her house. The twins are delighted. You're needed there."

"Mom. Come on—no way I'd let you spend Christmas Eve and Christmas by yourself. Not on your life."

"As a matter of fact—" For the first time I could remember, my mother sounded evasive. "My friend from Oak Hills insists on driving down to get me. He's asked me to spend Christmas with his son and family this year. I think I may take him up on it."

"Dr. Lund?"

"James, yes. And we *will* celebrate Christmas together, Kate. Even if it's in January."

I tried protesting, but my mother wouldn't listen. "No, darling. You're needed in England."

She was right.

Chapter Thirty-Nine

~

Tuesday, December 22nd

The day I'd planned to be on an airplane, flying home to spend Christmas Eve with my mother, I was with Tom, sitting on a bench outside a hospital room in Bury St. Edmunds. Alex Devereux was well enough to have an occasional visitor.

"Tell me about that text," I said. "The one you sent, telling me not to let Christine out of my sight."

Tom stretched out his long legs. "We'd just gotten the lab results. The DNA under Tabitha's fingernails was Mugg's. We knew he was the killer."

"Who was the father of Tabitha's baby?"

"Peter. As we thought."

The door to Alex's room opened, and a middle-aged man wearing jeans, a tweed sport coat, and an open-collared striped shirt came out. He had a head of thick silver hair and a slightly tanned face.

"Frightfully kind of you to come," he said in a clipped, cut-glass accent. "I'm Paul Devereux, Alex's father."

When we'd introduced ourselves, he said, "I'm off to the canteen for a spot of breakfast. Don't stay long, will you? She needs her rest."

Tom rapped softly on the door.

Alex lay propped on a pillow, her hands limp on the white cotton spread. A plump gauze bandage covered the right side of her head, which looked like it had been shaved. Monitors blinked and beeped.

"Hello, Alex," I said. "We heard you were awake. We wanted to see for ourselves that you were all right."

"The headache's the worst," she said weakly. "And the loss of memory. The doctors say it will return. I'm not sure I want to remember."

"You should know that Mugg has pled guilty to your attack," Tom said. "There's more, but we won't go into that right now."

"Lady Barbara sends her love—and all the interns," I said.

"Kind of them." Her tone bore no trace of sarcasm.

"We met your father just now," Tom said. "We understand your mother is on her way."

"Mummy's had to cut short her holiday in the south of France. Too bad of me, isn't it?" She raised a hand to brush back her hair but stopped when she felt the bandage.

"Your parents aren't together?"

"Never were. Daddy makes sure she has enough money to keep her from being a nuisance. I don't care if she comes or not." Her attempt to appear nonchalant was less than convincing.

I looked at that beautiful, pale face. "Lady Barbara says your job is waiting for you the minute you feel able to return."

Her eyes glistened. "Tell her I'm grateful."

"Of course." I laid my hand on hers. "I think we should go so you can rest."

"One more thing." She shifted her position and winced. "Tell Christine I'm sorry."

* * *

315

After dropping Tom at police headquarters in Bury, I caught the road south to Long Barston. I hoped Alex would decide to stay on at Finchley Hall. With Mugg out of the picture, Lady Barbara needed her.

I thought of the other interns. Would they stay on and finish out their internships? What would Christine do?

Late the previous night I'd spoken to my mother again. She'd sounded stronger. Charlotte was at the house packing a suitcase for her. My mother was waiting at the hospital for Dr. Lund to pick her up in his big silver Mercedes. They planned to stay the night at my house in Jackson Falls and leave in the morning for one of the Chicago suburbs, where his son, also a physician, lived with his wife and three daughters. I'd asked if the three-hour car trip would be too much for her. She'd laughed. "He's a doctor, Kate."

Signs for Finchley Hall and St. Æthelric's told me I was nearing the village.

Christine had insisted on completing the inventory of the documents in the 1934 file before the holidays, so I'd invited Lady Barbara and Vivian Bunn to meet me for lunch at the Three Magpies. I glanced at my watch. First I'd stop at the Cabinet of Curiosities.

The bell jangled as I entered. Ivor stood in his usual position behind the counter.

"I hear I missed all the fun," he said with a pointed look.

"You're not going to tell me I shouldn't have done it, are you?"

"Certainly not." He huffed on a glossy cobalt-blue bottle and polished it with a felt cloth.

"Mugg is the one who stole your copy of Swiggett's book. Why didn't you tell me he was in the shop?"

"You asked about strangers. Mugg wasn't a stranger. He said he was looking for a Christmas gift for Lady Barbara." Ivor set the blue glass bottle on the counter.

"Is that what I think it is?"

"Take a look."

The glass was hand-blown, translucent, few air bubbles. The body was pear-shaped with a flattened bottom and a cylindrical neck. "It's an unguentarium," I said, "a bottle for the perfumed oils used in bathing."

"Roman, second century. I'm mailing it to a chap in Shrewsbury today. Lots of cotton wool and bubble wrap." He set the vase on the counter. "How is your mother?"

"Fine—at least that's what she tells me. She's spending Christmas with a friend near Chicago. And I'm staying in England until after the holidays."

"Really?" He turned pink. "In that case, perhaps . . . well, perhaps you and your young man would join me on Christmas for a celebratory toast. Something I've been saving for a special occasion."

Knowing Ivor, this could be anything from a bottle of Veuve Clicquot to a cask of nineteenth-century French cognac.

"The carolers from St. Æthelric's stroll round the village between four and six PM. We could pull Christmas crackers." He looked as hopeful as a little boy, anticipating a bicycle-shaped package under the tree on Christmas morning.

"There's nothing I'd like better. I'm sure I can answer for Tom—unless he's called out. And I want you to meet my daughter."

"Yes, yes, a real celebration. Bring Christine along. Bring them all." He clapped his hands. "This will be the merriest Christmas since the Amazon rain forest when the fireworks went awry and burnt down the local wine bar."

I laughed. "That's a story I must hear, but not today. I'm lunching with Lady Barbara and Vivian Bunn at the Three Magpies. I'll invite them, too, if it's all right."

"The more, the merrier." He stopped and raised his hands in surprise. "Dear me, I nearly forgot. Do you remember F. Redfern, hmm?"

"The name on the slip of paper in that tortoiseshell snuffbox. You were trying to find a connection with the poet Alexander Pope."

He opened the drawer behind the counter and removed the snuff-box he'd shown me on the day we met. "Now where is that paper?" He shuffled through a stack of documents, sending them flying. "Aha." He waved a paper at me. "'The Last Will and Testament of Alexander Pope.' A photocopy, of course. The original's in the Bodleian." He stabbed at a paragraph. "Pope left the bulk of his estate to his friend, Martha Blount. Look." He squinted at the miniscule writing. "'I give and devise to Mrs. Martha Blount, younger Daughter of—'"

"What does this have to do with F. Redfern?"

"Excellent question. Martha Blount left a will, too. It's here—on the opposite side. Martha Blount bequeathed the sum of one hundred pounds to her faithful cook and companion. Read it for yourself."

He had bracketed a paragraph with red pencil: —TO MRS. FANNY REDFERN, WHOSE DEEP ADMIRATION FOR THE WORKS OF ALEXANDER POPE RIVALS MY OWN.

"Well done, Ivor." I tucked the episode away to impress my mother. I gazed around the shop and the amazing objects he'd bought over a lifetime. "You've got a gold mine here."

A shadow crossed his face. He sighed deeply.

"Do you regret parting with the Egyptian glass head? You could have sold it for a lot more than sixteen thousand and a book."

He huffed. "Don't be silly. I bought the thing for the equivalent of thirty pounds. Not a bad return on investment, even after forty years, hmm?"

"Then what's wrong?"

"I got a letter from the National Health. I'm scheduled for bilateral hip surgery at the end of April. Both hips at the same time."

"Good news, right?"

"They say I'm a good candidate." He pulled at his ear. "But the rehabilitation will take longer than I expected—a week in hospital, then a residential clinic for some weeks."

"That doesn't sound too bad."

"No." He frowned. "Best place for me. Only what shall I do about the shop?"

"Close it down until you recover?"

"I can't afford that—no, it's true. My cash is tied up in inventory. Meanwhile I have taxes to pay, utilities, interest on a loan, not to speak of normal living expenses. Sales like the cobalt vase don't come along every day. I sell very little to the walk-in trade. Most of my sales are online. That means keeping abreast of the market, contacting potential buyers, listing items for sale in online auctions."

"Couldn't you do that from the rehabilitation center?"

"After a few weeks, perhaps. But that's only part of the work. Once an object is sold, I must arrange for payment, check credit, decide how best to ship the object. Organize delivery. Be prepared to accept returns—that happens more than you'd think. And then, if the place looks deserted, there's the danger of theft. Someone must be here at the shop."

"Could you get someone to fill in?"

His eyebrows flew up as if I'd just uttered an oracle. "It would have to be someone I trusted, obviously." His blue eyes took on that childlike innocence I'd come to recognize as a sign of scheming and deception. "Someone with the knowledge to pull it off. Who could possibly step in at this late date, hmm?"

I'd heard that one before.

* * *

I found a parking space on a side street between the Finchley Arms and the Three Magpies. The dueling signboards were up. The Three Magpies was advertising an elegant champagne brunch on Christmas and New Year's Day. Not to be outdone, the Arms had countered with a few twigs of holly in chalk and the words UPHOLDING TRADITION: CHEAP ALCOHOL, LOW STANDARDS, AND POOR DECISIONS.

The Three Magpies felt lively, with customers in both the bar and dining room. Lady Barbara and Vivian sat at a table in front of the fireplace. Would Lady Barbara's patronage overcome the villagers' resistance to the Three Magpies, I wondered, or would her defection trigger all-out war?

Jayne Collier hovered around Lady Barbara like she was the Queen. "Care for tea? Glass of wine, perhaps? Champagne?" She'd already set down the sourdough with lemon and coriander olives.

"This is quite pleasant," Lady Barbara said when she saw me. "I've never been in a public house before." Having recovered from the previous day's ordeal with near-miraculous rapidity, Lady Barbara was reminding me more and more of my mother. She spread her napkin on her lap and speared one of the small purplish-brown olives. "To be fair, I should probably put in an appearance at the Arms as well. What do you think?"

I smiled and kept my mouth shut. I'd give a lot to see that.

After we ordered—we all chose the lunch special, smoked salmon with warm goat cheese on a caramelized onion tart—Vivian surprised me by nudging Lady Barbara. "Tell the girl, Barb. No time like the present."

"Yes, of course." Lady Barbara wiped a slick of olive oil from her chin. "I've made a decision, Kate—thanks to you." She took a sip of mineral water. "I think I've known for a long time that Lucien is gone. I just didn't want to face it."

"How did you know?"

"The letters. Oh, I put the speech patterns down to the natural changes that occur when one lives in a foreign culture. But I knew. I won't be receiving any more letters. Lucien will not be returning to England one day. The Finchleys end here—with me."

Vivian rolled her hand. "Get to the point, dear."

"The point is, I knew we needed cash. I didn't know just how desperate my financial condition really is." Her hand flew to her mouth, stifling a sob. "What wicked things Mugg did to conceal the truth from me."

It hurt me to look at her face.

"While Cedru was alive, he took care of all that. When he died, Mugg took over the finances. I should have been more vigilant."

"Tell her what you've decided to do," Vivian said.

"It's a case of what I've already done. This morning I directed my solicitor to draw up an agreement, transferring ownership of Finchley Hall to the National Trust."

Her words were clipped, decisive, but what was she feeling? I searched that pale, lined face and those dim eyes. Finchley Hall had been her life, a legacy entrusted to her by all those smug faces rendered in oils. She'd made a promise, a promise she could no longer keep.

A great loss.

"Don't look so sad," she said, reaching out to touch my cheek. "I'm not losing Finchley Hall. I'm *giving* it to the nation. I'll remain in my private quarters—a few familiar rooms is all I need—until I'm no longer able to live on my own. Francie has agreed to stay on, bless her." She laughed. "Three for the price of one, eh? Peter will finish the garden. And I'll have Vivian to keep me company. I don't know what I'd do without her."

"Nonsense," Vivian said, but I could see she was pleased.

"And the interns?"

"Those here now who wish to stay are welcome, but they shall be the last. If Alex decides to remain, I can just about afford to keep her on. All good things come to an end."

Jayne brought our food, and we spent the next few minutes savoring our first mouth-watering bites.

"What about the Hoard?" I asked.

"I believe I shall give the Hoard to the Museum of Suffolk History—in honor of Catherine Kerr and Tabitha King."

"Would you like to see it again? We could walk over to the archives building."

"No, dear. The Hoard has brought nothing but death. I'm through with all that, and good riddance."

"Well said." Vivian brought her fist down on the table, nearly toppling her water glass. "No point living in the past. Move forward is my motto."

Move forward. I'd told Tom I wasn't ready. What I hadn't told him was why.

You can't move forward when there's no place to step.

I smiled at these two old friends. They were pointing the way.

Because quietly, without fuss or fanfare, a door had appeared.

Chapter Forty

Thursday, December 24th
Christmas Eve

Tom and I were curled up on the sofa in his cottage outside the village of Saxby St. Clare. Lights twinkled on the Christmas tree. Candles glowed in the windows. I stretched my toes toward the fire. "I have a confession."

"Another one?" He gave me that half smile that always makes me melt. "You already told me you insulted my mother, not that I blame you. She deserved it."

I winced. "Are you sure I'm not the reason she's spending Christmas in Devon?"

"She spends every Christmas in Devon with Uncle Nigel."

"In the castle."

"In the large house I thought of as a castle when I was a child."

"I'm really not the reason she left Suffolk?"

"Really. But you are the reason I didn't. If you don't believe me, come here, and I'll convince you."

A few long minutes later he touched my cheek. "Back to the confession—the latest one."

"Here goes. When you took Christine into custody, I was angry. I know, I know. You were doing your job. But all I could think about was my daughter spending the night in a jail cell and possibly accused of assault. I blamed you, Tom, and that wasn't fair. I know the decision wasn't yours. I know Christine brought it on herself by refusing to speak. The point is, I didn't trust you. And I should have."

"But you—"

"No, just listen." I touched his mouth. "With the exception of my son, every man I've ever loved in my whole life has left me without warning. Not that they wanted to. My brother didn't want to die when I was five. My father didn't want to die in a car accident when I was seventeen. Bill didn't want to have a massive heart attack three years ago. The logical part of my brain accepts that. The other part, the irrational part, tells me I've been betrayed and abandoned."

"Oh, Kate." He slid his hand down the back of my hair.

"When you arrested my daughter, it felt like one more betrayal, one more loss. All I wanted to do was run. But I can't run from life. I know that. Life is a risk. Loving someone is a risk."

"Not with me."

I laid my head on his chest and listened to the strong, even rhythm of his heart. "Yes, it is, even with you, because you can't promise not to die. And there's no reason on God's earth why I should ask it of you. I doubted you in Scotland, and I doubted you here, and the reason was fear. The fear of trusting someone with no reservations. The fear of giving my heart, only to find it broken. What I want to say is this: I don't know what our future looks like, but I do know this—I will never doubt your character, your integrity, your intentions—or your love."

I took a shaky breath.

"Come here." He pulled me into his arms. "And this is what I want you to know, Kate. Whatever happens between you and my mother—or between you and Olivia, if she ever comes home from Africa—you are and will always be my first priority."

We sat, not speaking, listening to the flames hiss and pop. What we'd just said to each other had consequences. I'd come to England one person. Soon I'd leave, another person entirely.

In an effort to move in a less fraught direction, I said, "Any leads on the gang of thieves?"

He laughed. "Enough of the commitment stuff? All right. We've tracked down the so-called Danish couple. They are married—just about the only truthful thing about them. They're from Manchester. She did have a Danish grandmother who lived with them for a while. They met on the stage and turned their acting skills to felony. In aid of theft, they've impersonated everything from a Pearly King and Queen in London to a pair of Russian refugees. They'll be spending time in prison, less if they're willing to give up the leaders of the gang."

"I feel sorry for her. She was kind to Danny. And she had great taste in clothes."

He laughed. "That coat came in handy. When she went to the car to get the medical bag, she left the ring there. That's why our search turned up nothing."

"What about the collector in Bury St. Edmunds? I liked him, Tom."

"Honest as the day is long, as it turns out—a victim of fraud. He's cooperating fully with the police. If we ever recover the ring stolen from the exhibit, we'll reunite it with the blood-red ruby and the other Hoard items he purchased unwittingly."

"Oh, look, Tom." Outside the windows, fat flakes of snow drifted down. "Come on, get your coat. Let's watch."

We stood under the latticed wood canopy that sheltered his front door. He wrapped his arms around me from behind. I laid my head back against his shoulder and took it all in. A childhood dream come true.

Lights from nearby cottages twinkled like a thousand candles. In the distance we heard church bells, calling the villagers of Saxby St. Clare to Christmas Evensong.

"I'm having my English Christmas," I said, turning to look at him. "The only thing missing is wassail."

"I'd make you some if I knew how." Then he grew serious. "What's next for us?"

"Drinks with Ivor Tweedy, remember? Then dinner at the Trout."

He turned me around to face him. "Take pity on me, Kate. I'm a lost man."

I grinned. "I'm sorry. You're just so easy to wind up. When will you have time off?"

"Spring. Shall I go to you, or will you come to me?"

That was one question, as it happened, I could answer.

I took his hand. "Come back inside, and I'll tell you all about it."

Acknowledgments

My heartfelt thanks goes to the Suffolk Constabulary in Bury St. Edmunds for their help in understanding methods of policing in Suffolk—crime scene investigator Lisa Skelton; custody sergeant Sarah Bartley, who showed me all over the Custody Charge Station in Bury; and most especially DI Tamlyn Burgess, who took one of her rare days off to answer all my questions and more. Any errors are mine alone.

As always, I'm grateful to Faith Black Ross, my editor at Crooked Lane Books, and Paula Munier, my agent at Talcott Notch Literary. Thanks are also due my critique partners, Lynn Denley-Bussard, Charlene D'Avanzo, and Judy Copek, for their advice and suggestions—and to all those who read and commented on the manuscript in its various stages. This book would not have been written without the encouragement of my family—my sons, Dave and John, and especially my husband, Bob, who listened to endless talk of bodies and clues, drove me down narrow lanes and over blind summits in the English countryside, and (in the name of research) followed me into more stately homes than I had the right to expect.

Soli Deo gloria